For all the girls
who think they aren't enough:
Nobody storms the castle for the prince.

love is music ♡

PLAYER

SPITSHINE

VAL

S am turned me into a walking contradiction.

His ability to make me feel simultaneously mortified, stunned, and exhilarated was an act of sorcery I'd come to both look forward to and avoid at all costs.

In fairness, I didn't interact with many men, particularly not men who were of the tall, dark, and handsome category. More the short, awkward, and swipe-left category.

But *typically* I could maintain at least a tentative sense of normal around the opposite sex. Thing was, Sam was anything but typical.

I'd felt his presence from the second he entered the orchestra pit for sound check and through every song in *Wicked* from "No One Mourns the Wicked" to "For Good."

It was ridiculous really, just how obsessed with him I was.

I wished I could have said *obsessed* was too strong of a word, but there I was, playing on Broadway, and my dream job was the last thing on my mind. I'd spent the last month—ever since I'd secured my chair—daydreaming about Sam. That, and trying not to make an ass out of myself in front of him.

I'd been failing miserably on both counts, in case you were wondering.

The pit buzzed with chatter as musicians packed up their things. But above it all, I heard him laugh from behind me, near the enclosed drum booth where his buddy played. The velvety timbre of his voice plucked a string in me, setting it vibrating, humming a note only he could produce.

On that recognition, I did my level best to turn my focus anywhere but on him.

I polished off the brass bell of my trumpet, watching the blur of my distorted reflection in the curving metal. Once it gleamed, I pointed the bell at the ground, brought my lips to the mouthpiece, pressed the lever to open my spit valve, and emptied my lungs. The accumulated moisture in the tubes shot out of the little hole in a brilliant, disgusting fan of saliva and DNA.

The shoe wasn't there, and then it was, glistening with my spit and stopped dead in front of me. It was a *big* shoe, the leather of his high-top oxfords dotted with condensation. In a protracted turn, it shifted until its toe pointed at me in accusation, its mate following suit.

Horror rose in my chest.

My eyes climbed the length of his long body, cataloging every detail in the hopes it wasn't him. Because if the face I found at the top was the one I thought it might be, there was a very high likelihood that I would be leaving the theater on a stretcher.

His legs went on forever, his dark jeans tight enough to see the cords of his calves and thighs, loose enough that they still bunched artfully at his ankles and knees. His narrow waist, his belt punctuating a place my eyes wanted to linger. His torso widened to a broad chest that was still lean but strong—the discs of his pecs were visible under his shirt, the proportion of waist to wings to shoulders mathematically perfect. I mean, if I did math. Which, in that moment, I most definitely did not. I couldn't have counted bananas unless they were hooked in his belt.

If he hadn't already scrambled my wits, the second I laid eyes on his face, my wits would have willingly grabbed a whisk and scrambled themselves.

Dark. Dark and hard, from the cut of his jaw to his ebony hairline. From his stubbled beard to his strong brow.

Soft and light, his skin tan and glowing—actually *glowing* like a commercial for miracle cream that turned you into an immortal. His lips were a dusty rose, thick and luscious—the bow strong, the curve gentle, the corners curled up in amusement.

But it was his eyes that knocked the air out of my lungs. They were the color of sand, a burnished brown so light, they defied logic, the color contained by a dark ring circling the irises. His lids were edged with lashes so black, so thick, they looked like they were lined with kohl.

He was far, far above me, figuratively and literally.

"Oh my God," I breathed, setting down my trumpet and swiping my towel in the same motion. Without thinking, I hit the floor on all fours and mopped at his shoe with my towel. "I am so sorry," I said as I scrubbed with far more vigor than necessary. "I-I didn't see you coming, or I never—I mean, I wouldn't have ever intentionally—"

He chuckled through closed lips. "A good spit shine never hurt anybody."

My cheeks flamed, and I crawled to the side a little so I could get the outside of his shoe. "I can't believe I did this. I can't believe I didn't see you."

"Maybe I should wear a bell."

A small, singular laugh escaped me.

Like that would help keep my mind off you.

He paused. I kept at it, cleaning his shoe off like a maniac.

"Really, it's fine. Come here." A hand dipped into my periphery, a big, wide hand with long fingers.

There was something about the way he'd told me to *come here*, like he was going to take me to bed or to France or to heaven. My heart thundered as I reached for his hand. The moment our skin brushed, a zing of awareness shot up my arm and straight to my heart. My fingers slipped into the curve of his wide palm, and when he closed his fingers around my hand, it disappeared.

He pulled me to stand, squeezing once before letting go.

I swear to God, I almost hit the deck again, this time in a fit of histrionics.

I made the mistake of looking up and experienced a momentary lapse in time. His lips were together, tilted in a smirk.

"Thirty seconds more, and I would have had to pay you for the shine."

An awkward laugh crackled out of me. "Please, I probably should be paying you. I'm really sorry. I don't usually spit on leather shoes. Or any shoes. I don't usually spit. I mean, aside from my spit valve. Or when I brush my teeth. Or after I puke."

Oh my God, stop talking. STOP TALKING NOW.

I clamped my mouth shut.

The tilt in his smile angled higher. "No harm done, Val."

He knows my name? Holy shit, he knows my name.

Heat burst across my skin, climbing up my neck and to my cheeks.

Sam shifted away from me. "See you tomorrow. And maybe watch where you point that," he said, nodding to my trumpet. "Wouldn't want to lose you to the shoe shine industry."

The laugh that left me was unrecognizable. I lifted my hand lamely. "Bye."

Somehow, I found the wherewithal to stop staring at his backside as he walked away. I took my seat to finish disassembling my trumpet, packing the mouthpiece and horn away in its bed of cobalt velvet. And all the while, I sank into that familiar feeling of abject horror and the feverish thrill that accompanied every encounter with him.

He'd touched my hand. He'd smiled at me. He knew my name.

And in my book, that was a win regardless of how much drool it had taken me to get there.

SAM

I felt her eyes on me while I put my upright bass in its case. The weight of her stare didn't go unnoticed as I dragged my fingers through my hair when it fell out of place.

I probably shouldn't have lifted the massive case with one hand, an action that engaged every muscle in my arm from fingers to shoulder—back, pecs, and abs as a bonus.

But I did, and I did it without a shred of shame or remorse.

It seemed like we never got through a curtain call without Val crossing my path, and every encounter was more unexpected. Once, when she'd walked by, her toe had caught my music stand and taken it down in a hail of sheet music. Just the other day, she'd tripped on my foot and ended up in my lap, thanks to some quick maneuvering on my part. I hadn't forgotten the feel of her ass seated snugly against my thighs. And I couldn't help my amusement. I didn't even try, as innocent as it was.

Like the asshole I was, I soaked up every ounce of her attention.

I knew who she was—no one could miss her. A head of curly hair in shades of caramel to chestnut. A heart-shaped face set with big, dark eyes. Lips like a little Cupid's bow, small and full. Her body, short and stacked, with curves like a roller coaster. I noticed every one even though I wasn't sure she wanted anyone to—she hid her body under baggy clothes.

I wondered if she was ashamed. If she thought men didn't want a body like hers, with curves reminiscent of the mahogany bass I'd just locked away. If so, she had no idea how wrong she was.

I was an aficionado of women; I admired them, valued them, appreciated them always. And there was a lot to appreciate about Val.

Ian chuckled, his arms folded as he leaned against the wall beside me, twirling a drumstick in his fingers. "Man, that chick is so into you."

I hadn't realized I was smiling until my lips began to fall. "She's a cute kid."

"A girl with a body like *that* is no kid." Ian watched her with a wolfish expression on his face, nothing but teeth and eyes.

Ian Jackson, asshole extraordinaire. We'd met at a prep school for the gifted and filthy rich when we were fifteen and had been friends ever since, through Juilliard and into Broadway. We were two of a kind in our way. He was as fair as I was dark, with blond hair and cool eyes and a smile that brought girls running like the Pied Piper of Hamelin.

They didn't usually figure out they were on their way to their own funerals until it was too late.

And that was the difference—I was clear about my rules, and he wasn't. He'd tell a girl he knew it was sudden, he knew it was too soon, but would it be strange if he thought he might love her?

Anything to close the deal.

I, on the other hand, had never lied to a woman about what I could be to them. I'd never made promises I didn't intend to keep.

I had no problems closing deals either.

Ian had slept with every eligible member of the orchestra and half of the cast and crew, where I was much more interested in women I didn't have to see at work.

Not that I didn't have the opportunity.

As if I'd willed them to appear, three flutists walked past us, batting their lashes and fawning.

"Hi, Sam," the blonde one sang.

I swore I heard a collective sigh when I jerked my chin in lieu of a greeting.

"Hey, ladies," Ian said.

They soured in unison and picked up their pace.

"Seriously," Ian said, unfazed, "that little trumpet player is a rocket. I bet she's never even had a boyfriend."

My frown deepened. "You don't know that."

"She's got that look about her. You know what I mean—the good girls, the innocent ones. Pay them a little attention, and they worship you."

I shot him a look. "You're a dick."

He laughed, flashing a brilliant smile. "I know. I swear to God, man—when she was on her hands and knees scrubbing your shoe, I thought I was gonna have a heart attack."

He hadn't been the only one.

Dumbfounded, I'd looked down, my eyes roaming from her curly head down to the curve of her ample ass as she scrubbed. The motion set her body moving toward and away from me in a borderline pornographic wave that reminded me of something much more intimate than a shoe shine.

"I think I'm gonna go after her," he said, watching me.

Something inside me jerked in surprise, but I kept still, kept my voice light. With a laugh, I said, "No, you aren't."

"Honestly, I don't know why I haven't before. I shoulda hit on her the second she walked in. After her little display, I wouldn't mind getting her on all fours so she could spit shine my D."

My head swiveled around to eye him. "Assuming she'd be interested."

He gave me a look. "Why wouldn't she be interested?"

"She's too smart to fall for your bullshit."

His face lit up with humor. "Aw, what's the matter? You don't like her, do you?"

I rolled my eyes. "Of course not."

"No, of course not," he echoed pointedly.

A pause. "I don't want her. I just think she's sweet, too sweet for you. There are plenty of girls out there for you to fuck up, but *that* one you could fuck up permanently."

"Who says I'll fuck her up? I just want to fuck her. I mean, if you want her, she's all yours. After the shoe shine, you've got dibs."

"Thanks," I said flatly.

"But if you don't, I will."

My jaw clenched. I tried to smile. "Not a chance, man. No way would she fall for your line."

He shrugged, the picture of apathy. "That sounds like a bet to me."

I rummaged around in my bag, avoiding his eyes. Because if I looked directly at him, I might actually hit him. "You're the fucking worst. I'm not putting down bets on some girl."

"Not what you said last week about … Charmaine?"

I stood, scowling. "*Charlene.* But a girl at a bar with her skirt barely covering her ass is a different story than Val."

"*Val.* Well, well, well. You *do* like her."

"Don't be an idiot." It was inexplicable, the irrational bout of anger that sparked in my ribs.

Very few people could make me feel transparent the way he could.

In fairness, he wasn't usually *this* much of a dick. Competitive, sure. Egomaniacal, absolutely. But we'd grown up together, come into our careers together. We'd played the field together and conquered a mountain of ass in the process.

In truth, he knew me better than just about anyone. And I knew him.

Ian watched me with cool, calculating eyes. "That makes things more interesting. You don't think she'd be interested in me, but you don't want me to take a shot. You like her. So why not go after her? And don't say work. That's a bullshit rule, and you know it."

"And *you* know I won't do it. Work chicks. Good girls. That's your thing, not mine."

"Well, you know what I think, Sammy boy?" he said with his most winning smile. "Not only do I think she'd *happily* sleep with me, but now you've convinced me you want a piece of her, too."

My eyes narrowed.

"Tell you what," he offered. "I'll make you a deal."

"You couldn't just decide not to be a piece of shit?"

Another laugh, cheery and light. "Where's the fun in that?"

I folded my arms but said nothing.

"I bet you can't date her for a month. If you do it, if you last an *entire* month dating Susie Spitshine, I'll leave her alone. And if you don't, she's fair game."

A dry laugh burst out of me. "Come the fuck on, Ian."

"Come on yourself," he joked. "Get on my level, Sammy—it's nice down here in the dirt. Sleep is easy when you have no conscience." When I didn't respond, he added, "It's just a bet. What, are you afraid of losing after the other night?"

"I won that bet."

"Bullshit," he said on a laugh. "You were supposed to take her home without buying her a drink."

"I didn't buy her a drink."

When he rolled his eyes, his whole face went with them. "No, *I* did. You putting her drink on my tab was smooth, I'm not gonna lie, but I still won. Come on, a little wager on the spit shine. You say I can't have the ass I want, so this is my compromise—I get to watch *you* make an ass out of yourself while you try to figure out how to date."

"I know *how* to date. I just don't do it."

"Oh, yeah? When was the last time you saw a girl more than three times?"

My brows drew together. "That's not the point."

He pushed off the wall, his face full of amusement and challenge. "That's *exactly* the point. And those are my terms. How bad do you want me to leave her alone?"

I imagined him toying with her, stringing her along, hurting her like he would. He always did.

I could have named a dozen times off the top of my head that he'd hurt a girl, an unsuspecting, trusting girl. He spaced them into his conquests with an almost methodical precision, knowing how I hated it. I'd done my best to get him to quit leading on the innocent ones at work. The last one had been so upset when things fell apart, she'd wrecked her part during a show the next day and was fired on the spot.

But he was Ian, and nobody told Ian what to do. I could goad him, guide him, but that marked the end of my power.

I imagined Val coming to work with her face swollen and eyes bright with tears, unable to concentrate, potentially losing her job. Because as much as I wanted to believe she was too smart to fall for him, I'd seen him lie his way into enough hearts not to doubt him.

The thought seized me by the guts and twisted.

And judging by the familiar challenge in his eyes, there was only one way out.

"Swear it," I said, my voice low. "Swear that if I hold up my end, she's off the table. You won't touch her, talk to her, ask her out—nothing. Swear it, Ian."

He smiled. "I swear."

I stuck my hand out for a shake, but instead of taking it, he punched me in the shoulder and laughed that carefree laugh of a man with no soul to burden.

"God, you're such a pussy. Good luck. Clock starts tomorrow. Not gonna lie … I'm hoping you lose. I'd *love* me a little taste of that girl."

"I fucking hate you," I said lightly.

He clapped me on the arm. "I love you too, man. I love you, too."

With that, he walked away in the direction of the flutists. When I picked up my bag and turned for the exit, I caught sight of Val, who was watching me again. Her eyes darted away the moment I looked at her, the gesture as sweet and endearing as it was worrisome.

Reluctance pressed on my shoulders in layers, and in between every one was another emotion—relief, frustration, anticipation.

My only comfort was that she'd be better off dealing with me than with Ian.

At least I wouldn't hurt her.

PROOF POSITIVE

VAL

"Good news, bad news."

I closed the door to our brownstone with a neat click.

The faces of my three roommates turned to the sound of my voice. They sat scattered around the living room, listening to music—Rin with her computer resting on her never-ending legs, Amelia with a book in her small hands, and Katherine with a ball of yarn in her lap and knitting needles clutched in her fingers.

I felt my expression quirk in confusion. "Are those...knitting needles? Are you knitting?" I asked stupidly.

She shrugged. "I've always wanted to learn. Plus, I'm the only librarian in the New York Public Library system who doesn't. Even old James does it, although I'm pretty sure it's just so he can get into Esther's pants."

"Isn't she, like, eighty?" Amelia asked, frowning.

"I know. He has a thing for older women. He's barely pushing seventy-five."

Rin snorted a laugh and closed her laptop. "Bad news first, Val. Always the bad news first."

I sighed, dropping my bag behind the couch and walking around to sit next to Katherine. "It happened again. I swear, I cannot share air with him without somehow making a fool out of myself."

"Oh no," Amelia said, her voice soft and face sad. "Sam?"

"Who else?" I picked up Katherine's ball of yarn before it rolled off the couch. "This time was the coup de grâce... I emptied my spit valve onto his shoe."

Amelia gasped. Her hand flew to her mouth.

Katherine's needles stopped moving. "You spit on his shoes?"

"Just one shoe, and I didn't *actually* spit, but yes."

"What's the good news?" Rin asked, her face drawn in concern.

My sickening embarrassment lifted with my smile. "He knows my name."

Giggles erupted out of all of us. Well, except Katherine, but she was *almost* smiling, which was her equivalent to a full-blown grin.

Amelia beamed. "Okay, tell us the whole story."

"Well, I was trying not to pay attention to him, and I guess it worked a little too well. I didn't even see him coming when I emptied my spit valve and ended up blowing all over his shoes. For a split second, I thought I was going to have a heart attack. But instead of cardiac arrest, I lost my mind. I got on the ground to clean it off like an idiot. And my mouth—my God, my *mouth*—would not stop going on about spit and vomit and... *ugh*," I groaned.

"Vomit?" Now Katherine was definitely smiling, which consisted of a sardonic tilt of her lips, nothing more.

"Vomit. But then he helped me up, held *this hand*"—I lifted it in display, palm out—"and said my name! He knows my name!" I laughed, pressing the hand he'd held to my warmed cheek. "God, I am such an idiot for him."

"What do you think it means?"

"Nothing, I'm sure. He's so far out of my league, he might as well live on Jupiter. He probably only remembers me because I fell on him last week. But man, oh, man—does he have a *great* lap."

"Maybe he likes you," Rin said hopefully.

A laugh burst out of me. "Please, Rin. I know you've never seen him, but trust me when I say he's so gorgeous, it hurts to look at him. Like, it gives me physical pain. I'm pretty sure I have permanent retinal damage from looking without sunglasses on."

"So what if he's gorgeous?" Katherine asked matter-of-factly. "He's always so nice to you even though you almost broke his bass that time."

I groaned again at the memory. "Don't remind me. Or the time I was joking around with the French horns and laid a full-force high note right in his face."

"Well, it's only fair you busted his eardrums after what he did to your retinas," Rin said.

I couldn't even laugh. "Honestly, there's no way a guy like him would *ever* consider a girl like me. He dates skinny little size two models."

"You don't know that," Katherine added.

"I mean, why wouldn't he?" I asked honestly. "A guy like him could have anybody he wants. And I mean that. Single, married, straight, gay, man, woman. I'm convinced there's not a single human on the planet who would turn him down."

"No one is that good-looking," Katherine said.

I shook my head as I pulled my phone out of my back pocket and opened my photo app. "Fine. You don't believe me? Here." I shoved my phone at her.

She put down her needles and took it, leaning in, squinting her eyes. "It's kind of blurry. Is that your music stand in the way?"

I snatched my phone back. "Well, I was trying to be covert."

"Does he have Instagram?" Amelia asked.

I worried at my bottom lip. "I've never looked."

Katherine snatched my phone back again. "Well, why not?" She opened up the social app and clicked on the search.

"Because I'm afraid if I watch his life, it'll make the obsession worse. It's bad enough that I have to see him every day and know I can never, ever have him. If I start following him, I'll feel like I know him. It's better for everyone this way."

"Fine, you don't have to look, but I'm going to. What's his last name?"

My nose wrinkled up. "I don't want to say."

Katherine rolled her eyes. "Oh my God, Val. Don't be a baby. If you really want me to believe he's that gorgeous, I need proof. Now spill it—what is his last name?"

"Haddad." The word was almost a sigh.

Her fingers flew as she typed, and I leaned over to look. Rin and Amelia hurried to the back of the couch to look over our shoulders.

I thought I was prepared for photos of him. I mean, how could a photo be more disarming than the real-life version?

Answer: a million ways to Sunday.

His feed was a grid of images that did something unexpectedly intense to my insides, a hot stirring that twisted in my chest and slithered all the way down to low, low in my stomach. There wasn't a single photo that wasn't utterly perfect. Sam jamming with his friends. A top-down shot of a frying pan of eggs and bacon that displayed his shirtless abs in the process. A shot of his fingers brushing the ivory keys of a piano. Sam reading a book—*a book*—a big, fat hardback. Shirtless Sam sipping his coffee. Sam lying in his bed, looking into the camera like he was gazing across the pillow at me.

Katherine drew an audible breath and opened a picture that held the four of us perfectly still.

The image was of Sam playing his bass, one foot on the ground, the other hooked on the rung of his stool, his thighs parted to make room for the curving wooden instrument. I knew it was massive, but somehow he made it look small, natural, as if it had been fit to him exactly. His left hand pressed the strings with strong fingers, and his right held the bow with delicate grace, the veins visible, primed with blood and oxygen and vitality. His head angled to the ground, his eyes down, his dark, angular face caught in a moment of emotion, of connection to the music we couldn't hear.

"Wow," Katherine breathed. "You win. I get it."

"Can we agree now that he's totally unattainable?"

Katherine made a face. "Not totally unattainable. *Someone* could attain him."

"But *I* am not that person."

"You can't know that, Val. You like him. He's handsome and treats you with kindness, even when you spit on his shoes. I think you should ask him for coffee. See if there's something more to it."

I laughed, a nervous sound that betrayed the dread I felt at asking him for *anything*. "I can't talk to him at work. How would I get through an entire coffee date with him? I'd probably pour my latte in his lap by accident and damage his jock, which I bet is as flawless as the rest of him. And then I'd have to live with the fact that I maimed the most perfect penis on the planet. I'd owe all humankind a public apology."

Amelia nodded thoughtfully. "I think Katherine's right. I mean, what could it hurt? It's not like you could be any more embarrassed than the time you—"

I whirled around and clapped my hand over her mouth. "I cannot even believe you would jinx me like that, Judas."

But Rin was nodding, too. "I think it's a good idea, Val. You can

PLAYER

see if there's something more there than a pretty face. Ask him for coffee. Maybe there's some reason you could give him, something you wanted his advice on."

My blood pressure spiked at the thought of actually asking him to go on a coffee date with me. "He won't want me. I might think he's amazing, but no universe exists wherein a guy like *that*"—I gestured to my phone—"wants a girl like *this*." I flung a hand in the direction of my hips. "Why would he want a size sixteen with cellulite when he could have a size two with thigh gap?"

Katherine's face was stern, her eyes flaming. "Because you happen to be incredible, Valentina Bolivar. And if he can't see that, then he's a fucking douchebag and he doesn't deserve you. A guy like *that* would be *lucky* to have a girl like *you*. And if you like him, then you have to at least try. Of all of us, you are the one who is brave enough, who is confident enough to go after a guy and get him."

I gave her a look. "To be fair, we are not the bravest bunch. Four glorious wallflowers. Amelia can't speak to strangers, you scare everyone to death, Rin would rather eat a live snake than speak out of turn, and I am just too extra. It's like saying I'm the head bunny tamer."

"Come on, Val," Rin said on a laugh. "What's the worst that could happen?"

I held up my hand and began ticking things off. "I could faint, I could cry, I could start speaking in tongues. He could say no, he could laugh at me. He could pity me. Should I go on?"

No one spoke. Katherine was still pissed.

"I love you guys for believing in me. I do. But this is just *madness.* It'd be like, *Hey, you should just ask Chris Pratt out. He's recently on the market.*"

"Too soon," Amelia groaned.

"I'm just saying, he's not on *my* market. In fact, I don't even know if Sam's on the market at all. He could totally have a girlfriend, and I might make an irreparable ass out of myself for no reason."

"It's coffee, Val," Katherine said flatly. "You're not asking him to elope."

I opened my mouth to argue, but Rin cut me off.

"I know it's scary," she said, her face soft. "But what if he doesn't say no? Wouldn't it be worth asking if the answer was *yes*?"

I took a breath to respond, but this time, Amelia cut me off.

"Like Katherine said, it's just coffee. Ask him if he'd answer some questions for a blog post."

"I don't have a blog," I said, feeling my resolve crumble at the prospect of him saying yes.

"Well then, tell him it's for mine," Amelia volleyed.

"You blog about books," I shot back.

"He doesn't know that."

The temptation of spending a little time alone with him filled me with anticipation and a flurry of nerves—What would I do? What would I say?—but I imagined he'd know exactly how to soothe me. Maybe his charm would bring me down to normal levels, and we could actually have a real conversation. Maybe he'd even be charmed by me, too.

Maybe, in that dream world, I would have a shot with a guy like him.

More likely, my crush would turn me into a stalker, and his would never even start.

But that fantasy played itself out in my head, leading me to tentatively ask them, "Just coffee?"

"Or drinks," Katherine added. "A little social lubrication never hurt anyone."

"And it's not lame of me to ask him out?"

"You're not really asking him out," Amelia said. "Not if you use my blog as cover. But maybe you won't have to do that. Maybe he'll just say yes, and you won't need to explain. And anyway, we're far enough into the millennium that asking a guy out isn't weird. Feminism for the win!"

"I cannot believe you guys are talking me into this. I haven't been on a date since college—almost *five years* ago. Guys don't ask me out. I don't date. Even then, I didn't date. Pizza, bad oral, and lackluster missionary in a dorm room with the lights out doesn't count."

"Just ask him," Rin said. "If he says no, I don't think he'll be cruel about it. He's always so charming that I bet he'd find a smooth way out of it. And then you'll know for sure it's a no."

"You should wear your lipstick," Amelia said with a smile.

"Oh, I'm definitely not ready to bust out the Heartbreaker. First, he'd know something was up if I came in wearing lipstick the color of a fire truck. And second, I can't play the trumpet with red lipstick on or I really would look like a clown. Or a hooker. Either way, it wouldn't get me a coffee date."

"So, you're going to do it?" Rin asked.

With a sigh and a smile, I gave up. "I'll think about it."

Which we all knew meant I would do it.

GENETICS

SAM

Notes layered in my mind to the beat of the train as it clacked through the tunnel. The voices of the commuters. The sway of the car. The melody rose in me too quickly to write down. But I tried anyway, scribbling in my notebook resting on my thigh.

I did some of my best composing on the subway. I didn't know what it was about it—the crunch for time maybe, the riot of senses engaged, the rhythm—but sometimes I'd hop on the train and ride with no destination, just to write, just to feel the rush of creation.

When I looked up, it was just in time to see the 103rd Street station slide into view.

I'd missed my stop.

"Fuck," I hissed, scrambling to hang on to my notebook as I wound through people.

I barely cleared the doors when they closed, and the train pulled away, whipping the air around me in its exit.

Fortunately, my parents' place was right between the stations, so rather than take the train back a stop, I climbed the stairs, stowing my notebook in my bag as I stepped into the crisp fall afternoon, heading west, toward the park.

It was always quieter on this side of the city, with Central Park on one side and a stack of old buildings on the other. Trees stretched up, obscuring the sky in sheets of gold, fiery oranges and brassy reds, dropping occasional leaves bigger than my hand. Soon the trees would be bones, asleep for the winter. The thought made me preternaturally sad.

My lungs filled with cool air when I sighed.

I thought forward through my day, from the visit with my parents to the pit tonight where I'd see Val.

A bet. On the last girl I would have chosen.

Not because I didn't want her. With that smile, that body? If I'd met her anywhere but work, I'd have asked her out already. But girls like her weren't meant for guys like me. I went after the girls who knew exactly what they were getting and exactly what they weren't. The girls I couldn't hurt. Wouldn't hurt with my disinterest in a relationship.

A girl like Val needed a guy she could take home to meet her parents. A guy who'd buy her flowers and binge-watch Jane Austen movies. A guy who'd treat her right.

Like I'd said, I knew what I was and what I wasn't. And I wasn't boyfriend material. One-night material? Hundred percent. Weekend material? I was here for that.

Anything beyond that, and I'd only let her down.

And now I had to pretend to date her for a month.

Fucking Ian.

I couldn't figure out his angle. Val wasn't his type. He was much more prone to girls who nibbled salad at dinner and laughed at all his stupid jokes. But he'd known me long enough to pick up on my attraction and wanted to push me, get me to step out of line, betray my own code.

And I'd known him long enough to know he'd go after her just to prove his point.

We always did this, though the stakes hadn't been this high in a while. I'd tug on his leash, and in turn, he'd test my fences like a velociraptor.

I'd taken the bet, and my objective was clear.

Goal number one: protect her from Ian.

Goal number two: protect her from me.

There had to be a way to keep her away from Ian without leading her on, and I intended to find it. So my plan, which wasn't so much of a plan as it was an action point, was to ask her to come to the club where I played and wing it once she got there.

Things would work out. Something would land in my lap. It always did.

It crossed my mind that she might say no. But the signals she'd sent were received, loud and clear. The flush in her cheeks, her lingering gaze, the near-constant tripping she did around me. She was interested.

I was an arrogant prick to assume. But I just so happened to be a professional player, and reading women was at the top of my résumé. Val wanted me, plain and simple. But I had yet to figure out the context of her attraction. What exactly did she want from me? Something temporary or permanent?

Because if she was looking for a boyfriend, goal number two was fucked.

First things first. There was a way out, I knew. I just had to figure out what that was.

The club would be the perfect place to start.

I smiled to myself at the rightness of it all. I'd swing her around the dance floor. Make her laugh and make her happy. I'd fill myself up on those sweet smiles and her joy. And I'd find a way out of this bet with her virtue and my integrity intact.

My smile widened, my tongue slipping out to draw my bottom lip into my mouth. Ian was right about one thing—innocent girls had their appeal.

I suspected he was right about more than just that when it came to Val. That she couldn't smell the danger all over me was the first clue to her inexperience. And when it came to girls like her, there was one of two ways you could take it.

You could be the guy to worship her, or you could be the guy to ruin her with lies.

Case in point, Ian would wreck a girl like Val, show her the ugly side of the world, of love, of men. And I'd only seek to make her happy. I'd show her things she'd only read about. I'd make her world better, not ruin it.

Yeah, you're so fucking noble, Sam. A regular old Casanova.

A small laugh huffed out of my nose as I reached my parents' building. The doorman waved me inside and deposited me into the gilded elevator before sending me up to one of the penthouse floors my parents occupied.

The foyer to their floor was a marble affair, rich without being pretentious, which was a feat for any Fifth Avenue penthouse. Within seconds of knocking, the door swung open to reveal my mother, smiling brightly. I barely had time to brace myself before she flew into my arms.

"Oh, Samhir," she cooed in Lebanese, leaning back to look at me as if she hadn't seen me in a year. "It has been too long."

I laughed. "I missed you, too."

"Why do I feel like you look older? It has only been a month."

"I don't know, Mama. You only look younger every day."

It wasn't a lie. Her hair was the color of midnight, pulled back in a loose bun at the nape of her neck, her body slender and small. Her skin was smooth, the only sign of her age the wrinkles at the corners of her dark eyes, forced in place by the high, round apples of her cheeks when she smiled, which was often.

She laughed and cupped my cheek. "Flatterer. Come inside and say hello to your papa." She took my large hand in her small one and pulled me through the door.

"How was the book tour?"

"Lovely and exhausting. There were days when I'd wake up, not sure what city I was in. But it was brilliant. Just brilliant. I am very glad to be home though. Papa is glad, too. He gets grumpy when I'm away too long."

"I listened to Oprah's podcast with you last week. I hope she's treating you well. I'd hate to have to talk to her again."

She tsked and swatted at my arm. "She asked after you, sent me back with a gift. It's a Burberry peacoat."

I chuckled. "I don't think you were supposed to tell me what it is."

"She made me promise I'd send her a picture of you in it. You, my darling, have charmed every woman you've ever met, haven't you?"

"I can't help it. I take after you."

She smirked at me, her eyes twinkling with mischief. "It's how I caught your father."

"Clearly you've never seen him look at you. He required no subterfuge."

Her laugh, the sound so familiar and warm, I felt my smile all the way through me. That laugh was home.

She towed me out to the balcony where my father sat at the table with his paper. He lowered it enough to see us over the top, his smiling eyes the same dusty brown as mine.

"Ah, my son returns now that his mother is home."

He feigned apathy for as long as he could hold out, then stood, abandoning his paper on the table as he strode toward me, extending his hand. We clasped forearms, and he pulled me in for a hug, cupping the back of my neck.

"Hi, Papa."

He leaned back, smiling. "Samhir, I am happy to see you. Come. Sit."

I did as I'd been told, and they sat with me.

"How is work?" Mom asked.

"Still going well. No one has stolen my job out from under me, so that's something."

"And Ian? How much trouble is he in today?"

I chuckled. "As much as always."

"He must come see me. I brought him cheese curds from Madison like he asked, and corn from Lincoln. I tried to tell him it tastes the same as anywhere, but…" She shrugged.

"He never does listen, does he?"

A sigh. "Maybe someday. And how is the band? The club?" she added.

"The club is great. My favorite four nights of the week."

Dad humphed. "A swing band. You were top of your class at Juilliard, and you play at a nightclub. You know, you could have played with the New York Philharmonic."

"Yes, I remember getting that job. I also remember turning it down."

"Ahmed, leave him alone," Mom chided. "You made your choice to be a surgeon, and he made his to play on Broadway."

"Top of his class, Hadiya! Top of his class!" His tone was teasing and his lips smiled, but his eyes held that familiar hardness. Disappointment.

"I know, Papa. I just have too much fun watching the girls at the club when they spin around and flash their panties."

He rolled his eyes.

"Really. You don't see that at the symphony." I earned a twitch of his lips as he tried not to smile. "Broadway and the club make me happy. My life is good, Papa. Don't worry."

"I don't worry about you, Samhir. I just want you to be the best you can be, that's all."

"I am always the best I can be, at everything I do. I get that from Mama."

"I was also top of my class," she added helpfully.

"And I get it from you too, Papa."

"Summa cum laude," he said.

"Really, everything is good. I have everything I've ever wanted and things I didn't know I did. Like a Burberry coat from Oprah." I turned to Mama, effectively changing the subject. "Sounds like we need to have a photo shoot. I don't want to keep her waiting."

She chuckled and stood, shaking her head. "She blushes like a girl when she talks about you, you know."

And I smirked at my father. "Ah, then she takes after Papa, too."

He made a face but laughed—they both did.

Happiness. My life was exactly what I wished it to be, free of chains and full of living. I had music and dancing, a career I loved, and a life brimming with experiences.

And I couldn't think of a single thing more I could ask for. Not one.

SUPER BREEZY

VAL

There's no way I can pull this off.

I swear, through our entire rehearsal, I could *feel* him. The only lights under the stage were islands of music stands, the conductor on her podium, and the video monitors showing us the stage and the actors as the show went on. Several rows of musicians separated me from Sam, including a tuba, two French horns, the drum booth, and the percussion box. But every molecule in my body zinged with anticipation and reached in his direction.

Coffee. Ask him for coffee.

It's beyond lame. He probably goes to nightclubs with models. Coffee with a dumpy trumpet player isn't even at the bottom of the list. It's not on the list at all.

Seriously, don't be a baby. Maybe I could just try talking to him. Talking couldn't hurt.

I could bite my tongue. That would hurt.

Or I could say something dumb, which would hurt my ego.
Ugh. There has to be an easier way.
I mean, I don't have *to talk to him. I don't have to ask him out.*
Right. Let's just skip it. Maybe tomorrow. Maybe the next day.
Maybe on the 24   of never.

The director held her baton up, slowly raising her hands, her face open as she brought up the final crescendo, held it, and brought us to a close. There was a moment of shocking silence created by us just as much as the music had been. Goosebumps ran a path up my arms, as they always did.

The crowd above us roared their applause, and we launched into the music for the curtain call. Those final minutes were controlled chaos—the cast taking their bows, the audience clapping and cheering, the orchestra zipping through our final number. And then it was done.

The pit hummed with energy and noise, kept close by the low ceiling. Keys clicked, papers shuffled, gentle taps against wood, and an occasional string of notes from one instrument or another.

They were some of my favorite sounds in the whole world.

I sighed with contentment, gathering up my music, not realizing that, for a moment, I'd forgotten all about Sam.

Until he walked right past me, close enough to catch a hint of spice I imagined belonged to him. His head was turned as he said something to that douchebag Ian Jackson, drumsticks stuffed in his back pocket as they headed across the pit. The lights under the stage had come on, casting hard shadows across Sam's body. His back was a topographical map of masculinity, with hills and curves and valleys that made no sense to my female mind. I wondered absently what it looked like naked. I bet it was smooth and tan, sculpted in muscles, like his forearms and biceps and triceps. All the 'ceps, covered by smooth, tan skin. Big, juicy, muscly 'ceps.

Yeah, I should definitely ask him out.

His bass was shaped like a woman, tucked under his arm like it was nothing; the neck rested in the curve of his, his arm slung over the ribs, his fingers hooked in the notch at the waist. The instrument was propped against his narrow hip as he walked across the room, thirty pounds under his arm that appeared to apply no strain beyond the tension in his arms and shoulder and *that back.*

No, I definitely cannot ask him out.

I sighed, slipping my music folder into my bag, and began the process of putting my trumpet away. I made sure I took a good look around before emptying my spit valve. Sam stood at the other side of the pit, watching me with smoldering eyes and a twitch of a smile on his lips. Ian was saying something from behind him, but Sam didn't seem to be listening.

My pulse doubled. I snapped my attention back to my instrument. He was probably laughing at me. Reminding himself of the time my sweater had caught on the back of a chair when I passed and almost ripped the neck clean down the sleeve. Maybe he was making sure I'd finished with my saliva so he could safely pass me, nothing more.

I polished the bell of my horn, watching the blob of my curly head in the brass, and in the middle of my internal talk-down, another blob appeared next to mine.

My eyes moved. My head followed.

And to my absolute surprise, there he was, my crush and the object of my obsession.

"Hey, Val."

"Hey, Sam." The words were a disbelieving croak.

His smile widened.

I was staring at his mouth, my brain on emergency function. Which was why I lacked the control to stop myself from blurting out, "We should go on a date."

The only surprise that registered on his face was the uptick of one dark brow, the one that notched in the thickest part. I didn't give him time to speak before I burst into high-pitched, tremulous laughter that was at least three decibels too loud.

"That's not what I meant. I mean, coffee could be a date to some people, I guess, but you're not some people. I mean, you're people, but not like regular people, but I thought we could get coffee because my friend has a book blog, but she was wondering about string musicians, and I thought, *Hey, Sam could answer those questions better than me*, so I thought we could have coffee and—" I took a breath. My heart and stomach swapped places. I swallowed the only moisture in my cottonmouth in a sticky lump. "We definitely shouldn't go on a date. Like, at all. That would be crazy." Another laugh, this one as insane as the accompanying thought of Sam agreeing to leave the building in my presence without a bodyguard.

I imagined his responses.

I was wondering if you could sign this restraining order.

You've got a little drool on your face, right there.

I only have coffee with stalkers on Tuesdays.

His eyes sparked with amusement. "I have a better idea."

I blinked. "I'm sorry?"

"I'm playing at Sway tomorrow night with my band. Come to the show."

This time when I laughed, it actually sounded like me. "Wait, you're in a band? Like…rockabilly?"

"Swing."

"Is there dancing?" I asked hopefully.

Something in his face changed, and it upped his hotness by at least fifteen percent. "You dance?"

"I don't know how to swing dance, but I *love* to dance."

His smile tilted, and a sliver of his teeth showed. They were, to no one's surprise, brilliantly white and in perfect alignment. "I'd love to teach you how to dance. The show starts at eleven tomorrow night. Tell me you'll be there."

Something in my chest exploded like a whistling spinner. "I'll be there."

"Good," he said. "Let me give you my number."

"Okay, let me get my ph—"

He took my hand and flipped it over, cradling it in his as he pulled a pen out of his back pocket. He scrawled his number on my palm, his fingers brushing against my skin as he wrote. His face was close to mine as he watched his work, so close I could smell him, a mixture of spice and musk and male so delectable, I had to stop myself from drawing a long, loud breath through my nose.

Sam returned my hand. "Text me if you need anything." He straightened up and took a step back. "And, Val?"

I forced my eyes from my hand to meet his gaze. "Yeah?"

"Wear red." His eyes flicked to my oversized crimson sweater. "I like you in red."

My cheeks took the suggestion and rose to the occasion, the blush so intense, it almost hurt. "Deal," I managed to say.

He winked—he actually winked at me, and it was the sexiest thing I'd ever seen—before turning to walk across the room.

A date. So much better than coffee, better than dinner or drinks or anything I could have thought of.

Sam. On a stage. In a band. Dancing with me.

It was beyond comprehension.

And my only cohesive thought was that I'd better do my damnedest to find a red dress.

SAM

Goddammit, she was cute.

Cute and ridiculous.

And absolutely into me.

My eyes met Ian's, and every good feeling I had was doused and left hissing in the dark cavern of my chest.

"Did you do it?" he asked when I approached.

"Of course I did. A bet's a bet, right?"

"Good boy." A smirk. "What'd you write on her hand?"

"My number. Phone was in my bag. She's coming tomorrow night."

One of his brows rose with his smile, which had all the humor of a shark in chum. "Did you tell her to bring a friend?"

"Give it a rest, man."

He laughed. "We'll see how Susie Spitshine handles the club and if you can seal the deal. Wonder how long until you get into her pants?"

I punched him in the shoulder a little too hard to be playful. "Shut the fuck up, asshole."

He took the hit and rubbed his arm jokingly. "Don't have to be so touchy about it. But if I can't sleep with her, it's only fair that I get to hear about it when you do."

"Well, if I do, you'll be the last to know." I clapped him on the shoulder and left him behind me.

Val watched me as I passed, and just before I was to the exit, I turned back to flash her a smile. A blush smudged her cheeks, her smile bright and hopeful.

That hope gutted me.

You're an asshole, Sam.

I walked out of the theater and out into the city, trying not to think of the curve of her shoulder peeking out of her giant red sweater. Even at its size, it hugged her collarbone and hung off that one tanned shoulder that was smooth and unmarred with even a single freckle. Which was interesting, given the smattering of freckles on her cheeks and bridge of her nose I'd noticed when I wrote my number on her hand. I could smell her hair, the coconut and vanilla mingling in a mouthwatering combination that made me want to bury my face in her curls. Even the way that gargantuan sweater clung to the curves of her breasts, the width of her hips, was enticing.

I pictured the sweet, optimistic surprise on her face when I asked her to come to the club.

Technically, she'd asked me out first, shocking me in the best way. At least, I thought she had asked me out somewhere in her rambling nerves.

God, she was almost too much—she disarmed me completely.

One of the upsides of the bet was that tomorrow night, I'd get to hang out with her. I'd see her at the club.

I imagined her in a red dress, swinging to the music. I imagined pulling her around the dance floor in my arms, imagined her small hand in mine. Imagined that look of hope on her face that made me feel like a king and a crook.

But I wouldn't hurt her. No matter what, I wouldn't hurt her. If I did, I'd be no better than Ian.

And she deserved better than that.

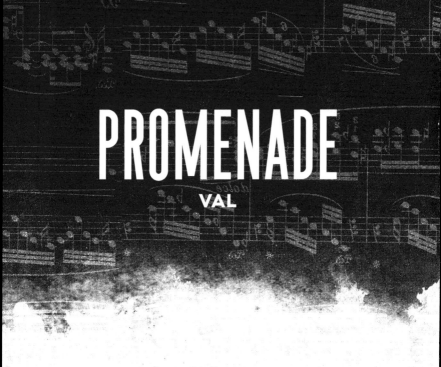

PROMENADE
VAL

I held my breath, my eyes locked on the tip of my lip liner as I drew a tenuous line along the curve of my bottom lip.

On inspection, it wasn't so bad. I went over it again with a little more confidence.

The lipstick had never been used, the angled surface smooth and perfect. I'd bought it months ago, at the same time my roommates bought theirs. It had been my idea. Correction—it had been the idea of our favorite waitress at our favorite bar, but I had been the whip-bearer who brought the plan to action. I'd had to drag the girls into Sephora and practically handcuff them to the makeup artist's chair, but I'd done it.

Rin had been the only one to embrace it, and that had inspired us to start the Red Lipstick Coalition.

The idea was to wear that lipstick, unabashed and unafraid, in an effort to be bold and brave as their names implied. Rin's lipstick was called Boss Bitch, and she'd lived up to the title.

Who would have thought one of the shiest women I'd ever known would have the stones to take her internship by storm and slay the heart of her beastly boss? Not me, that was for sure. And I couldn't have been happier to be wrong.

Katherine, Amelia, and I hadn't had the courage or occasion to wear ours yet. My little tube of Heartbreaker had been sitting on top of my dresser long enough that a thin layer of dust coated the embossed cap. But tonight? Tonight called for red lipstick and victory rolls.

Tonight, I was going to a swing club.

With Sam.

On a date.

I think.

I was the literal worst at dating.

In high school, my brothers had scared off every guy who opened his mouth to speak to me. And honestly, I hadn't minded. Being the only girl with boobs in the fifth grade had ruined me. Boys groped. Girls name-called. I hated my body with a deep, burning passion. And by the time I got to high school, I was done with the whole thing for life.

My current roommates were also my college roommates, and the second we met, we became a unit. Well, almost the second we met. Amelia—a tiny, pale, platinum-haired introvert—was so shy, she couldn't even call the dentist to make an appointment, and when I first met her, she didn't speak to any of us for two weeks. Katherine was her opposite—a taller, darker emotional robot with a broken filter—and we were all sure she hated us.

Rin and I were the most alike, though she used to be so much softer and shier than me. She hadn't wanted anyone to see her, would curl into herself with the slightest attention. I was more likely to twerk in line at Taco 'Bout It than to shy away from attention, given that the right Nicki Minaj song was playing.

But guys didn't ask me out. The four of us were so insulated that no one could infiltrate our defenses, which was part of the problem. We went to girls' night at our favorite bar every week with the intention of socializing. But we never left our table, and no one ever came to talk to us.

Of course, in college I'd gone on a few dates and hooked up with a few guys. They'd all been magnificent duds, which hadn't inspired me to keep looking. I had a vibrator and internet access. What more could a girl want?

That *had* been my model at least. Until recently.

I pressed my lips together, inspecting my reflection once more before stepping into my room.

"That dress is *incredible*," Amelia breathed.

I did a little twirl and laughed.

We'd spent the day shopping, looking for outfits befitting a swing club. Amelia wore black high-waisted pedal pushers with a short-sleeved tailored shirt, tied in the front. A black-and-white polka-dot scarf was tied around her platinum hair and knotted on top. Katherine wore a tailored shirtdress the color of rust, dotted with little mustard flowers.

And I had found a dress that nearly brought the three of us to our knees.

The silk chiffon shirtdress was the color of a ripe, juicy apple with a spaghetti-strap shell. But the sheer, fitted bodice boasted little pleats in front, a Peter Pan collar, and puffed sleeves with elastic hems. Shiny red buttons marched down to the thick waistband, which gave the illusion that my waist was much smaller than it typically appeared.

But the skirt was the best part. Layers of chiffon spilled off my hips in a circle cut so brilliant, the featherlight fabric swayed joyfully with every motion.

"I can't believe we found something like this in my size," I said, pressing a hand to my stomach. "Well done, Amelia."

She flushed, red lips smiling. "One of my best and most useful skills is manipulating Google. It has all the answers—best new vintage clothing in Manhattan, how to do victory rolls, Lindy Hop for beginners."

"I'm so glad you guys are coming with me. I don't think I could have done this alone." I followed them out of my room and down the stairs.

Katherine shrugged from the front of the line. "It'll be fun. Plus, we get to wear our red lipstick without feeling weird about it."

"Seriously," Amelia added. "Mine's been sitting next to my toothbrush for forever, and the thought of wearing it actually makes my fight or flight kick in. But I didn't think twice about putting it on tonight. And I actually kind of love it." She made a kissy face over her shoulder at me to prove it.

"You in red lipstick is the highlight of my life. Thank you, by the way—you did such a great job on my hair," I said to Amelia, smoothing a hand over said victory rolls. Only the front was up; the back was a riot of curls. And my lips, like my friends', were shockingly red.

Rin and her boyfriend, Court, were waiting in the living room, and the second we entered, Rin hopped out of his lap and bounded toward us, beaming.

She was a vision, all six feet of her, in high-waisted sailor pants and a corset top. She looked like a Korean pinup girl, her dark hair pinned in, rolled up, and tied with a red scarf. Her alabaster skin against the ebony of her hair and the ruby red of her lips were the embodiment of art and beauty.

"Oh my God, Val—*that dress!*" Her eyes moved down my body, red lips gaping. "Spin around."

I did with a laugh, and she clapped, laughing with me.

Court stood, and I bit my tongue.

He would *not* have appreciated my wit in the moment.

The man was a Roman marble statue with a heartbeat—intense and chiseled to perfection. Except instead of a toga or the suit as he typically preferred, he was stiff-backed in slacks, a button-down, suspenders, and a fedora.

He looked about as comfortable as a roller skater approaching a cobblestone street covered in ice.

Court caught my eye and held it with suspicion, like he was waiting for me to tease him and had a response locked and loaded.

I couldn't help but laugh. "Don't worry—I'm not gonna make this any worse for you than it already is."

His shoulders relaxed, and a smile flickered at the corner of his mouth. "Good. It's bad enough that I'm wearing suspenders. Aren't these on your Never Will I Ever list you put together in college? By law, these are strictly banned." He hooked a thumb in one of the elastic bands and snapped it.

Rin turned to him, smiling. "Well, if I were still abiding by those laws, we'd have been over a long time ago. *Dating an asshole* was at the top of the list."

"It's true," Katherine offered helpfully.

"It's like I said," Rin continued, "think of it like Halloween. See? All of us are dressed up, and this is just your costume."

The second she touched his chest, he curved into her, his eyes warming and lips smiling. His hand slid into the small of her back to pull her to him. "Only for you would I wear a hat that makes me look like Jason Mraz on *TRL*, Cocoa Beach."

I rolled my eyes. "That show has been off the air since 2008."

"That's funny, since that was the last time Jason Mraz was cool."

Amelia's face pinched in offense. "Sir, I will have you know that Jason Mraz is a musical genius, and not only is he still cool, but he is essentially the king of all singer-songwriters. That hat is an icon, and you should feel good—nay, *privileged*—to don a fedora worthy of comparison." She pointed at him to punctuate her sincerity.

Court laughed and put up a hand in surrender. "All right, all right. I'm sorry."

"Thank you," she said curtly, folding her arms. "Apology accepted."

Rin chuckled, reaching up on her tiptoes to kiss him on the cheek, taking the hat off him in the same motion. "Leave it here if you don't like it. I much prefer your hair where I can reach it anyway."

"Come here," Katherine said, motioning to Amelia. "Let's practice some more. I need to work on the promenade."

"Okay," Amelia answered, taking Katherine's hand.

Katherine was, of course, leading. "And … rock step, triple step, step, step, triple step. Ba, pa, promenade, pop out, promenade."

With every syllable, their feet moved in step with each other.

"You guys look great," Rin said.

"I'm not doing that," Court insisted.

She chuckled and leaned into him.

Katherine spun Amelia around, and Amelia couldn't stop giggling.

"I hope you have on hot pants, Val," Amelia said. "Otherwise, everybody's gonna see your chonies."

I popped my butt out and flipped my skirts to flash my tiny black shorts. "Bam!"

She feigned blindness. "Your heinie is too shiny!"

I laughed, spinning again. "I can't believe this is happening. I feel like Cinderella on her way to the ball."

"And you've got a prince waiting for you and everything," Amelia said as Katherine pulled her into a slide, hands over heads to trail down their arms. Katherine yanked her for a spin, and Amelia squealed. "God, this is too much fun."

I sighed, my smile faltering. "I'm not sure what this even is. Technically, I asked him out but then told him I *wasn't* asking him out, and he suggested I come to the club. He might still expect me to ask him about Amelia's fake article. I have no idea."

Court frowned. "You don't know whether or not it's a date?"

"It's complicated, Courtney."

He rolled his eyes.

"Law of attraction," Katherine said, triple-stepping, pulling Amelia in and pushing her out in counts of five. "Believe it's a date, and it's more likely to *become* a date."

I laughed. "Who knew it was that easy? I'd have been believing Ryan Reynolds was going to date me for years."

Amelia missed Katherine's hand and stumbled backward with a *whoop!*

Katherine laughed, panting from exertion. "It's gonna be fun, Val. And after tonight, it'll be clear what he wants. You'll know for sure soon enough."

I humphed, but my cynicism was short-lived. A spark of anticipation took its place. Because I was about to see Sam on what might or might not be a date. Outside of work and in a club. A club with jazz music and swing dancing and drinks and my friends, even pouty Court and his suspenders.

And, if I played my cards right, I might get to dance with Sam.

If I never got another thing from him, I'd still die happy.

A half an hour later, we were climbing out of the cab and stepping onto the curb in front of Sway. Muffled, bouncing swing jazz couldn't be contained by the building walls. An echoing bounce lightened my step as we made our way toward the line at the door. The whole lot of us was grinning with the exception of Court, who looked suspicious and mildly threatening.

"Ah, excuse me, miss?" a deep voice said, but we kept walking, never even considering we were being addressed. "You, in the red dress—Val?"

I stopped so fast, Katherine and Amelia bumped into me. I turned to find a bouncer with a clipboard waving me over. His jaw was shaped like a brick, and his head was bald as a cue ball.

My face quirked as I approached. "Yes?"

He smirked. "Sam told me to look out for you. Curves for days, red dress, goes by the name of Val. No need to wait in line, sweetheart. Sammy's got you on the list."

A tittering laugh escaped me. "You're kidding."

He gave me a look. "Well, I'm not psychic, cupcake. These your friends?" He nodded to Amelia, Katherine, and Rin, narrowing his eyes for a second when he reached Court.

"Uh, yes. They're with me."

"Just need your IDs," he said, smiling at me as he unhooked the red velvet rope.

The twenty people in line glared at us like we'd just kicked a litter of puppies. I smiled apologetically. And once we proved our legal age, we were past the ropes and on our way in.

The bouncer followed us, leaning into the door to tell the ticket girl, "They're on the house."

A pretty girl with russet hair smiled. "Have a good time."

We stepped into the club, laughing, Katherine's arm in mine and Amelia's hand in my free one. It was too loud to talk, but once we were inside, it didn't matter.

I had absolutely no words.

The club wasn't a club at all—it was a grand, gorgeous ballroom. The ceilings were plastered with geometric moldings that sang of the thirties and forties. Edison bulbs hung in clusters all around the room, their glow dim and orange, painting the room—which was a wave of bopping bodies—in golds and shadows. Every surface shone with polished wood and brass. Leather and luxury, velvet and vice. But it wasn't so elegant or extravagant that the music didn't feel exactly right, that the bobby socks and saddle shoes didn't make sense. It all made sense, perfect sense, from the architectural details to the bopping beat. From the bodies jumping and spinning on the dance floor like tops.

We'd stepped back in time.

I watched the bodies as they came together and apart, the raucous joy punctuated occasionally by a set of feet and pettiskirts, flashes of hot pants as girls were flipped. There wasn't a single face on that dance floor that wasn't smiling.

Scientific fact: anyone who doesn't feel absolute bliss watching swing dancers has no soul. Swing dancing is single-handedly the most jubilant act to ever exist. It only exists for joy, nothing else. How many other things in the world can say the same?

Katherine grabbed Amelia's hand, laughing as she towed Amelia out onto the dance floor. Rin lit up like a floodlight, snagging Court's hand, and he followed her onto the dance floor with a lovesick smile on his face.

I laughed at the big sap and made to follow them, my smile so big, my cheeks hurt. But then I looked up to the stage, and my feet came to a stop.

My face slipped into a slack, surprised O.

Above the sea of bouncing dancers was the stage, and on that stage stood the jazz band with every member playing his absolute heart out. A pianist behind an upright piano, a guy sitting on a box with an acoustic guitar in his lap, a sax and clarinet player next to a trumpet player and a trombone. Ian behind his drums, carrying the hopping beat with an ease that shouldn't have been legal.

And in the middle of them all was Sam.

He held his bass with expert ease, his heels bouncing in time with his fingers as he plucked the strings. His hair, black as pitch, was combed back and shining, his lips smiling as he looked down the line at the other musicians like they could have been playing in a garage and not in a ballroom full of several hundred people, almost all of who were dancing. God, he was tall, his gray tweed pants low on his hips, black suspenders over his broad shoulders, his white tailored shirt cuffed up his forearms that fluttered with every move of his fingers.

The instruments, I realized, had been taking turns soloing, and the light shifted to Sam, who took over the stage, the band, the club. The universe.

He spun his instrument around, catching it just in time to stay on beat as he launched into a rowdy solo. At one point, he reached behind him to dingle a ditty on the piano between phrases, and once, he hit the cymbal of Ian's trap set to punctuate a run. The noise of the crowd rose in a wave. When he really leaned into the solo, he tilted the bass on its side, holding the neck at a forty-five degree angle, and in a balance of perfect physics, he climbed up on its ribs, one foot on the shoulder, one in its waist. And there he stayed, perched on his bass like he was staking a claim, shaking his head to the tune. His fingers worked his way up and down the neck of that instrument like he was making love to it, sliding his fingertip along one string in a long, falling slide in the end. And at the break, he hopped off the bass with a kick of his legs, picking up the beat the second his feet hit the ground at the precise moment the rest of the band joined in.

I was pretty sure every woman in the room lost her drawers to him in that moment.

Katherine materialized by my side, breaking my attention.

"We're crossing *No guys with suspenders* off the list," I said definitively.

"Agreed. Now, let's dance!"

And then she swept me onto the dance floor.

For the next hour and a half, Amelia and I took turns dancing with Katherine. And when she wasn't swinging me around, I watched Sam play. If it hadn't been for him hamming it up every time he was in the spotlight, I wouldn't have even known he was aware of the crowd. The entire band deferred to him—he was the center of it all even though he was at the bottom of the sound, the foundation of the music.

Once, somehow, he caught sight of me in the ocean of people. It might have been the dress, bright as a stoplight on the edge of the dance floor, but he saw me and flashed the most brilliant, breathtaking smile. Strictly for me, he angled his bass like a guitar, the stand still on the ground, and played it with a flourish and a wink in my direction, picking it back up to spin it around just as the song picked up for the chorus.

I could barely stand it. I wanted to watch him play forever, but I was *dying* for him to get down here and dance with me.

After a while, their set ended, and the crowd erupted in cheers and whistles as the band headed offstage, instruments in hand. The piano player stayed put, plinking out a swinging jazz tune that got everyone dancing again as stagehands cleared the set for the next act.

I took a breath, pressing my hand to my stomach to try to still my nerves. "How do I look?" I asked Amelia.

She beamed. "Like a million and one bucks."

"Don't worry," Katherine said. "It's gonna be great. *Here he comes.*"

I swallowed hard and turned to find Sam winding his way through the crowd toward me, smiling in my direction. Hands reached out to pat him on the shoulders, smiling faces praised him, and every female—plus several men—in his path stopped to watch him walk by. He was a magnet moving through metal shavings.

I almost didn't believe it when he stopped in front of me. "You made it."

"I did," I said, trying to keep my cool. "That was incredible! I had no idea places like this even existed!"

He laughed. "You can't unring that bell. Looks like we've got ourselves a new regular."

Ian stepped out from behind him, his face too angular, too sharp. He was technically handsome—strong jaw and bright blue eyes, golden hair and a gorgeous smile. But something about him sang the warning of a predator, a man with little care for others, especially of the opposite gender. I'd heard enough chatter from the woodwind section to know he was a player through and through.

"Hey, Val," he said. "I don't think we've officially met. Ian Jackson. These your friends?"

I tried to smile at him, but it felt about as genuine as the Flendi bags guys sold on the street in Midtown. "This is Katherine, Amelia, and Rin—my roommates—and this is Court, Rin's boyfriend."

"Nice to meet you," Sam said to the group.

Katherine stuck out her hand stiffly. "Nice to meet you, too."

Sam took it, amused, and she gave it a pump. Amelia gave a timid wave and took a step behind Katherine.

Ian slithered around Sam to stand by Katherine. "So, Katherine, is it? And what is it you do for a living?"

"I'm a librarian."

"You're kidding. Tell me you have glasses and wear your hair in a really tight bun. You stick your pencil in it, don't you?" He was practically frothing at the mouth.

Court's eyes narrowed to slits, the muscles at his jaw bouncing. He shifted like he was going to take a step, but Rin stayed him with a hand on his arm and a smirk on her face.

"I have twenty-twenty vision, and I only use pens."

He laughed. "Let me buy you a drink, Dewey."

Her brows drew together. "As in the Dewey decimal system? That's not terribly clever."

Another laugh as he tried to put his arm around her. "Man, you are too good to be true. Come on, what are you drinking?"

She shrugged out from under his arm. "Your request implies a desire for sex, but I'm a lesbian," she lied with a completely straight face. "See?"

Katherine turned on her heel to Amelia, grabbed her face in both hands, and planted a sloppy, closed-mouth kiss on her lips.

Amelia's hands flew out and windmilled, but Katherine held her still while she finished the job. When she broke away, it was with a pop, a curt nod, and a clinical brush of the corner of her lips.

I thought I actually heard the thunk when Court's jaw hit the ground.

Amelia stood stock-still, her blue eyes wide and blinking and her face the color of my dress.

"So, there you have it," Katherine said matter-of-factly. "Very much gay. Thank you for your kind offer, but I think my date would be offended if I accepted."

Ian's mouth gaped like a trout, and a single *ha* burst out of him. "Well, my mistake." He turned to Sam, who seemed like he was trying very, very hard not to laugh. "I'm off to the bar. Don't get into too much trouble now. Okay, kids?"

Sam gave him a look. "We'll try to be good."

"But not you two," Ian added with a glance at Katherine and Amelia.

Amelia still hadn't moved other than her eyelids, which still blinked like a camera shutter.

And with that, he left.

I found myself breathing a little easier once he was out of sight.

Sam extended his hand, and when I placed mine in his palm, he held it up, inspecting me. A long whistle left his lips. "Now, *this* is a dress." He spun me once, the chiffon lifting away from my legs, lighter than air. "I've been waiting all night to dance with you. Would you do me the honor?"

My heart did a back handspring. "I'd love to." My smile slipped. "I'm not very good. I've never really danced like this," I warned.

With a solid tug, I was in his arms. One steady hand held my ribs, and the other held mine to the side as if it were the most natural thing in the world, to hold me like that, to sway this way. The smell of him invaded my senses, spice and musk and clean, masculine sweat.

"All you have to do is stay on your toes. I'll do the rest."

I must not have looked certain because he added something that hit me deep in my chest.

"Trust me, Val."

To dance with him. That was what he meant. I knew it in my brain, but my heart heard something else entirely.

"All right," I breathed.

He smiled.

His grip tightened.

The beat picked up.

And I flew.

In Sam's arms, things like physics and gravity no longer existed. I didn't need to do anything but trust him as he spun me away, my arm flying out in a mirror of his. Another tug and I was back in his arms and spinning with him, then again, he let one hand go and swung me out. He knew exactly when to push and when to pull, how to use the force of our turns to keep me moving, spinning, stepping. I felt like I was in a centrifuge, my weight and his balanced so perfectly. Every time I misstepped, he was there, snagging my hand, my waist. And I settled into the motion, bouncing on the balls of my feet and laughing as he whipped me around the dance floor.

He pulled me in close after a minute, pressing me against his long body and bopping me around a little slower. I couldn't stop giggling.

He smirked down at me. "See? Told you. Nothing to it."

I shook my head, smiling up at him. "Easy as pie."

Sam's eyes shifted to my lips and stayed there. "I love this lipstick. I've never seen you in it before."

"Well, I can't exactly play the trumpet in it."

A chuckle. "No, I guess not."

"Honestly, I used to be scared to death of it. But thanks to Jeffree Star's YouTube tutorials, I'm basically a pro. I'm not usually a red lipstick kind of girl. More like a Chapstick-and-a-dash-of-mascara kind of girl."

His smile tilted, his eyes still on my lips. "Oh, I definitely think you're a red lipstick kind of girl." Before I could faint from the compliment, he said, "I'm glad you came tonight."

I felt myself brighten. "Me too. I swear, it's impossible to be sad at a place like this."

He laughed and spun me out, then pulled me back in and bounced us in a quick circle. "This club is my favorite place in the whole world for that reason."

"Thank you. For inviting me here. For telling that guy at the door who I was."

"I'm glad Benny found you. I realized too late that I hadn't gotten your number, and I was a little worried he wouldn't pick you out of the crowd. But when I saw you in this dress, I knew he'd have spotted you easy."

I was glad it was dark so he couldn't see me blush. The golden light highlighted the bridge of his nose, the angle of his cheekbones, the ridge of his brow, casting his eyes into shadow.

"I kind of can't believe I'm here," I admitted.

"Why not?"

"Well, because," I said, as if that explained everything.

A chuckle rumbled through him, and he triple-stepped us in a circle before slowing us down again. "Well, that clears it up."

"I…I honestly didn't mean to ask you out or anything. I didn't think you'd be interested in hanging out with me."

He frowned. "Why wouldn't I want to hang out with you?"

God, he's going to make me say it.

"Well, because…I mean…well, *look* at you."

My hand rode his shoulder as he shrugged. "Look at you. Every guy in the club has been watching you tonight."

I laughed like he'd just told a side-splitter. "That's sweet, Sam, but—"

"But what? I wouldn't lie to you, Val. You're beautiful. A little clumsy and without much of a filter, but you're interesting. Different."

I tried to take a breath but couldn't. *Different.* That hadn't sounded like a good thing.

He read my mind or my face, adding, "You're not like other girls. I'm just glad I finally got you to relax around me. It was making me jittery."

Another laugh. "This is you jittery? You should teach classes on how to be cool. I'd be first in line."

"You don't need classes. I like when you say exactly what's in your head. It's refreshing."

He pulled me into a sweetheart hold, my back to his front, our arms crossed in front of me like a prom picture. I followed his lead as we kicked our feet out in time to the music, and he spun me out, spun me back, and whipped me in a circle again.

When I landed back in his arms, I felt a little dizzy, and it had nothing to do with the spinning.

"So," he started, "did you actually have questions for me for your friend's blog?" His smile was conspiratorial. Crooked and charming.

"No," I admitted. "God, I'm the worst at this. I don't have any idea how to date—" My eyes snapped up to his. "Not that this is a date. It's not. I mean, unless you thought it was, and then that would be rad—" *Rad? When the fuck have I ever said rad?*

I took a breath in the hopes it would quiet the buzzing in my ears. It didn't.

His expression was unreadable. "When was the last time you went on a date?"

I swallowed. Hard. "Five years ago," I confessed quietly.

He said nothing at first, instead taking a moment to swing me around. "I have a hard time believing no one has asked you out in five years."

"Well, believe it," I said with a little more snap than I'd meant to.

He pulled me a little closer. "Where have you been going to meet guys, a Braille library?"

My brows came together in confusion, and he laughed, flashing his teeth before leaning in to press his lips to my ear.

"They must have been blind."

I laughed and covered my face with the hand that had been on his shoulder. "I can't with you, Sam. I can't with any of this. I really have no idea what I'm doing at all. Know of any tutors? Because clearly I could use some tips."

He spun me out and twirled me around for a couple of measures, then zipped me back into his arms with a laugh. "I can teach you. I don't know if you know this, but I'm a professional dater."

"Teach me?" I echoed stupidly.

"Teach you. Let me tell you something, Val, there's no reason you couldn't have any guy you wanted. If you want to know how to snag a guy, how to pick him up, small-talk him, charm him, I can teach you."

"Oh." My heart, my hopes, my happiness sank like a stone in a river. "I…I guess you have a lot of experience, huh?"

"Loads." His face was the picture of calm confidence. "One month of lessons. We can meet here at the club as often as you want, go on a few dates so I can show you the ropes. What do you say?"

I took that stunned moment to twist the dial on the telescope so I could see things for what they were. And everything became clear. Sam was just being a nice guy, trying to find a way out after I made an ass out of myself yesterday. He had no intention of dating me. Of course he didn't. Why would he?

This made much more sense.

My first instinct was to refuse, to immediately leave the club with my friends and polish off the pint of mint chocolate chip in my freezer. Maybe a solid cry for good measure.

But then I took it a step further. What he was offering was tempting. A month of dancing with Sam in the club. A month of fake dates and drinks and laughter. A month of Sam's smiles just for me.

I knew how pathetic it was even then, in the moment. But I'd never have another chance to pretend like that with a man like Sam, not as long as I lived.

So with a smile that hurt as much as it displayed my hope, I said something I knew I'd come to regret, deciding then and there that I didn't care. "When do we start?"

COCKSURE

SAM

I smiled into my whiskey, spinning my glass in a slow circle on the bar.

I'd wandered back into the club after putting Val and her friends in a cab to pull a seat up to the bar for a celebratory drink.

I'd solved all my problems.

The answer had fallen in my lap exactly as I'd anticipated, thanks to Val's admission. She didn't know how to date, and I was a serial dater.

She had no idea that, with that one little fact, I held the power to shield her from Ian without putting her feelings on the line.

It was the loophole of the century.

We'd be together for our lessons, which meant I'd be spending a lot of time with her. And given the nature of our lessons, we'd be doing a lot of *fake* dating. Ian would think we were together, and I could help her, teach her a thing or two so she could find a guy. I could teach her the difference between guys like me, guys like Ian, and the good guys. Show her how to recognize a man who would appreciate her, help her spot the kind of guy who was everything Ian and I weren't.

I still couldn't believe it had been so long since she'd been on a date and found myself wondering what the real story was. Because there was a story—I knew that as well as I knew the color of the sky or the C scale. How in the world a girl like Val hadn't been snapped up was beyond me.

As an added bonus, I would get to hang out with her for an entire month. I was probably far too happy about that to be considered wise, but I couldn't help it.

I couldn't tell you what it was about her exactly. I was attracted to her. If I'd met her here at the club, she'd be in a cab with me right now. Alone.

Some guys picked a girl out by looks alone. Some simply by a single feature—body, smile, hair, eyes. But I found I was looking for something more. It was a feeling, an intuition, and it didn't discriminate. If the feeling was there, that thrum of connection… well, that was all it took.

And Val had it.

There was nothing I loved more than a girl who could make me laugh. A girl who caught me off guard. The fact that she was so goddamn cute was the best kind of bonus. I bet her pert little mouth was sweet and soft. I bet she sighed like an angel with a single touch. I bet her ass bounced like a porn star in bed.

A frown tugged at my lips. No boyfriends probably meant no sex. Poor Val had to be *starving*.

And man, did I wish I could be the one to feed her.

I sighed and took a drink, my spirits rising again. Teaching Val would be fun, and I imagined us being friends. I hadn't missed the flash of disappointment on her face the moment she realized what I was suggesting meant we weren't going to get together. I felt the sting of it myself, like walking past a case of fresh pastries and only being able to admire the display. But what she didn't realize was that it was for the best. We'd make great friends, and I could help her. I could teach her.

I could dance with her some more.

Spinning her around the dance floor was simpler than it should have been. Even the girls who knew how to swing always seemed to have an opinion on where they wanted to go and what they wanted to do, and unless you'd been dancing with someone for a long while, it was impossible to read each other's cues. The easiest thing when dancing with a new partner was to let the guy lead, which was exactly what Val had done. She gave over her trust, let me spin and trick her all over the place, let me pull her and turn her and hold her close. She'd done as she'd been told and stayed on her toes, trusted my direction, and the result had been absolute harmony.

She just sort of…fit. And if she kept taking my lead, tutoring her was going to be a piece of cake.

"What are you grinning about?" Ian said from my elbow as he took a seat. "Hey, Rico—pour me a scotch, would ya?"

Rico nodded, flipping his towel onto his shoulder before turning to the wall of bottles.

"Just feeling smug about sealing the deal with Val," I said with meaning he'd never guess, shooting him a smirk to drive it home.

He shook his head. "I don't know why I ever get my hopes up that you'll fail. Never once have I seen it."

"Not true. Kandi Koffman, junior year." I shook my head at the memory of her. "She shot me down like a clay pigeon."

With a laugh, he picked up the drink Rico had just set in front of him. "Damn, that's right. Cheers to the only chick who ever realized she was too good for you."

I clinked my glass to his, and we took a drink.

"You know," he started once he swallowed, "I can honestly say I've never had a girl pretend to be a lesbian to get out of a free drink."

I laughed, picturing the little one's face—Amelia. "First time for everything."

"When are you seeing her again out of work?"

"She'll be back in the club for our next gig."

"So we'll be seeing a lot of her. Good. I can keep an eye on you, make sure you're not shirking your responsibilities."

My spine straightened an inch, but he kept talking before I could respond.

"She looked good. That dress, man. She looked like a cherry with a smile. Too bad I can't have her for myself. Yet."

"Ever," I corrected and took a drink.

He chuckled. "We'll see about that, loverboy."

And with a hard smile, I said, "We sure will."

VAL

"This is a horrible idea," Katherine said, kicking off her shoes by the door.

I huffed. "It's not a horrible idea. It's *brilliant.*"

Amelia sat on the bench in the entry and untied her canvas sneakers. "I'm somewhere in the middle. If a guy like Sam proposed hanging out with me for a month, I'd have said yes. I mean, assuming I could have spoken to him at all." She wiggled her toes when they were free. "But I'm not gonna lie, Val—you're playing with fire."

I was glad Rin and Court had gone to his place because there was no way he wouldn't have some serious opinions about my situation with Sam, and I wasn't ready to hear them.

"Look," I said with some finality, "the big goal for tonight was to find out what I meant to Sam, and now, that's clear. Am I disappointed? Fuck yes, I am wildly disappointed. But now I know. And he's offered to help me. There were a hundred cute guys at the club tonight, and I wouldn't have had the guts to talk to any of them. But maybe, with a little help, I could figure out how to pick up a guy. And the club is the *perfect* place. I could test-drive them with a dance, see if we jive well. Like, actually jive. Or jitterbug. Or maybe a little Watusi."

Amelia laughed, but Katherine didn't look amused.

She hung a hand on her hip and gave me a look. "Do you honestly think you can spend all that time with him and not want *him* to be the one you're dating? Six hours ago, you were borderline obsessed with him."

My heart lurched. "Well, trust me when I say that his offer to tutor me instead of to take me home was a bucket of ice water on my hope. Sam's offering to be my friend, which is exactly what I should expect. Plus, he's going to keep teaching me how to dance. I had so much fun tonight—I'd hate for that to end."

Amelia sighed, her cheeks pinking with a flush. "It really was more fun than I've had in ages. I was worried boys would try to talk to us, but Katherine took care of that." She gave Katherine a look.

Katherine shrugged. "It worked, didn't it?"

Amelia looked at the ceiling and shook her head.

"So will you guys come back to the club with me?" I asked hopefully.

"I will if Katherine will. Since she's my girlfriend and all."

Katherine wore an impressive frown. "I don't know, Val. I'm not going to pretend like I approve of you getting tutored in dating by the guy you have a crush on."

"Don't you believe me?" I asked, hurt. "I can do this without getting hurt. I know where we stand now. Sam wants to be my friend, nothing more. It makes perfect sense. The idea that he might actually like me as more than that is just too ridiculous for words. I can't believe I was deluded enough to ever consider it in the first place."

I took a breath and smiled. "I'm excited to learn. In fact, I think we could *all* benefit from his tutelage."

"Ooh, good word," Amelia said.

Katherine still didn't look convinced. "You're not going to see it any other way, are you?"

"Nope. To be honest, I'm actually a little relieved. The performance anxiety might have sent me to an early grave. If I'm gonna have a heart attack, I'd prefer it to be much beyond twenty-six and triggered by a slab of bacon."

Katherine assessed me for a long moment before releasing a resigned sigh. "All right."

Amelia and I cheered.

"But only because I really, really want to go dancing again."

I scooped her up in a hug and pressed a kiss to her cheek. "Thank you," I said, accepting her support, along with everything else, for as good as I would get.

ON LOCK

VAL

"Who knew you had all the moves, Val?"

The pit the next night was constant motion, the show over, my face in my case as I packed my horn away. When I looked up in surprise and confusion, I found Ian smiling down at me. That smile was anything but easy.

I made myself smile back. "Not me, that's for sure. Sam did all the heavy lifting."

"He does that. He was right—you look great in red."

"Thanks," I said, not knowing how else to respond. Was he hitting on me? Making fun of me? I was oblivious. Oblivious and instantaneously uncomfortable.

"You're welcome. Have any friends who aren't pretend lesbians? I'd love somebody to dance with who spins like you."

The scent of spice and *Sam* invaded my senses as his heavy, warm arm came to rest on my shoulders, as if it were the most natural thing.

My pulse spiked in a surge of awareness.

"I bet you would, Ian."

He was smiling—I could hear it. He was too close to see. If I'd turned my head, I might have accidentally kissed him. For the duration of an inhale, I let myself imagine what that would feel like, and on the exhale, I let it go.

"Don't let him hound you, Val. He's relentless."

"It's true," Ian admitted. "I never give something up once I set my sights on it."

Something about the way he'd said it made me uneasy.

Sam picked up my trumpet case for me and steered me away from Ian. "Yeah, well, cheaters never win."

"And good guys finish last," Ian volleyed enigmatically. But he flashed his shark smile at me. "See you tomorrow night, Val."

"Ah, okay. See you then."

"Can I walk you to the subway?" Sam asked, his face turned to mine—I could feel his breath on my cheek. It smelled like mint and infatuation.

A surge of irrational frustration rose in me at the fact that he didn't have a single flaw. Maybe he had disgustingly long toenails or bellybutton funk or smelly ears. Something. Anything.

"Sure," I said lightly, waiting on him to release me.

He didn't. Instead, he tucked me into his side as we strode out of the theater. I reminded myself that it didn't mean anything. He'd told me without rejecting me exactly where the boundaries were. He was just affectionate, that was all. He did this with all the girls, friend and floozy alike.

"I really did have a great time last night," he said when we stepped outside, turning for the Midtown station. "I thought about you all night. You're a great dancer."

I smiled down at my shoes. "Thanks. I mostly only dance in my kitchen. If it wasn't for your lead, there's no way I would have known what to do, so thank you for teaching me."

He chuckled, hooking his arm around my neck and drawing me in for a hug. "You're a model student."

My arm wound around his waist, slipping under his coat. It was beautifully cut, as was everything he wore, henley to Levi's to oxfords. The feeling of his hard torso shifting as we walked did something vital to my insides.

His arm slipped away, and when we parted, my cheeks were on fire.

I kept on topic. "I have to admit, I'm feeling a little obsessed with swing after last night. I've been listening to Caravan Palace all morning on repeat."

"That's one of my favorite bands. Genius, like if Daft Punk had a Lindy Hop baby. Have you heard of Parov Stelar?"

"No. Should I check him out?"

He smirked down at me. "Only if you feel like dancing."

"I always feel like dancing."

"You and me both."

"Really, you might have ruined me for all other clubs."

A shadow flickered in his eyes. "I'll teach you everything you want to know, Val." He looked to the subway entrance and jerked his chin at it. "Which way are you heading?"

"South. I live in the Village."

"Me too. Washington and Barrow."

I smiled. "Hudson and Charles."

"Just around the corner from Smalls. You been there?"

I shook my head. "Is it a bar?"

That smirk tilted higher. "A jazz bar. It's a great little spot. Small dance floor but always bopping. We should go sometime."

"Sure," I said, pressing down my excitement at the prospect as we trotted down the subway steps.

"So, what's Val short for?" he asked once we passed the turnstiles.

"Valentina."

"Exotic. Makes me imagine you as a flamenco dancer."

I laughed. "Not far off. My grandparents emigrated from Spain. My *abuelita* danced flamenco. *Abuelo* plays guitar. It was love at first *braceo*." I held my arms up like a dancer and snapped my fingers to illustrate.

"No wonder you look so good in red."

I shook my head at him, amused as we stepped onto the train. "How about you? Somehow I get the feeling you're not a Samuel."

"Samhir. My parents moved here from Lebanon in the eighties. Got their doctorates from Columbia and never looked back."

Sadness slipped over me. "Do you ever see your extended family?"

He shook his head, his face closed. "I've never met my grandparents."

"I...I'm sorry. Or wait, should I not be sorry?"

He chuckled. "It's okay. They weren't thrilled with my parents embracing the west so completely."

"Do you have any siblings?"

"Nope, just me. They're too busy for more. Dad's a surgeon, and Mom's a psychiatrist."

He'd said it like there was more to the story, but I didn't press him.

"I can't imagine what it's like to have a family so small. I have four older brothers, and my grandparents lived with us growing up. We're a mix of Spanish and Irish."

"That explains the freckles."

"Our house is always loud. Either someone is debating something irrelevant, getting in trouble, laughing too loud, or telling somebody what to do. It's literally never quiet. My brothers talk in their sleep."

His smile quirked. "Do you?"

"They say I do, but I don't."

"How do you know?"

"I have three roommates, and none of them have told me I do. Thus…" I shrugged.

Sam laughed.

The conversation ebbed, and as I took a breath, I summoned the courage to bring us back to the heart of things, the only reason he was hanging out with me in the first place. "So, what's our first lesson?"

"Flirting. It's the basis for everything—pick-ups, conversation, wooing in general."

I giggled at his casual use of the word *wooing*. "All right. I'll bring my A game. Dust off the old tricks." I buffed my nails off on my shoulder.

One of his dark brows rose, that notched one I found I loved so much. "Should I be concerned about protecting my virtue?"

"Oh, you definitely should. I know I play it all awkward and weird, but I'm a regular jezebel."

The smile he flashed was almost blinding. "In that case, I think you'll be a natural."

The train stopped, and we exited, heading out to the street where we paused, face-to-face. He was heading south. I was heading north.

"Well," he said, offering me my instrument, "see you, Valentina."

I took it, slinging the strap over my shoulder with a smile that fluttered at the prospect of seeing him again. "Make sure you prepare yourself for all my moves." I did an awkward karate chop, which earned me a laugh.

"I'll try to brace myself." He turned and walked away, glancing back over his shoulder with a half-smile that hit me in the chest.

With a sigh, I waved and headed home, reminding myself that I knew what I was getting into. That we were friends, nothing more. And I ignored the quiet whisper in the back of my mind that reminded me what a fool I was.

MODEL STUDENT

SAM

"Is there a mirror in your pocket? Because I can see myself in your pants."

A laugh burst out of me as I swung Val around the dance floor to the beat of a slow song a couple nights later, her body flush against mine. Her smile was so pleased, and I found myself pleased too, pulling her a little closer.

"Seriously, I wish I were cross-eyed so I could see you twice."

I spun her out, laughing again. I couldn't help it. She wore red again—a tailored short-sleeved shirt with puffed sleeves and a black high-waisted circle skirt. When the hem rose, I caught a flash of red hot pants that set my blood simmering.

I pulled her back into my arms.

"Come on, Sam—level with me. I keep wondering if your middle name's Google because you're everything I'm searching for." Her cheeks were high. I couldn't stop laughing. "No? Maybe it's Wi-Fi because I'm really feeling our connection. Or maybe you don't have a name, and I can call you mine."

I shook my head. My face actually ached from smiling. "Is this honestly how you think people flirt?"

She shrugged, innocently batting her lashes. "Is it not working?"

Better than you know.

"The art of flirting is the nuance. Some things are simple, intuitive. Like making eye contact and holding it," I said, illustrating by holding her gaze. Her eyes were velvety brown, her long lashes casting shadows on her irises. I didn't miss her pupils dilate. "Touch him. Not in a weird way, but his forearm or shoulder." I squeezed her waist with one hand, running my thumb on the back of her palm with the other. "Smile," I commanded.

She did, her small mouth drawing up in a sweet crimson curve.

"Good." I smirked, the motion catching her eyes and holding them. "Draw attention to your favorite feature. You try."

"I don't know how to show you my ankles from here."

A surprised laugh escaped me. "Your ankles? Really?"

She nodded earnestly. "They're like the only part of my body that's slender. Look." She held out her foot, pointing her saddle shoe to the side so I could admire the admittedly curvaceous joint.

"First," I said when her foot was back on the ground and we were swaying again, "being slender is not all there is to life."

Her lips turned down at the corners. "That's easy for you to say. Look at you."

I wore a frown to match. "What do you mean?"

"I mean…" She let out a frustrated sigh, glancing around us. "Sam, have you ever looked around you? You have to know everyone's watching you. Everyone wants to know you, wants to be you, or wants to be *with* you."

"How do you know? Maybe they're looking at you. Maybe it's

you they want to know."

She laughed. "It's no secret I'm a bigger girl. You're built like a goddamn supermodel who's addicted to protein shakes and kale."

I pulled her to a stop and pinned her with a sobering stare. "Val, listen to me when I say this." I paused, waiting for a response, but she only looked up at me with her doe eyes, big and brown and soft. "Are you listening?"

She nodded.

"There is not a single thing wrong with your body. The curve of your ankle is as gorgeous as the curve of your waist, your hips, even your chin and cheeks." I caught that little chin in my thumb and forefinger and tilted her face up. "I can't decide what my favorite feature is of your face. Your eyes, wide and dark and deep. The length of your lashes—I swear, they're a mile long. Your lips—the swell of the bottom is just … *juicy*. That's the word I always think of because they're always shiny, like a freshly washed apple. I never know what it is. Lip gloss? The consequence of your tongue sweeping it? Or are they just always wet?"

The lips in question parted to speak, and somehow, I found myself. I pulled her to me and turned us to start the dance again, breaking the moment with a regrettable snap.

"So you could sell any one of those features, easy," I said matter-of-factly, ignoring the blush on her cheeks. *Reel it in, man.* "Compliment him, something unexpected. Let him catch you looking at him, smile, look away. He'll get the hint, I promise. And if he doesn't, he's too stupid for you."

Val laughed, but the sound was small. "Are you sure I can't use my pick-up lines? I have so many good ones."

"I'm sure."

She fanned herself. "I dunno. I mean, is it hot in here, or is it just you?"

I laughed. "I was wondering, do you believe in love at first sight, or should I walk by again?"

She blinked dramatically. "I thought something was wrong with my eyes."

"Yeah?"

"I can't take them off of you."

The beat picked up, and so did our feet. She executed a particularly epic spin, one that gave me a full view of her ample ass, and a second later, we were cheek-to-cheek.

I said into the shell of her ear, "You're hotter than the bottom of my laptop."

Her lips were next to my ear too, her breath hot and humid. "I wish you were my big toe."

I leaned back to eye her.

She smirked at me. "I'd bang you on every piece of furniture in my house."

"Goddammit, Val." I laughed, the sound so easy. I hadn't laughed so much in forever. "You never answered my question, by the way."

"What question?"

"Do you really think people flirt like this?"

She shrugged and looked off, avoiding my eyes. "Isn't that what you do? You're the player, the pick-up artist. The guy who gets all the girls. I've heard all the stories about you and Ian. That's why you're the perfect person to teach me. You can show me how not to be… well, *me*, so I can pick up guys."

I full-on frowned at her. "I'm not teaching you how not to be you, Val. It's not fake—it's marketable. It's figuring out how to send the right signals, how to sell your favorite parts of yourself, show them to him so he can see them and want them."

"But this is what dating is, right? Playing a game. You're teaching me the rules." She was so sincere, something in my chest twisted painfully. It must have shown because she hung on to me a little tighter. "No, it's good though. I'm excited. I didn't mean it in a bad way. I appreciate you, Sam."

I took a minute just to dance with her, pulling her around in a series of moves, one to the next, with no time to speak in between while I gathered my wits.

"Let me fill you in on a little secret," I said when we were in the clutch again. "This isn't about playing a game—it's about confidence. It's about practice. It's about figuring out what you want and going after it. If you want a guy, you have to let him know. *That* is what I'm teaching you. How to get what you want." I paused, watching my words sink in. "I'm teaching you how to be brave, not fake."

"All right," she said quietly. "Well, I'm ready to learn."

"Pop quiz. Try it on me."

She blinked. "All of it?"

"Not all at once. I don't want you to hurt yourself."

Val laughed, the tension lifting. "Okay. Give me a minute though. Can we just dance?"

I pulled her into me and turned us in quick, bouncing circles, her hand clutched in mine, resting on my chest. "We can dance all night if you want." The ring of truth in the words echoed in my rib cage.

And for a while, that was all we did. We danced.

She was already improving, learning my cues, picking up moves by observation.

Val was a natural.

I didn't know exactly when she turned it on, but after a little while, I found myself watching her lips as she pulled the bottom one into her mouth, her lashes as she fanned them, her hand on my shoulder or in mine, lingering, squeezing.

"Dancing with you is too easy," she said. "You know exactly what to do with me."

That was when it hit me. My smile was broad and proud. "Valentina Bolivar, are you flirting with me?"

Her cheeks flushed with her little smile, lips together. "Maybe a little."

"Practice makes perfect," I said. "Just like dancing. You just keep getting better and better at both."

She swatted at my arm. "Samhir Haddad, are you flirting with me?"

I laughed and pulled her close. "Maybe a little."

"So what's our next lesson?"

"Practical application. How about after the show tomorrow night, we go to Smalls? We can have a drink, dance a little, and have you pick up a guy."

Her throat worked as she swallowed. "I mean, it's a little soon for that, don't you think?"

"Like I said, practice makes perfect. I can tell you all day long what to do, but until you do it on your own, it'll never stick."

"Okay," she said, though she looked unsure of herself.

"You trust me, right, Val?" I asked, watching her.

She drew a long breath. "I do. It'll be fun. And if I bomb, you can dance with me to make me feel better."

All I could do was laugh as I brought my lips to her ear. "You've got yourself a deal."

BEASTS & BRUTES

VAL

My hangover the next day was nonexistent, thanks to the bag of chips I'd polished off with Amelia when I came home. I'd been relieved to find her up reading. She was on a deadline and couldn't come to the club, and Katherine was still catching up on her sleep from the first night. Rin and Court had to work early too, and so I'd been blissfully alone with Sam.

Blissfully, longingly alone.

Sam had walked me home, leaving me with a hug I felt the ghost of an hour later. When I'd walked through the door, I was so wound up, I needed a distraction. Not that I'd really told Amelia much of anything that was happening inside my brain or heart. Instead, I'd entertained her with stories from the night.

If my lessons with Sam were going to continue, I'd have to maintain my solid stance in the friendzone. And there was no way to do that without also remaining solidly in denial.

Admitting how I really felt would have been pointless and self-destructive. Plus, I was having too much fun to ruin things with the truth, not when I knew exactly where the boundaries were.

By the time I reached my parents' place on the Upper West, I was practically skipping. In a few hours, I'd see Sam at work. I'd spent all day cataloging the things I wanted to talk to him about, thought of a few things he'd think were funny. I wanted to hear him laugh, wanted to see him smile.

God, what a sucker I was for him. I'd never had so much fun with a man as I had with Sam—it was almost too much. I wondered if I really would be ruined for all other guys.

My standards were all kinds of fucked up, thanks to him.

I unlocked the door and followed the noise into the kitchen, which was stuffed to the gills with the Bolivar clan.

The commotion comforted me—tiny *Abuelita* at the stove in front of a massive, simmering pan of paella, her silver hair with a scarf the color of absinthe tied in a little bow on the top, and *Abuelo* in the breakfast nook with his straw fedora cocked on his head. His skin was as dark as a saddle, and his glittering eyes rested on his worn, old copy of Pablo Neruda poems. Mama manned a stockpot with a lid, her curly hair loose and thick, her smile bright and easy as she took direction from *Abuela*. Dad sat across from *Abuelo* with a spread of cards in his hand, tall and smirking, his skin fair and hair black as midnight.

And then there were my brothers.

The four brutes were scattered around the room—Alex sitting on the counter next to *Abuelita*, earning occasional pops on the back of his hand for sneaking a shrimp out of the pan; Dante and Max flanking Dad, hiding behind masks of apathy, which meant they both had shitty hands; Franco, who I only saw the ass end of, as the rest of him was in the fridge.

I bumped him hard with my hip as I passed. "Don't fall in."

He tried to stand up in surprise and thumped his head on the shelf with a yelp. "Dammit, Val," he said, rubbing his head.

I stuck my tongue out at him, and he sprang into motion so fast, I squeaked, pivoting to try to get away from him.

But I wasn't quick enough. He snagged me around the neck and flexed his Herculean arm, awkwardly bringing me into his ribs.

"Now, say you're sorry, *diablilla*."

"Ugh, Franco! It's not my fault your ass is so big."

He squeezed, cutting off my air. I twisted my fingers into his kidney, and my six-foot, two-fifty big brother squealed like a piglet and relaxed his grip enough that I could slip out of his hands.

Franco scowled, betrayed. "You're lucky you're cute, *conejita*." Bunny, their nickname for me since always.

"You're lucky you're muscly, *toro*."

"Mess with the bull, get the horns, *chiquilla*." He cracked his knuckles to illustrate, but he smiled.

I made my way around to Mama, kissing her cheek, then *Abuelita's*. "Hi. God, it smells good in here. You're magic, *Abuela*."

She laughed, abandoning her wooden spoon in the pan to wrap me up in a hug that was surprisingly fierce for such a tiny woman. She leaned back and cupped my face. "Valentina, *mi amor*, you are too skinny. We will feed you," she said to herself, nodding as she turned back to her task. "Mama's got *patatas bravas* and *ablóndigas*. Promise *Abuelita* you will eat, *cariño*."

I chuckled. "I promise," I said before heading to the small table where everyone else sat.

"Heya, babe," Dad said, angling his cheek in my direction. "Knock me a little one right here."

I gave him a kiss and peeked at his cards, which were abysmal. "Wow, Dad. Are you supposed to have them all in a run like that?"

Dante and Max groaned and threw their cards on the table.

"Fold," Dante said with a huff.

I laughed. "How's it going, guys?"

"Could be better since I just lost twenty bucks to Dad." Max folded his arms.

"Thanks, pumpkin," Dad said in my direction, reaching for the cash in the pot. "What's new?"

"Not much," I answered, setting down my trumpet bag as I took a seat at the bay window bench. "Working a lot and—oh! I started going to this swing club, Sway." I felt myself light up. "It's so much fun, swing-dancing and jazz and *gah*. I haven't enjoyed myself this much in forever. My legs haven't worked this hard since marching band. I think my pants are even a little loose."

"*Too skinny*," *Abuelita* called from the kitchen.

Mama laughed and shook her head.

"Who are you going with?" Dante asked, his expression dark.

Four brothers, all utter beasts—an ox, a bear, a bull, and a puma. I had a brother in every grade above me, and Franco was in mine— our birthdays were ten months apart. Irish quints we were, and for an entire year, my poor high school had housed all five of us at once.

As such, no guy would come near me. It had been as much of a blessing as it was a curse, though I'd generally found myself more relieved than offended.

Attention from the opposite sex hadn't interested me. Not then at least.

"Not that it's any of your business, nosy, but I'm going with Katherine and Amelia."

"All right, then who are you dancing with?"

My cheeks warmed. "There's a whole club full of guys to dance with."

Max joined in, mirroring Dante. Separately, they were brutes. Together, they were a hurricane. "And who's dancing with *you*?"

I made a face. "I have some friends from the pit who go. They play in the jazz band. It's not a big deal. Can't you just be excited I have a new hobby I love?"

"You take your mace with you, right?" Max asked.

"Always."

"What about the knuckle keychain I got you?" Dante pressed.

"This one?" I slipped my hand into my bag and brought it out with the black rings on my middle fingers, triangular cat ears out and thirsty for blood. "Come here. I've never gotten to try them out."

I lunged for him, and he laughed, shifting out of the way to pull me into a choke hold, just like I'd escaped from Franco.

"Ugh, I hate you guys."

"Liar," he said, digging his knuckles into my scalp.

I wriggled, pressing the cat ears into the soft skin under his arm. He let me go with a hiss.

"Oh, good. They do work."

He rubbed his arm. "Very funny, *conejita*."

"You asked." I deposited my keys back in my bag and set it on the bench.

"How's it going on *Wicked*?" Dad asked.

Dante shook his head, smiling proudly. "I can't believe you landed that spot. I mean, I can believe it—you're too good not to get a regular spot—but damn if that wasn't unexpected."

I beamed. "Trust me, I'm more surprised than anyone. Thank God Julien got the flu and was out for a week. If I hadn't been subbing for him—"

"Val, they canned him after a day and gave you his job. You've been working on the *Wicked* music for years in the hopes of getting a spot. I bet you can play it in your sleep."

"Better than reciting limericks when I'm in the throes of REM," I teased.

Dante's brows flattened. "Seriously, I've been trying to get on that crew for what feels like forever."

I laughed. "I guess you'll just have to settle for *Phantom. Pobre* Dante."

He rolled his eyes. "I'm just saying, you earned the spot on merit alone. You hadn't met Jason McAdams before subbing for Julien, right?"

"Nope."

Another shake of his head. "Seriously, that contractor is one of the most nepotistic assholes in the industry, and that's saying something. It's no wonder he won't hire me."

"Well, maybe if you hadn't punched him in the face at Delmonico's—"

"Well, maybe if he hadn't been fucking my girlfriend—"

Abuelo's hand flew out faster than a man of his age should have been capable of and whapped Dante upside the head. "Watch your mouth, Dante."

Dante rubbed the back of his head, cowed. "Sorry, *Abuelo*. But that guy's the worst."

"No," he countered, "*Jessica* was the worst. Blame her."

Dante grumbled something I couldn't hear but let it go, changing the subject. "So, who's going to Sway that you know? If it's that dickhead Jackson, we're gonna have a problem."

I huffed and rolled my eyes. "God, you act like I'm not an adult, Dante."

Again, his arms folded, his biceps fanned out and eyes narrowed.

Max took the cue and mirrored him. "Who is it, Val?"

I brushed invisible lint off my pants. "Sam Haddad," I said under my breath, not looking up when Dante shot up in his seat.

"Are you fucking *kidding* me?"

Another *fwap* from *Abuelo's* hand. Dad laughed, but his eyes were hard.

"Haddad is just as bad as that douchebag Jackson he hangs out with."

"God, don't be dramatic, Dante. We're just friends."

"There's no such thing as *just friends* with Haddad. He's slept with half of Manhattan, Valentina."

The men of my family leaned in and gathered around with flinty eyes, Alex and Franco appearing at Max's elbows. *Abuelo* had put down his book. I caught sight of Mama as she leaned back to look between my brothers, offering me a sympathetic glance.

My face was on fire. "I told you, we're just friends. He doesn't want anything to do with me, not like that."

Max's face twisted in a snarl. "Screw that guy. He should want *everything* to do with you. He must be an idiot."

The rest of the wolf pack nodded their agreement.

I scowled at them. "Well, which is it? He should like me, or he should stay away?"

"Both," they said in unison, then glanced at each other and laughed.

"You're impossible, you know that?" I asked the room. "He's my friend. I'm having fun at the club learning to swing. The band is brilliant, and I'm not gonna quit going, if that's what you're getting at."

Dad shook his head. "Nobody wants you to quit going. We just don't want you to get hurt."

"Well, it's like riding a bike. If I'm ever gonna find someone, I'm going to probably get hurt. You can't protect me from everything, or I'll never learn."

My brothers all opened their mouths to argue, but Mama interjected. "Go set the table, boys."

No one moved.

"Now, please." Two syllables of firm Mom voice that brooked no argument, and their mouths snapped shut.

They pushed away from the table and dispersed, though not without pinning me with looks that told me it wasn't over. The boys gathered up plates and silverware and glasses, and Dad sidled up behind Mama, wrapping his arms around her waist and burying his face in her neck. *Abuelo* was the only one who hadn't moved.

"You know, *cariño*, the first time I ever saw your *abuela* was in a *tablao*. But before I saw her, I *felt* her. I felt the music. You don't feel it in your heart or your mind, you hear it here," he said, sitting up straight, puffing his chest, pressing his fist to his stomach. "In your guts. It's the softest part of you, the place where your fears and hopes live. And I knew her right then. She was under the only light in the room, her face still and hard and beautiful. She was mine. She didn't know it then, but she was."

I smiled, leaning in, the band on my lungs relaxing with every word of the story I'd heard a thousand times. "What happened, *Abuelo*?"

"I watched her dance and lost my heart. All of Madrid had lost their heart to her, including her partner. But she didn't love him. She didn't know, but she was waiting for me. I had nothing but my guitar and my love. And that was enough. Valentina, *alma mía*, you are perfect. And one day, you will meet a man who sees you, who knows you. You'll meet a man who needs you, just like I need Valeria. Just like your papa needs your mama. Don't ever give your love to a man who won't give you everything he has to his name in exchange, heart and soul in hand."

I swallowed to open up my tight throat, nodding.

He smiled, his eyes deep and velvety, his face worn and smiling. He patted my hand, his paper-thin skin soft, the calluses on his fingertips hard as stone. "You deserve happiness, *mi cielito*. Nothing less."

Happiness. Such a simple thing to ask for and such an impossible thing to find.

But for the first time, I had hope.

THE TASTE OF VICTORY

VAL

I scanned the Smalls Jazz Club as I took a drink a few nights later. "How about him?"

The guy standing at a high-top table near us was a tall drink of water with a nice smile. I was encouraged by my chances when I saw his spindly arms. It made him more approachable than most of the other guys at Smalls that night, who were as rich in the 'ceps as Sam was.

"Not him," Sam said shortly.

I frowned at him. "Well, why not?"

"Because he's an asshole. What about him?" He nodded to a guy at the bar, one with an apple pie, all-American football vibe going on. He was way out of my league.

I shook my head. "He's too…" I shook my head again, not wanting to explain. "Not him."

"You're hot enough for him but okay." He looked across the room, his eyes golden and hard as a hawk's. "Okay, what about this guy?" He turned me to face the dance floor, leaning over my shoulder to bring his cheek close to mine. "That one, in the newsboy hat. He can jive, check him out. And you know they say a guy who can jive is great in the sack."

I laughed, ignoring the zing of awareness at his hands on the tops of my arms or his face so near. "I dunno, Sam. He's pretty… well, pretty."

He turned me around again. "So are you. Look, he's coming to the bar. Now's your chance. Your mission, should you choose to accept it, is to pick up Newsboy and convince him to buy you a drink."

I nodded, pumping myself up. "Okay. Easy. Eye contact. Smiles. Bite my lip. Laugh. Compliment him. I can do this."

He held my shoulders like the coach from *Rocky*. "You can definitely do this."

"I can do this!" I said again, slamming the end of my drink and straightening my spine. The whiskey and Coke slid down my esophagus, filling my belly full of warm anticipation.

"Go get 'em, tiger," he said with a smirk.

And I turned to meet my fate.

Smile. Make eye contact. Don't be weird.

I sidled up next to Newsboy at the bar and shifted to face him. He was handsome, strong nose and jaw, his forehead dotted with sweat from dancing. When he noticed me looking, he met my eyes—his were the most brilliant shade of blue and green.

"On a scale from one to America, how free are you tonight?" I asked.

A laugh burst out of him, and it was such a nice sound, I found myself smiling.

Good. Check that off. Eye contact, too. The weird part you just can't help.

"What are you drinkin', sweet cheeks?"

I wondered whether he was talking about the cheeks on my face or my ass and tried not to flinch. Instead, I kept that smile in place. "Maker's and Coke."

He leaned over the bar and whistled. "Two Maker's and Coke, would ya?"

The bartender jerked his chin in acknowledgment.

He turned to face me, his smile affectatious. "What's your name?"

"I'm Val," I said, sticking out my hand.

Newsboy laughed and took it. "Ricky. I've never seen you here before." He looked down at our hands as I pumped them. "Quite the grip you've got there."

"Thanks!" I said proudly. "It's my first time here."

"Ah, poppin' your cherry? Tell me you dance so I can die and go to heaven."

My smile split wider, not because I actually liked him—he seemed like kind of a creep—but because it was working. "Oh, I love to dance. I'm just learning. I'm nowhere near as good as you are. I saw you out there…you were really something." I touched his forearm that rested on the bar.

His hand slipped around my waist. "Boy, would I love to teach you a thing or two."

Our drinks appeared on the bar in front of us, and I was thankful for something to do with my hands. More grateful he had something to do with his other than put them on me.

I shook off the feeling—like I'd turned a corner into a dark alley, alone—and was grateful Sam was watching.

"Cheers," I said, holding up my drink, and he clinked his to mine.

"To cherries poppin' and solid handshakes."

The whiskey went down easier this time. Drink number three agreed with me. "So tell me, Ricky, what do you do for a living?"

"I'm a logistics consultant."

I blinked. "Oh. Like, something with numbers?"

He chuckled. "I help improve customer service operations and develop cost-effective solutions for things like supply and distribution issues."

I swear, I was looking at his mouth and listening with my entire brain and both ears, but I didn't understand a word he'd said. "That sounds riveting."

"It's a veritable adrenaline mine, logistics consulting," he joked. "So, who's your friend giving me the hairy eyeball?"

He nodded over my shoulder, and when I looked behind me, Sam wore an unreadable expression.

"Oh, just a buddy of mine. Don't worry—he's totally gay."

A short, loud laugh of surprise left him. "He doesn't look too keen on you being over here with me."

"Psh, please. It was his idea."

That seemed to surprise him, but he didn't comment. "So, how about you? What do you do?"

"I'm in a pit orchestra on Broadw—"

"*Ricky Santolini, you useless son of a bitch!*"

Her voice came from behind me, shrill and high, cutting through the music and murmur of the crowd like a siren. His eyes darted behind me and shot open like he'd been zapped with electricity.

"Oh, shit. Jeanette, baby, what are you doing here?"

"What am *I* doing here? What the fuck are *you* doing here?" Her blonde hair was in a mostly ruined ponytail, and mascara pooled under her eyes, running in long streams down to her chin. "You told me you had to work late, but I knew you were a liar, you fucking lying liar!" She pushed his shoulder. "Stupid, stupid liar. Well, I'm not as stupid as you." With every *stupid*, she pushed him again. "If you wanted to dump me, you should have just said so. Stupid! You stupid, stupid, stupid, cheating liar!"

Once I picked my jaw up off the ground, I tried to slither out of there unnoticed. But the second I moved, Jeanette turned her bloodshot eyes on me. I froze dead to the spot.

"I...I'm sorry. I was just lea—"

She launched herself into me, throwing her arms around my neck. "Don't be sorry. Just run away from this piece of shit as fast as your legs will take you, okay?" She leaned back, her face bright with concern as she waited for me to respond.

"Ah...um...okay. Thanks, Jeanette."

She hugged me one more time and let me go, and I slunk away and back to Sam's side as Jeanette and Ricky's argument escalated to nuclear proportions.

I plopped into the seat next to Sam, still blinking. A sip of my drink helped me collect myself. Sam's face was enigmatically closed.

"Well, mission accomplished. Newsboy's name is Ricky, as the entire bar heard. He's a logistics consultant, which is something so boring it didn't even sound like English when he explained it, and I got a drink." I held it up in display. "Victory tastes...unexpected."

Sam chuckled and shook his head. "Teachable moment. Eighty-five percent of all guys you meet will be duds. But you'll learn to spot the good ones on sight. Sorry I picked a loser. I'm much better at picking out women, if it makes you feel any better."

I giggled. Then I put my drink down because if I was giggling, I should probably quit drinking. "Why are you apologizing? I just won! I checked all the boxes—I smiled, complimented him, got a drink, and I even got to use one of my pick-up lines." I beamed like a spotlight.

Sam shook his head again, but he was laughing.

"I know I wasn't supposed to, but you told me to be myself. And myself loves cheesy pick-up lines."

"Well, cheers to that, Val." He raised his drink and brought it to mine. "Now, finish that drink. I promised you a dance, and I intend to make good on it at least four or five times tonight."

I took a gulp, then another, and paid for my enthusiasm with a deep cough against the whiskey.

"Question," he said while he waited.

"Answer," I responded automatically.

He smirked, amused. "What'd he say when you looked back at me?"

"Oh! He asked who you were and I told him not to worry because you were gay." I laughed a little too loud at myself.

Something in his face changed, darkened, even though he was smiling. His eyes were molten gold.

"I could show you how *not-gay* I am, but I feel like that would be against the spirit of our lessons." He was leaning toward me, and I found that I wasn't breathing, my unblinking eyes on his lips. "So not-gay," he whispered, his lips close enough to feel the words against my mouth and smell the sweet whiskey riding his breath.

And in a snap that left me reeling, he was a foot away, knocking back his drink and sliding off his stool.

"Finish that drink, Valentina, so I can take you on a turn around the dance floor."

I pounded my drink, even though I shouldn't have. It was just that I couldn't say no to Sam, hangover be damned.

He held out his hand, and the second my fingers were in his palm, he towed me out to the dance floor. There was nothing in the world so freeing as being twirled around by Sam like I was weightless.

The night flew by, time speeding up and sliding past with nothing to mark the hours but his laughter and my smiles and our bodies bouncing around the parquet like we had nothing in the world to do but dance. I had no idea how late it was until "New York, New York" came on with the house lights.

Sam hooked me under his arm and guided me out into the chilly fall evening. Like an idiot, I'd come without a jacket, and I tried to play it off like I wasn't cold. A shiver wracked down my spine, betraying me.

He shrugged off his leather jacket. "Here, wear this."

"B-but then y-you'll be cold," I said, shifting away from him in an effort to stop him. "Look, it's n-not even cold. It's f-fake cold. It's only what—like, sixty out? M-my body is j-just being drunk and d-dumb."

"Val." The word was a gentle warning. He held out his jacket like a matador. "Put it on."

"N-no," I said with a laugh.

He shook it once like he was taunting me. "*Toro.*"

I giggled, stumbling a little as I brought my hands to the top of my head, pointer fingers to the stars. "*Olé*!" I cheered as I charged. But instead of running through his jacket, I found myself in his arms.

I didn't know how it happened. The jacket was there, and then it was gone. But instead of being laid out on the sidewalk like I should have been, Sam's arms were hooked around my waist, our bodies winding together and twisting from the force of his catch. And then I looked up, and time stretched out in a long, still moment. His eyes on my mouth. Mine on his. His nose millimeters from mine and his mouth so close, if I turned my head just right, our lips would brush. The warmth of him was everywhere.

I wasn't cold anymore. I was on fire.

So I said the first thing that entered my empty mind.

"Are you going to kiss me, or am I gonna have to lie to my diary?"

The moment broke with our laughter, filled the air around us, stopped my chugging heart. He pressed his lips to my forehead.

I sighed. "I guess that'll do."

He hooked his jacket over my shoulders, taking a moment to look over my face, watching his fingers as he tucked a loose curl behind my ear. "Come on. Let's get you home. You did good tonight, Val."

"Thanks to your expert advice."

But he smiled. "Pretty soon, you'll figure out you didn't need me at all."

And I smiled back and pretended like it was possible that statement held an iota of truth.

PRACTICAL APPLICATION

SAM

The melody sang in the air around me, the same melody that had been following me around for days. My eyes were closed, my fingers moving on their own across the ivory keys. Each time I started the phrase over again, I would find another layer of depth, another expression of the music in my mind. It was the truth, uncovered like bone rising from sand.

I paused, snagging my pencil from behind my ear to jot down a few more notes. In my mind, it wasn't a piano, but a full orchestra, the rise and fall of the music filled to the edges with a host of sound and harmony.

In my heart, it was my dream.

In my life, it was my secret.

It had started in college, an errant thought that had led to my favorite pastime. That pastime had turned into an obsession, hijacking my brain, thieving my spare time. Some people knew I made music—I always had my music notebook on me, and I'd written plenty for the band—but no one knew I was working on symphonies or scoring nonexistent screenplays of novels I'd read.

I set down my pencil and stretched, straightening my spine, arms overhead, glancing around the room. It existed only for music—my black baby grand in the center of the room, instruments dotting the space in front of the wall-to-wall bookshelves. Tall windows with wide molding cut the room in thirds with wedges of light stretched across Persian rugs that were stacked and layered on top of each other, extending to every corner. Mahogany and brass, wool and paper. The room was texture and sound.

I got up and walked over to my guitar, lifting it to my torso, thrumming a few chords as I made my way to the small, low-backed couch. The melody found its way to my fingers again, as if it wanted to be communicated in every instrument, in every way.

My ownership of the music was defensive and fierce. It was mine and mine alone, meant to be hidden, protected. Because no one would love it like I would. No one else could understand it the way I did.

I'd never even considered sharing it.

Sometimes, I wondered *why* I didn't feel compelled to put myself out there. It wasn't as if I didn't have connections; between Juilliard and successfully working in pit orchestras for six years, I knew almost *everyone*. Our community wasn't big, and we'd all worked together at some point or another. It wasn't even that I was afraid of failure.

No, it was much more complicated than that.

I didn't like to walk into something I wasn't absolutely sure I would succeed at. What if I put my heart and soul behind something and couldn't perform? If I put my hopes and dreams on the line and it fell apart? If I couldn't meet the expectations? My responsibilities?

What was more terrifying than the failure itself was the damage that failure would do.

Expectations. I was familiar enough with them, duly doled out by my father on the regular. At least this way, I was failing him on my own terms than by my own shortcomings.

If I were being honest with myself, it was one of the reasons I didn't get serious with anyone. I couldn't be all things to a woman. I knew my capacity, and I gave what I could. Of course, I was rarely truly honest with myself, which suited me just fine.

Either way, I'd never found a woman who inspired that kind of devotion, and for that, I was thankful.

Things were easier this way. And my life was *the* life, a life full of art and money and women. My life was full of pleasure, and I couldn't have wanted for anything more. I was happy and independent, untethered and unbound.

Val rose in my thoughts like a siren. Sweet Val with her doe eyes and bright smile. The realness of her struck a chord in my chest as honestly as my hands on the guitar.

I smiled to myself, thumbing the strings, feeling the vibration in the bones of my hands.

I'd expected Val to falter when it came to picking up a guy at Smalls, but the truth was, it'd been *me* who ended up agitated. Not only had the guy been a jerk, but the sight of his hand on her waist had had me imagining how many bones on his body I could break. His nose, easy. Jaw, probably. Cheekbone—with a solid head-butt, all things were possible. His hand had so many bones, I could rack up a pinball score with a well-placed boot, especially if he was still on the ground from the head-butt.

I'd also been irritated that she wouldn't go for better-looking guys. She didn't think she was desirable—it was clear in every little way—and the thought maddened me. Somebody had *told* her she wasn't desirable. Someone had made her this way.

The thought made me want to find whatever man had told her

such lies and rack up a bone count on him, too.

Fucking assholes.

My new mission in life was to convince Val of just how desirable she was. If the circumstances were different—if I didn't like her so damn much, if I didn't worry I'd inadvertently hurt her—I'd show her *exactly* how appealing I found her. But instead, I'd settle for teaching her confidence. She didn't need lessons on dating because, just like with dancing, she was a natural.

Good guys finish last, and cheaters never win.

So who would get the girl?

I was beginning to hate Ian's lurking. At work. At the club. In the back of my mind.

Ten years we'd been friends, ever since he had been kicked out of another prep school and accepted to mine with the help of his musical talent and an obscene donation from his parents.

It was just about all they' were good for.

Ian had been raised by nannies, a long, miserable string of them. He'd always been an unholy terror, but even then, it was easy to see what he really wanted—attention. But his parents ignored him, and so he continued to act out.

The prank he'd been kicked out of his first school for—writing a choice swear word in the rugby field with bleach—was both harmless and destructive enough to get him expelled.

But when he showed up, I think somehow I knew. I knew he needed a friend, knew he needed someone to have his back. And I figured maybe I could temper him a little in the process. For the most part, I had.

I wouldn't go so far to say he hadn't been a terrible influence on me, but the truth was, he was almost like a brother to me, or what I imagined one to be. Somebody to spend time with, someone you'd known forever and shared history with. Someone you accepted without condition, who would put up with your bullshit, no matter what.

Although I was beginning to wonder if the feeling was mutual.

He was antagonistic by nature, but lately, with Val, his bite had taken an unfamiliar edge. Maybe it was because he'd temporarily lost his wingman. Or maybe I was just hyperaware of Val.

Either way, I didn't like it.

I brushed the thought away like a fly, checking my watch with a sigh before standing to hook my guitar back on its stand between a French horn and a mandolin. We were a few hours from showtime and then the club.

And after that? Well, after that, I had big plans. And I hoped Val had been studying.

Because it was time for a date.

VAL

"A date?" I squeaked, clearing my throat.

Sam laughed, the sound so easy and kind and *good* that I didn't feel embarrassed. "A date," he said as we headed out of the pit. "Getting a guy to buy you a drink is one thing, but getting through a meal with him is a real testament of skill."

I blinked and made myself smile against my fear. "Okay."

"Anything you don't eat? Meat? Sushi? Peanuts? Dairy?"

"Oh God, please give me all the meat," I blurted, rolling my eyes and thinking of steak.

To his credit, he didn't laugh, though he watched me fighting a smirk.

"Steak," I clarified, cheeks steaming. "I love steak and meat and chicken and sushi and all the dairy. Peanuts I could take or leave."

"Loves steak—got it."

I looked down and then back up, suddenly unsure of myself. "I don't … I'm not sure …" I took a breath. "What do I wear?"

"How about I come over and help you decide?"

My mouth opened, then closed, then opened again, like a goggle-eyed goldfish. I imagined Sam stretched out in my bed while I dug through my closet, and something hot and tingly happened in my stomach. "Is that … I mean, is that part of my lessons?"

"Sure, if you want it to be." Sam leaned in. "I like to think I know what men like."

I chuckled and tried to act casual.

He extended his hand. "You ready for the club tonight?"

My hand. He was holding my hand and towing me toward the theater exit. I did my best to wrangle my wits.

"Yeah. I'm heading home to change and get Katherine and Amelia, so we'll be right behind you."

"I'll ride home with you."

"You don't have to do that," I said, blushing.

He shrugged. "I don't mind. Anyway, I'm swinging by home too."

I laughed, relieved. Of course we were already going in the same direction. He wasn't offering to go out of his way.

Stupid.

"Oh. Well, in that case …" I took a thick breath when he let my hand go to open the door for me. "So, what kind of lessons will I be learning on our … date?"

"Anything you want to know. Like what to wear. Plus general conversational tips and rules of thumb. Like, don't get too drunk."

"Not a bad rule of thumb for life either."

He laughed. "I meant to ask where you were the other day before work. You smelled incredible."

"Seafood dishes are your scent of choice? Interesting," I teased.

"It wasn't that. It was the spice or the … I don't know. I couldn't put my finger on it, but it made my mouth water."

I resisted the urge to fan my cheeks. "I can't say I blame you. Paella is my favorite. I went to my parents' for dinner, which was the usual. It was fun and enlightening and maddening. My brother Dante was being an asshole, but that's his primary function. I don't know why I'm ever surprised."

Sam's face flattened. "Dante? Dante Bolivar is your brother?"

I sighed. "Yeah."

He scrubbed a hand over his face like he'd made a grave mistake. "Does he know you're hanging out with me?"

"Hence the extra dickishness."

"He's one of the most talented trumpet players on Broadway."

I chuckled. "I'll let him know you said so. Maybe it'll earn you brownie points."

"Doubtful. Dante's black and white, yes and no. There's no middle ground with him. And hanging out with you is definitely gonna be a no from him."

"How do you guys know each other?"

One dark, notched eyebrow rose as we stepped onto the train. "He didn't tell you? Interesting."

I made a face at him.

"Nothing really. We know some of the same girls, and we might have gone after some of the same girls."

"Oh," I said, trying to sound light and failing. The syllable was tight, tinged with sadness. "He used to only date girls in the business, but that got … complicated."

"Yeah, I imagine it did. It's one of the reasons I never date girls in show business. The only thing it's good for is coordinating schedules."

"Are you … are you dating anyone now?" The second the words left my mouth, I wished I could reel them back in. I didn't want to know the answer.

"No," he answered without hesitation.

"Right," I started. "I mean, how could you? I'm taking up all your free time."

"Val, it's fine." He was smirking, amused again. The gesture both relieved and embarrassed me. "I like hanging out with you."

"But…I mean, you should have a girlfriend or at least some steady ass."

His laughter was comforting. "I don't do girlfriends."

"Wow, tell me there's more to that. You know, so you don't sound like a douchebag."

Another laugh, this time surprised. "I know what I can and can't be to somebody. I can be a date. I can be a night. I can even be a weekend. But I can't be more than that."

"Can't or won't?"

He caught me in a glance. "Maybe a bit of both. Or maybe I just don't. Truth is, I don't want to hurt anyone, that's all."

"And you don't want to get hurt."

"Who does?"

I shrugged. "I just figure the risk is worth the reward."

"I see it from the other side—nothing lasts forever. Why take someone's heart in my hands when I know I'll just let them down?" He shook his head. "Better to be honest with myself and with women."

I sighed. "I see your point, I guess. I'd rather a guy be honest with me than lie and string me on."

"Exactly. That way, everyone knows what they're getting. No surprises."

"Right," I said firmly, seeing him more clearly than I had before. And I told myself this was him. That he was honest. That he wouldn't hurt me or anyone else, not on purpose. So I echoed his words, steeling myself against anything else I might feel. "No surprises."

JUST ONCE

SAM

"Not that one," Val said, her voice tight.

I held up the houndstooth circle skirt, frowning. "Why not?"

She reached across her waist to cup her elbow. "I shouldn't have bought it. It's too...much."

I glanced from her back to the skirt. "Try it on for me." I reached into her closet, returning with a tight, red, three-quarter-sleeved boatneck top. "With this." I scanned her shoes, snagging a pair of black heels with peep toes. "And these."

I pushed them all at her. Begrudgingly, she took them, snagging a wide black belt before leaving for the bathroom to change. I heard her sigh through the closed door.

While I listened to the shuffling fabric and tried not to imagine Val naked on the other side of that thin piece of wood, I wandered around her room. Every color, every fabric was rich and saturated—

deep magentas, heavy teals, emerald greens, luxuriant amethyst. It was loud and chaotic in a way that sang perfect harmony.

I found it to be so very *Val*. I wondered if it was something she'd consciously decided or if it had just come together naturally. Somehow, I had the feeling it was just an extension of her, happening without thought, which made more sense.

Val just *was*.

She was the most refreshing woman I'd met in years.

The bathroom door opened, and when I looked up, she stood in the doorway, looking terrified.

She was stunning, from the sliver of her shoulders to the red swells of her breasts. From the notch of her waist, accentuated by the thick belt she'd grabbed, to the sway of her houndstooth skirt's hem at her knees. Her calves were elegant curves, rolling down to those ankles she so prided herself on, her little toes sensually peeking out of the tip of her shoes.

I stuffed my hands in my pockets and whistled, swallowing hard when it was done. "I don't want to live in a world where you don't wear this outfit to dinner. You've gotta tell me why you look like you'd rather throw those clothes on a bonfire than wear them out."

Her face pinched in discomfort as she looked down at herself. "The skirt is too busy and the shirt is so…tight. You can see…you can see stuff I don't want people to see."

I frowned. "Like what? Because from where I'm standing, you look like a winning lotto ticket."

She shook her head and sighed.

My frown deepened. I took the steps to meet her, lifting her chin up so she'd look at me. "Tell me."

Another sigh. "My…my arms are too big—they look funny."

I turned her a little, taking her elbow in one palm and her hand in the other to inspect it. "I don't know what you're talking about. I don't see anything wrong, Val. They're in perfect proportion with the rest of you."

"Maybe that's part of the problem."

My teeth ground together. "What else? Is there something else?"

Her cheeks flushed pink and pretty. "My back."

I stepped around to the back of her, but all I saw was the twist of her curly hair, the curve of her neck, the span of her waist, the spread of her hips and ass. My hands found their way into my pockets again to keep her body safe from their touch.

"What about your back?"

She reached behind her and adjusted her bra strap. "Just…all this. It's so lumpy and…fat."

"Don't say that word."

She frowned at me as she turned to face me. "Why not? I am."

"No, you aren't."

"You wouldn't understand," she said, containing her frustration. "I bet you've always been this beautiful, and you've only been with pretty, skinny girls. But when you're built like this"—she gestured to herself—"you catalog all the things about yourself that are shaped wrong. Too big, too much, too *fat*. That's what they call it, Sam. It's not a dirty word."

"It is, and you know it is. Even when you say it, you sound like you're trying to hurt yourself. You know, everyone has their things. Some people think their noses are too big. Or their chins. Their teeth are crooked or their eyes are too small. And you want to know the real secret?" I took a step toward her. "They're all way more worried about their own insecurities to pay any attention to yours. If I saw you on the street, I wouldn't see what you see. I'd see your neck, this curve." I brushed my knuckle in the bend where her neck met her shoulder. "I'd see your waist, your pretty ankles."

She chuckled softly at that, though her cheeks were still flushed with emotion.

"There, that smile. That's what I'd see. It's what you should see, too. You're beautiful, Val. Anyone who doesn't see that needs to get his eyes checked."

I caught myself before I said more—or worse, before I did something I shouldn't. I turned back to her closet and absently flipped through the hangers.

"I don't want you to wear that outfit if you're not comfortable though. The lesson is about confidence more than anything, and how gorgeous I think you look doesn't matter if *you* don't feel gorgeous."

She drew a long breath from behind me. "You really think I look okay?"

I turned again and met her eyes with heat I hadn't intended and couldn't have stopped. "Val, you could stop a man's heart dead in his chest. I wouldn't lie to you, not about this, not about anything. I only wish you could see yourself the way I see you."

Val held her head up, her eyes shining, her throat working as she swallowed. And her small mouth smiled, lips together. "All right. Let me just finish my makeup, and we'll go."

"Put on the red lipstick," I suggested.

"Really? I mean, it's so…costumey."

I gave her a look. "You're wearing a houndstooth skirt. Wear the lipstick."

She chuckled, rolling her eyes. "Whatever you say, professor."

With a smirk on my face, I watched her walk away.

She'd get there. She'd see herself like I saw her.

I just had to show her.

VAL

My salivary glands exploded when I read the steak menu.

Every topping known to man was available to smother your meat in. Spinach. Garlic butter. Mushrooms. Onions. Pico de gallo. Cheese. Olives, chimichurri, herbs—the list went on and on and on.

I frowned, dragging my eyes to the salads with a sigh.

"What's the matter?" he asked over his menu.

"I should probably get a salad, huh?"

He met my frown with one of his own. "Not unless you want one."

"What I *want* is this ribeye smothered with *everything*."

"Then that's what you should order."

"But won't a guy be grossed out by me stuffing my face with meat?"

A slow smile crept onto his face. "Absolutely not. All any man wants is to watch a girl stuff her face with meat. Besides," he said, looking back at his menu, "there's no polite way to eat a salad. I've seen enough girls pick at a salad over dinner to know."

I laughed. "I never thought of it that way. There really isn't a way to eat it aside from shoveling lettuce in your mouth like hay."

He wrinkled his nose and shook his head. "Get the steak."

"Done." I closed my menu and set it on the table. "So, where should we start?"

Sam met my eyes and laid his menu on top of mine. "Well, the first thing you need to figure out is, what do you want? What are you looking for long-term and short-term? A relationship? Love? Sex? Nothing? You won't always know until you're sitting across from them."

"Well, I don't know if I ever want to date anyone just for sex."

"You say that now. But what if you were at dinner with a great-looking guy, total charmer, loads of chemistry. Only problem is, he's dumb as a bag of hair. You're attracted to him, but you don't want to take him home to meet your mom."

I nodded. "Okay, I see your point. Why does it feel so much less…predatory for a woman to do that? When I think about you thinking some girl is too dumb to date, but you'd sleep with her, it makes me want to sit you down and get you to come to Jesus."

He shrugged. "Because men are notorious predators. But this is another reason I tell women what they won't get from me. They can take it or leave it. I don't lead anyone on. You've got to know that plenty of guys aren't like me though. Don't believe their lines. Make them earn your trust."

"Okay. So, figure out what I want."

"But don't settle. Just because a guy buys you a steak doesn't mean you owe him anything."

"Or I could just buy my own steak."

"Or that. If lesson one and two were a success, you'd have found yourself a date, which is a crucial part of the whole dating thing. So, what kind of guy makes it into this chair? What kind of guy are you looking for?"

"Well," I said, unrolling my silverware to give myself something to do with my hands, "he'd have to be funny, smart. I don't think I could date anyone who didn't have a good sense of humor. He should be passionate about something."

"Anything?"

"Sure. Music. Movies. Magic."

"I mean, who doesn't love an illusionist?"

I laughed. "Depends. I can handle some sleight of hand, but if he's pulling quarters out from behind my ear while we're having sex, we might have a problem."

He choked on his water, bursting out laughing once he swallowed. "I imagined him pulling a quarter from somewhere else."

"So did I. I just didn't want to say vagina at the dinner table."

"What else?" he said on a laugh.

God, he was handsome, his suit dark and tie to match, his shirt crisp and white. His black hair was pushed back from his face, those finger ruts deep and inviting. And his eyes, golden and glinting with amusement and something else, something I couldn't place and wanted to badly.

Did he even know? Did he notice the girl from the table next to us had dropped her napkin no less than three times next to his chair to try to get his attention? Did he feel their eyes on him, sense that they wanted him to look, to see them, or if nothing else, to see *him*?

Did he know, or did he just not care?

"Well," I said, turning back to his question, "it would be nice if he liked to dance since now I know how much I love that. Someone understanding of my schedule and life. I'd barely ever see a guy with a nine-to-five. Someone who wanted me just for me, who loved me for exactly who I am without wanting to change a thing. So basically, a unicorn. Or a jackalope."

His brow quirked. "A what?"

"A jackalope. You know, a jackrabbit with antlers?"

Sam blinked at me. "A … what?"

I laughed. "The unicorn of the American South. Mythical creature found in folklore. Taxidermists' paradise? Breeds during lightning flashes? You catch one with whiskey, which is honestly my kind of animal."

He still looked confused.

"No? Anyway, it's not important. What I mean is that they're not real, much like my expectations."

"There are seven billion people in the world. I'm sure there's a guy out there who fits the bill."

The waiter appeared before I could argue.

"I'll have the fourteen-ounce rib eye, mid-rare, with spinach, mushrooms, garlic butter, and caramelized onions. Oh! And could you bring me some olives on the side? And I'd like mashed potatoes and broccoli, please."

He took my menu with a nod. "And for you, sir?"

"I'll have the same."

I smiled at Sam, shaking my head as the waiter read it back and headed off.

"Is this another practical application? Are you flattering me or trying to make me feel more comfortable by ordering the same?"

"You got me—I really wanted the Waldorf salad."

I couldn't help but laugh, but when it died down, I found myself shaking my head, marveling at the moment. At the beautiful man smiling at me from across a candlelit table with eyes like whiskey and a face like an ancient prince. I was lucky to have earned that smile, to have this time with him. I reminded myself not only to enjoy every fleeting second, but not to waste it.

"So, what else? Do you have any conversational tips for me?"

"Think up some questions you can lock and load if the conversation dies. But not the typical old *what do you do, do you have any siblings* type questions. It's not an interview."

"Okay." I only had to think for a split second. "What's the one song that you love, but you'd die of embarrassment if anyone caught you singing it in the shower?"

He laughed and answered without missing a beat, "'Mercy' by Shawn Mendes. I can't help it, man. That kid kills me. You?"

"Well, not much music could embarrass me, but I know all the words to 'Bodak Yellow' and have been known to twerk whenever it comes on within the privacy of my home." I smiled at his smile and said, "If you could be the absolute best in the world at one thing, what would it be?"

His eyes twinkled with amusement. "Composing. You?"

"You compose?" I asked, my eyes widening with my smile. "What do you write?"

"All kinds of stuff. What about you? What would you be the best in the world at? Let me guess," he said, avoiding my questions. "Roller derby. No, reigning twerk queen—that is something I need to see before I die."

I laughed. "Don't hold your breath."

"Seal trainer? Tap dancer? Pastry chef?"

"Kisser. I'd like to give a man a kiss that makes him fall in love with me."

Something in him stilled. "Dangerous request. What if you kiss the wrong man? You'll never get rid of him."

"Then I guess I'd have to be sure about the men who get my kisses." I changed the subject with another question. "What's the most exciting thing that's happened to you lately?"

"Asking you to the club."

I smiled. "Well, mine was going to the club, so I guess we're on the same page."

"Guess so," he said quietly, though his smile was still in place.

"So," I started, aching to relieve the tension between us, "what *shouldn't* I do on a date? There has to be a list, right? Don't talk about myself too much? Don't ask too many questions? Don't accidentally be nosy or rude?"

He shook his head. "Two rules: don't drink too much, and don't be anyone but yourself. That's it."

I frowned. "Except *myself* empties spit valves on shoes. What about my flaws? Shouldn't I…I don't know. Hide them? I don't want a guy to see the bad things about me until I've had time to snag him."

"Everyone's flawed. I guarantee whatever man sits across from you has more shortcomings than you could ever possess. All you're gonna have to do is show up and be yourself. You've got a rockin' body. You're talented and smart. You're funny and young, and your body is rockin.'"

I chuckled. "You already said that."

"It's worth repeating. I just…" He gave his head a little shake. "I can't figure out how you haven't dated."

My insides squeezed painfully. "It's always been this way, Sam. It's okay. It's just what it is. This is just *me*." I gestured to my body. "Guys aren't interested."

Another shake of his head, this time angry. "I don't understand why you don't believe me. Do you think I'm bullshitting you, Val?"

"No, it's… it's not that. It's just… it's hard to explain."

"Try."

I twisted my napkin in my lap, squeezing until my knuckles ached. "Do you remember when you first started noticing girls?"

His frustration dissipated, his face softening with it. "Junior high, seventh grade. That was when I really started looking."

"I was the only girl in the fifth grade who needed a bra. A *real* bra with underwire. It was almost overnight and *bam*. Hips and boobs at eleven. Kids… kids are cruel. In seventh grade, the girls had all discarded me and quit calling me by my name—they called me a slut instead. Then the rumors started about things I'd done with boys, things I'd never even heard of until they started accusing me. In the eighth grade, it was the boys. They didn't just *ask* if they could touch my boobs, they touched them when they wanted, usually when their friends were around to laugh. In class. In the cafeteria. At my locker. By then, the girls were just calling me fat. And the sad thing was that I was relieved. I'd rather be fat than sexualized."

Sam watched me, his face calm and his eyes on fire.

"Then I went to high school. My brother Franco was in my grade, and freshman year, he filled out. He couldn't have done much of anything before that—I think he weighed half what I did. But Alex, Max, and Dante were in every single grade above me. The name-calling, the advances—all of it stopped overnight, and I don't think I'd ever been so relieved in my life. I found my friends in band, and that was a safe place, too. Dante made sure of that. By the time I thought I might want to give boys another chance, they'd all been scared off to the point that I was untouchable."

"I'm sorry, Val," he said with a gentleness that made my heart ache.

"It's all right, really. I went to prom with my best friend, and we had way more fun than I would have had with some bass clarinet player," I said on a laugh. "He'd asked me, but Franco eavesdropped on a call wherein the poor kid sang 'Closer' by Nine Inch Nails and got his face beat in for saying he wanted to fuck me like an animal." Sam laughed as I continued, "And by the time I got to college, I was fine. I'd had plenty of time to get used to myself and learn to love myself. To be independent and self-sufficient. I dated some in college, but nothing serious. Just enough to lose my virginity and have at least a *little* experience. So, there it is. That's why. I'm not gonna pretend I'm not a little fucked up. But this is why I need your help."

"You sure I'm helping?"

"Are you kidding, Sam? The last few weeks have been some of the best of my life, and it's thanks to you. You were right—practice makes perfect. I'm less scared at the prospect of dating than I've ever been, and it's because you make me brave."

"I didn't have to do much, Val. You're braver than you know."

We were interrupted by our waiter and two steaming plates. And Sam turned the conversation to lighter things. But I didn't miss his gaze, heavy with what, I didn't know. As curious as I was, part of me knew how dangerous finding out would be.

AN HOUR LATER, WE FOUND ourselves walking toward my place, Sam's arm around my shoulders, my body tucked into his side. I had learned not to question his affection, chalking it up to another teachable moment, the feeling of what a date *should* be like. It was all part of the lessons, that was all.

I wondered how far our lessons would extend. How many dates would we go on? How many lessons would we have? And how far would the pretense go?

Would it turn to the physical? Because for all my worldly experience, I was wildly unpracticed.

My arm wound around Sam's narrow waist, the scent of him all over me. And I realized I wouldn't hate those kinds of lessons. Not one little bit.

The brownstone stoop came closer with every step until there we were, standing on the sidewalk. I faced him. He faced me. The air between us crackled with anticipation.

We both moved at once, him opening his arms for a hug and me offering my hand for a shake. With a laugh, he brought his hand down to meet mine as mine rose for a hug.

"Come here," he said, still laughing as he grabbed me and pulled me into his chest. His arms wrapped around me, the feeling so divine, so comforting and right, a sigh of contentment slipped out of me and into the cold autumn night.

For a long moment, we stayed just like that, saying nothing. I finally loosened my grip. He didn't.

And then I made a terrible mistake.

I looked up from the circle of his arms and met his eyes.

Polished wood. Honey in sunshine. Sand in the sunset. Those eyes were on fire, his pupils open and black as ink. His lips, wide and dusky and masculine, his breath catching in his chest.

I couldn't breathe at all.

"I think you should teach me how to kiss." The words left me in a breathy rush so fast, they bounced off his lips and brushed my face again.

His big hand slid up my ribs, up my arm, and cupped my cheek. "Val," he said, the word thick with emotion—regret, refusal, wishes, desire.

"Hear me out," I said, taking a breath. "It's important to know when there's chemistry, right? How do I know if there's more there? If I should want to kiss him, if I should want to sleep with him? How do I know it's even a good kiss? I don't know, but I think you could show me."

His eyes darkened. "You don't know how to tell a good kiss from a bad one?"

I shook my head. "I've been kissed, sure. Dozens of times. But I can't seem to remember a single one."

His inhale was sharp. Somehow, we were closer.

"Please," I begged softly. "Will you teach me? Will you show me, just once?"

"Just once," he said like a prayer, his eyes on my lips as he inched closer.

"Just once," I promised, the words hanging between us for a heartbeat.

And just when I thought he'd refuse, his lips crashed into mine.

For a moment, I was lost in the shock of sensation, the fact of his mouth on mine, the demand and sweet relief. And I parted my lips to grant him entry, sighed into his mouth as his tongue tangled with mine. Our bodies were caught in an updraft, twisting together, burning like a torch. His lips—my God, had I gone my whole life without his lips on mine?—opened wider, his hand turning my face to an angle that let him in, let him take what he wanted, anything he wanted. And I couldn't breathe without breathing him, couldn't feel my heartbeat without feeling his against my ribs, mine thudding from inside of me like it was reaching for him.

The depth of the kiss ebbed, then slowed. And, to my deepest regret, stopped with the coming together of his lips, the tilt of his head to bring his forehead to mine. His nose brushed the bridge of mine, and I wanted to open my eyes, wanted to see his lips, his face, his eyes. But I didn't want to find out it hadn't been real.

Just once.

And that would have to be enough.

I finally parted my heavy lids with the regret of a thousand lifetimes.

Sam leaned back, his face shadowed and eyes burning coals. "When you get a kiss better than that, you'll know."

And I knew for a fact that I never would.

FOR SCIENCE

SAM

The icy-cold shower stream hit my back like freezing cold nails. The tiles under my palm were warm by comparison, the frigid cold in my marrow, in my shaking bones, in my clattering teeth. Even then, there was no banishing Val from my thoughts. There was no forgetting the impression of her body against mine. There was no denying the memory of her lips, of her hands, of the pleasure in her eyes or the flush in her cheeks when I'd kissed her like I'd been dreaming of for so long.

Just once.

I slammed the lever with the meat of my fist, stopping the water.

I'd fucked up. And I'd fucked up *bad*.

Girls like her are off-limits to guys like you, player.

I wasn't even sure how it had happened. She had been there in my arms, just like she'd been so many times before, but *this* time?

I'd been dangerously close to kissing her long before she asked me to.

Begged me to.

I swiped the towel off the rack on the wall and scrubbed it over the length of my still-trembling body, clenching my jaw to stop the rattling in my skull, but it was no use.

I shouldn't have done it. I shouldn't have crossed that line. Because now I'd opened the door, and not walking through the fucking thing was going to be impossible. Impossible and absolutely imperative.

You can't have this girl.

I hadn't yet abandoned my objective—keep Val safe from *me* just as much as Ian. What I wanted should have been secondary to that. And I'd jeopardized the entire operation by agreeing to kiss her.

No, not agreeing. *Surrendering.* I'd yielded to my desire, submitted to my wishes, and in doing so, I'd put her in front of the firing squad and placed her last cigarette in her lips.

She deserved everything I wasn't.

Just once.

I brushed my teeth, flipped off the bathroom light, padded through my apartment with goosebumps still prickling every square inch of my skin. I felt like I might be cold forever, wondered what it was like to ever feel warm. Even my sheets were cold, chilled, deserted.

I shivered as I threw the comforter over me, my hair soaking my pillow. My room was comprised of indistinct shades of blue, the ceiling dark. I searched it for answers all the same.

How didn't she know what constituted something so simple as a good kiss? How could she have thought she needed any practice?

Val needed no practice. Val was a fucking expert.

I'd like to give a man a kiss that makes him fall in love with me.

Touché, Val. Tou-fucking-ché.

It was rare to have a first kiss be so perfect, without hesitation, our lips and mouths and bodies and minds in unexpected harmony. How she'd worried she'd be anything less than breathtaking was beyond me. That she didn't know a good kiss from a bad one confounded me.

In fact, the realization that she'd been kissed so poorly made me want to find every incompetent fuck on that list and tell him to fix his life and do better.

The knowledge that she'd been sexualized as a child did nothing to cool my simmering anger. To know that she'd been punished for something she couldn't control only fanned the flames.

I knew something had happened, that something had shaped how she saw herself, but I couldn't have imagined just how cruel that something was.

But it didn't change the fact that she was beautiful and bright and brilliant. Any man could see that—her scars were only visible on close inspection—and I just couldn't comprehend how no one had snapped her up and laid claim on her.

I pushed away the thought that it could be me.

With a noisy exhale, I shoved my hand in the freezing mess of wet hair on my head and left it there. My fingertips curled against my scalp like I could pluck thoughts out of my brain and put them somewhere they couldn't plague me. Like the way her breasts felt against my chest. The weight of her arms around my neck. The heat of her mouth and the sweet eagerness of her kiss.

I still felt that heat even now, after a full hour and a long, subzero shower.

Just like that, the chill in my bones was replaced with simmering warmth that pumped through my veins.

Goddamn, I was in so much trouble.

Just once.

I drew a heavy breath and let it out in a noisy huff. So I'd learn a lesson in willpower—it wouldn't be the first time.

I frowned. Maybe it would be the first time. It wasn't often that I didn't go after exactly what—or whom—I wanted. But Val was different. I never wanted to hurt anyone, but with her, it was a directive I couldn't ignore. I had to protect her. She was too innocent, too good not to.

She couldn't possibly know what she was getting into with me. Not really.

But I did. And so the responsibility fell on me.

Just once.

And that would have to be enough.

VAL

"Once is never going to be enough."

Amelia's face was stern. Well, stern for Amelia at least. Her face was pinched, her hands on her hips and her cheeks flushed in determination.

She looked about as menacing as a Precious Moments figurine—all she needed were some ill-fitting overalls and a cowlick to polish off the look.

"Well, it's gonna have to be enough. I shouldn't have asked him for that much in the first place."

Her arms folded across her chest. "How can you say that? That kiss blew your mind."

"I know."

"It rearranged the stars. It permanently affected your gravity. It set the bar somewhere around Pluto."

I sighed. "I know."

"It almost gave you a heart attack. It straight-up ruined your panties—"

"I *know*. But I betrayed the rules he *very* firmly put in place."

Katherine interjected, "I mean, they weren't *that* firm—"

I cut her off with a look. "This wasn't part of the deal. I took advantage of his help and good nature."

Katherine's brow rose. "You took advantage of *his* good nature?"

"I did. He gave me a mercy kiss. A pity kiss."

"Doesn't sound like a pity kiss to me," she said pointedly.

"How would I know? I have very clearly *never* been kissed for real in my life. Not if that's what I've been missing. I'm sure it was totally lukewarm to him. Mediocre. Average. As unexceptional and bland as cold tofu."

Katherine nodded her understanding. "Sort of like if you've never seen a penis. The first one could be totally average, but you'd panic, wondering how in the world it would fit in you. A turgid penis is nothing to scoff at."

"I'll take your word for it," Amelia mumbled, not having seen one in person. "I'm just saying, if it was *that* good, why wouldn't you do it again?"

"Because he doesn't *want* to."

"You can't possibly know that," Amelia argued.

"Well, I—"

"She's right," Katherine said, though she didn't at all look happy about it.

Our faces swung in her direction, Amelia's smug and mine betrayed.

"You can't actually be suggesting—"

She cut me off, holding her hands up, palms out. "I'm not suggesting anything. I'm only saying, you can't know for sure that he doesn't want to kiss you again."

"It's…it's ridiculous. Why would…he could never…I mean, it's *me*, and he's *Sam*, and…no," I sputtered.

Katherine watched me for a beat. "It's not a bad idea. He's

already showing you the ropes of dating. Why not the physical part of relationships, too?"

I blinked at her. "You can't be serious."

She made a face. "When am I not serious?"

"That's fair," Amelia chimed in.

"So you're saying I should sleep with him?"

"Well, I think you should consider *asking* if he wants to sleep with you, but if that's what you want, then yes. You know, for posterity."

A laugh bubbled out of me. "So I should sleep with him for science? Assuming he's interested. Also assuming he doesn't laugh me out of whatever building we happen to be in."

"From what you said about the kiss, it definitely sounds like he'd be interested."

"This is also assuming I could get naked in front of him. I'd be too busy cataloging my flaws to enjoy myself."

"Let me tell you a little story," Katherine said studiously. "Once, when I was fifteen, my parents dragged me to a water park in an effort to, in their words, *normalize* me."

Amelia snorted a laugh.

"Exactly," she continued. "So when we got there, I pulled off my cover-up and looked down, and there it was. A stray pube, black as ink, on my pale upper thigh."

"Oh my God, no!" I said, giggling.

"Oh, yes. I mean, it wasn't long enough to curl, but it was long enough to grab. I know, because I panicked and tried to pluck it with my fingernails."

Amelia and I groaned in unison.

"It wasn't coming out—no way, no how. So I looked around at everyone, imagining them all staring at my stray pubic hair, laughing and pointing. And that's when I realized something."

She paused. We waited with bated breath.

And with a smile, she said, "No one was looking at my stray pube. They were worried about their own pubes."

My mouth fell open in awe. "That is the most profound thing you have ever said."

"I know. It was one of the great epiphanies of my life. Everyone has flaws, and that's all they see. But other people, they don't see your flaws. They're way too concerned with their own. So don't worry about Sam. I bet he doesn't see a single thing you see."

I narrowed my eyes in contemplation. "I thought you said this was a terrible idea. That it would all go down in flames. With tears. And a whiskey binge."

"I would never use a metaphor. And anyway, that was before. You've proven you can be around him without being obsessive or unhealthy."

"We're literally discussing sleeping with him so I can take notes. What about this is healthy?"

She rolled her eyes. "I'm saying that I think you've established an interesting relationship with a man who has the ability to teach you more than some basic social skills. The boundaries are such that you could graduate into a physical relationship with him, and as long as you maintain emotional distance, you could find yourself very fulfilled."

Amelia snickered. "Oh, she'll be full *and* filled all right."

I shook my head at the two of them. "I cannot believe I'm hearing this right."

Katherine shrugged. "It's just sex. Do you think you can mess around with Sam and not get your heart involved?"

I frowned, considering it. I was actually considering it, and I wondered briefly if I'd lost all touch with reality or if I still had a tenuous grip.

They weren't wrong—kissing Sam might have been the greatest mistake of my life. Because now I knew what I was missing, and I wasn't inclined to let it go despite the promise I'd made that it'd just be the once. Maybe there was a way to keep it going. I very obviously had *a lot* to learn.

Would Sam be open to teaching me? Would it be worth asking? What if he said no?

What if he said *yes*?

The thought of kissing him again sent a bloom of heat through my chest that sank low in my belly. If he could do what he did to me with just a kiss, I didn't even know if I'd survive the onslaught of his hands. Never mind his body. Might as well just pick out my tombstone now.

Here lies Val. She wasn't ready for his jelly.

He'd been so eager to teach me so far, even to kiss me. Sure, I'd had to do a little convincing, but it really hadn't taken much. There was no risk to his heart—he didn't get involved, and if he did, it wouldn't be with me.

But there was a risk to *my* heart.

I knew without even needing to think about it that he'd ruin me for life. But I was already screwed for kisses. Why not make it a sweep and give him the win across the board?

All I had to do was ask.

Katherine was right. We were in a unique position, one where I could propose the advance in our lessons. If he agreed, there would be more kissing. Some heavy petting. And possibly, potentially, the best lay of my life, past or future.

And just like that, I knew exactly how to word it so I wouldn't sound like a creep and he could let me down without fear of hurting my feelings.

I took a breath and smiled. "For science."

JUMP

SAM

I saw her the second she walked into the club.

It was like I'd known she was standing there, as if the crowd parted at the opportune moment, like the club had pointed its lights in her direction by instruction of the universe.

She was a vision in navy and red, her skirt almost black with white piping and sailor buttons on the front. Her shirt, the red tailored one with the puffed sleeves. Her saddle shoes pointed in my direction.

But it was her smile that made my heart skip a beat, made my fingers miss a note. Her cheeks, alight with the same joy I found when I walked into the club. Her eyes, sparking so bright with her happiness, I could see from across the room. Her smile, lips red and stretched and beaming.

Just once.

A string in my heart thrummed with a string on my bass as I picked up the beat. And when she met my eyes, I gave her the best smile I had.

It was honest, instinctive. It was a smile for her, just as much as hers was for me.

I turned my attention to my instrument, tuning out the crowd. But not her. No, I played for her and her alone, jumping in for a solo when it wasn't my turn. The guys let me—all I had to do was shift, and they knew I was taking over. I was the closest thing to a conductor that we had.

I spun my bass, dragged it across the stage without my fingers losing their place, playing harder, faster than I usually did. Tilted it to forty-five degrees and climbed on top in a feat of skill that looked like it defied gravity but was simply a matter of physics—the neck in my left hand, my foot in the waist, the weight on my back foot holding the base to the ground. When I jumped off, it was with the kick of my feet out behind me, and when I landed, I swept my instrument into my arms to play it like a bass guitar.

The screaming and whistling reached me through a haze. I jerked my chin to Chris, our trumpet player, who joined me in a seamless duet. He walked to my side, facing me as he played, the two of us riffing off each other like we had a hundred times. When I widened my stance and gave him a nod, he picked up his pace and brought the melody up to the top. And when it hit the height, just before the rest of the band joined in, he jumped on my back and pointed at the ceiling, ripping the high note right on cue.

The crowd lost it, yelling and whooping and bouncing. Feet were in the air, skirts flying, smiles, smiles, smiles *everywhere.*

And I was high on the feeling.

Val was there, on the edge of the dance floor, jitterbugging alone, while Katherine and Amelia swung each other around. We started a new song, and I took my place back in the middle of the group. But I couldn't stop watching her.

Fucked beyond repair. That's what I was.

She's not for you. You can't have her. Find another girl before you do something stupid.

A wave of aversion rushed over me at the thought of hooking up with anyone.

I found myself wearing a mighty frown.

It happened like this sometimes—I'd meet a girl I wanted, and she'd be *all* I wanted until I saw things through.

That explained what this feeling was. That was all it *could* be, all I was capable of. Attraction. Possession. Acquisition. Nothing more.

The thought erased my discomfort. And with my conscience clean, I gave myself license to watch Val without remorse.

The set felt forever long, and by the end, I was itching to get my hands around Val's waist. From the confines of the stage, I'd witnessed a string of guys ask her to dance. But she'd turned them all down.

The teacher in me shook his head. She'd missed the point.

The player in me thumbed his suspenders, nodding his approval. I had an itching notion I wouldn't take kindly to watching another man twirl her around the dance floor.

I rushed off the stage, hurrying my instrument into its case, taking the stairs down to the floor in a leap, eating up the space between me and her in a series of strides and a handful of heartbeats.

She didn't see me coming, not until I was almost on her. I stepped into her seamlessly, slipped one hand in the notch of her waist and grabbed her hand with the other, spinning us in a single motion. And just like that, we were dancing. Around and around, into me and away from me, her skirts flying and smile bright, her laughter in my ears and her body against mine.

I quit tricking her around so we could catch our breaths, and she fit into the frame of my arms with precision and grace that always surprised me, no matter how many times I'd held her like this.

"Having fun?" I asked.

"Always. Is there any other way to swing?"

"Nope," I said as I sped us around in a little triple step, spinning her around before slowing us again.

"The band was on fire tonight. You guys were feeling it, huh? The crowd was *hoppin'*."

"We were definitely feeling it."

A pause breathed between us, and something akin to guilt rose in my chest, a dreadful, sinking feeling.

She's not for you. Just once. You promised.

I opened my mouth to say something—anything—to reinforce the fences, to keep her away, but she spoke first.

"So, I've been thinking about our lessons."

"Have you?" I asked, praying my voice was devoid of hope.

"Mmhmm," she answered with a nod and a smile. "I've been thinking about them a lot. I learned something very valuable last night."

I swallowed hard enough to make my Adam's apple ride from jaw to clavicle. "Oh?"

"Yup. And that lesson was that I have no idea what I'm doing."

I laughed my relief. "I don't know about that, Val. Seems to me you don't need any lessons at all."

"That's sweet, but I'm pretty sure it's like dancing. You're good enough for the both of us."

God, she was so pretty in my arms, her face shy and devoted and laced with levity. "You have no idea how wrong you are."

Her cheeks flushed, but she didn't waver. "So I have some ideas about my next lessons."

"All right. Shoot. What do you want to know?"

"How to give blowjobs."

I tripped over her feet, and we took a dangerous tilt, but I caught us, somehow spinning us so the dance didn't break.

"I'm sorry, what?" I asked once I had us righted. My heart was louder than the music. My mouth watered with anticipation that I'd heard what I thought I'd heard.

"Blowjobs. I mean, for one. I'd also like to experience sex in several positions and cunnilingus by a man who actually knows where a clitoris is."

That time, my feet just quit. I stood stupidly in the middle of the dance floor as a hundred people danced around us, looking down at Val's face, which was the picture of calm determination.

"So you…you want…you're saying you want to…"

She waited for me to finish, but I only kept stammering. "I want our lessons to extend to the physical. For science."

"For…science?"

"You're clearly an expert kisser, which leads me to believe you're an expert…well, everything else. I've only been with two guys, and neither of them knew what to do with my body any better than I knew what to do with theirs."

"Val…" Everything in me screamed both yes and no at equal decibels.

"Before you say no, I want you to know there are no strings. This is just for educational purposes. You've already helped me so much, and I'm eager to learn. If you aren't interested in sleeping with me, I totally understand. No hard feelings. But I had to ask."

Her face was so full of hope and resolve. Something in my chest split and ached. "Val, if I wasn't interested in sleeping with you, I'd need to have my pulse checked."

She drew in a breath that seemed to give her confidence. "Good. Then—"

"Hang on," I started, sobering. "This…this isn't like going to practice dinner. It's not so easy to separate your feelings when you're hooking up. I don't want to hurt you, and this complicates things in a way I'm not sure you're ready for."

That confidence shifted to fury in the span of a heartbeat. "Now, hang on just one fucking minute, Sam. You don't get to decide what I'm ready for and what I'm not. Don't tell me what I'm emotionally capable of handling. I mean, I appreciate you being the white knight and all, but who the hell do you think you are?"

I opened my mouth, found no words, and closed it again.

"I've thought through this, and I know the risk. My terms, if you'd have let me finish, are to give *you* the topics of education in an order *I'm* comfortable with. And if something happens to change the dynamic of our relationship or how I feel, I'll tell you so, and we can end the lessons. You said you're always up-front, and you've been upfront with me. I don't have any misgivings or expectations of you."

She took a breath and straightened her spine, lifting her little chin to meet my gaze.

"So, what do you say? Will you teach me?"

I knew what to say. I knew what to do. I knew right from wrong and black from white and good from evil.

I just didn't care.

I stepped into her, cupped her face in my hands, eliciting a gasp of surprise from her plump lips. "Let's just start with kissing. I don't want to have to tell you I told you so." She parted her lips as if to argue. But I didn't want to hear it. "And school is in session starting *right now.*"

Her mouth was hot and soft, her surprise lasting only a millisecond before she submitted. Her arms wound around my neck, her body stretched long on her tiptoes. She was sweeter than I remembered, and I tasted her deeply, determined not to forget a single detail.

The twenty-four hours since we'd kissed had been shades of gray, and I was seeing in Technicolor.

Whistles and laughter erupted around us, and we broke the kiss to look around, remembering we were in the middle of the club. We executed a perfect bow-curtsie, and the second she was upright, I tugged her hand, bringing her into me. I grabbed her free hand and pushed her away, kicking us into the song, spinning her until she couldn't stop laughing.

And I shouldn't have felt like I'd just made all the right moves, not when I'd unwittingly hammered the last nail into my coffin.

VAL

He said yes!

It was my only thought, and it had the enthusiasm of a cheerleader celebrating a winning touchdown with a back handspring that spanned the full hundred yards.

Kissing. Kissing and touching and Sam. Naked. Naked Sam. *Kissing me.*

I squealed when he twirled me faster, so fast, I almost lost my footing. Everything had sped up, my heart and his, the energy between us effervescent, cracking and bubbling against my skin with anticipation. But no matter how fast he spun me, no matter how I faltered, he was always there, steady and strong, his hands waiting to catch me, fitting to me, moving me and molding me and putting me exactly where he wanted me.

Which was exactly why he was so perfect for the job.

My bar very clearly needed raising.

The crowd around us began to part, to stop and form a circle around a couple. They were *incredible*. She was a little rocket, a tiny thing that her partner tossed around like she was nothing. The *tricks*. I couldn't get over the tricks. There were times I didn't know where she'd even end up, and wherever I figured would be wrong. Instead of landing on her feet, she'd slide under his legs. Instead of flipping over his back, she'd land on his shoulders.

We were all stopped and clapping and cheering and whooping, our faces open and smiling and awestruck.

"God*damn*, they're amazing!" I laughed the words to Sam, who smiled down at me like he was watching me experience Disneyland for the first time. "I wish I could do that!"

"You can," he said.

I laughed so openly, it made him frown. "That's funny, Sam."

"Don't do that, Val. You can trick, easy."

My smile fell. "No, *you* don't do *that*. That girl weighs ninety pounds. There's no way you could flip me like that, not unless your superpower is manipulating the laws of physics."

Sam folded his arms and turned to face me. Everything about him was stern. "I can flip you."

"Stop it. Can we just dance again?" I asked, resigned and regretting bringing it up.

"Sure, if you let me show you how to flip."

I huffed. "Please…I don't want to embarrass myself. Can't you see that?"

His jaw flexed, but his eyes were soft. "I guarantee you can flip. If I'm wrong, if you're embarrassed, I'll let you call in a favor of choice. Anything you want, anytime you want it."

Several naked physical acts crossed my mind, and I looked him over, the strict sincerity in his face disarming me.

He offered his hand. "Trust me, Val."

I took a breath and slipped my hand into his palm, knowing at least if I regretted trying, I'd get naked favors out of it. "I trust you."

At that, he smiled. He towed me to the edge of the dance floor where there was more room.

"All right. Here's how it goes."

We were face-to-face, and he took my hands in front of me and pulled, turning me under his arm. The twist put us in a sweetheart hold, his arms around my waist, my back to his front.

"Now," he said as he unwound me without releasing my hands, "when I let your hand go, leave it here on my arm, and hang on. I'm gonna grab you here." He hooked his left hand under my left knee, and his other arm locked my waist in the hook of his elbow—his bicep around my stomach, his forearm in the small of my back, and his hand gripping my waist on the other side.

That arm was the fulcrum I was going to spin around.

He was going to spin me. Around his arm. Over his shoulder.

Fear shot through me like lightning. "Sam, I don't—"

He stayed me with a squeeze of his hand and a gleam in his eye. "I'm not going to let you get hurt."

I swallowed and took a breath, but I couldn't speak. So I nodded and hung on to his bicep.

"Okay," he continued, "when we get here, you've got to kick off. Jump as hard as you can with me hanging on to you like this."

"Okay," I said, memorizing everything he'd said and repeating it back in my head.

"Oh, and Val?"

"Yeah?" I met his eyes.

He smirked. "Don't let go."

I laughed nervously as he brought my hands to the starting position again.

"Let's do it a couple of times without flipping just to get the rhythm of it."

So we did. We took it slow a couple of times with him talking me through it, then fast a couple more, always stopping just before I jumped.

"All right," he said, facing me. "You ready?"

I nodded. "No."

With a laugh, he pulled me into him and pressed a kiss into my hair. "You can do this. You can do anything."

The breath I took almost fortified me. Nerves wriggled around in my stomach like worms.

"Okay. Here we go," he said and whipped me around.

My pulse quickened. In seconds, I was hanging on to his arm, and he was hooking my knee and then—

He tried to lift me, and I barely budged. The only thing he managed was bringing the knee in his hand up.

Shame washed over me, pricking my skin like static from my chest out to every limb, climbing my face painfully until it reached the corners of my eyes. Tears sprang, clinging to my bottom lids as I tried desperately to keep them at bay.

I laughed. It was the only thing to do. "Well, you officially owe me, and don't think you're gonna get off easy, Sam. I told you so."

His face was inexplicably hard and soft all at once. And when he cupped my cheek and looked into my eyes, I thought I might just go ahead and sink into the floor and disappear.

"I don't owe you a single thing." He paused, searching my face for understanding. And then a smile brushed his lips. "You forgot to jump."

"I—" I blinked. "Wait, I what?"

"You. Forgot. To jump," he said slowly.

"I…oh my God," I breathed on an incredulous laugh. "I didn't, did I?"

He shook his head, his smile spreading. "Again."

My heart thumped so hard, it felt like I was going to have a heart attack as he spun me around, left my arm on his, which I grasped, and hooked his hand under my knee.

"Jump," he commanded.

I sank and kicked off with all my strength. And for a moment, I was weightless. The world turned upside down. My insides mixed up and switched places. My skirts flew. And then my feet solidly hit the ground, Sam's arm still at my waist, steadying me.

And then I exploded. I shot off my feet, jumping up and down, throwing myself into his arms, the two of us laughing as he spun me around. He brought me to a stop, smoothed my hair, smiled down into my face.

"See? I knew you could do it. All you had to do was jump."

And before I could speak, he kissed me.

STEADY AS SHE GOES

SAM

"I swear, she'll be here any minute," I hoped, checking my phone for a message to prove me a liar. The screen only showed me the time.

The guys in the band shared a look.

"I don't understand why you couldn't just call Tommy," Mike said, adjusting his sax strap on his shoulder. "He always fills in for Chris."

"I'm still pissed he didn't just suck it up and come in." Ian's eyes were on his drumstick as he rolled it across his knuckles.

"You didn't hear him on the phone," I said. "His fever was so bad, at one point, he started speaking Hebrew."

Ian shrugged. "I'm just saying, take some Advil and show up."

I shook my head. "You're a dick."

Nick spun around on his piano stool at a lazy pace. "This chick had better be good. We haven't had to rehearse in months. I'm missing brunch for this."

Josh stopped strumming his guitar, one brow rising at Nick. "Brunch? What the fuck, man?"

"You don't know living until you've had the chicken and waffles at Splits. I dream about that meal."

I checked my phone again, wondering how long I could hold off a mutiny. When the door burst open, I was relieved I wouldn't have to.

Val's cheeks were flushed and glistening, her chest heaving from exertion. Her eyes met mine, and her smile could have powered a New York City block.

"Hey, I'm sorry I'm late. I got here as fast as I could."

"Don't worry about it," I said before anyone could be an asshole. And by anyone, I meant Ian. "Guys, this is Val. Val, meet the guys."

Said guys stepped forward, extending their hands to meet her. Except for Ian. He sat behind his trap set and raised one drumstick in lieu of a greeting.

She set her things down and unloaded her trumpet while I spoke.

"Thanks for coming down at such short notice. There's not much to practice today—we just want to get a feel for playing together. Almost everything we play is in E or A with a base melody. Then, we just jam. You'll come after Matt, the clarinet, and keep an eye on me for cues."

"Got it," she said as she stood.

I tried not to stare at her lips when she brought her instrument to them and blew soundlessly to warm up the pipes.

"All right. Nick, kick her off."

Nick plinked out a melody on the piano, and one by one, we joined in. Val came in last, the cherry on the sundae, the tip of the top. And from the first note, the energy in the room rose like a wave. Everyone turned to her like she was the center of the solar system, myself included. I made no attempt to hide my smile, which was smug as fuck.

We took turns soloing, and when it was her turn, she played with unexpected fierceness and unsurprising gusto.

In short, she was phenomenal, just like I'd known she'd be.

When I closed off the song, everyone broke out laughing and praising Val, who blushed again, her face beaming.

"Damn, that was *fun*," she said, smiling as she brushed her curly hair back.

Nick shook his head at me. "Where have you been hiding her, Sammy?"

"I only just found her myself," I answered, my eyes catching hers for the briefest of moments, which was just long enough to have me considering how I could maneuver her out of the room to kiss her.

"If I hadn't known Chris for a decade, I'd say we should really consider replacing him," Matt said.

"That's exactly how she landed her permanent chair on *Wicked*. Never miss work if your sub is better than you," I said on a laugh.

Val's blush flared brighter. "Well, you guys sure know how to make a girl feel welcome."

I laid a hand on the small of her back and smiled down at her. "I think you're gonna fit in just fine."

She mirrored me, and I didn't miss Ian pinning me with a questioning look. I did, however, ignore him.

For the next hour, we rolled through our favorites and a few new melodies I'd come up with. That was all the time we needed to make sure the show that night would be a hit. With Val on the docket, it was guaranteed.

I was just about to call it when Nick asked, "Are you gonna show her any tricks?"

"Oh, I couldn't," Val said.

I frowned. "Sure, you could. It's easy—I do all the work."

She gave me a look. "You mean like Chris did the other night at the club? Because there's no way—"

"*Val*," I started, and she clamped her mouth shut. "Come on, let me show you. Just jump, remember?"

With a sigh and a softening of her face, she answered, "Yes, I remember."

"Good." I turned to my bass and tilted it to forty-five degrees, putting almost all the weight on ribs of the instrument's base. The neck rested in my left hand, and the waist hooked on my left thigh. "All right, come here. Nick, spot her, would you?"

"You got it," he said, bounding over to us.

Val approached me warily.

"Okay, put your right foot here"—I patted the notch at the waist of the bass—"and take my hand." I offered my right hand.

She did as she'd been told, her foot fitting into the curve. Her knee hitched, her calf resting against my ribs. I found myself smiling. Val didn't look amused.

"All right, now, I'm going to duck, and I want you to use my hand for leverage to swing your leg around my neck. Put your left foot on the shoulder of the bass. Right here." I patted the curve where it met the neck of the instrument.

A breathy laugh escaped her. "I can't—"

"You *can.* I've got you, Val. If I can hold Chris, I can hold you, easy."

She took a deep breath and looked behind her at Nick, who offered an encouraging nod. "Okay."

"On three. Ready? One, two, *three.*"

Her clammy hand bore down on mine, and I ducked so she'd have a shorter distance to throw her leg. She placed her foot on the shoulder, right where I'd said, and just like that, she was standing on the ribs of my bass with her thighs around my neck.

There were a grand total of zero places I'd rather be than between Val's legs.

She let out a triumphant whoop, and I couldn't help but laugh.

"See? I told you. Again."

"Yeah, yeah, you told me so. What's new?"

"How do you feel up there? Steady?"

"Surprisingly steady. Have you got me?"

"Rock solid. Think you can play like this?"

"Absolutely. But…" She paused. "How do I get down?"

"Jump."

She laughed, but the sound stopped abruptly when I craned my neck to give her a look. "Oh, you're serious."

"I can help you down, but it's cooler if you jump."

She took a noisy breath. "Any tips?"

"Yeah, don't fall."

"Thanks," she said flatly.

"Put your hand on my shoulder and use it to steady yourself."

"Okay. One, two, *three!*"

I grabbed the neck and held on tight as she kicked off, and it must have been a good one because the guys broke into whistles and cheers.

When I turned to look at her, I found her grinning at me. "Again!" she crowed.

And with a laugh, I assumed the position again, offering my right hand for her use.

As far as I was concerned, she could use me all she wanted.

I thought back to her request—to extend her education to the bedroom—and a flash of desire washed over me in a hissing *yes*. God, the things I wanted to teach her. To show her. I knew in my marrow she'd never been subject to body worship, and I wanted to worship every curve. I wanted to go to church, get on my hands and knees and pay homage to every warm, wet space in her body.

It's dangerous, I reminded myself. *You'll hurt her.*

Be honest, the devil said, disguised as an angel. *Just tell her you can't give her anything more. Then you're free and clear.*

Lies, all of them. And I believed every one.

EVERYTHING EVERYWHERE

VAL

An ocean of people rocked in front of me, bouncing and spinning and flipping to the beat of Ian's drumsticks.

Sam looked over at me, his smile so utterly perfect. I closed my eyes, my cheeks high as I blasted a riff that hit a note so high, I could feel it zing all the way through me.

Adrenaline pumped through me as it had since we'd stepped onstage. I'd imagined this feeling, but reality didn't come close—it was a religious experience. It was what I'd been born to do.

Sam, I'd discovered, was a doorway to a world I'd only dreamed of. A world of kisses and touches and music. A world of dancing and flipping and laughter. A world where I was onstage in front of hundreds of people, doing the thing I loved most.

It was every version of me that I'd wished existed come to life.

Our set was nearly over, which I would have hated if not for the fact that afterward, I'd be bopping around the dance floor with Sam.

My Sam. For the time at least.

My heart flung itself against my breastbone when Sam spun his bass with the help of his foot and stepped into the open stage in front of us. I let him ham it up, and he did. The instrument rested between his legs, and he shifted his hips like he was dancing. Or fucking.

Oh, the things those hips could do.

Oh, the things I wanted those hips to do *to me*.

When he tipped the bass and the verse wound toward the break, I walked over, still playing. Until the four-count break hit, and in a flash that shocked even me, I grabbed his hand, stepped on the waist of the bass, and kicked my leg over his neck. My red dress flew—the same dress I'd worn on that first night—and just like that, he straightened up. We hit the chorus at the exact same moment. His hand slapped that bass like he was punishing it, and my horn pointed at the ceiling in exaltation as I made my way through an epic, barely planned run. All the lights were on us, the crowd absolutely wild, my heart blindly racing and the man between my legs playing as if the devil himself were spurring him on.

When we split back into the verse, I laid a hand on his shoulder and jumped, kicking my feet out behind me. I jumped into the verse, jitterbugging around Sam in a circle—hips swaying, shoulders shimmying, twisting on the balls of my feet—before heading back to my spot. A few minutes later, the song was over, along with our set.

The crowd broke into applause and cheers, everyone stopping to face us, hooting and whistling and smiling their thanks. We stepped out and bowed. Sam and the guys turned to me, applauding me from the stage, and I thought my heart might stop from shock and the overwhelming humbleness it evoked. The noise from the crowd rose, and not knowing what else to do, I stepped out and curtsied, waving to them all before following the guys offstage.

I'd barely passed the deep navy velvet curtains when I was

scooped off my feet and spun around by Sam. His arms clamped around my waist, and I flung mine around his neck in an effort to hang on while he madly spun us backstage.

"You were amazing," he said in my ear, and I buried my face in his neck to hide my smile.

"Thank you for that, Sam. Thank you so much."

He nuzzled his nose into my hair. "No, thank you."

He set me down, but his hand found mine and clasped it. The guys congratulated me as Sam took my trumpet and set it on its horn next to where his bass lay on its side. And the second they dispersed, he towed me behind the stage to an alley of curtains. The next thing I knew, we were behind them all, completely alone in the almost dark. The curtains rippled against us from the disturbance, the brick wall biting at my back. And, when I took a breath, Sam's body held me in place, his hips pinning mine, his golden eyes on fire.

"Pop quiz," he said. And before I could wonder what he meant, his mouth covered mine.

Hot and wet. Supple and sweet. He kissed me until we were coiled around each other with no breath, no air, no space between us.

To my disappointment, he broke away, his lips swollen and eyes smoldering. I couldn't help but smile.

He smiled back, tracing my face with his gaze. "You are incredible, Valentina." His voice was rough, his calloused fingers rougher as they brushed my chin, my jaw, the hollow behind my ear.

"Takes one to know one."

He chuckled softly. Now his fingers were at the nape of my bare neck. "I like your hair like this. I love to see this curve. Here," he said, trailing those damnable fingers down the stem of my neck to the point where it met my shoulder. "And I love the magnolia," he said, running a petal of the flower behind my ear between his thumb and forefinger. "It kisses your ear right here, right where I've wanted to kiss all night."

Before I could speak, he did just that. His mouth closed over my earlobe, his tongue wet and dexterous as he sucked. I went limp in his arms, my eyes fluttering closed with a sigh.

"God, how do you do that?" I muttered.

He hummed from deep in his chest, the sound so close to a moan, my body responded in every erogenous zone I had, plus a few I hadn't known existed.

His lips moved down my neck. "What's our first lesson?" he asked between kisses. "Tell me what you want to know."

I wondered how I was supposed to answer with his face buried in my neck. "Everything," was all I could manage.

Another hum, this one edging on a growl. His hips rolled into mine to press his hard length against a very, very sensitive part of me.

"When you say things like that, I want to touch you everywhere," he said as his hand skimmed my collarbone, then down to the curve of my breast. "Here," he said, his thumb brushing my nipple once before his hand moved down my ribs, down my stomach, to the aching point between my thighs. "Here," he said, cupping my sex once, gently, that thumb brushing my clit too softly before his hand moved on, skating to the outside of my thigh. He hitched it just a little, settling himself between my legs again.

I was covered in goosebumps, my body shivering against his and my breath trembling. "When you say things like that, I want to let you touch anywhere you want."

He lifted my chin as he came in for another kiss. "Don't tempt me, or I'll make you come right here."

I smiled, blinking slowly up at him. "I can't."

It was Sam's turn to blink, but his was from confusion rather than drunk from kisses. "Can't what? Let me?"

"No—I can't come. No one's ever been able to do it other than me."

With a laugh, he kissed me. "You've been dating the wrong guys, Valentina. You just need someone who knows what they're doing."

My eyes rolled involuntarily. "That's what they all say. My body just doesn't work that way."

His smile shifted, his eyes hardening along with the boa constrictor in his pants. "You *can* have an orgasm, which means I can give you one. In fact," he said with a shift of his hips that had me slow blinking again, "I could make you come right here, right now, in less than three minutes. And I wouldn't even have to take your panties off."

Now it was me who was laughing. "Sam, you're crazy. We're in public, and I've literally never—*oh*."

His hand—oh my God, his *hand*—had trailed up my thigh and under my skirts, not stopping until his fingertips were skimming the length of my center and his thumb was pressed against my clit.

My hand slithered from the back of his neck to cup his jaw. "Sam," I whispered desperately as he stroked me.

His forehead touched mine, his lips millimeters away. "Shh—clock's ticking."

He held me in place against the wall, his hand working my body through the fabric of my hot pants for only a moment before they skimmed up to the hem and dipped inside.

My heart thumped like a bass drum, rattling my chest as he inched down. And when his fingers actually connected with my clit, my entire body contracted, toes to core to eyelids.

This was the point at which I lost all sense of time, space, and self.

The sum of my universe was cupped in Sam's palm, at his fingertips as he sank into me to the knuckle. His palm squeezed and relaxed against my clit, his finger slipping in and out of me with every flex. His breath against my skin as he whispered things that sounded like prayer and poetry and pious praise. Some was filthy. Some was reverent. All was a blur, the sound underneath the thundering of my heart and the rasp of my breath.

A flex of his hand, and my body involuntarily squeezed his finger so hard, he hissed a single word.

"*Fuck.*"

Another pulse at the sound.

His hand tightened again, grinding, reaching for the depths of me. My body wanted him there so badly, it drew him in as a wave of heat spread from my chest and raced for every extremity.

His free hand cupped the bend of my neck. My mouth opened with pleasure, and his lips brushed mine.

"Come," he said, his lips grazing mine without the connection I wanted. The sensation drove me mad. "Come right here." His hand between my legs squeezed, his finger curling inside me.

A moan, my hand on his face, my thumb brushing his bottom lip.

His hips pressed into the back of his hand. "Come for me." His voice, deep velvet, dark as the curtains around us, the sound rumbling from his chest into mine. "I want to feel you." It was a whisper, a command, a demand and a request.

And I had no choice but to say yes.

As the world around me exploded in a blinding flash, I said *yes* many, many times, along with his name, a call to a higher power, and several swear words that would have impressed me if I'd been at all coherent.

I'd had orgasms before. I'd had sex before. But never before had I been reduced to primary functions and relieved completely of my senses.

I sagged against Sam—his hand slowed but didn't recede. And then he kissed me.

He kissed me so deeply, I couldn't breathe, couldn't think about anything beyond the seam of our lips, the tangle of our tongues, the juncture of my thighs where his hand nestled. That kiss held a thousand things I wanted to say, a hundred things I wasn't allowed to feel, a dozen thank-yous, and a handful more yeses.

Eventually, depressingly, he slowed his pace. Closed his lips. Reclaimed his hand. Leaned back. Looked at me in a way that made me feel more beautiful than I'd ever felt. And he said, "I told you—you just had to find a man who knew what he was doing."

I laughed, knowing all too well that he was right and knowing even better that I'd never find another man like him. Not as long as I lived.

CLITOSAURUS SEX

SAM

Val whooped as she jumped into my side and onto my thigh, and I tipped her, dipping her head almost to the ground. Her legs hugged the back of my arm and kicked over my head, her toes pointed at the Edison bulbs overhead.

And all the while, my thirsty eyes drank in the sight of her smiling face.

Her joy, I'd found, was inescapable.

I straightened up and swung her around, putting her feet back on the ground, mourning the loss of her body curled around mine.

That smile, red and lush. I'd watched her put on her lipstick backstage after I proved my point.

Fuck, I would have loved to prove that point again. To relish in her sweet surprise, to experience all the firsts she wanted and the ones she had no idea existed.

Everything about her was perfect, top to bottom.

Especially bottom.

Her skirts twirled when I spun her out, and when she returned to my arms, I reveled in the feeling of her flush against me. A few weeks of dancing together, and our bodies were in perfect sync. She anticipated every move and stepped into it, knowing by the pressure of my hand or shift in my feet which direction we'd go and where I wanted her.

It was a strange comfort, the natural accord that came only from time and practice, trust and partnership.

I'd never experienced togetherness like this before. And, oddly, my only desire was for *more*.

The thought should have made me uncomfortable. Instead, I found myself smiling at Val, reveling in the sound of her laughter as I flipped her with ease.

The song came to a close, and the band slowed down. Val brushed a loose lock of hair back, her chest heaving and face light.

"I'm gonna go grab a drink," she said breathlessly.

"Let me get it. What do you want?"

She laughed. "I'll grab it on the way back from the ladies.'" Her hand brushed my arm and squeezed my forearm, and then she headed away.

I stuffed my hands in my pockets, smiling. Amelia and Katherine swayed together, lost in conversation, oblivious to me. And with nothing to do, I moved for the edge of the dance floor, watching the crowd while I waited.

Their faces were familiar, though I didn't know their names other than the girls I'd taken home. Jenny in the pineapple-yellow pedal pushers, who made that sweet little moan when I kissed that spot behind her ear. Jana, who had been so nervous, she talked about her cat all night, up until the moment I got my hands on hers. BB with the punk-rockabilly pink hair and all the hidden piercings I'd become so familiar with.

Their eyes brushed over me with a silent request, one they knew would be denied, judging by the look behind them. They said hello when it was appropriate but otherwise kept their distance, abiding the boundaries I'd set from the jump.

And then there were girls like Patrice.

I spotted her platinum hair weaving through people on a direct track for me. And when her eyes came into view, they were set with determination, her red lips curled into a seductive smile.

Predictable.

Patrice and the like were rare in my world—I'd developed a sense for them and learned to avoid them. They were the girls who believed the rules didn't apply to them. The girls who thought they were different, that they were the exceptions.

They all placed expectations on me, which was the equivalent of chains.

Patrice elbowed her way through the crowd and nearly charged me, hips swinging in black capris, her tailored shirt knotted just above her belly button.

"Hey," she said, sidling up next to me. "What's shakin', Sam?"

"Not much," I answered, scanning the room for Val. "You?"

"Oh, just the usual. I've been looking for a dance, but you've been with your new girl nonstop. What's the story?" she asked, attempting to mask the bite in her words.

"No story. She's a friend."

"You're pretty chummy for friends."

I swiveled my head to pin her with a glare. "Yeah, we are."

Her hands rose in surrender, palms out. "I'm not judging. I'm just surprised is all."

"Why's that, Patrice?" The question came out bored, but I hid the bite in *my* words about as well as she had.

"She's just…not your usual type."

"I didn't realize I had a type."

She squirmed just a little. "You know what I mean."

"Obviously I don't."

"She's…I dunno. She's not a small girl. Doesn't seem very confident either."

"An hour ago, she was center stage under a spotlight, jumping on my shoulders like a circus performer. How much more confident can she get?"

Patrice blushed but opened her mouth to speak.

I cut her off. "And if you say another word about her size, I swear to God, I'll make sure you can't get into Sway for a month. I thought you were better than that, Patrice."

At that, she blanched. "Fair enough." Her eyes darted behind me and narrowed. "Ugh, Ian. That's my cue."

"Hey there, Patsy," Ian said with an unfriendly smirk.

"Don't call me that, asshole."

He laughed. "Aw, don't be sore, sugar. Come on, let me buy you a drink."

Ian reached for her, but she shrugged out from under his arm.

"In your dreams," she shot, turning to me once more. "Let me know if things change, all right, Sammy? You know where to find me."

Before I could permanently decline, she turned and walked away.

Ian watched her go with open admiration of her ass. "Look at you, turning down pussy left and right."

"Yeah, well, I'm only one man with two hands, which just so happen to be full."

He snickered. "With Val's ass, I'm sure they are."

My hand twitched at my side with an involuntary urge to pop him in the nose. "Why are you such a dick?"

"Can't help it. I've got so much to spare." He glanced over the crowd, unimpressed. "Nail her yet?"

"What's it matter?"

"It doesn't. I'm just curious. I have this nagging feeling that she's a virgin, and the thought of that ass of hers getting punished is too much to resist."

My simmering anger flared. "She's not a fucking side of beef."

"Aren't you noble." He turned to me and laughed with condescending certainty. "Man, watching you wriggle around on the hook is too much. Just don't go falling in love, Romeo."

"Shut the fuck up, Ian." It sounded like I was kidding. I wasn't.

"I mean, seriously," he said, turning to face me. His face was smiling. His eyes were not. "Look at you. Moral ambiguity looks good on you. Better than the bullshit you always put on. Always Mr. Cool, always have your shit together. Always the good guy. What you don't realize is that we're the same, you and me. All you've gotta do is get on my level, give up the act."

"You keep saying that. But it's not an act, and I'm nothing like you."

"Not an act? Who's the one lying to Val? Who's the one leading her on? Tell me it doesn't feel good. Tell me you don't like having her on the string."

I stepped into him, shoulders square, jaw clenched. "I haven't lied to her. I'm not stringing her on. And you're fucking heartless."

He shook his head, the corners of his lips curling. "And you're fucking hopeless."

I caught the scent of her hair just before I felt her hand on my arm. "Is everything okay?"

I didn't break eye contact with Ian. "Everything's fine."

He laughed, a sound I was coming to hate. It shocked me that I hadn't noticed before.

"Speaking of fine," Ian said, the tension easing, but I could still feel the tug. "I'm off to find tonight's lucky girl. You kids have fun."

And with the tip of his hat, he turned and disappeared into the crowd.

I exhaled slowly and counted to three, scooping Val into my arms to whirl her around. She held on to me like she might fly away from the force. As mad as I was, she might have.

"What were you guys talking about?" Val asked after a moment, her dark eyes troubled, her brows knit to form the smallest crease.

"Nothing," I said, trying to will the word into truth. Because it wasn't nothing. Not when it came to Ian, and not when it came to Val.

She didn't seem convinced. "Really? Because you looked pretty upset. Did he say something? I mean, I imagine he did. He's always so…"

"Annoying? Disgusting? Misogynistic?"

Val laughed. "I was going to say forward, but that works, too."

"I don't know if he can help it. He's always loved attention, especially from women. I keep trying to tell him he doesn't have to be so…well, *Ian*. But honestly? I think he enjoys it. Like he gets a rush from deceiving people, from manipulating them." I shook my head and stopped talking. I'd already said too much.

Worry tugged at her lips. "Does he manipulate you?"

I laughed. "All the time. Every day. But he's the closest thing I have to a brother. That's what they do, right?"

Now she wore a full-blown frown. "No. I mean, my brothers fuck with each other, but it's always harmless. Well, *usually* harmless. They've been known to throw their fair share of punches. But true deceit and manipulation? Never."

And then I was frowning, too. He'd been my closest friend for what felt like forever, the one I spent more time with than anyone else. As I recounted the last few years, I realized we didn't hang out with anyone else. Every other friend I'd had, he'd teased, pointed out every bad quality, and-or been an asshole to them. Which left him and me very much on our own.

I think I'd known somewhere in the back of my mind that he'd done it on purpose, but I hadn't fully recognized it until right then.

And now, he was after Val.

Ian pissed me off on the regular, but the bet had taken him to a level I didn't like. I wondered briefly if he'd betray me but pushed the thought away the second it touched me. He wouldn't. We'd been through too many years together for that.

"Ian's a dick, but you don't have to worry about him. He's like a dog with no teeth. All bark."

She laughed, the joke easing the strain in the air. But not the strain in my chest.

So I did what I could—I kissed her and hoped I was imagining things.

Nobody'd ever accused me of being smart.

VAL

"So, I maybe got finger banged in public tonight."

The door slammed shut behind me, and I turned in our entryway to find Amelia and Katherine gaping at me with twin expressions of shock. Katherine swayed a little, reminding me just how drunk she was.

"No. Fucking. Way." Amelia blinked at me with owl eyes.

I nodded, lips between my teeth, trying not to gloat. Problem was, I was honest-to-God proud of myself. Not that I'd done anything but stand there and hold on to him for dear life.

"In public?" Katherine asked like she hadn't heard me.

"Backstage, just after the show. He pulled me behind the curtain and..." I shrugged, not knowing what else to say.

"But... how... I... like..." Amelia stammered.

"Sit," Katherine commanded, pointing at the couch.

We obeyed, and by the time we were seated, it seemed we'd all found our tongues.

"Okay, how in the world did that happen?" Amelia asked.

"I can't keep my mouth in check around him and admitted a guy has never given me an orgasm. He set out to prove me wrong."

"Did he?" Amelia's eyes widened, her breath quickening. "Prove you wrong, I mean."

My smile curled up on my face. "Oh, he did. In less than three minutes. With my panties still on."

They broke out in laughter and squealing and exclamations, and I joined in with hot cheeks that were sore from grinning.

When we calmed down a little, I said, "But I need a game plan. I'm supposed to be guiding the lessons, and I'm afraid I'll keep having orgasms in public without one."

"Where's the problem with that?" Katherine asked, smirking.

I rolled my eyes. "You know what I mean. I just…I just want to regain a little control."

The effort required for Katherine to haul herself off the couch in her drunken state was exceptional. "This is a job for the whiteboard."

Amelia groaned and flopped back on the couch. "God, you are such a buzzkill. Diagrams are not sexy!" she called, her volume climbing as Katherine left the room.

When she appeared again a few seconds later, it was with a whiteboard under her arm and a dry erase marker in her mouth.

"Prease," she said around the marker butt. "You have nevew sheen my diagwams." She propped the board on the mantel and removed the marker from her mouth, uncapping it. "All right, let's talk about sex."

Amelia and I broke into the chorus of the Salt-N-Pepa song of the same name.

Katherine rolled her eyes. "This is serious, guys."

I gave her a look. "You're about to make sexual charts and diagrams to give to my sex tutor. This is *not* serious. If this *is* serious, we should seek professional help."

She ignored me and turned to the whiteboard. "Okay, let's list off the things you want Sam to teach you." With a few swipes of her hand, she created a section for the list itself with subheadings for foreplay, positions, and geographic locations. "Just call them out," she said after a second. "I can keep up."

Amelia and I giggled, curling our feet under us.

I thought for a second. "Hand jobs. Blowjobs for sure."

"Ugh, that just sounds like the worst," Amelia groaned. When we made faces at her, she said, "Don't look at me like that. My palate is exceptionally small."

"You have to relax your throat and hold whatever you can't fit in your mouth with your hand," Katherine offered matter-of-factly as she demonstrated with her hands, her mouth stretched in an O.

We then made faces at *her*.

To which she said, "Now, don't look at *me* like that. *Cosmopolitan* might be setting women back forty years, but they have some solid sex tips."

"All I know is, I'm exceedingly bad at blowjobs," I said.

"How many have you given?" Katherine asked.

"Two, and I had no idea what I was doing with any of them. Both guys stopped me after a few minutes and told me it was okay, that they didn't really like blowjobs anyway. Pretty sure they were lying."

"I'm pretty sure they were, too," Katherine agreed. "I've given a few, but I couldn't understand why I wasn't enjoying it. The girls on Pornhub *really* look like they're enjoying it. I feel like I'm doing something fundamentally wrong."

"I just don't get why it's called sucking dick," Amelia said. "Do you actually suck it? Like a skin lollipop?"

"No, I don't think you actually *suck*," Katherine added thoughtfully. "Although I don't think a little suction is frowned upon. I definitely know you don't *blow* during a blowjob."

I sighed. "Well, that explains some things."

"It's intimidating," Amelia said, crossing her arms with her face drawn. "You've got to get down there with his smelly junk in your face and jam it down your throat. I've never seen a penis in real life, but I'm a hundred percent sure the average dick and my mouth are not the same length."

Katherine and I snickered.

"And then, after you…I don't know what—gag on his dick for however long?—then he comes and fires a huge load down your esophagus." Hysteria rode the words like a bronco. "How do you not choke? Or drown? I don't think I could swallow. I just don't!"

"Don't worry," I soothed. "When the time comes, you don't have to do anything you don't want to do. You don't even have to let that nasty thing near your exceptionally small palate, and you certainly don't have to swallow his load. Okay?"

She nodded and sighed. "Okay."

Katherine scrutinized our very short list for a moment. "Well, in the way of foreplay, that's about all you can do. There are, I suppose, addendums to blowjobs—like testicle juggling, perineal massage, or anal penetration—but I think you should maybe just start with the basics."

Our faces twisted in disgust, and we shared an uncertain look.

Katherine continued, unfazed, "So, what about positions?"

Amelia whipped out her phone. "We should consult the internet. None of us have the experience to really answer that question without research."

I leaned to look at her screen, and Katherine moved around the back of the couch.

"Ah, okay. This one has illustrations and—*oh*."

She'd landed on a sketch of a girl who was upside down with all her weight resting on her shoulders and her legs in the air. The guy stood behind her, holding one leg in the air by the calf while pushing the other down like a jackknife, opening her up so he could nail her where she was split.

Our heads tilted to one side in unison.

"Is that seriously called a Piledriver?" I asked the universe.

"Oh my God, the next one is called the Prison Guard," Amelia said, clicking the link.

We burst into laughter at the drawing. The girl was hinged at the waist with her hands behind her back, and the guy held her wrists in the small, like he was handcuffing her, while he did her from the back.

"I will never have sex imitating incarceration," Katherine said flatly.

"Never say never," I volleyed as Amelia skipped further down the alphabet. "Holy shit, look at that one."

I pointed at a thumbnail, and she clicked it.

I could barely understand what I was seeing. They were in a sixty-nine but upright, which was the first point of confusion. Secondly, they were *backward*; her legs were hooked over his shoulders, putting her ass against his chest and her junk where a necklace would go. And the last straw was that, to gain access to his dick, her neck was twisted around like a flamingo.

Nothing about it looked doable or enjoyable.

"I'm absolutely positive that would never work," I said, unamused.

"Maybe if she were eighty pounds and a contortionist," Katherine offered.

"I mean, sixty-nines are the worst anyway," I said with the shake of my head. "Isn't the whole point of oral to get to lie there and do nothing? Never mind doing it like *that*. The amount of concentration and strength that would take would leave the whole thing devoid of fun."

"Thumbs down on the Snake," Amelia said. "Ew, Mexican

Halloween? That's just racist." We leaned in, reading the description. "*The male lies down on his chosen one*—what the fuck is this website?"

"Maybe we should start with some more basic stuff. Like Reverse Cowgirl and easier," Katherine suggested. "There," she said, pointing at the search results. "Click that article from *Cosmo*."

Amelia opened it and started scrolling.

"Hmm, the Hobby Horse looks fun," I said, encouraged by something that actually looked within the laws of gravity. I burst out laughing. "Is that actually called the Clitosaurus? I can't!"

"Who knew there were so many cowgirl options?" Amelia asked. "Regular, Reverse, The Hot Seat, Slow Burn—*oh my God.* The Pinocchio! Look—you get on your toes and bounce."

"I don't think I'd like to have sex in a position named to insinuate you fuck a beloved Disney character's nose," Katherine said.

I frowned. "There are too many to choose from, and they're all so ridiculous. I can't suggest to Sam that we do the Thigh Master. Or the Bucking Bronco. Or the Squeeze Box." I leaned in a little. "Okay, that one actually looks kind of fun, and it gets bonus points for the clever name, but still. How am I supposed to pick? And how many?"

Katherine moved back to the whiteboard, uncapping her marker again. "Well, let's think about this methodically. You should probably experience you on bottom and you on top, plus a clitoral orgasm and a G-spot orgasm."

My frown deepened. "But this isn't about me, not exactly. Not like that. I'm not doing this for the orgasms. If he can give them to me, that'd be a bonus."

One of Katherine's dark eyebrows rose. "If?"

I sighed. "You know what I mean. Shouldn't my objective be about driving *him* crazy? I mean, I can't learn how to make a guy have sex with me better. That's kind of up to him. Right?"

Katherine's face pinched in thought, but it was Amelia who spoke.

"Maybe you should just ask Sam. Isn't that the whole idea? Who better to tell you how to drive a guy crazy than an actual guy with an actual penis?"

"Good point," I said. "Okay. So, hand jobs, blowjobs, and recommendations on positions for us to try? I can do that." My stomach flipped upside down at the thought of having sex with Sam. Actual naked nipple-bare sex with Sam. Part of me wondered if it were even truly possible in this universe or any other.

Katherine frowned. "But I didn't get to make any diagrams."

"Would it make you feel better if I read off some sex statistics so you can make a pie chart?" I asked.

She brightened up. "Actually, yes."

"Oh," Amelia started, "and I'll search some statistics over the last decade so you can make a line graph."

"You're really the best friends a girl could ask for, you know that?" she said with a broad smile, for Katherine. I could almost see her teeth.

"You're not so bad yourself," I said with a laugh. "Now, get up there and draw me a bar graph, but instead of bars, I want penis."

"I want penis, too," she said, turning to the whiteboard.

"You guys can have all of mine," Amelia offered.

"See?" I said, leaning into her side to rest my head on her shoulder. "Best friends *ever*."

HOT FOR TEACHER

SAM

"**S**o, I've been thinking about those blowjobs."

I stopped dead on the sidewalk so I could focus wholly on dislodging the hot dog I'd inadvertently inhaled on the heels of her proposition.

She stopped, turning as she arranged two hot dogs in one hand so she could slap me on the back. "Oh my God, are you okay?"

My hand rose, palm out. I swallowed hard. "I'm fine," I croaked.

"Here, have some water." She passed me a water bottle from her bag, and Iy took it gratefully. "Anyway, I've always been bad at blowjobs and hand jobs, too. I was thinking that for our next lesson, we could practice. I mean, if it's still okay that I handle your penis." She said it with clinical detachment, as if she were talking about how to do laundry or wash a car. The thought had me picturing Val in a G-string and a tiny triangle top, washing a Maserati with the curves of her body slick and covered in soapy bubbles.

And then she unhinged her jaw and took an ambitious bite of her hot dog.

Until that moment, I'd thought her mouth was small. It was not. The sight of her deep-throating a hot dog, coupled with her talk of handling my dick, arrested all thought.

She chewed, watching me curiously. "Are you okay?" she asked once she swallowed.

I cleared my throat. "Yeah. Yup."

"I have a lot of questions. You know, for educational purposes. Like, do you like it when a girl plays with your balls? How do you feel about your perineum? I read that butt plugs can really enhance male orgasms. Have you found that to be the case?"

A single, strangled laugh shot out of me. "Sometimes, the things that come out of your mouth astound me."

She flushed, embarrassed, and launched into a rambling apology. "I'm sorry. Is that too personal? I just figured, you know, since we're about to… well, *you know*, that I should ask. I clearly have no idea how the male body works beyond the basics, and I just—"

I stepped into her, cupped her face with my free hand, and kissed her until her body was soft against mine, our lips in unison, the rhythm easy and right and good.

When I leaned back to look at her, she was lust-drunk, her lids half-closed and lips swollen.

"Now, first," I started, now that I had her undivided attention, "that's a big step. Are you sure you're ready?"

Just like that, her face hardened, her brows drawing together with her frown. "Listen, don't go all Lancelot on me again—I don't want to hear it. I'm not doing this for you, I'm doing it for *me*. I am a grown woman, goddammit, and I—"

My lips descended again, cutting her off. This time, her free hand slid up my chest, my neck, her fingers slipping into my hair. A soft moan climbed up her throat and into my mouth.

This time when I pulled away, she looked like she might melt into the sidewalk.

I smirked. "I wasn't going to say no, Val. I just had to ask. If you say you're ready, I trust you." I ignored the little voice in my head that asked me if *I* was ready.

She looked up at me with those big brown eyes and asked, "So, you'll teach me?"

If I hadn't already had a hard-on, I would have at those words from her lips, knowing what it would mean for both of us. "Yes, I'll teach you. And then it's my turn."

At that, her cheeks flamed hot and bright. "Oh no, it's not about me. You don't have to do that."

"Maybe I want to." The words were low and rough. "Here's another secret—pleasure isn't just about receiving. It's about enjoying someone else's body. It's about making them feel good, knowing it was by your hand. Or mouth. It would *please* me, Val. It would please me a great deal."

"Well, I don't know how I'm supposed to argue with that," she breathed.

"Then don't," I said before I kissed her again.

Breaking the kiss was almost impossible now that I knew I was about to have her naked and at my disposal. But I did it with all my willpower at my back. Her eyes were still closed, her lips parted like she was waiting for more, and with a chuckle, I kissed her nose.

We started walking again, turning back to our hot dogs. Thankfully, I had on Oprah's Burberry peacoat so no one could spot the anaconda in my pants.

"So, when should we have our lesson?" she asked, avoiding the word *blowjob*.

I found myself both disappointed and relieved—I didn't really want to choke to death on a hot dog.

"Tonight," I answered without hesitation.

"Tonight?" she squeaked.

"Well, our lessons are almost up," I said, ignoring the flash of disappointment that followed the words. "No time to waste. We'll go to my place after work. Unless you have plans?"

I didn't miss the look on her face, which matched that sick feeling in my chest. "No...no plans. But...well, do you mind if I swing by home first? To...freshen up?"

"You don't have to do that, you know."

She paused. "It would make me feel better. Plus, I'm wearing my granny panties."

A laugh burst out of me. "Doesn't matter to me. They're not gonna be on long anyway."

VAL

When the opening notes of *Wicked* filled the theater, my nerves hummed with anticipation.

By the time intermission rolled around, the hum had turned into a buzz that echoed in my brain like a swarm of murderous wasps.

And when the show ended, I was almost positive my guts had turned into snakes and that I should really consider a visit to the ER.

At least that way Sam wouldn't see me naked.

Not that I didn't want to be naked with him or see him naked. I would have climbed a moderately sized mountain if it meant naked Sam was waiting at the top of it. But the thought of him seeing me exposed, with all the things I hated about my body on display, was almost too much to bear. And that was just when I was *thinking* about it. Never mind actually stripping naked and standing there in front of him to be scrutinized.

You don't have to do anything you don't want to do, I reminded myself as I packed up my things.

Sam was watching me, just like he had been all night. I could feel his eyes on me as plainly as if he were touching me.

Did I want him to touch me? Abso-fucking-lutely. Did I want him to bury his face between my legs and write his name with his tongue? Without a single doubt. Did I want him to nail me into the next century? Indubitably. I'd even let him Piledrive me—*if* we could figure out the mechanics of it and *if* I didn't get a cramp.

I just had to get over the extraordinary vulnerability that would accompany it, that was all. Easy-peasy. No sweat.

Well, maybe a little sweat.

I took a breath and stood, my back as straight as I could get it without looking like I had a red-hot poker up my ass.

Sam was right there, waiting. His amber eyes were aflame, his lashes black as ink, soft as a raven feather.

Waiting for me.

He leaned against the wall with the easy grace of a panther, lithe and beautiful and utterly dangerous.

I slapped on a smile and commanded my feet to move me in his direction.

"You ready?" he said when I approached.

That innocuous question held a dozen more that were far less innocent.

Ready to show me your secrets? Ready to kiss the places no one sees? Ready to feel me inside you? Ready to fuck? Are you ready?

My brain simultaneously gasped *no* and screamed *yes*.

"Let's go," I said, hoping I sounded brave.

His answering smile sent a rush of heat through me that pooled at the point where my thighs met. It was then that I realized I *was* ready. Scared, sure. But I was ready.

Sam pulled me into his side, tucked me under his arm, kissed the top of my head. And as we headed out of the theater, I sighed, breathing the clean, spicy scent of him with the inhale and releasing the top layer of my fears with the exhale.

We headed toward the subway station.

"Want to grab anything to eat before we head home?" he asked as we passed another hot dog stand.

I shook my head, nestling into him. My arm wound comfortably around his narrow waist.

"What's the matter? Not in the mood for another dog? We could get kabobs instead, if you're hungry."

"It's not that. It's more that I couldn't choke down another hot dog knowing I was about to choke on *your* hot dog."

A free, easy laugh burst out of him. It was becoming my favorite sound, that laugh.

"I don't know. I've been thinking about eating your bun all night."

It was my turn to laugh, amused even though my face was on fire. "The last person to call my ass *buns* was my Grams."

"Who said I was talking about your ass?"

I chanced a look up at him, a little confused. He smirked down at me.

"Think about it. A hot dog bun isn't shaped anything like an ass. It's long, plump, and it has that slit in the middle, built for meat." His voice had dropped to a whisper. "No, it's not your ass I want, Val, although I'm planning on acquainting myself with that, too."

My eyes, I realized, were locked on the thick swell of his bottom lip, distracted by the occasional view of his tongue in the darkness of his mouth.

"I've never known anyone who can make food sound so

incredibly pornographic," I said half to myself.

"Well, I've never known anyone who can make cheesy pick-up lines work."

I chuffed. "Well, we all have our talents."

He pulled me closer. It always astounded me—just when I thought we couldn't get closer, he'd squeeze a little tighter, pressing me into his body a little deeper.

Regrettably, we reached the turnstiles and had to separate, though we came together again the moment we were through, like magnets. When we stepped on the train, we didn't sit even though there were plenty of open seats. Instead, he leaned against the rail with his legs split just wide enough to pull me into the wedge of space and against his chest.

For a minute, he just held me. "You nervous?"

"A little." I paused. "A lot."

"Tell me what you're afraid of."

I wanted to tell him, and it was the last thing I wanted to say. But I couldn't seem to deny him. So I took a breath and spoke.

"I'm afraid I'll be terrible. I'm afraid I'll fail. I'm worried something horribly embarrassing will happen and you'll never want to see me again."

"What else?" His big hand skated my back, up and down, slow and reassuring.

"I…I'm afraid to…to be naked in front of you." How I found the courage to admit it, I'd never know.

I rode his chest as he sighed. "I won't tell you not to be afraid of that—I know by now that'd be pointless. But I want you to know that's something that only exists in your head. I swear to you, whatever you're afraid of will be the furthest thing from my mind."

"It's easy for you to say, Sam. You're with beautiful girls, thin girls, girls with long, straight hair and flat stomachs."

"How do you know?"

I started to speak but could find no argument. "I…I don't know. I just figured."

He was quiet. "Do you want to know the first thing that I look for in a girl?"

"What?"

"Her smile."

I leaned back to look at him but said nothing.

His eyes roamed my face, as if he'd find an explanation written somewhere there. "You can tell almost everything from a smile. How easily it finds its way to her face. How sincere it is or isn't. How it changes her eyes. How it makes me feel. Everything else is secondary to that smile." He brushed the line of my jaw with the backs of his fingers. "You, Valentina, have one of the most brilliant smiles I've ever seen. It finds your lips almost as if that were their natural state. Even when you frown, the corners turn up like they can't help but be happy. And when you smile, your eyes shine. Your face shines with it. And that hits me in all the right places."

I took a breath that skipped in my chest.

"The girls you idolize and idealize and compare yourself to so very rarely interest me. But *you* interest me. I just hope one day you'll believe me when I say it."

Every vital organ in my body melted, except my heart. That thumped hard, sending waves of appreciation and adoration lapping against my ribs.

"And," he continued, "you don't have to be afraid it'll be bad. I'm here to teach you, remember? I'll tell you what to do."

"Okay," I said on a breath and a flicker of hope.

The train pulled into our station just as he kissed me, a hot, brief melding of our mouths to occupy the time until the doors opened. Hand in hand, we headed up the stairs and to the sidewalk where we stopped, facing each other.

For a second, we just stood there, the air between us thick.

He stepped into me, tipped my chin, and pressed his lips to mine with gentle affection. "Hurry," he whispered.

A zing of anticipation shot through me. "I will."

He kissed me once more before letting me go, but he didn't move to walk away. Instead, he stuffed his hands in his pockets and watched me go as the taxis drove by, their taillights the color of desire, casting a halo around him like an angel of mercy.

BELL CURVE

VAL

t's a blowjob, not brain surgery.

That was the sound of the impatient voice in my head, which had been berating me since I'd walked away from Sam. All while I'd shaved my legs, it had reminded me that this wasn't a big deal and that I was overreacting. While I groomed my other bits, my brain was too busy trying to make sure I didn't nick something important to reprimand me for my nerves. The silence was appreciated. When I'd stood in front of my underwear drawer, sifting through sports bras and panties with frayed elastic and faded fabric, it'd gotten back to admonishing me for not owning something sexier.

Although, when I'd put on my favorite red dress, it'd actually complimented me, which was a welcome change of tune.

And now I was standing on Sam's doorstep in full hair and makeup and a fancy dress, which seemed so silly, considering my makeup was about to get wrecked, and if things went according to plan, my clothes would be in a pile on the floor within the hour.

Naked. Naked with Sam.

My stomach climbed up my chest and into my esophagus.

God, you are such a baby, Val. Knock on the damn door already.

It was the final kick in the ass I needed. My fist rose to bring my knuckles to the wood in a succession of raps that sounded far less confident than I'd intended.

Three seconds. That was how long it took for the door to open. I knew because I'd started counting the moment the last knock sounded.

And there he was, standing in the doorframe, tall and dark and gorgeous. And smiling. At me.

The apartment behind him was dim. Music floated out to greet me, though it was too soft to make out. Something that sounded a little like instrumental hip-hop but with more soul. Slower, easier. Sexier.

Sex. Naked sex with naked Sam and naked me and—ohmygod, what am I doing here?

His face changed the second the thought entered my mind, his eyes determined, smoldering and decisive. And without a single word, before I could even register what happened, he swept me up in his arms and kissed me.

It seemed to be a favorite trick of his—to read me, understand me, and soothe every fear with a touch, a kiss, a word. He knew exactly what to say, exactly what to do. It was his version of a magic trick, and I was the lucky lady from the audience chosen to join him onstage.

By the time he broke the kiss, my wits were too scrambled to think of much at all. One of the many things I'd learned was that it was hard to be afraid when you were making out. And the escape from my skittering thoughts was impossibly enticing.

"You wore my favorite dress." His voice was rough.

I wasn't even sure I had one to use at all, so I nodded.

He thumbed my chin. "Don't be scared, Val," he said gently, with reassurance I felt all the way through me, calming me like a snake charmer would a cobra.

When he kissed me again, I sank into him, let my fears go. And they floated away.

I didn't notice much beyond the places where our bodies touched—the shuffle of our feet, the click of the door closing, the rasp of fabric as he took off my jacket. I didn't know where he put it.

I couldn't have cared less.

Through his apartment he guided me, though I didn't see a thing. My eyes never opened. Our lips never parted.

It wasn't until he closed his lips and backed away that I finally pried my eyelids apart to meet his gaze.

This room was almost dark as well, the lights turned low, the music the same volume as it was in the other rooms. The furniture sat low to the ground, clean and simple, modern without being cold. Luxurious without pretension.

We stood in his bedroom, at the foot of his bed, which was swathed in dove grays, creams and whites, soft and downy and inviting.

I kept my eyes on his, my thoughts turning to the task at hand. *My* task.

"I…I don't know how to start," I said tentatively, quietly.

"Lesson one." His hands ran over the curves of my shoulders and down my arms. "Don't overthink it. What do you want to do, Val? What do you want to feel?"

My hands slid up his chest as I searched my mind. "Your skin," I said, testing the words. "I've imagined what it's like to feel your skin under my fingertips. How it would feel against my skin."

"Then find out." He took my hand and placed it on his chest.

I took a breath to slow my heart. Down his torso my hands skated until they reached the hem of his shirt, hesitating for only a beat before slipping into the space between.

Skin, warm against my palm, soft to the touch and hard underneath. Fingers sliding up the planes and valleys of his abs. His shirt hem hooked in my wrists, riding them as my hungry hands roamed higher. To the curve of his pecs, the disc of muscle, the hard tips of his nipples.

He reached back between his shoulder blades and grabbed a handful of shirt, pulling it over his head. A current of his scent followed the motion, more soap than spice. But I could smell the man underneath, a hint of something indistinguishable and wholly male, something that sank into me and twisted.

Sam's hands were on my waist, my hips, moving but never interfering. My eyes could only scan the topography of his body, the cords of muscles that made the curves of his shoulders, his biceps, his forearms.

I had seen men naked before. But Sam wasn't a man. He was a myth or a god, an ancient prince. A fable.

"Now what do you want?" he asked, his voice rough and low.

His callused fingertips caught the chiffon of my dress, and the fabric clung to them didn't want him to let go. I found I knew the feeling

"Kiss me," I answered, not knowing where to go next, "and do something you want."

He drew in a breath. I leaned in, my hands resting on the swells of his chest as he brought his lips to mine.

I could have lost myself in that kiss like a ship in a hurricane, never to be heard from again.

He only released me to trail kisses across my jaw to my earlobe, down my neck. But it was his hands that drew all my attention as they trailed up my ribs and to my breasts. For a moment, he held them both, squeezed his fingers, his palms pressed them to each other, tested their weight and give and density. One thumb brushed my nipple, drawing it tight before disappearing on a track for my zipper at the back of my dress.

The vibration as it lowered echoed through my ribs in a shudder.

"I want your skin," he said, closing his lips over the flesh just under my ear. His tongue swept, his teeth grazed. "I want this," he whispered into the curve of my ear as he palmed my breast, "naked in my hand. Can I have it?"

"Yes," I whispered, my nipple tightening even more against his palm, answering for itself.

"This dress. I love this dress." His hand slipped into the gap of my zipper. With the snap of his fingers, my bra was unclasped and loose. "I'll love it even better when it's on the floor."

My thighs clenched. His hands moved. My heart thudded. His fingers hooked the back of my dress. My breath hitched. He pulled.

With aching slowness, he skated the dress and my bra over the curves of my shoulders until my clavicle was bare. He stopped with his hands cupping my upper arms, the fabric twisted between his fingers.

His eyes locked on mine, searching the depths as I searched his.

Are you ready? read his pupils, wide and open and bottomless.

"Don't stop." The words spilled, trembled, begged.

His lips, strong and intent, pressed against mine, urging them open. His tongue, slow and persistent, warm and wet, tangling and teasing. His hands, light and easy, steady and unwavering, sliding my dress down my arms and to the ground in a whisper of silk.

The room was cold, but I was not.

His hands were everywhere, roaming the curves of my ass, tracing the valley of my spine, trailing up my neck, cupping my jaw. We wound together, my arms around his neck, fingers buried in his midnight hair, my breasts pressed against his hard, hot chest, skin to skin, heart to heart. And I wasn't afraid.

Our bodies were flush, his hands finally finding a place they wanted to stay—my ass. His fingers flexed, the flesh spilling and tight between them, fingertips skating the edges of my panties. He dipped them into the hem at the very base of my spine and broke the kiss, panting.

"We'd better get to your lesson. If we don't do it soon, I won't be patient enough."

"Okay," I breathed, leaning against him, certain that if he let me go, I'd hit the ground like a sack of hammers. "Tell me what to do."

A sound somewhere between a moan and a hum rumbled in his throat. "Take off my pants."

I swallowed hard and nodded, my hands on a track for his waistband. First, the button. Then, the zipper. I felt the zing of it all the way up to my elbow. My eyes were on my fingers, on the V the zipper made, the dark thatch of hair inside. He wasn't wearing underwear. The shape of his cock in his jeans caught all my attention, thick and straining.

I slipped my hands into the waistband at his hips, feeling the indentation of his glutes, the heat of his skin, the tight muscles of the tops of his thighs as I dragged his jeans down. The flap of his zipper held his cock for only a moment before it was free and bouncing gently from the force.

My eyes widened, my hands freezing, my gaze locked on the tip of his crown and the slit, beaded with a milky drop.

"Oh my God," I whispered in reverential fear.

"Don't be afraid," he said, gripping his base. "Give me your hand." His free palm was up, waiting for mine.

I did as he'd asked. He turned my hand over in his, threaded his fingers between mine in a fan of fingertips, and wrapped our hands around his shaft.

"Feel it," he commanded as he stroked.

I did. I felt the impossible hardness and softness of it, the length and weight shocking. I tried not to think how it would fit in my mouth—how it would fit *anywhere*—and instead explored the ridge of his crown, the veins of his shaft, the way his skin moved against the turgid flesh underneath. The slick, curiously weeping crown, the feel of it as I spread the slickness with my thumb.

"Lesson two," he panted, his voice almost a whisper, "if it feels good to you, it feels good to me."

He kissed me before I could speak, his mouth opening wide, his hands angling my face so his tongue could delve as deeply as possible. And all the while, my hands stroked, my fingers learning the lines, the ridges, the length of it until his hips rocked in rhythm.

He turned us around and backed us into the bed. My knees hit the mattress and bent—I sat with a surprised *oof* that broke the kiss.

It also put his cock at eye-level.

The urge to wrap my fingers about it and taste the tip of him overwhelmed me. But before I could reach for it, he lowered his lips to kiss me again, guiding me back. We crawled onto the bed, me backward and him on top of me, until we reached the pillows. Another inexplicable urge to pull his body down to mine, to feel the weight of him on top of me, to feel the length of him between my legs, was almost too strong to resist. But again, I was denied. He lay next to me, pulling me onto my side by my hip to face him.

For a moment, the kiss broke, and his gaze rested on my breasts. His fingers followed, tracing the curve, cupping, squeezing, kneading. But I couldn't be still. I reached for his cock, eager to hold it again.

He pumped his hips once I had ahold of him. "Lesson three." He pumped again slowly, intentionally. "I'm going to tell you what I want, what feels good, but only do it if you want."

"I don't think there's anything I wouldn't do, if you asked me."

I didn't mean it like it sounded. Or maybe I did and didn't realize it. But his eyes caught fire at the implication all the same.

"Kiss me," he instructed. "Starting here." He touched his lips. "Ending here." He flexed his hips into my hand.

My heart skittered in fear and anticipation, but I brushed it aside and leaned in, meeting his lips. Once we were connected, he slipped his hand into my hair and shifted to his back, pulling me with him in a twist, my hips still by his side.

I ended the kiss to move to his jaw, the bristle of his scruff scratching at my lips, my skin. But I couldn't reach him, not like I wanted. So I moved.

I moved between his legs, avoiding straddling him—if I did that, we'd skip this lesson completely. Instead, I kissed down his chest, nestling my hips between his thighs. They were so *big*, the thick muscles clamping my ribs, squeezing my breasts together.

The feel of being locked between his thighs was one of the most satisfying sensations I'd ever experienced.

My hand was still on his shaft, stroking him gently, though with less concentration now that I was moving and kissing and multitasking. But down I went until my chin bumped his crown. My heart chugged, a jolt of anticipation racing up my spine. I kept kissing down his stomach alongside his cock; my cheek brushed it, my nose.

His fingers dove into my hair, gathering it so he could see. I glanced up at him. Met his eyes. Stuck out my tongue and dragged it up the salty, satiny length of his cock.

He hissed, arching his back just a little, his fingers tightening in my hair. "Hold the base. Like that. Kiss the tip."

I took a breath. Opened my mouth. Placed the crown in my mouth. We both moaned. Mine rumbled down his shaft.

"Mmm," he said through lips pinned shut, the bottom between his teeth. "Feel it with your tongue. Taste it. Do what you want, whatever you want." The words were almost lost.

So I did. I felt the skin on my tongue, unable to compare it to anything, the slick softness, the salty taste of skin and seed. My tongue found the notch of his crown, tested the firm ridge where the flesh changed consistency. It rolled around the tip, rested him against the flat of my tongue.

"Stroke," he said.

My hand pumped in rhythm to my mouth.

"Now, take it deeper."

I closed my eyes and bowed my head, lowering my mouth until it was so full of him, I could barely breathe.

"N-not too deep. Don't ... want to hurt you." His hips moved gently, like he wanted to pull out, so I did as he'd said, stroking what I couldn't take with my hand as I rose and lowered my mouth again. "*F-fuck*."

I wanted to ask if I was doing it right, but ... well, my mouth was occupied. I opened my eyes and looked up the line of his body.

Sam was stretched out before me, arm behind his head, face bent in pleasure, eyes hooded and dark but for the ring of gold of his irises. Every curve, every plane, every angle was a feast for my eyes, for my senses. For my mind and soul. And my body responded, from the rush of heat between my thighs to my aching nipples. From my hands around his cock to my tongue that wanted to taste every inch of him.

"Raise your ass up," he said. "I want to see it."

I pulled in my knees, arched my back. He reached for my breast, his fingertips searching for my nipple to tease it, twist it. My pace quickened, my tongue flat against him.

"Suck. Gently."

I did, tightening the force of my tongue just a little, just enough, judging by the intake of breath and force of his hips. Faster I moved, humming, purring. Faster his hips moved until my jaw ached.

I slowed, and he slowed with me. I pumped him, spent a moment with the tip in my mouth, licking him, my tongue sweeping around his crown. My mouth was so strangely full, so oddly wet with spit and seed and Sam.

I pulled away, stroking him to buy myself a second to swallow the riot in my mouth. My voice was gravelly when I spoke. "I'm sorry my mouth is so wet."

His hips bucked into my hand. "Let it be wet. Let it be messy."

So I did. I lifted his cock, dropped onto it again. Let the fullness of my mouth spill over, drip down his shaft, let him watch.

I'd never felt so beautiful, so desirable. I'd never felt so wanted as I did when I watched Sam watching me.

His cock swelled. I took him deep, and it pulsed. Bigger it grew, impossibly, until I could barely hold him. He was close, I realized. And my enthusiasm sparked, my excitement, the build of his orgasm fanning the flame of something inside me. My body rolled like a figure eight, ass and hips, shoulders and neck, mouth open, head bobbing, hand stroking his base, sliding down to cup the soft, cold sack, slipping back up to his dripping cock.

"I'm close." He fought to speak. "You don't"—he moaned— "have to swallow."

My neck worked, keeping pace, going as deep as I could without gagging, already knowing exactly what I'd do when the time came.

"Fuck, you're beautiful," he groaned as he fucked my mouth. "You're perfect. You don't need me, Val. You're fucking perfect."

My eyes watered from the act, from his words. His hands twisted in my hair, moved it from my face, cupped the back of my head, gripped my hair again.

A hot throb. A massive pulse.

He exploded in my mouth with a grunt that made my core flex, pumped into me as I closed the back of my throat and sucked in air through my nose so I wouldn't drown. And all I could do was watch him. Watch the wave of his body as he slammed into my mouth with all the control he could muster, I imagined. The pinch of his brow. The crescents of black lashes on his cheeks. His lips, parted and stretched into an O of ecstasy. The sharp line of his jaw when his face tilted up to the ceiling.

He was the most beautiful thing I'd ever seen in my life.

When he was finally spent and empty, I sucked all the way to the top and closed my lips, my mouth full. His eyes were barely open, but he looked at me, shifted to reach for me. And I swallowed once, twice to finish the job. Pleasure passed across his face at the sight, and those hands cupped my cheeks, pulled me on top of him, kissed me desperately, hard and hot. His tongue dove into my mouth to taste himself in the depths.

And I had the undeniable, intoxicating feeling that I'd passed the lesson with flying colors.

CUNNINGLINGUIST

SAM

Her mouth, deceivingly small, unexpectedly skilled. Absolutely perfect.

The tang of my body on her tongue drew a moan from deep in my throat. The taste mingled with the slickness of our mouths until there was no distinguishable difference—it was her and me and sex, all joined together to make something solely ours.

Val needed no instruction. She needed no one to tell her what to do.

She'd blown my mind on her own.

The echo of my orgasm pulsed through me. I'd had blowjobs, sure. But Val...she was like nothing I'd ever seen before or would ever see again.

After a moment, she ended the kiss. Her lips smiled, but her dark eyes betrayed her uncertainty.

"So...did I pass?"

I chuckled, tucking her curly hair behind her ear. "A-plus. You wrecked the bell curve."

The tightness around her eyes melted away. "Oh, thank God. I mean, I figured it couldn't have been the *worst* since you ... you know."

I slipped my thigh between her legs, shifted my hips to align them with hers. "Since you made me come?" I asked, my voice low.

Her cheeks flushed, so pretty, so sweet. "Yes, since you came."

"How did it feel?"

Her brows came together in thought. "I get it now, what you said about pleasure. Making you feel good made me feel good. Thinking about what I wanted to do to you felt good. Touching you felt good. Lesson learned."

My hand skated down her back, over her hip. I chuckled softly as she continued.

"Every time I've ever done it, it felt like a chore. I mean, I wanted to do it, but I wasn't *into* it. I ... I don't know why exactly it was different with you. Honestly, I think you just turn me on," she said on a laugh.

"That makes all the difference. No one wants to get head—girl or guy—from someone who isn't enjoying themselves. And no one wants to give it to someone who demands it or seems bored. Sex is more than two bodies. It's two minds. Sex is giving pleasure because it's pleasurable, when it's done right. Any man who isn't just as concerned with your pleasure as he is his own isn't the man for you."

"Should I get my notepad? I feel like I should be taking notes."

I pulled her a little closer, kissed her lips gently. "You're not leaving my bed. Not yet."

Her gaze dropped to her fingers where they lay on my chest. "Sam," she said softly, "really, you don't have to—"

"Oh, that's not how this works." I shifted my thigh, pressing it against her sex. The wet heat of her settled against my skin through the thin barrier of her panties. "After watching you suck my cock, after watching your ass sway out of my reach? After the feeling of you pressed against my thighs?" I cupped her breast, the curve too big for my hand, the weight heavy and soft and warm. "I know I don't have to. I *want* to."

I kissed her, shifted, rolled her underneath me. Pressed her into the bed with my body, tasted her skin with my fingertips. Waited for the tension to dissolve from her limbs, waited until her lips were pliant and open. Waited until her doubt was gone.

I was a patient man. Especially when it came to Val.

My thigh was still between hers, her body soft beneath mine. My hands full of her and hers all over me.

I broke the kiss to leave her panting up at the ceiling, my lips on a trail down her body. Her jaw and neck. The soft hollow of her clavicle. The valley of her breastbone. And for a moment, that was where I stayed, listening to her sigh with her breast in my palm, riding the rise and fall of her chest, languidly licking her skin. Thumbing her tawny nipple, teasing it to a peak.

Her fingers dug ruts in my hair, curled against my scalp, tightened the closer my tongue came to her nipple. A flick of the tip, and her thighs squeezed mine. A hot breath, and her back arched, bringing her nipple to my lips. I parted them, brought the flat of my tongue to her breast, closed my mouth, drew her in. Relished in the mewl she rewarded me with.

I didn't move on until the mewling graduated to impatient moans. Her hands sought traction, moving from my hair to my neck to my shoulders, her hips rolling impatiently, grinding against my thigh, searching for pressure.

Down I kissed, one hand unwilling to relinquish its claim on her breast. I pinned her legs together with my thighs, holding them still. Her hips shifted, her body squirming, her thighs clenching and releasing, trying to open. But I wouldn't let them. Not as I kissed down her stomach or the outside of her hip, dragging her panties down her legs. Not as I clamped her restless thighs with my forearms and trailed my nose up the seam of her thighs. Not when my nose grazed the tip of her sex and I could smell her sweet heat. My mouth watered. I parted my lips. Brought the flat of my tongue to meet her. Closed my lips as she gasped. Sucked as she sighed.

Her thighs trembled in my arms, and all I wanted to do was spread them wide and bury my face in her. But like I'd said, I was a patient man. I took my time navigating her body, my tongue seeking the slick creases of her flesh, teasing the bundle of nerves, tasting her. Around her hood my mouth roamed, sucking, shifting side to side, drawing out her desire with every flick of my tongue, every flex of my lips.

She whimpered, and I looked up her body, over the sensual curves of her stomach, her breasts, round and heaving, her nipples reaching, tight and strained. Her face was there between them, her brows drawn and cheeks flushed so hard, they splotched at the edges, down her neck and shoulders. Her lips parted, gasping.

"Please. Oh God. *Please*, Sam." Her legs writhed against me in an effort to get free.

My hand moved up her thigh and between to hook the back in my hand. "Is this what you want?" I spread it, only the one. The other pushed against my forearm, wishing to mirror its twin.

"Yes. *Yes, please.*"

My gaze locked between her legs. I couldn't look away.

"I want it, too," I said half to myself, inching closer, debating where to start. I pushed her other thigh up, spread her as wide as her hips would let me. My hand trailed to the center of her, stroked the line, slipped the very tip of my finger into the dip without breaching her.

She bucked, an involuntary jerk of her hips, at the contact.

"No one's ever touched you like this, have they?" I asked as I spread my fingers and opened her up.

"N-no," she whispered.

"I hate that, you know," I said quietly as my fingertips stroked her, felt every secret place but the one inside her. "I hate that no one has ever appreciated your body the way I do. But I'm glad, too. Ask me why."

A shuddering breath as I circled her clit with slick fingers. "W-w-why?"

I edged closer until my lips were millimeters from the edge of her desire. "Because the first time gets to be all *mine*."

I closed my lips over her clit at the same moment I sank my middle finger into her heat.

Her sweet, whispering moan spurred me, the relief of touch releasing something in her I didn't know she'd ever be able to bottle back up. It was free and wanton, her body unencumbered by fear or thought, only feeling. She trusted me; I'd disarmed her, left her defenseless and vulnerable, naked and writhing, a slave to touch. My touch. And I didn't take that responsibility lightly.

I found a rhythm that made her breath pick up, found the places that made her whisper pleadingly to the sky. I learned what she wanted. Like when I teased the left side of her clit, her thigh would jerk in pleasure, and when I shifted to apply pressure to that place— always with more attention to that side—her hips would roll, their agenda their own.

Her body squeezed my finger, drawing it deeper, and I slipped another in to better fill her. I learned what she liked, and every time I started over, it was a little faster, a little harder. She came closer. With the rhythm of my fingers, I sucked, my lips latched to her hood. My tongue drew her in until she was bucking, murmuring, her fingers twisted in my hair like reins as I fucked her with my mouth.

And then she came with a thundering pulse, squeezing and flexing and panting and sighing affirmations and rocking her body and—*God*, she was so perfect. So fucking perfect. And she had no idea.

As she rode the end of her orgasm, I kept her pace, though I couldn't be soft. Because my own orgasm pulsed in my cock, thick and hard and aching. I propped myself up with one knee, my face still between her legs, my hand reaching between mine, closing around my length and pumping. I groaned against her.

"Come here," she panted, pulling at my shoulders, shifting to reach for me.

I climbed over her, bracketed her hips with my knees, pressed my forehead to hers as I looked down our bodies. Her hands on my cock. Her breasts jostling as she pumped. Her hand disappearing between her legs, coming back wet. Those fingers slicking the tip of my cock with her sex.

And that was all I could take.

Electricity detonated down my spine as I came like thunder, spilling in hot bursts all over her—a creamy drop on her tan nipple, a milky stream across her stomach, another filling the cup of her belly button. The sound of her sigh filled the room. It was only a breath, but it held the weight of a thousand yeses.

And then I kissed her. I kissed her with possession and relief, with deliverance and demand. I kissed her and thanked her, kissed her and told her I wanted to keep kissing her. I kissed her and kissed her, told her my secrets with my lips and my tongue and my hands and my noisy breath. There were no words to explain how I felt, not even to myself. Only kisses. A hundred of them, a million of them, not enough of them.

Her arms draped around my neck, and our kisses became lazy and languorous, unhurried and easy. When I finally returned her lips to her, they were swollen, plump and pink and smiling.

"Did I pass?" I asked with a smirk, my voice rough from disuse.

"Summa cum laude. You'll need to prepare a speech for graduation."

I laughed and kissed her again, a soft, brief pleasure. "How do you feel?"

"My heart feels like it just finished a marathon without leaving the comfort of bed. The rest of me feels like I could sleep for at least twelve hours without moving."

"Not in my bed."

Her smile fell, the light in her eyes dimming.

But I smiled, cupped her face, and finished the thought.

"There's no way you'd sleep for twelve hours in my bed without me fucking you again."

She laughed, and somewhere in the sound was a sigh of relief.

"Question," I said.

"Answer," she replied.

"What gave you the idea to touch yourself to lube me?"

Her face fell. "Why? Was that not okay?"

I chuckled. "Val, that was so okay, I came all over you within a heartbeat. It just surprised me with its … ingenuity."

She rolled her eyes. "Well, I mean, I watch Pornhub like any other red-blooded American. It's a treasure trove of filthy sex tips."

This time, I didn't chuckle. I laughed, a deep sound that bounded through my chest. "You are something else, you know that?"

"Look who's talking."

"Want to shower?" I asked with a smirk, thumbing her cheek.

She glanced down at the mess between us. "Oh. I probably should."

I kissed her nose and rolled off of her. "Come on. I'll show you where everything is."

I padded through my room and into the bathroom, swiping a washcloth off a stack on the shelf to run under the sink faucet. Val came in a second later, and when I looked up, my lips sank in a frown.

Her confidence had been hushed, taking her courage with it.

Her arms cradled her breasts, arranged as if she was trying to hide. Everything about her posture screamed discomfort, from her sloped shoulders to her turned-in toes.

But the worst was that she wouldn't meet my eyes.

I shut off the faucet and ate the space between us with two paces. Her face was in my hands, angling it so she would look at me. She didn't fight it.

Her eyes were impossibly sad.

"Tell me," I commanded gently.

"Nothing." She tried to smile.

"Don't do that. Don't lie. Please, Val."

"It's stupid, and I already know what you'll say," she said, the admission coming faster with every word. "You'll say you've already seen me from every angle, that I'm beautiful and whatever. It's one thing to be in your bed, but…I don't know. Walking around in front of you naked is different. I…I hate my body. I hate it, and I don't want you to see it like this."

I didn't say anything for a second, processing her words, thinking about how to respond, holding her small face in my hands like she were a fawn set to bolt.

"You didn't seem to mind a minute ago," I said gently. "I know I didn't mind then, and I don't mind now. I'd take you into that shower and show you just how much I don't mind, but that's not what tonight was meant for." I searched her eyes, wishing I could undo what lay behind them. "I hate—*hate*—that this is how you see yourself. That you think everyone sees you the same way, that *I* see you this way. All I can do is tell you that you're wrong and hope someday you trust me enough to believe me."

She shook her head and tried to look away as her eyes filled with tears. "You're just saying that, Sam. This is your job, isn't it? You're not just here to teach me. You're here to make me feel beautiful. To give me confidence. It's not real."

Anger blew through me like a hot desert wind, dry and rough with sand. "Is that really what you think? That I'm patronizing you? That I was what, *faking* it?" I shook my head, holding her face still so she'd have to look into my eyes when I said what I had to say. "In that case, I deserve a fucking Academy Award. I'm not an optician or a magician—I can't make you see something you don't want to believe."

I let her face go and turned for the door.

"Towels are on the shelf. Use my bathrobe, if you want. It's on the back of the door," I said just before I hooked the doorknob and closed it behind me.

Frustration scratched at ribs as I blew into the kitchen to clean myself up. I didn't understand how she could be so clueless, that she couldn't grasp how this worked. Men weren't robots. We couldn't fake attraction, fake interest, not at that level. Or at least *I* couldn't. It was there, or it wasn't.

Maybe it's that I feel misunderstood, I considered as I stormed back into my room, throwing on sleep pants and nothing more.

I righted my blankets and found Val's clothes, folded them, and stacked them on the foot of the bed, thumbing the silky fabric of her panties before laying them on top.

She thought I was faking it. That I was a liar. That I was lying to *her*.

But it wasn't me she disbelieved, I realized. It was the *world*.

My anger dissipated, leaving me with nothing but sorrow. Because Val didn't know any better. She'd never had anyone want her this way, treat her with care, touch her with desire. She didn't know how badly I wanted her and didn't understand how I possibly could.

Those fucking jerkoff, lowbrow, plebeian motherfuckers. They didn't deserve to touch her. They don't deserve to touch anyone. I should find them and cut off all their fingers.

I raked a hand through my hair as I padded back out of my room, stopping to pour a drink on my way to my music room. I flipped on the lamp next to the piano, taking a sip of my whiskey.

When I sat, I heard the melody, the one that had been haunting me, but with a new stanza, a continuation I hadn't considered before. The notes rang in my head, sang in my bones, left through my fingers, filled the room.

And in my mind was Val.

The shadows of her body, the sound of her sigh. The feel of her against me, the heat of her skin. The smell of her, rich and lush, clinging to me.

My pulse picked up in anticipation of every brush of my fingers against the ivory keys. The tune felt familiar, as if I'd heard it before, though I knew I hadn't—at least, not with my ears. I'd heard it with my heart instead.

I paused, picking up my pencil to jot on the sheet music. Then again, I played the stanza, made more notes.

An immeasurable amount of time went by—I was lost inside a slipstream—before the bench under me creaked, and I felt her next to me.

My fingers finished the phrase they had been caught in as she silently watched on. Normally, I would have stopped at the first sign of an audience. Normally, I wouldn't have even entered this room when a woman was in my place. But there I was, playing the symphony no one had heard but me as Val sat at my elbow, her eyes on my fingers and her fingers toying with the tie of my black robe.

The final notes hung in the air, and I let them breathe, let them fill the room and the space between us. And when they finally faded away, I released the keys.

"That … that was beautiful," she said with an air of wonder, her fingers brushing the edge of the sheet music on the rail. "What's it called?"

"It doesn't have a name. No one's even heard it but you."

"Why not?"

I shrugged. "It's not finished. And anyway, I'm just messing around."

"It's really good, Sam. I mean it." She gathered up a few pages and flipped through them. "Seriously, have you ever considered doing something with it?"

I took the pages from her gently and set them back on the stand. "No. I just do it for me."

"Oh," she said, threading her hands back in her lap. She glanced around the room. "I didn't realize you collected instruments."

"I don't collect them. I play them."

Her head swiveled around to meet my eyes. "Are you serious?"

My lips tilted in a smile. "Pick an instrument. Any instrument."

She turned around on the bench and stood to wander around the room. "The French horn," she said, pointing at it.

I met her at the horn, took the mouthpiece off, and blew in it a few times, cupping it in my hand to warm it up. Then I popped the piece back on, picked up the instrument, and played a verse of Strauss's Nocturno, Op. 7 horn solo, slow and haunting. I'd always loved it.

Her eyes widened, but she was smiling. She walked across the room and pointed at the oboe. "This one."

I chuckled, setting the horn back on its stand before making my way to the oboe. "All right, but you have to gimme a second." I opened a reed case and popped one in my mouth. "Gotta get this nice and wet."

She laughed, making her way around the room again, touching some of the instruments. I watched her, followed her fingertips as they traced the brass and wood and string.

I put the reed in its place and brought the instrument to my lips, pursing my lips tight. The opening bars to Tchaikovsky's *Swan Lake* solo filled the room.

The shock on her face was priceless. "The oboe? No way."

"Way," I said as I set it back where it belonged.

"Okay, this one." She pointed to the guitar. "No way can you also play something badass, too."

I picked up my Gibson and tuned it, then pretended to fumble through a bit of "Hotel California." Her face fell a little.

So I dropped the act, plucking out a song I'd written. The notes rose and fell, fast and then slow, the tune both happy and sad, in A-flat major.

Her lips parted, her eyes on my hands as my fingers moved without thought up and down the frets, up and down the strings as I strummed and picked the tune. She sank into the armchair, mesmerized, and there she sat until the song was finished. I set the guitar on its base, uncomfortable with her silence. She was so rarely silent. And I so rarely played for anyone.

I stepped toward her, knelt at her feet. Took her hands in my own. "I'm sorry, Val," was all I could say.

"Please, don't apologize." She took a breath, turned her hands in mine so she could hold them. "You're incredible, do you know that?"

I huffed a dismissive laugh.

"No, I mean it. Not just because you can play the oboe either."

Another laugh, this one lighter, the tension between us easing.

"You're patient and kind. You always have my back, always want my happiness. You're always telling me what you think of me, and I never listen. But it's not because I don't believe your conviction. It's just hard to imagine that you—beautiful, gorgeous *you*—could think those things about me. It feels like…like a deal you make with the devil. You might get what you want, but there's always a catch. The guy gets the girl, but she dies in a car crash. You get all the money he promised you, but you lose all your friends. Your wish was granted, but you're still not happy. There's always a catch, Sam, and I just can't figure out what this one is."

I frowned, shaking my head. "You've idolized me, Val. I'm just a guy, a normal guy."

"You are anything but normal," she said on a laugh. "Just…bear with me as I occasionally slip into my crazy pants. I wish I could fake how I feel, pretend not to be insecure or needy, but you see right through me. You always do."

I slipped my hand into her hair, smelled the mix of vanilla and coconut and my soap, wished I could somehow change how she felt. But that would have changed who she was, fundamentally, irreplaceably.

"Believe me when I say that I think you're the most beautiful girl I've ever seen," I said to the depths of her eyes and the reaches of her heart, and I meant every word. And I told her so with another kiss.

There were never enough kisses.

She wound around me, twisted into me, and my arms welcomed her, pulled her into my chest as best I could, which wasn't very well at all. So I stood, bringing her with me. Even through the thick fabric of the robe, I could feel the shape of her body. And I wanted her again. I wanted all of her full of all of me.

So I did the only thing I could.

I broke away. "Come on," I said, wishing there were anything else I could say but, "let's get you home."

THE RLC
VAL

"Jizz tastes like a roll of pennies."

My roommates burst into laughter, and I shrugged. It was true.

Rin shook her head, her red lips smiling. "Oh, man—please tell me that wasn't the size of his dick because, if so, I am so sorry."

Katherine snorted. Amelia blushed.

I leaned on the high-top bar table. "No, no. More like..." My face quirked. "An aluminum can?"

Amelia gaped. "But how... how would that... where would you even put..."

"Okay, okay... a steel pipe," I amended.

"There it is," Rin said approvingly. "That's a visual I can get behind."

I sighed, smiling. "I honestly didn't think I'd be so into it. But there he was, naked as sin and lying there, exposed and at my disposal. And it was hot. He's beautiful. I would gladly put any part of him in my mouth, if he asked me to."

"Well, cheers to a lesson well learned." Katherine raised her glass, and we mirrored her.

"And to steel pipes," Rin added.

"And to not choking!" Amelia chimed.

We laughed and took a drink.

"Sam's angling to go to the club for your birthday," Amelia said pointedly. "Have you decided what you want to do yet?"

My nose wrinkled. "Please don't make a big deal about it."

Katherine rolled her eyes. "You know we will. We always do."

I sighed, smiling because I secretly loved the attention while also not wanting to get my hopes up. A wise man once said, *low expectations are the key to life*, and I was inclined to believe him.

"I don't know what I want to do, and I can't tell Sam no, so I'm sure we'll be at the club."

"Yay!" Amelia cheered, even throwing her little fists into the air. "I love it there. I'm so glad you met him, Val."

"Me too." My mind drifted back to the night before, and that touch of uncertainty that always followed me around when it came to Sam prickled. "Do you…do you think it's bad that he told me I didn't have to swallow?"

Rin's and Katherine's faces softened into gentle smiles.

"Not at all," Rin said. "Trust me, he wanted you to swallow. I don't know what weird, primal part of their brains that hits, but they *always* want you to swallow. He was just thinking about your comfort, which is so thoughtful. Polite."

"A polite blowjob," Katherine said on a laugh. "Sounds like an instructional at charm school."

I chuckled. "He really is so polite. Holds open doors, compliments me, pays for my drinks, reciprocates oral. Like, he didn't have to go down on me after I went down on him. Not that I minded. At all."

Feverish heat slithered through me at the memory. "How have I gone my whole adult life without *that*?"

"Amen," Rin said, briefly raising her glass before taking a drink.

Katherine assessed me for a minute. "What you listed out sounds a lot more like dating than it does a friend or a tutor."

That heat in my belly flamed at the suggestion. "I can't even entertain that thought, Katherine."

"Ignoring it doesn't stop it from being true," she countered.

"How long has it been?" Amelia asked. "How much longer before the lessons are over?"

I chewed my lip. "I don't know. I'm afraid to look."

"Why?" Katherine asked.

"Because I think it's soon, and the thought makes me sick to my stomach. I don't know what happens next. I don't feel tutored enough. I don't feel ready. Will he still want to be friends? Will he still want to hang out with me?"

Katherine's eyes narrowed in thought. "Then it sounds like it's time to make a decision about what *you* want next."

I snorted a laugh. "I have a choice?"

"There's always a choice," she answered. "Do you still see him as just a friend and tutor after last night?"

The flame in my stomach flared painfully. "By all outward accounts, yes."

"And the inward accounts?" Rin asked gently.

My shoulders slumped. "No. Not at all. But this is what I signed up for. These are the rules of engagement. I can't change how he feels any more than I can change the way I feel."

"And how do you feel?" Rin didn't move, didn't pick up her drink, just asked the question and watched me.

"Like I put my heart in a blender and hit Pulse."

Katherine frowned, confused. "I don't understand if that's a good thing or a bad thing."

"Bad. Very bad."

"Got it," she said with a nod.

"What if he has feelings for you, too?" Rin asked, ever the optimist.

"He doesn't. I mean, he *couldn't*."

"Sure he could," Amelia interjected. "Katherine's right—everything you two do sounds like dating."

"But we're not. He's *teaching* me, not actually *dating* me. They're two very different things."

"Well, they look a whole lot alike from the outside," Katherine said flatly. "Dating seems vacuous. I think I'd rather not do it. Ever."

"No one uses vacuous in casual conversation," Amelia told her with a comforting pat of her hand.

"I do," Katherine answered with a shrug. "Anyway, have you considered asking him how he feels?"

"Nope, not once." I took a sip of my drink to punctuate my definitive certainty that I never would.

"I know it's scary," Rin started, "but you have to be brave. We made a pact." She straightened up, reaching into her purse and returning with her tube of Boss Bitch. She set it on the table with the snap of a gavel in a courtroom. "I hereby call a meeting of the Red Lipstick Coalition to order."

Amelia and Katherine straightened up in their seats like traitors.

Rin picked up the lipstick and held it like a beacon. "We do so solemnly swear to use this shiny little tube of power to inspire braveness, boldness, and courage. We promise to jump when it's scary, to stand tall when we want to hide, to scream our truth instead of whisper our fears. May we be mistresses of our destinies and to hell with anyone who tries to tell us otherwise."

"Hear, hear," we cheered.

Well, they cheered. I grumbled.

Rin smiled, looking mightily pleased. "You're the one who said it first, Val. You're the one who inspired us to get this red lipstick in the first place. You're our fearless leader, the girl who isn't afraid of *anything*."

"The girl who started all this hadn't yet met Sam."

Rin rolled her eyes. "Val, you solemnly swore to be brave and bold. You promised to jump when it's scary. So put on your red lipstick and jump. Tell him how you feel. Or, at the very least, ask him how *he* feels."

"Do you guys honestly think he has real feelings for me?"

"What happened after the oral?" Katherine asked. I could almost see her mentally lick the tip of her pencil to take notes.

"Well... we talked for a minute, and he showed me to the shower. We got into a little... argument, I guess you could call it."

"About what?" Amelia asked with a frown.

My nose wrinkled, and I felt myself shrink in my seat just a little. "I was feeling self-conscious, and when he told me all these wonderful things, I... well, I didn't believe him. And that made him mad. I might have accused him of bullshitting me just to be nice."

Rin flinched. "Ouch."

I sighed. "Yeah. He stormed out, and the whole time I was in the shower, I just felt like scum. When I came out, he was gone. I found him in his music room and listened to him play piano for a while. And then he apologized."

"He apologized to you?" Katherine asked. "After you called him a liar? Val, he likes you."

I flushed, flustered. "I just... he couldn't. He *can't*. It's not possible. Besides, if I let myself even *think* it only to find out he still just sees me as a friend..."

"I don't think a guy would go down on you like a porn star if he didn't like you as more than a friend," Katherine said with authority. "Back me up, Rin."

Rin shrugged apologetically. "She's not wrong, Val."

Fluttering surprise lit through me. "But he said…"

Katherine's face flattened. "People don't always say what they think or what they want. Case in point—you have withheld your feelings from Sam since the very beginning. The idea that he has indisputably said exactly what he means is ludicrous on its own merit."

Rin reached for my hand, and my panic eased marginally when I met her eyes. "You don't have to talk to him right away. But it might be time you considered your feelings and his. Maybe he likes you."

"Maybe he doesn't," I volleyed.

She nodded. "Maybe he doesn't. But can you honestly say that things are the same as they were before last night?"

When I really considered it, my heart sank and filled up all at the same time, the feeling of stretching and falling almost too much to withstand. I clutched my drink in my clammy palm. "No," I answered quietly. "It's not the same."

"Things change," she said. "That's life. We change. The people we love change. *Everything* changes, which is a blessing as much as it is a curse. There's a chance that the man of your dreams could have feelings for you. I think you just have to be open to the possibility."

"But then I'll have hope. And hope, as sweet as it is, has the power to break my heart."

"And it has the power to inspire you, Val. You just have to let it in."

I looked around at the faces of my friends and did just that. And even though that hope was held inside a heart with a false bottom, I wished for its truth all the same.

BECAUSE, OF COURSE

SAM

I shouldn't have been thinking about Val in the shower, but there I was in a full lather, standing with my face in the shower stream and her on my mind.

It wasn't like *that*, although I'd be a liar if I said I hadn't taken matters into my own hands twice since we parted ways last night. And once more the second I'd stepped into the shower after my workout.

I chalked my appetite up to the fact that we hadn't slept together. I'd had her naked and spread eagle in my bed and hadn't fucked her. Not with the one part of me that wanted her most, at least.

She was irresistible, from her body that gave and gave to the innocence of her pleasure. I could have kept her in my bed all night, occupied the long hours with the sweetness between her thighs, the softness of her sighs.

Those sighs aren't yours to keep.

I let out a sigh of my own and turned off the shower.

I'd gotten close. Too close. Close enough to know what I was missing.

Close enough to count the abundant reasons I couldn't have her.

Frowning, I dried off. Antsy, I dressed. But when I picked up the phone to call my mom, I only felt relief.

She'd know what to do.

She answered on the second ring. "*Habibi*. Hello, Samhir."

"Hi, Mama. How's your day?"

"Good. Papa and I started ballroom dancing. I didn't know the phrase *weak ankles* before today."

I chuckled. "Well, maybe they'll beef up with a little working out."

"I hope so. In a few weeks, we'll be practicing swing. Maybe Papa and I can come to your club and dance."

"Maybe," I said noncommittally, uncertain how I felt about the prospect of my father hearing me play there.

"But that isn't why you called, *qalbi*." She changed the subject with purposeful, professional ease. "How are you?"

"Fine. I actually wanted to ask you about a friend of mine."

"Of course. How can I help?"

I sighed, deep and noisy. "I don't know what to do about her."

"Something needs to be done?"

"Yes. I think so at least, and I think I'm the person who needs to do it."

"And why is that?" she asked, psychiatristing me.

Normally, I'd evade. But desperate times and all that.

"Well, she developed young, really young, and the other kids sexualized her. I think she just…shut down. I know for sure her brothers earned her some breathing room, thanks to a few well-placed fists. But she never really got over it. And now…I don't know, Mama. She doesn't believe me. She doesn't know how beautiful she is."

For a moment, there was silence as she gathered her thoughts. "And you want to be the one to change her mind?"

"No, I *need* to be. I can't explain it. I just … I think I might be the only person who can see it. Who sees her."

She didn't speak through my pause, so I kept talking.

"She's never dated, not really. She's never been in love or had someone cherish her. Worship her. She doesn't understand her worth, her value."

"How does that make you feel?"

I laughed at the blatant therapist question, but I answered it. "Frustrated. Angry—not at her, for her. It motivates me. I have to do something. She deserves to be with a man who sees her the way I see her. Who appreciates her the way I do. Who will treat her with the respect she deserves."

I shook my head, dragging my hand through my hair. The vision of her trying to cover her body in shame haunted me, materializing like it had between the moments of unslaked desire. I meant what I'd said—I *hated* that she felt the way she did. I hated whoever had contributed to her insecurity, hated that she couldn't love her body the way I did.

That was all she needed—to be worshipped until she believed she was worthy of every reverent touch.

There had to be someone.

An idea sparked and caught fire.

"Thanks, Mama."

She laughed. "I didn't do anything but listen."

"I know, but it worked," I said as my smile climbed. "I know just what to do."

VAL

"So, I had an idea."

Sam pulled me a little closer, his arm hanging on my shoulders, our strides aligned—mine stretched a little longer, his shortened to match.

I smiled, hoping his idea involved nudity. "Tell me."

"I think it's time for a real date."

"You do?" My heart hopped on the Tilt-A-Whirl and rode it around like a screaming loon.

A date. A date with Sam. Sam and me. Dating.

Dating!

This is it.

Don't freak out.

Don't blow it.

Don't—

"I do. And I have the perfect guy in mind."

I laughed, nestling into his side. My fingers toyed with the waistband of his jeans, eager to get them off of him. "I bet you do."

"So his name is Adam. He's a buddy of mine from Juilliard—"

I didn't hear what else he said. My brain was wholly occupied with processing the name *Adam*, which was definitely not the name Sam, and thus, I could not comprehend what he was saying.

It dawned on me slowly, like waking from a dream. He wanted to set me up on a date with someone named Adam. Because he and I weren't dating. We weren't anything but friends with an unconventional arrangement. An arrangement with rules. Boundaries.

Boundaries I'd selectively forgotten.

Something inside me simultaneously broke and snapped back into place like a bone that had healed wrong.

"And you guys are going to be great together. I know him. He's perfect for you."

Perfect for me.

I took a painful breath and smiled. "I'd love to meet him."

"Good, because he's already agreed to a date. Tomorrow night, if you're free."

"Yeah, I'm free." I was always free. Every night for weeks had been reserved for Sam.

"I'll let him know." Sam pulled me to a stop and turned to face me. One hand snaked around my waist, the other cupped my cheek, and his face was smiling and pleased. "This is your final exam. He's gonna take care of you, Val. And if he doesn't, let me know so I can teach *him* a lesson or two."

I chuckled, though my heart sank on a slow track for my stomach. "So, I guess our lessons are finished?"

He tightened his grip on my waist, bringing me flush against him. "The month ended yesterday."

My lungs caught in a hitch. The ache in my heart was unbearable. "But you want to know the truth?"

"What?" I asked breathlessly.

"You didn't need any lessons in the first place. I just count myself lucky to have been here while you figured it out for yourself. You knew what to do. You proved that to both of us last night."

The memory flashed through me, through *all* of me, heart to heel and everywhere in between. Pain drifted in its wake at the knowledge that I wouldn't have a night like that again, maybe ever.

"Thank you, Sam. For"—*wanting me, showing me, helping me, teaching me*—"everything."

"Don't thank me, not for doing something that was such a pleasure. I…" Something darkened behind his eyes, something he wanted to say. Something I desperately wanted to hear. But then he blinked, and it was gone. "I'm glad we're friends."

"Me too." My smile was as heavy with loss as it was honest with appreciation.

He angled my face, tipped it to his, lowered his lips to brush them against mine in a kiss that was featherlight and fringed with goodbye. And when he stepped back and pulled me into his side once more, the world was colder than it had been a few minutes ago.

And for once, the heat of his body couldn't chase away the chill.

SOMEONE LIKE ME

VAL

I smoothed my skirt, ignoring the three worried faces in the mirror behind me.

"I don't like it." Katherine's words were flat and definitive.

"Honestly, it's *fine*," I said for probably the seventy-second time in the last twenty-four hours. I had been asleep for at least eight of those. "It's like I said the other night—you know, when I *told* you guys he wasn't into me?" I laid a look on all their faces to make sure they'd heard me. They had. "This is what I signed up for. Sam's just my friend, and I knew when I asked him to kiss me that this was all it would ever be. He's my friend, and he cares about me. So much in fact that he hand-picked a guy to set me up with. His standards are so high, I have no doubt Adam will be not only handsome, but well mannered and respectful. If he has a good sense of humor, I might just throw my panties at him the second I have the chance."

Rin frowned. "I'm sorry, Val. I'm honestly just so surprised. I was banking on a declaration and possibly a proposal of marriage."

I laughed. "Not everyone is like you and Court with the breakneck relationships. Especially not Sam. I've never known anyone so unattached. How he could spend this much time with me, be this affectionate and share this much of my life, all while keeping his heart on lockdown is beyond me. I know my heart hasn't been."

"No, it hasn't," Amelia said softly.

"If he told me right now he wanted to see me, I'd blow off my date and run straight into his arms. If he said he wanted to be with me, I'd dive in without thinking twice. But I'm … I don't know how to explain it. I'm not under any delusions about him. I know exactly what we are and what we're not. I know what's available to me and what isn't. And Sam's heart is not on the table. It never was. He did exactly what we set out to do, and now, I'm graduating. We should be celebrating."

"Then why do you look so sad?" It was Rin, and her eyes, when I met them, were as downtrodden as my own.

I attempted a smile. "Because that doesn't mean I don't wish things were different." I sighed. "But this is exactly how it should be. And that's just *fine*."

"Every time you say the word *fine*, I believe you less and less," Katherine said.

A laugh huffed out of me. I turned to face them, holding my hands up in display, palms up. "Do I look okay?" My skirts flared a little when I shifted.

Their affirmations made me feel a little better about the whole mess.

When I looked at the clock, I hissed a swear. I was about to be late. "I've got to go. Wish me luck," I said, scooping up my purse and phone.

We headed out of my room with me leading the charge like we were on an expedition. Although the most gusto I could muster would max us out at conquering a ball pit at Chuck E. Cheese's.

"Crush it!" Amelia cheered, then amended, "I mean, don't crush his dick. Except maybe with your vagina." She sighed. "You know what I mean."

"Break a bed frame!" Katherine encouraged. We gave her a look. "You know, because the sex is so savage."

I laughed as we approached the front door.

Rin pulled me into a hug when I turned to face them. "You're going to be great, Val. I hope he's funny and smart and gorgeous."

"And that he has a fire hose in his pants," Amelia said with a waggle of her brows.

"I love you guys," I said on a chuckle.

"We love you, too," they said in unison, and we all burst into laughter.

And with that, I could stall no more. I pulled on my coat and stepped outside to meet the evening, wishing I could just go back inside and climb in bed with a bowl of guacamole the size of my face and a bag of chips. And some tequila. I wouldn't have thumbed my nose at tequila at all.

Before I took three steps, my phone buzzed with a text from Sam. *I would wish you luck, but you don't need it.*

I smiled down at my phone, ignoring my speeding pulse as I texted him back. *I wish I had your faith in me. I'm nervous.*

Don't be. Tell me what you learned in lesson one.

I took a breath and messaged him back. *Eye contact. Compliment him. Touch him, not weirdly. I guess I won't have to use a pick-up line since we're already going on a date.*

You forgot the most important thing.

What's that?

Be yourself. It's what makes you so beautiful.

Warmth bloomed in my chest, the edges touched with pain. So I made a joke. *You sure it's not my red lipstick?* I paused on the sidewalk to take a ridiculous selfie, kissy face and all, and fired it off.

The dots that indicated he was typing started, then stopped, then started again three times before the text came through. *That definitely doesn't hurt.*

Another message came through right after.

When is he picking you up?

He's not, I answered. *I'm walking there now.*

He didn't come pick you up? Why didn't he come pick you up?

I rolled my eyes, but I found myself smiling. *Because I didn't want him to know where I lived until at least the third date. Wasn't it you who told me eighty percent of men are assholes?*

Eighty-five, and it's true. But Adam isn't one of those guys. That's why I picked him. Well, that, and I knew you'd love him.

Hopefully he loves me, too.

If he doesn't, he's a fucking idiot, and you should send him to me so I can tell him so to his face.

I laughed, already feeling less nervous. Sam had a knack for that. *All right, I'm almost there. I'll talk to you later.*

Message me and let me know how it went.

Okay. Thanks again, Sam.

Anytime. Oh, one last thing.

What's that?

Don't forget that you're the prize. Not him.

My cheeks flamed hot, and I shook my head at my phone, smiling. *If you say so.*

I say so.

I slipped my phone into my purse, warm and giddy. Problem was, I was walking into a date with a guy who wasn't the one who'd made me warm and giddy. I did my best to shake it off in that last block, and by the time I reached for the brass door handle, I was almost ready.

Almost.

No amount of preparation would have readied me for the man waiting inside.

He stood the second I stepped in. Adam was tall—*gorgeously* tall—with dark hair that he wore a little long. It curled at the ends, licking the collar of his leather jacket.

"Val?" My name was a question on his sculpted, smiling lips.

Surely, *this* wasn't the guy Sam had set me up with. He was almost as out of my league as Sam.

"Adam?"

He stepped to me, extended his hand, took mine when I offered it. His skin was warm, his hand strong. "Sam said you were a stunner, but I had no idea you were this beautiful. It's nice to meet you, Val."

"You too," I said from behind a blush.

"I got us a table by the window. I hope that's okay."

"Of course." I followed him to the table, pausing for him to pull out the chair for me. "Thanks," I said as I passed him and sat.

He smelled good, I noted, and he had a nice handshake, but neither affected me. It didn't linger in my mind, and I didn't feel the ghost of touch on my skin. Not like Sam.

Stop it, Val. He's not Sam, primarily because he's actually available.

"So," I said as he took the seat across from me, "you know Sam from school?"

He smiled, sitting back in his chair. His eyes were bright and friendly, happy eyes to match his happy smile. "Everyone at school knew Sam. He's never met a stranger, you know?"

I chuckled. "I do."

"We were roommates for a while. You guys play *Wicked* together, right?"

"Yeah. I just recently got a permanent chair."

"Congratulations. That's no easy feat."

"Trust me, I know," I said on a laugh.

"Did you know the contractor?"

I shook my head. "I was subbing, and they gave me the chair. I'd never been so shocked in my life."

He nodded, impressed. "On merit alone. Not only rare, but difficult. Congratulations."

"Thanks. Finding subs has been interesting. I'm terrified to choose someone inadvertently who's better than me. One cold, and I could be out of a job."

Adam smiled. "Well, if you were good enough to earn the chair, I'm betting they'd be hard-pressed to find someone better."

I laughed. "Oh, I doubt that, but thank you for the vote of support. What about you? Sam didn't tell me what you do."

At that, he smiled, the genuine smile of a man who loved his job. "I teach elementary school music."

My insides melted, and my face melted with it. "Oh my God," I cooed. "Are you serious?"

"Serious as a number two pencil." He leaned in and said conspiratorially, "In case you didn't know, those pencils are *very* serious. Ask any Scantron."

I laughed, settling back in my seat as he continued.

"Best job in the world. I don't think I have a single student who hates my class. Do you know how impossible that average is? Ask any teacher and they'll tell you."

"I believe you. It's almost impossible to hate music."

"I'm with you. But you'd be surprised at how many kids *hate* it. When you don't have rhythm or are tone deaf, music class is only a reminder of a failure. So I do whatever I can to make sure those kids find something to love."

Seriously, my insides were about as solid as nougat in the backseat of a Jetta in August.

He smiled. "Anyway, almost everything I do involves music somehow. I even compose in my spare time."

I brightened up. "Oh! Have you and Sam ever written anything together?"

His brows quirked in confusion. "Sam? No, as far as I know, he doesn't write music. Although I've never seen anyone pick it up like he did. He made all of us look like idiots in composition class. Thank God he didn't decide to go that direction. I'd never live down my inadequacies."

I smiled to cover the truth, not wanting to betray Sam's secrets, not having realized they were secrets to begin with.

"So, shaper of young minds during the day, composer by night. What else do you do?"

"I love to read. Is that dorky of me to say?" he asked, rubbing the back of his neck.

"Uh, no. Absolutely not. You should tell every woman you meet how much you love to read."

He laughed.

"I mean it. Put a picture of your bookshelves on Tinder and see how many hits you get. Mention the fact that you teach elementary school and watch all their panties combust."

Adam's eyes twinkled as he leaned on the table, angling toward me. "Sam was right."

"Right about what?"

"You're pretty amazing. I'm glad you came, Val."

I smiled, wishing I weren't lying when I said, "There's nowhere I'd rather be."

SAM

This is fine.

I turned on my heel and paced across the room again, raking my hand through my hair.

Fine, perfectly fine.

Val was on a date. With a great guy. Who would treat her right.

Fine.

On paper, he was perfect. On paper, he was *the* guy. The guy who would give her everything she needed, everything she could possibly want.

This was exactly what should be happening. Val knew everything she needed to know. Lessons complete. I'd hung up my chalkboard and sent her out on her own. Everything was just as it should be.

I turned again, chugging across the room, my legs eating the distance at a distressing rate. Nerves scratched at my skin from the inside, metallic and abrading. The urge to take off running and sprint until I collapsed overcame me.

Fine, fine, fine.

I'd texted her to make her feel better.

I'd texted her to make *me* feel better.

I didn't know what I'd expected. I thought I'd been looking for reassurance, a sign I'd done the right thing. I thought maybe I'd miraculously feel some sort of relief at talking to her before her date.

Wrong.

Somehow, I felt infinitely worse.

She was sitting across from him right now. I knew the restaurant well—I'd fucking suggested it. I'd have chosen the table by the window where the lighting was best and you could see the city. She'd be sitting there in the low light with some romantic acoustic bullshit playing on the speakers, laughing at something he'd said. He'd touch her hand. Tell her she was beautiful. They'd kiss, his hand on her cheek, her fingers on his chest. He'd pull her close, feel the curves of her body against him.

Sheer and absolute abhorrence ripped through me, tore me open, left my guts on the floor of my music room.

He'll take her upstairs, my masochistic mind continued, *undress her. He'll taste her and have her.*

And you just taught her how to give blowjobs.

I stopped in the middle of the room, my lungs in a vise and my heart locked in an iron maiden.

He's going to get your blowjobs.

My dinner charged up my esophagus.

He's going to get her sighs. Her kisses. Her laughter. He's going to get her smiles.

I willed my feet to move. They carried me toward the door.

He's going to get all of her, my mind said.

I scooped up my keys and ripped the door open.

No, he's not, my heart answered. And I flew down the stairs, realizing what my mind had been blind to.

Those kisses and sighs and smiles? Those were *mine*. And I was going to go get them.

VAL

I laughed at Adam's joke, setting my fork on my plate so I wouldn't drop it.

His smile is so nice, I thought, ignoring the sadness underneath.

He's not Sam, the other voice in my head whispered.

When Adam reached for my hand, I felt…

Nothing. I felt nothing.

But I smiled back, determined to give it my best shot.

A month ago, I would have been over the moon to be on a date with a guy like Adam.

But a month ago, I had been a different person.

A month ago, I hadn't known Sam.

He's your friend. That's all he'll ever be to you, and you know that.

I fought the urge to sigh. It was true. I'd known this was how it would be, and I'd walked into it willingly. And now, walking away, I was thankful for what I'd had.

That didn't make it any easier. It didn't mean I was happy about it. It was just what it was.

Adam's hand was warm, strong, his fingers long enough that they covered mine easily. He'd started talking again, this time a story about a little boy in his music class that kept calling castanets *nutcrackers*. His thumb shifted against mine in slow, easy strokes.

I was thinking about Sam.

In fact, I was thinking so hard about Sam that I thought I caught sight of him out the window in my periphery. I looked, not comprehending the vision of his face on the other side of the glass. He couldn't be real, standing there on the sidewalk with his chest heaving under his leather jacket like he'd run a mile. I had to have conjured the apparition, his eyes liquid gold, hard and heavy on mine.

Adam turned to the window. "Sam?"

I blinked.

Sam glanced down at our hands, and his face tightened. He met my eyes again only for a split second before he took off for the door of the restaurant.

The chime of the bell was loud enough to startle me. Slowly, I turned in my seat to look behind me.

And there he was, as real as my pulse thundering in my ears and the swampy damp of my palms.

I pulled my hand out from under Adam's, confused by my guilt, confused by Sam's presence, still half-wondering if I was daydreaming.

"Sam?" I asked stupidly, squinting up at him like he might change into someone else if I looked hard enough.

"Hey," he said breathlessly. His face was a dichotomy of desperation and discomfort.

"What's up, man?" Adam asked. His smile almost completely hid his confusion. His tone did not.

Sam shifted his weight, his hands opening and closing at his sides like he was trying to grip his own reins. "Do you ... ah, sorry, could I ... ah ... borrow her for a second?"

"Sure, so long as you bring her back," Adam joked. A thread of seriousness lay underneath.

I grabbed my napkin out of my lap and set it next to my plate as I stood. "I'll ... be just a second, Adam."

He tried to smile, but when his eyes darted to Sam, the veneer of his certainty cracked. "Yeah, okay. Well, I'll be here."

Sam grabbed my hand and took off for the door, towing me behind him like a Radio Flyer. Once outside, he pulled me in the direction opposite the window where my table had been.

"Wait," I said, pulling him to slow his pace. "What's going on, Sam? Is everything okay?"

He stopped, turned to face me, pinned me with a gaze that brought time to a brief, heavy halt. "No, Val. Everything is not okay."

Worry overtook my heart. I stepped into him, touched his chest. "What happened? What's wrong?"

He covered my hand with his own. A jolt of possession and desire shot through me at the contact. "I've made a mistake. A stupid, blind mistake."

My brows drew together in confusion. "I don't understand."

"I didn't either. Not until you were here. I ... I don't ... I can't ..." He drew a long, noisy breath and sighed it out in frustration as he sought the words. And then he reached for my face and whispered, "Oh, fuck it."

His lips connected with mine in a shock of pleasure that slipped over me like a sip of whiskey—a long burn, a sting, the sweet taste on my tongue, warming me from my chest to every extremity.

I leaned into him. He wrapped himself around me, breathing me in until I was dizzy from lack of oxygen.

When our lips finally slowed, we were twined around each other in the middle of the sidewalk, oblivious to anything beyond the tips of our noses, which grazed each other when we parted.

"He doesn't get my blowjobs," Sam said roughly, drunkenly, his lids half-closed. His hands flexed, gathering the fabric of my dress in his fingers.

A laugh burst out of me. "What?"

His smile, sideways and seductive. "He doesn't get my blowjobs. Or my smiles or sighs. He doesn't get your body because that is *mine*."

My heart tripped at the word, hanging in the air for a long moment before falling at his feet.

"I should have seen it sooner." He searched my face like he was seeing it for the first time. "All this time, I wanted to help you find a guy who would see you the way I do. Who would want you the way I do. Who would appreciate you the way I do. The way *I* do, Val. Thing is, no one will. No one can. No one will ever care for you the way I do."

I couldn't speak, my throat thick, the words lodged somewhere in the column of my throat. My lips parted. No sound came out.

"I know I'm not good enough for a girl like you. I'm not the guy you take home—I've only ever been good for a fling. A night. But I want to be more. It's just that I've never..." he started, shaking his head almost imperceptibly. "I've never wanted to try before. I've never even considered it. But, with you, tonight, I *had* to. And I mean that literally—all I could do was blink, breathe, and get to you. But now...now, I don't know what to do." He cupped my face, looked deep into my eyes, and I lost myself in his. "Tell me what you want, Val. Tell me what to do."

Shock. Disbelief. Unbridled joy.

Sam wanted me.

Confusion. Astonishment. My wish come true.

I only had one cognitive thought in my addled mind. "Kiss me again."

A laugh, a single, soft puff of air against my lips, and he did just that. For a long moment, that was all either of us needed or wanted. It was the only promise we could offer.

When the kiss broke, he waited to speak. Waited for me to tell him what to do, which was funny, considering he was supposed to be the expert.

"I thought you didn't date," I said, still stupefied.

"I don't. But the thought of you with someone else makes me crazy, far crazier than the thought of dating. Being with you is easy. I don't have to think. I don't have to try. I can just be me, and you can be you, and we're happy. I don't want you to see anyone else. Only me."

"I don't want to see anyone else. I only went out with Adam because you set it up, and you were so excited. And…well, you said it was time, and I trust you. But this—whatever this is—is what I've wanted from the beginning, from the first."

His face softened. "Me too." He took a breath, straightened his spine without separating our bodies. "No more lessons. No more pretending. No more just friends. I want you, Val. I promise I'll do everything I can to make you happy. I want to bring you flowers and take you to dinner. I want your toothbrush in my bathroom, and I want to spend all my time with you, just like we have been but *more*. I want more. I want to be the best fucking boyfriend on the planet."

I stilled completely. "Did you just say *boyfriend*?"

A flickering smirk. "I did."

Gaping. I was gaping. "I'm not dreaming, am I? Did you *actually* just say that?"

He laughed, thumbed my bottom lip, stared at it for a second.

"Everything I want from you fits into that box. And I've never been a boyfriend before, but I'm pretty sure I'd be the best at it. I don't like to fail, and I don't do anything halfway."

I searched his face for a moment. "I don't even know what to say."

"Say yes." A plea, soft and hopeful. When I didn't speak, he pulled me closer. "You told me once that you wished you could kiss a man and make him fall for you. Well, check that off your list, Valentina. Be mine."

There was only one answer, and my lips whispered it right along with my entire heart and soul. "Yes."

I couldn't get out anything more than a whimper before he kissed me again, a kiss so deep, I had to hang on to him to stay upright.

When he broke away, I was breathless, speechless, witless.

"Come on," he said, his nose grazing mine. He kissed the tip of it. "Come home with me. Right now." Without waiting for an answer, he took my hand and started off down the sidewalk.

I took three steps and stopped, pulling him back. "Wait. Adam." My heart sank. "Oh God. What will I say?"

Sam kissed my forehead. "I'll take care of it. I got you into this. I'll get you out of it. Wait here."

I watched him stride away. He walked into the restaurant, and when curiosity got the best of me, I edged out on the sidewalk so I could see in. Sam had taken my seat and was leaning on the table, speaking to a stoic Adam, whose hands were in his lap, his face drawn but not angry. He nodded as Sam explained. I watched his admission, the subtleties in his posture—a small shake of his head in wonder, a disbelieving smile, a sigh, a raking of his hand through his hair. Through it all, he looked happy, elated, even as he apologized.

Fear crept into my mind, cold and dark. It was too good to be true. It couldn't be real. Not that I didn't believe Sam felt exactly as he said he did—*right now*. But tomorrow would he wake up and have lost the feeling? Would he get me out of his system, slake his desire and be done with me? Was he motivated by something he wasn't aware of, like jealousy of Adam?

I trusted him, I did. But I worried that, in his own way, he was as naive as me.

The only difference was, I *knew* I was naive. Sam had all the confidence of a professional lion tamer laying his head in the mouth of the beast.

I took a breath and let it out. And then I made a decision that might hurt me later. I'd lost all sense of self-preservation.

Tonight, Sam was mine. If I never got another night, I'd have this one. And I intended to live every moment completely.

Adam and Sam stood and shook hands. Sam laid cash on the table, and a brief argument about the check ensued before Adam finally conceded. And then Sam turned and nearly bolted out of the restaurant.

He was grinning like a kid, hurrying toward me. He scooped me under his arm and swept me into a kiss.

When he let me go, he said four words I felt all the way down to my toes.

"Now you're all mine."

FACTS & FIGURES

SAM

Val's hand in mine was victory.

Her smile was my triumph.

Her lips against mine were my elation.

The light changed, and we crossed the street, Val's arm around my waist. Our pace was not a patient one.

Two blocks.

"Can I ask you something?" she asked as we crossed the street.

"Anything."

"When did you realize it? How you felt about me."

"Five minutes before I got to the restaurant."

A soft laugh.

"But you know something? I think I've always known. Since the very first day you subbed."

She chuckled as we stepped onto the curb. "Me too. I wasn't sure you even saw me."

"You ran into a music stand and took down three more like a chain of dominoes. Really loud metal dominoes. Everyone in the pit saw you."

She buried her face in my chest. "Oh God."

I laughed, tightening my grip on her.

"Why me, Sam?" she asked quietly.

"Why not you?" I asked her back.

I swear I heard her roll her eyes. "I won't state the obvious, but past all that … after all that time we spent together, you never made a move. I mean, I had to *beg* you to kiss me. You never told me how you felt."

"Neither did you."

She sighed, but she didn't answer, and for a handful of footsteps, neither did I. I didn't know how to explain.

"There are so many reasons why it's you, Val. Almost too many to count. Your smile. Your honesty. The way you say exactly what you think when you think it. Your laugh. But more than anything, it's how you make me feel. You make me want more than I have. You make me want to be more than I am." I paused. "Did you know I have a rule?"

"What kind of rule?"

"I've never hooked up with anyone I worked with. It was just easier, cleaner, not to mix business with pleasure. You know how much drama there is in theater. This way, I could avoid any hard feelings. I never broke the rule. And then I met you."

She didn't say anything, just nuzzled closer.

"If we'd met anywhere else, I would have asked you out a long time ago. But I'm glad I didn't."

"You are?" Two disappointed syllables.

"I am. Because I wouldn't have let myself get this close to you. And if I hadn't gotten this close to you, I wouldn't have understood what I was missing. I've never met someone I wanted to date. I've never met someone I *had* to have. The thought of you with Adam made me so crazy, I ran three blocks to bust it up before he could kiss you, just so I could kiss you myself. There wasn't a choice to be made, Val. You and I have become a fact. We were long before tonight."

One block.

"I'm just glad you didn't say no," I continued. "I don't know what I would have done with myself if you had." Phantom loss slipped over me. I pulled her closer to ward off the chill.

But she laughed, a happy, hearty sound. "Me? Say no? To you? That's…" She burst out laughing again.

I smiled and kissed her curly crown of hair. "That's how I feel about you. I just feel like an idiot for not realizing it sooner."

I spotted the entrance to my building and picked up my pace.

"I'm glad you realized it at all."

"Me too," I admitted, my relief complete.

We hurried inside and up the stairs and into my apartment. I clicked on a light and dimmed it. The room was golden, as if it were bathed in candlelight. And in the center was Val.

Her chestnut hair spilled over her shoulders in wild curls, framing the shape of her face. It was a heart, her narrow chin and small mouth at the tip, up the soft curves of her cheeks and to her eyes, big and wide, dark and deep. She was sweet innocence, a diamond found in the dark. And with fierceness that washed over me like a wave, I knew I'd do anything to protect her, to shelter her. To keep her safe.

This chance I had was a gift. God knew I wasn't enough.

You're going to disappoint her.

Maybe, I answered that voice in my mind. *I might not know what I'm doing, but I'll be damned if I fail. I won't fail.*

Another surge of relief filled me from boot to breastbone. Because nothing could keep me down. Beyond all comprehension, I'd found a girl who made me so happy, I'd taken a risk I'd never considered before. And she wanted me, too. She'd said yes.

I'd gotten the girl.

She was mine.

And now I would claim her.

VAL

One second, I was caught in his stare, lost. And before I could breathe, I was in his arms, the space between us gone. Our breath mingled, our lips a seam. His hands searching my face, my hair, my body, guiding my thigh up the length of his. Over my ass and under.

He picked me up like I was nothing, but he held me like I was everything.

My legs wound around his waist, and my arms hooked around his neck, our hips locked and our lips never parting as he carried me to his bedroom.

He laid me down.

I was aware of everything. The feel of his shirt under my hands. The weight of his body pressing me into bed. The taste of his lips. The soft cotton of his sheets against the backs of my arms. The rough calluses on his fingers rasping against my thigh. The beat of my heart as it raced in my rib cage. The hard length of him shifting pleasurably against the center of me.

And the kiss went on and on.

Everything had shifted. A few words, and the thin boundaries we'd held in place were gone. Against all reason, he wanted me.

Me.

You and I have become a fact.

It couldn't be real. It had to be a dream, some brilliant dream where it rained chocolate sprinkles and broccoli tasted like birthday cake. Where snow wasn't cold and girls like me got their wishes.

And oh, how I had wished for Sam. I'd wished on every star and eyelash. Every eleven eleven and every dandelion. I'd wished for him before I knew I was wishing for *him*.

When he relinquished my lips to kiss down my neck, I sighed my contentment. He hummed against my skin in answer.

In a feat of strength and skill, he grabbed me and twisted, pulling me into his lap as he sat. I gasped in surprise as his lips connected with the hollow of my throat, his hands up my skirt, my ass in his palms. He squeezed.

"God, I want this ass," he whispered against my skin. "It's perfect. I know you don't believe me, but it is." He pulled, grinding my core against his cock.

My arms rested on his shoulders, forearms cradling his head, fingers slipping into his hair. "If you think it's perfect, that's all that matters, isn't it?"

A chuckle. A wet kiss on my neck. My skin drawn into his hot mouth. "Is that all it takes to convince you? I've been going about this all wrong."

His fingertips trailed up, traced my hip, found the bend of my thigh. With one hand, he lifted my skirt. The other stroked me through my panties, eliciting a whimper and a shift of my hips, seeking connection.

"So many firsts I've claimed," he said between kisses, his thumb doing some magic on the hood of my clit. "Tell me. Tell me what's mine only."

My chest heaved, the motion inadvertently bringing my breasts into his face, then away, then back again. "F-first swing dance. First real kiss. First real date. First real everything," I breathed.

"More," he demanded.

"F-first orgasm by a m-m-man—*oh*!" I gasped, my core clenching when he squeezed my clit. "First real b-blowjob. First time coming from a man's mouth. *Mmm—ah*!"

He popped my ass with his free hand, and my hips swung into his from the shock and pleasure.

"Say blowjob again." His voice was gravelly and raw, that free hand moving to my breast. He unfastened the top button of my shirt and buried his face in the valley of flesh.

"Blowjob," I whispered, rocking my hips.

His hips rose in answer, his fingers working my buttons until they were open. "I want another first."

"Tell me."

He slipped that hand under my shirt, and I shifted, helping him get rid of it altogether. "I want to be the first man to make you come, cock deep inside you."

"Oh my God." The words were barely intelligible. My hips were not my own. The point where his thumb connected with me ached desperately.

"Have I mentioned, I'm not a fan of failure?" He palmed my breast, squeezed and released, slipped around my ribs to the clasp of my bra, unfastened it with a snap of his fingers.

"Y-yes. I remember." My bra slid down my arms. I tossed it away, cupped his jaw.

His eyes lowered, his lids heavy, one hand cupping my sex, the other tracing my collarbone. "Once I make up my mind about something, I don't stop. Not until I have what I want." His hand, warm on my breast. His thumb, callused and rough against the tender skin of my nipple. "And I want you." He squeezed, the flesh spilling from between his finger. "I'll have that orgasm. I'll take a few more because I can. Because it's like I told you." His lips, millimeters from my nipple. His breath hot and damp when he spoke. "Your pleasure is my pleasure. And I want to take mine until I'm satisfied."

The sensation of his mouth on my nipple was a haze of feeling, too many nerves firing to decipher everything at once. It was the slick of his tongue. The pressure as he sucked. His lips parting, flexing, releasing. The very edges of his teeth grazing the tight peak.

"Sam," I breathed, already close.

My hips were too wild, the delicate crawl of heat across my skin bringing with it a dimming of the room as he pressed exactly as I wanted, sucked just like I needed, licked right where I desired.

He closed his lips, his hands disappearing from the places they'd been. They moved instead to my face, which he turned to his, bringing me down for a kiss that left me boneless in his lap.

My clumsy hands fumbled down his torso to the hem of his shirt. "Too many clothes," I mumbled against his lips.

He laughed against mine and reached back to grab his shirt and tug it off, mussing his hair on its way off his body and onto the floor.

It was my turn to stare, eyes down and hands roaming over his skin, so tan, so soft over the hard muscles of his chest.

"You're so beautiful," I whispered in wonder.

He held my face so delicately, tipped it to meet his amber eyes. "Every day, every minute I'm with you, any time of day, any day of the week, I feel the same. You're the most beautiful girl I've ever known, Val. Ever."

I shook my head, looked down my warm cheeks. Happily warm. But he couldn't have meant it.

I didn't even have to say it out loud. He knew. The air shifted, tightened. When he breathed, he breathed me into him.

"Every curve," he said, his hand skating down my arm. "Even the ones you hate." He traced the back of my arm, the flesh on my ribs that rolled just once. I flinched involuntarily. "You see it as a flaw. I see it as honest. It's *you*. And I want you just as you are. Every tiny freckle on your nose. Every curl on your head. Every soft place on your body. You call them flaws. I call it a signature. Because there is no one like you, not in the whole world. And I will love every curve until you realize you love them, too."

I couldn't speak, and I didn't have to. My lips crashed against his, my soft body against his hard one, our arms locked, my legs around his waist. There was no space. No air. Nothing in the universe but me and Sam and the words he'd etched upon my heart.

He lay back, taking me with him, twisting to put himself on top of me. Down my body he roamed, his hands leading the charge and his lips in their wake. Down my stomach, over my hips, his fingers hooked into my panties and slid them down my legs until they were gone.

His hands had an agenda, first to bring my thighs together, the action twisting my waist, turning my hips so one pointed at the ceiling. With his eyes between my legs, those hands trailed up the backs of my leg, thumbed the slick center of me. Without looking up, he knelt, disappeared behind my ass but for his hand gripping my hip. For a split second of anticipation, that was the only place we touched.

A humid breath against my waiting center was my only warning.

The heat of his mouth against the heat of me was the sweetest pleasure, their softness and slickness equal, though mine lay waiting and his sought. It sought every furrow, every crease, every ridge and every valley. It sought the dark places, sought the swollen, aching peaks. A moan, a rumbling sound that touched the tip of me, commanding attention I was helpless to deny.

His face nestled deeper. I was barely cognizant of the fact that his nose was dangerously close to my ass, and even that realization was dismissed without a second thought. He was far too into what he was doing to seem bothered. In fact, he moved deeper still, his tongue sliding into me, reaching for the depths of my body.

A whimper from my lips. A noisy breath from his nose. His

fingers squeezing my ass hard enough to sting, pulling to separate my cheeks, garnering him more access. And then he was turning me, twisting me again to put me on my knees, climbing up behind me, his face buried in the split of my body.

He backed away, panting. I laid with my chest pressed against the bed, looking back at him over my shoulder, up the line of my back and the heart-shaped curves of my ass as he palmed my cheeks, squeezed them, spread them. Licked his beautiful lips and lowered his body. Drew a line up the center of me with his hot mouth. Closed his eyes, his midnight lashes on his cheeks, taking his pleasure just as he'd said he would, giving me pleasure as he'd promised.

My lids fluttered closed, my breath shallow, my face turning into the sheets to burrow, needing pressure, needing to move, needing more. I was empty, achingly empty. His name on my lips, an unbidden plea.

With a final, deliberate, slow lick up the line of my center, his mouth disappeared and his hands along with them. I heard the clink of metal, a zing of his zipper. I willed my drunken lids to open as I rolled over, caught sight of him rummaging in his nightstand. The silver packet in his tan fingers. The open V of his pants. And then my eyes were wide open and hungry, watching him as he dropped his pants, taking in every shadow of his body. The indentation of his hard ass. The fluttering muscles over his ribs. The channel of his hips, hard and muscular. The dark thatch of hair just down and between.

His cock in his hand.

The condom in the other.

His fist closing over his crown, stroking his shaft.

His eyes meeting mine.

Flashes of motion like flickering heartbeats. And then he was crawling into bed with me, reaching me first with his lips, then with his hands, seeking nothing more than to hold me to him, those hands splayed across my back with gentle demand. His legs twined with mine, his thigh nestled at the point where my thighs met. And for a moment—one long, hot moment—that was exactly enough.

But our bodies wanted more, our hips searching for what only the other had. I moved up his body to gain access, spreading my legs to give him all the room he needed.

He took control, placing me flat on my back, spreading my thighs with his knees. He gripped his base, thumb extended to guide his crown to the split of my swollen lips. Between them he slid without breaching me, drawing his cock up the line, against my clit, down again, hovering over me all the while. Our faces were turned down, watching him toy with me.

And then he brought his lips to mine. The kiss seared me from the place our lips touched, through my heart, and down to the point our bodies would join, a kiss barely containing the anticipation, a kiss out of our control.

When he broke away, our eyes locked. His crown found the dip. His hips flexed. And he slipped into me slowly, so slowly, not stopping until he filled me completely.

Neither of us moved beyond the thundering of our hearts and the heaving of our lungs. Our gaze never shifted, his arms bracketing my head never tensing, his fingers in my hair still as stone.

And then he kissed me, pumping his hips. We swallowed each other's moans, the connection liberating, the slow grind of his body as he filled me again gave me the pressure I'd needed so desperately.

God, the feeling of his weight, his hips sinking into mine, the heaviness of his body, the cage of his arms. I matched his rhythm without knowledge or intention, my hips rolling in time to his, bringing my body where I needed. And he knew where I needed it too, knew the exact speed, the exact force. He knew when to slow and when to speed. He knew when to kiss me and knew when I needed to breathe and be and nothing more.

His hand hooked my leg, guiding it over his shoulder as he got on his knees, tilting my ass to him. And when he pumped, he went deep, so deep, my lungs contracted in a gasp of shock and pleasure.

"Tell me when you can feel it," he breathed, adjusting my leg as he thrust his hips again.

"Feel wha—-*homygod.*" My hands slapped into the sheets to brace myself when the tip of him hit a spot deep in my body I'd only read about. My fingers clutched at the sheets, back arched, offering my breasts to the sky. "*Yes,*" I whispered as he slammed into me, his hips waving to kiss my aching clit. I writhed, mad from the feeling so intense, I became a wild thing underneath him, around him.

And then there was only one objective, one desire. My nerves fired, burning a trail across my skin to the center of me, to my core so full of Sam.

Another thrust of his hips. A breath that skipped and shuddered in my chest. Another thrust, and my body contracted, squeezed, pulled him deeper into me. Another thrust, and I exploded in a blinding blaze of electricity, a pleasure so hot, so acute, I couldn't hold it all. It split me open and poured out in a bursting pulse, drawing him into me as air sawed out of my lungs with affirmations and pleas.

My body slowed, but he didn't. Faster he moved, the sound of his thighs slapping my ass ringing in the room. My breasts caught the motion, jostling in even circles, a whimper slipping out of me, my body still riding the last of my orgasm. His breath came faster, louder, a moan, a cry.

He swelled inside me, pulsed, and with a sweet sighing *yes,* he came, fingers digging into my flesh, brows tight, eyes pinned shut and jaw clenched.

I watched him release, watched him let go, watched his ecstasy, his pleasure.

His pleasure was my own, just as mine was his.

He pursed his lips and shifted, struggling for breath as he laid his body down on me, kissed me with the passion of a man who'd been liberated. He kissed me until our hearts slowed, kissed me until those hearts matched pace.

Only then did he break the kiss to look into my eyes, his fingers in my hair and his lips swollen and smiling. I was surrounded by him.

It was glorious.

"You must be a magician." My voice was rough from disuse.

His smile lifted on one side. "Why?"

"'Cause when I look at you, everyone else disappears."

He laughed, kissing me sweetly. "If I had a dollar for every time I looked at you, I'd be in a higher tax bracket."

A giggle burst out of me. "My name's Microsoft. Mind if I crash at your place tonight?"

Another laugh, another kiss. His nose brushed against mine. "Will you? Stay the night with me, Val."

I wound my arms around his neck. "You sure?"

"As your boyfriend, I respectfully demand it."

I chuckled. "How can I argue with that?"

"You can't," he said against my lips. "Because I have more orgasms to earn, and I'm pretty sure it's gonna take me all night."

And then he kissed me and made good on that promise.

BOYFRIEND MATERIAL

SAM

When I woke, I woke wrapped up in Val.

We were a tangle of arms and legs, her head tucked under my chin and her breath puffing against my chest. She rested on the curve of my shoulder, and my arm cradled her head, keeping her close. Even in sleep, my fingers needed to rest in her dark curls. I could smell the coconut. I shamelessly buried my nose in her hair and inhaled like an utter and absolute creep.

"Mmm-nanaman," she mumbled. "Banana man."

I pursed my lips, stifling laughter.

"S'sa Piledriver. Bronco, bucking bronco. Mmm, Hobby Horse." She giggled to herself, and the sound dissolved into a sigh.

A sharp intake of breath followed, marking the end of whatever dream she was having about horses, broncos, and professional wrestling.

She stirred, sighed, shifted to get us closer together.

"Morning," I said gruffly, my voice raspy.

"Mmm," was her only reply.

I couldn't see her face, but I somehow knew she was smiling.

Closer still I pulled her, shifting to twine my legs tighter around hers. Our calves were back to back—hers smooth and soft, mine scratchy and hard.

"Bad news," I started. "You do talk in your sleep."

She gasped and raised her head, her face red where it had rested against my skin and lips open in an incredulous O. "I do not."

"Do too. You were talking about Westerns and wrestling. And bananas. What do you know about Piledrivers?"

Recognition brushed away her disbelief, replacing it with embarrassment. "Oh my God. Nothing. It's nothing."

I laughed. "Nice try. Spill it, Valentina."

She seemed to steel herself. "It's a sexual position. Have you tried it?"

It took me a second to parse not only what she'd said, but the positions I knew of. "I'm...not sure what that is."

She huffed, her embarrassment swelling. "It's when a guy...he takes a girl, and he..." She groaned. "I can't explain it. Google it."

I shifted, doing my level best to reach for my nightstand without disrupting her. When I checked my phone, a string of messages waited on the lock screen from Ian, pestering me. I scanned them.

Ian asking where I'd been last night, if I'd been with Val. If I'd ditched her yet and found someone new.

Questions. A dozen questions, and the answers were all the same: none of his fucking business.

I ignored them, navigating instead to my browser where I searched for *Piledriver sex*. On finding an illustration of two people banging, I nodded.

"Oh, right. Yeah, I've done that. It's not all it's cracked up to be."

She laughed and rolled her eyes, but her discomfort was crystal clear.

"I'll show you a better one later."

That one earned me a real smile.

"So we have until sound check to do whatever we want. The world is our oyster." I toyed with her hair, fitting my finger into a curl. "What do you want to do?"

"Lie here like slugs all day."

I chuckled, pulling the coil until it was straight and letting it go. It sprang right back into a perfect curl. "Only if you stay naked and I get to touch you wherever I want."

She kissed my chest and shifted, setting one hand on my chest and resting her little chin on the back of it. "You've got yourself a deal, sir."

"How about tonight? We could go dancing."

"I have dinner with my family."

I frowned.

She frowned, too. "I know. But we have dinner every week. My whole family goes, brothers and all."

"How many brothers do you have?"

She sighed. I tried ineffectively not to pay any attention to her naked breasts against my ribs.

"Four. Dante, Alex, Max, and Franco."

"Are they as crazy as Dante?"

"Crazier."

I laughed.

"Okay, that's a lie. He's the eldest and thus the head of the wolf pack. Although I will say that all four of them together is much more terrifying than Dante on his own." I must have been making a face because she added, "Together, they're a hurricane."

"I should go to dinner with you."

Her face fell. "Did you hear anything I just said?"

"Sure, your brothers are either a scary natural disaster or a pack of hairy wild animals. Is there any circumstance that dictates whether I'll get one over the other?"

She laughed, rolling her eyes. "I get it. You're already regretting the whole boyfriend thing and looking for the sweet relief of beyond. Is that it?"

My jaw flexed. "I want to go *because* that's what boyfriends do. Isn't it? Meet the parents. Charm the mom. Take licks from the dad. And thunder-wolf brothers."

Val worried her bottom lip. "I don't know, Sam. I mean, you've only been my boyfriend for twelve hours. Are you sure you're ready to meet my entire family? That's not something people who are casually dating do, is it?"

"Who said I wanted to be casual?"

A pretty flush rose in her freckled cheeks. "Well, I…I don't know. I'm still trying to math how I'm here, in bed with you, never mind that you were serious about being my boyfriend."

"Of course I was serious. One of these days, you'll trust me."

Worry passed over her face. "No, I didn't mean—"

"It's okay. I'm patient. I'll earn it." I slipped a curl between my fingertips. "But just so you know, I don't really do things a little bit or even halfway."

"Well, what if…what if things don't work out? They'll ask after you. They'll know you, see us together, and when…if you…if *we* part ways, I'll have to answer for it."

"That was a lot of amendments."

She sighed. "Sam…"

"I get it. I do." I brushed her pink cheek with the backs of my knuckles. "But I'm not going anywhere. I'd like to meet your family. I'd like them to know me, to see us together. I'd also like to eat your *abuela's* paella."

"I hope that's not a metaphor."

"I don't know what I find more disturbing—the allusion to your grandma's lady parts or the comparison of it to a seafood dish," I said on a laugh. "Maybe I can even convince Dante that I'm not a total piece of shit."

She snorted a laugh. "I mean, good luck with that. That's what I'm saying. What if he…I don't know…gives you a wedgie or something in front of everyone?"

"How about I don't wear underwear, just in case."

"Oh my God."

At least she was smiling.

She watched me with eyes so big and brown, so soft and deep, her lashes impossibly long. "Are you sure? If you really want to come, I won't say no. *Abuelita* might actually drop to her knees and thank Saint Anthony for you."

I chuckled, my fingertips thirsty for her skin, tracing lazy lines up and down her arm. "I'm sure. What's the worst that could happen?"

"You could end up with your head in a toilet bowl. Or with a black eye. Or a broken arm. Or a—"

"Okay, okay, I get it. But I promise, that won't happen. I'll be on my best behavior, break out my prep-school charm and winning smile."

She didn't look convinced.

"It's a good smile," I assured her. "I'll have you know that smile won over Oprah."

Her eyes widened. "Oprah? As in, *My aunt has a dog named Oprah*, right?"

"No, as in *the* Oprah."

She blinked once, slowly. "May I ask how in the ever-loving fuck you know *Oprah*?"

"My mom is Hadiya Haddad."

Her eyes widened even more. It was a little alarming. "Your… your mom is *Hadiya Haddad*?"

I nodded, trying to keep my smile in check. Ninety-eight percent of the time, I loathed this conversation. With Val, I only found myself amused.

"As in *Be You* and *Finally Me*?"

Another nod.

"I cannot believe that. I watched her *Oprah* special about failure and cried the entire time. Does that…" It dawned on her, and her face softened. "Your family. They gave up everything… *everything* for their lives here. For your future."

My smile was gone, but it hadn't turned to a frown. It just simply *wasn't* anymore. One more nod. I brushed her hair over her bare shoulder, my fingers skimming the curve.

"Can we eat dinner at your house instead?"

The sound of my laughter surprised me. But that was one of the many things I loved about her—surprises. "Another time. Tonight is your family, my charm, and hopefully, a night without wedgies, swirlies, or any other *ies*."

Her face quirked. "Analogies?"

"Those are okay. Maybe no maladies though. Or tragedies, I hope."

"Definitely none of those." Her smile climbed lazily. "So we have all day, and you promised me we could lie here like wastoids."

"And *you* promised me I could touch you wherever I wanted." My hand found her breast and fondled it without shame.

As she laughed, I twisted us until she was beneath me, her face in my hands and her naked body soft beneath mine. And I collected payment in full.

PLAYER

SAM

I waited behind her on her stoop, shamelessly staring at her ass as she unlocked her brownstone door.

The things I'd done to that ass. The things there were left to do. And I wanted to check every one of them off my list. Twice.

My phone buzzed in my pocket again, and my mood soured instantly. Ian. Ian giving me shit.

I turned my phone off and returned it to my pocket without thinking of it again.

The only person I wanted to be able to find me tonight was Val.

She glanced back at me, and we shared a secretive smile before she pushed her door open.

I followed her in to the thundering sound of footfalls on the stairs.

"Oh my God, Val, what the hell? You didn't come home last night and I was worried to death and why didn't you call and did you sleep with Adam because—*oh*!" Amelia came into view, skidding to a stop so fast, the rug almost slipped out from underneath her. She went pale just before all of her blood rerouted to her cheeks. "Sam?" she squeaked. Her big blue eyes bounced to Val, then back to me.

I draped my arm over Val's shoulders, smirking. "No, she did not sleep with Adam. She slept with me."

Val laughed, but she pinched the tender skin of my ribs and twisted evilly.

"Ow!" I said on a laugh of my own. "What? We slept."

She rolled her eyes.

I kept on smirking at Amelia. "I'm her *boyfriend*." I rolled the word around on my tongue, felt the shape of it.

"B-boyfriend?" Amelia blinked, her brows sliding together in confusion.

"Boyfriend. As in I'm going to dinner to meet her family. And she's packing a bag because she's not coming back for at least two nights."

"T-two nights?" she stammered. She blinked again.

"*At least.*"

Val laughed again, swatting at me as she ducked out from under my arm. "Stop it, Sam. You're gonna give her a stroke."

"I … I can't … you left … you were on a date with *Adam*," Amelia insisted.

I stuffed my hands in the pockets of my peacoat and nodded. "She was. I interrupted and told her what a fool I'd been and asked if I could be her boyfriend."

"Well, you didn't really *ask*," Val said over her shoulder.

"No, I guess I didn't."

I stepped into her with an over-the-top look of earnest devotion—she didn't need to know the feeling was real. I took her hands, and with a dramatic flair and a stiff back, I got down on my knees at her feet. It was where I belonged anyway.

"Val," I said somberly, looking up into her laughing face, "will you do me the honor of being my girlfriend? I'll promise to always call when I say I will. I'll never forget your birthday—"

"It's tomorrow," she said on a giggle.

"I'll watch any sappy movies you want, even the period pieces where the guys wear those stupid neckties."

"Don't you dare make fun of cravats!" Amelia gasped.

I schooled a smirk. "And I swear to always leave you the last Oreo. Wait—you like Oreos, right?"

"Please," she said, rolling her eyes, retrieving a hand to gesture at her hips. "Body by Oreo."

"Thank God. I'd hate to have to end this thing before we really got started. So, will you? Twerk once for yes and booty pop twice for no. That way, no matter how you answer, I win."

With another laugh, she turned, and from my spot on my knees, I had a front-row seat to the show. Her back arched, her ass close enough to touch. Her hands dropped to her knees as she glanced over her shoulder with a smirk.

And then she properly blew my fucking mind.

I was momentarily stunned by the shape of her ass popping and shaking and opening and closing and moving in a way that broke some physical law of the universe. Which one, I had no idea, and I couldn't have cared less. When she rolled her hips and galloped her ass like a fucking pony, I almost had a heart attack.

In fact, in my stupor, I'd sat back on my own far less talented ass, riveted with the intensity of observing the moon landing.

I blinked up at her when she stopped, turning to me with a satisfied smile and her hands on her hips. "How's that for a yes?"

I stood and swept her into my arms. "Please always say yes, just like that."

I kissed her before she could say another word.

Amelia's small hands were over her mouth as she giggled. "I…I can't believe this."

"I almost realized it too late." The twist in my chest at the thought stung.

She chuckled. "Little dramatic, Sam."

"What?" I asked. "I set you up with the perfect guy. If I hadn't stopped it, you probably would have ended up marrying him, and where would that have left me?"

She laughed fully at that.

"Luckily, I have long legs. I got there pretty quick once I figured it out."

Val tugged me toward her room, still laughing. "Come on. Let's get going, or we'll be late."

I waved at dumbstruck Amelia, following Val through the house. When we reached her room, I shut the door and flopped onto her bed, boots hanging off the edge.

"So, Franco is nearly your twin," I recounted, hooking my arm behind my head. "He's probably the most likely to be on my side. Max and Alex defer to Dante, who's the shot caller. Right?"

"Pretty much." She pulled a weekend bag out of her closet and dropped it next to her dresser.

"So if I can win Dante over, I should be in. Easy enough."

She glanced over her shoulder with a laugh. "Right."

"You doubt me?"

"Trust me, I don't at all doubt that if you set your mind to win over my brother, you'll do it. But I'm a hundred percent sure it'll be anything but easy." She tossed a couple of lacy swaths of fabric into the bag.

"You underestimate me, Valentina."

"You underestimate him. Dante is the most stubborn ass on the planet." She moved to her closet and pulled out two dresses. When she turned, she held them up one at a time. "This one? Or this one?"

"The red one. Always the red one."

"Oh! And look at what I found." She rummaged around in a basket on her dresser, and when she turned around, two hair combs were in her hand. "Look! I can put them in my victory rolls." She turned around again, holding them up to her hair. They were gold, dotted with red glass. "They're just cheap little things, but I saw them and thought of you."

I smiled at the sight of them in her hair, at the hope in her smile, at the knowledge she'd gotten them with me on her mind.

"I love them. Bring them, too."

Her smile widened, and she dropped them in her bag.

"You know, my mom has a million of those."

"Does she?" Val asked as she picked out panties and pajamas, tossing things into the dark mouth of the bag.

"She gets them everywhere she goes, always has. I'll have to show you sometime." I switched gears, feeling inexplicably sentimental. "So, your grandma *is* making paella, right?"

Val laughed, tossing the red dress on the back of her chair. "Always. Tonight is *arroz negro*. Hope you like squid."

"Black paella is my favorite," I said stupidly. I couldn't think of anything else to say. As I watched her unbutton her blouse, I found my mind devoid of any other thought.

"Don't worry. Everyone will love you. I mean, with the exception of my brothers, and I know they'll come around."

The V of her shirt opened up, the sliver of her breasts becoming a wedge, then her top was gone completely. I stared at the lush curves of her breasts, the dark circles of her areolas, visible beyond the lace. My hands tingled imagining all the things they'd like to do.

"I'm not worried," I mumbled in a trance.

She didn't seem to notice, just went about undressing. She unzipped her skirt, slid it over her hips and ass. It hit the ground in a puddle of fabric. Everything she did was sensual, and she had no idea. The curve and point of her feet as she stepped out of the circle of her skirt. The hook of her thumbs as she slid her panties off. Her fingers as she picked up a new pair and stepped into them, giving the briefest flash of the valley between her legs I'd become so well acquainted with last night. The elastic of her waistband snapped when she let it go.

"…know what I mean?" she asked, turning to me for an answer.

"Hmm?" I hummed, tearing my eyes away from her ass to meet her eyes.

She blushed, laughing. "Wow, Sam. Really?"

"What do you mean, *really*? You realize you just stripped down naked, right? I can't be expected to listen when I can see your nipples, Val."

She made a face. I made one right back at her and stood, pacing toward her.

"So you're telling me that if I were to strip down right now," I said, shrugging off my coat and tossing it back in the direction of her bed, "you'd hear everything I said?" My hands moved for my belt buckle and unfastened it, and her eyes followed hungrily. "If I were to tell you the secret of the universe with no pants on, cock in hand, you'd hear every word?"

Pants unzipped and hanging off my hips. Her eyes on the dark sliver of hair, the straining bulge of my cock.

I stopped a handful of inches from her. Her eyes were down, her breath shallow, her breasts rising and falling. I palmed one like I'd been imagining a moment before. Her hands seemed to have a mind of their own, her fingers tracing the shape of my cock, hooking in the opening of my zipper, slipping between the denim and my skin.

"No, you wouldn't hear a word. I could tell you all the great mysteries of time, and you wouldn't catch a single one. Would you?"

"Would I what?" she muttered absently.

I laughed and kissed her, the weight of her breast in my hand, her fingers grazing my shaft. But before she could wrap her hand around me, I picked her up and carried her to bed where I told her a few mysteries of the universe in a way she couldn't help but hear.

"OKAY. ARE YOU SURE YOU want to do this? Now's your last chance for escape."

She stood on the sidewalk under a gigantic elm whose leaves had burned to russet and amber. With every rise in the wind, a few let go and swayed, twirling to the ground. Her eyes were as dark and soft as freshly turned earth.

"I'm ready. There's squid and noogies waiting for me upstairs. Now, let's go face the wolf-nado."

She laughed softly, and I bent to kiss her nose.

"Come on," I said as I took her hand.

And with a deep, fortifying breath, she turned for the door.

A shock of nerves zipped through me when her hand grasped the doorknob. Because despite my bravado and determination, I was worried. But only a little and only for that moment. I shoved the feeling back down where it belonged and lifted my eyes to the stairs.

The noise was the first thing to hit me. Laughter. A conversation in Spanish. Acoustic guitar, plucking an exotic tune. More laughter. Male voices chanting something in Spanish and another burst of laughter. Val's shoulders rose and fell with another sigh, her spine straight. Her hand tightened on mine.

I squeezed back.

She let me go as we stepped into the kitchen. It seemed to be the hub of the house, the center of everything, a room full of people and sizzling food and the sounds of togetherness.

Their faces turned to Val and lit in smiles. A tiny woman with deep lines in her face, a crimson scarf tied around her head. Another woman who looked to be an exact copy of Val in twenty-five years, with curves and chestnut hair and eyes like a baby deer. A tall man with black hair and broad shoulders, a friendly smile but suspicious eyes. A small man in a straw fedora, his aquiline nose hooked like his back, his dark hands weathered but his eyes glittering coals.

And four brothers wearing matching dubious expressions of discontent. Their arms folded across imposing chests in identical postures.

Dante I knew, the tallest of the four. His gaze was the heaviest, black as midnight's asshole. Max and Alex I deemed to be the two just behind him, the three standing like the head of a formation of bowling pins. Angry, immovable bowling pins. Franco *looked* younger than the other three, though it might have just been that his eyes shone more with amusement than a desire to decapitate. He stood just off to the side, as if he didn't want to commit.

I decided he was my favorite.

Val's grandmother held her face in spindly hands, smiled brightly. "Ah, *mi cariño*. You brought your appetite, *sí*? And a friend?"

"Yes, but I think he only came for your paella, *Abuelita*."

They all turned to me, and I stepped into the light of their attention. "It's true. I'm a sucker for paella, and from what Val's told me, I might be spoiled forever after tasting yours."

The old woman laughed, shuffling toward me with arms outstretched. I bent when she reached me, and she placed her hands on my face, her skin paper-thin.

"Tell me your name, *príncipe*."

"I'm Sam. Thank you for having me, *Abuelita*."

"Thank you for coming with our Valentina." She searched my face, her lips in a sly smile and eyes twinkling. "*Qué lindo*." Her hands moved to my shoulders, then my arms, giving them a squeeze. "*Muy fuerte.*" She leaned in, saying conspiratorially, "You know, *príncipe,* Valentina has hips made for babies."

"Oh my God, *Abuela,*" Val groaned. "Mama, please?"

Her mother laughed. "Come on, Mama," she said, taking *Abuelita* by the arms. "It's nice to meet you, Sam. I'm Victoria. This is my father, Matias, my husband, Sean, and our sons, Dante, Francisco, Maximus, and Alejandro."

Val's father stepped forward and extended his hand. "Good to meet you, Sam. I've heard a lot about you."

I took it, clasping it firmly, pumping it with a friendly shake and a sideways smile. "Pleasure to meet you, sir. If what you've heard is from Dante, I'll go ahead and see myself out."

He laughed, a genuinely amused sound, touched with surprise. "You'll learn soon enough that Val's opinion counts more than all four of her brothers put together."

Max faked a cough, masking the word *lameculos* with impressive skill.

I had no idea what it meant, but it couldn't have been good. This was confirmed by the look Val's dad shot at him.

"*Cállate,*" *Abuelita* said with the flick of her hands. "*Fósforo.* Don't listen to them. They are just matches, quick to flame, easy to put out." She snapped her fingers and gave her grandsons a look that had them glancing at their shoes.

"It smells incredible," I said, wandering over to the stove where a simmering pan sat, sizzling with black rice and seafood.

"Mama makes paella like I've never had before," Victoria said from my elbow.

Abuela waved her hand again and made a sound of dismissal. "When you've made it your whole life, it's not so hard. Have you ever been to *España,* Sam?"

"No, I've always wanted to go to Barcelona."

It was *Abuelo's* turn to make a dismissive noise. "Everyone wants *Barça*. Where you need to go is Madrid. *That* is where you find culture. Food and *cava* and flamenco." He curled his fingers in a wave, plucking the strings of his guitar without looking. I could almost see a dancer in my mind, stomping her heels to the beat.

"Dinner is almost ready," Victoria said. "Boys, will you set the table, please?"

"I'll help," I offered.

Val laughed, a tittering sound that indicated her nerves. "You don't have to do that."

"I want to," I said, reaching for a stack of plates as four hurricane-lobos descended like the thunderhead she'd warned me of.

"We'll help, too," Dante said, wearing a wolf smile if I'd ever seen one.

"Great. Grab the knives," I said, shifting to make room. "And I'll follow you in."

Dante humphed. "Maybe you're smarter than you look—" I almost smiled until he added, "—but I doubt it."

Her face pinched in fury. "Leave him alone, Dante, or I swear to God—"

"Val, come here and help me with this, would you?" her mom asked from across the room.

Val gave me an apologetic and mildly terrified look. Then, she pinned Dante with one that I was surprised didn't actually make him combust on sight.

"Coming," she said.

I waited patiently while they gathered up glasses and wine and cutlery, and one by one, they filed past me into the dining room. Each took the opportunity to eyeball me. Franco was last, his glare punctuated by a smirk and a small shrug.

We moved around the long, rustic table in a silent assembly line. Knife, fork, glass, napkin, and plate—me—last.

"So, what do you want with my sister, Haddad?" Dante's voice was as fiery as wood coals. "Because whatever it is, I know it can't be good."

Knife, fork, glass, napkin, plate, shift.

"Would you believe me if I said I just want to make her happy?"

A laugh from the quartet, dry and distrustful.

"Not a chance."

I nodded. "Figured. I also figured there's nothing I can say to convince you. Give me a little time, and I'll prove it to you."

Dante glanced at his knife, the light glinting off the blade. "Why do I have the sneaking suspicion you're full of shit?"

"Because you're a suspicious guy. It's the only reason I ended up with Shannon instead of you."

His square jaw clamped shut and flexed. "Fuck you, Haddad."

"I don't mean it like that. It's part of who you are, man. If you trusted people, you'd get the girl more often."

Knife didn't move, and fork, glass, and napkin waited, eyes shifting between us.

"Please don't stab me with a dinner knife. I don't think she'd ever forgive you."

A dry laugh through his nose eased the tension only marginally. We shifted around the table.

"If people were worth trusting, maybe I'd agree. But you don't know what she's been through. You don't know what bullshit she's put up with. And if you hurt her, I swear to God—"

"Listen, if I hurt her, I'll come back here of my own free will and let you put that steak knife to good use. I know I don't deserve her, and I know you don't have a reason to trust me, but I mean it—I just want to make her happy for as long as she'll have me. That's it. That's all. I know you've heard about me, but I'd bet you've never heard me to be a liar."

Dante assessed me, his jaw muscle bouncing. The other brothers shared a look.

"I'll beat your face inside out, *gilipollas*. You so much as make her *think* about crying, and I'll come and find you in your fancy apartment and bust your teeth like a stack of plates. You hear me?"

"Loud and clear." I found myself smiling.

When I set down my last plate, I stepped around the table and extended a hand. He rolled his eyes and swatted it away, though playfully.

"Don't press your luck, dickhead."

A chuckle rolled through them, and I realized I'd passed some sort of test. Tentatively at least.

Val burst into the room. Her eyes darted from face to face.

"Dante," she warned, "I told you to leave him alone."

"Please. When have you ever known me to leave a guy alone who wants to date you? Especially not an immoral fuck like Haddad." He shot me a look.

Pain flashed behind her eyes at the mention of my past, and for the first time ever, I felt a pang of regret. I'd done nothing wrong, deceived no one. But that truth hurt her all the same.

And I hated it.

I stepped to her side. "It's all right, Val. They're just looking out for you. If the tables were turned, I probably wouldn't have let me walk through the front door, never mind sit at the dinner table. No hard feelings. Right, guys?"

They grumbled their agreement.

She let out a worried sigh, her brows together. "You four have run off every guy who's ever come around. Please, leave him alone."

Max laughed. "Poor Sammy, you need *conejita* to stick up for you?"

My lips flattened. "I don't need anyone to stick up for me. But I really think you ought to respect your sister whether you agree with her or not. And if *you* make her unhappy, then I suppose you'll have to answer to me. I meant what I said."

Rather than argue, Dante watched me for a moment with a glint of—was that appreciation? "Fair enough." He jerked his chin at his brothers. "Come on. I think we could all use a beer."

They filed out just like they'd filed in—with a glare and a scowl. But we'd come to an agreement, shaky though it might be, and I was calling that a win. Or at the very least, a draw.

She sighed when the last wide back disappeared. "God, I'm so sorry. Are you okay?"

I laughed. "Of course I'm okay. We just had a little talk, that's all. I like them. They're scary as fuck, but I like them."

Val leaned into me and sighed again. "This is stressing me out, Sam."

I wrapped my arms around her and kissed the top of her head. "Hey, don't worry about me. I knew I was walking in to a firing squad, and I came willingly. If I'm remembering right, I think I even invited myself."

She chuckled. "I don't understand you."

I leaned back and captured her chin in my thumb and forefinger to tilt her face to mine. "What's there to understand? I want to be the guy you bring home to meet your mom. I want to be good enough for you. I want Dante to see I'm serious. There's nothing to understand beyond the fact that I want you, and I want to make you happy, whatever the cost. That's it. It's that simple. So just let me."

Everything about her softened—her body, her face, her eyes, her lips. And so, I kissed those lips and told her without words that truth once more.

I LEANED BACK FROM THE table, so full that if I'd had another bite, I was sure paella would have spilled out of my nose.

Her brothers wore similar expressions. Alex held his fist up to his lips and stifled a burp.

"Hands down the best I've ever had, *Abuela*. Val, tell me you know how to cook this and that you can teach me. Otherwise I'm gonna be banging on *Abuelita's* door for it weekly."

Abuela laughed, her cheeks high and round. "Or *conejita* could bring you back again. I'll feed you whenever you want, *príncipe*."

Without any direction, Val's brothers and father stood and began clearing plates. It seemed to be the way of things; the women cooked, and the men cleaned. I stood to pitch in, but Val stayed me with a smile.

"Let them," she said quietly. "You're our guest. It was bad enough manners that they let you help set the table. *Abuela* won't stand to let you help clean, too."

"It's true. I won't," *Abuela* interjected.

Val's mom laughed. "Come on, girls. Let's get the vermouth. Papa, will you play?"

"*Sí, cariño,*" he answered, shifting his chair back, using the arms to lift his weight.

The women left, Val last, offering the sweetest smile before she disappeared into the kitchen.

I sighed, sitting back, not realizing that *Abuelo* had returned until he was almost on me. In each hand was the neck of a guitar.

"Valentina says you play. Will you play with me?" His voice was old Spanish leather, tanned and smooth.

"I'd be honored," I answered honestly.

I took the guitar, a beautiful instrument. The strings were soft, the sound full and thick when I strummed.

Abuelo's head bent, his face untroubled. There was no concentration, only a flickering emotion on his brow, a hint of a furrow deepening, the crease between flexing, relaxing. And he played. His fingers stroked the strings in a blur, every note in perfect time, perfect harmony. For a moment, I watched a master in awe and reverence.

And then I joined him as he'd asked.

It was a simple addition, a quiet succession of chords to whisper under his melody. When he sped, I sped. When he crescendoed, so did I. When he slowed and let the notes sing for themselves, I followed every lead.

When the song ended, my throat tightened. Matias smiled at me.

"Love is music. It's learning when to be loud and when to be soft. It's riding the scales up and down. Learning the curves and strings to play the song of your heart. You have to know when to lead and when to follow. When you're wrong and when you're right. Love is music, *hijo mío*. It is the greatest music there is." He absently fiddled the strings, a brilliant melody exhaling into the room. "I won't scare you like my grandsons. I won't tell you not to love her. I'll only tell you to love her well. Love her like you love music, and she is yours. Love her any less than that, and she is lost. Love her with all of you, or leave her to love someone else."

My lips parted to speak, but the words caught in my throat. So I nodded just as the women entered the room again with glasses, oranges, smiles, and a bottle of vermouth.

He held my eyes and nodded back before picking up his melody. I followed him in, working only to complement him, feeling the warmth of her hand on my shoulder and the warmth of my heart in my chest.

Love. The word of a thousand sonnets. The word whispered across a thousand years. A word I'd never considered outside of my family. A word I'd never sought.

A word that brushed against my heart like fingertips.

Love is music.

The simple profundity of those three words struck me deep. And when I looked up into her smiling face, I felt the notes in my soul.

BELIEVER

SAM

The room was a chorus of noise once more as we pulled on our coats and said goodbye. *Abuela* kissed both my cheeks and told me to be a good boy. Victoria smiled as brightly as Val and sent me off with a container of paella for lunch the next day. Sean shook my hand with a nod and a smile of approval, and Matias tipped his fedora from where he sat.

The four horsemen scowled at me from the back of the room, and I touched my finger to my forehead in salute. Dante jerked his chin in acknowledgment.

We said our farewells all the way down the stairs, waving once more before the door closed.

Elm leaves crunched under our feet as we left the brownstone behind us.

All the way to the theater, we chatted, though my mind was occupied, processing the last few hours, the last few days. I didn't know how I'd gotten here, how I'd found this place. How my world had tilted just a little, just enough to change how I saw things.

No, I didn't know how I'd gotten here, but it was the only place I wanted to be.

The theater was bustling when we walked in, the pit already dark. Musicians played disjointed bits and bobs, the sounds floating over each other in streams, filling the air with anticipation of showtime.

I walked Val to her chair, spent a minute trying to make her laugh. And when I'd achieved my goal and gave her a long, searing, mildly-inappropriate-for-a-workplace kiss, I headed toward the back of the pit where my instrument waited for me.

Unfortunately, that was not the only thing waiting for me.

Ian was leaning against the wall, arms folded, ankles crossed, lips smiling.

Everything about him felt like a lie.

"Well, well, well. Look at what the Spitshine dragged in."

I ignored the insult to Val, contrary to what I wanted to do, which was put his head through a wall.

But that wouldn't help matters. So I smiled.

"How's it going?" I asked without giving a single shit.

"Fine. I didn't see you at the club last night, but I figured you had a date. I've gotta admit, Sammy—I didn't think it'd be Val."

"Well, I'm just full of surprises."

A laugh. "You're telling me. Imagine my shock that you were with her when the bet was done. I'd ask you what the story was, but after that kiss? Pretty sure the whole orchestra knows. You finally fucked Susie Spitshine."

Every muscle in my body tensed in unison. "Don't fucking call her that. And it's none of your goddamn business. Not anymore. Bet's up. Game over."

"Sure, sure. But what's your angle? To be honest, I'm floored you waited this long to nail her. Think you'll have her out of your system by the weekend? There's a pack of new chicks at the club, just aching to be taught a lesson."

"Guess you'll have them all to yourself. I'm staying put for a while."

One eyebrow rose with the corner of his mouth. "Good one, Sammy."

I shrugged and picked up my bass. He watched me tune it in silence.

"You're serious," he said after a minute.

"You're the one with a penchant for elaborate jokes, not me."

"You"—incredulous chuckling—"and Susie Spitshine. Dating. For real."

"Yes. And if you fucking call her that again, I'll break your nose," I said with the seriousness of a cardio surgeon elbow deep in a rib cage.

Another laugh, amused and a little too loud. "Come on. You're fucking with me, right?"

"Do I look like I'm fucking with you?"

"Not really, which is tripping me out. I mean, you can't actually mean to date her."

"Why not?"

He ticked off his fingers. "Because you're a player. Because you don't know shit about women's emotions. Because you don't know *how*."

"Maybe she's the perfect person to teach me."

His eyes narrowed. "You honestly think you can be one of those happily-ever-after people? That you can just change? That's never gonna happen."

"You're a fucking cynic."

"I'm a fucking *realist*. Guys like us don't get happy endings."

"Guys like *you* maybe. I don't subscribe to that line."

He watched me, the darkness behind his eyes hard and cold. For a long, pregnant moment, he was silent. Then, a smile meant to be genuine. But in the tight lines of his face was betrayal. "Well, I never thought I'd see the day. Sam Haddad, all settled down with the little awkward trumpet player and all their hopes and dreams and fucking rainbows and happily ever afters. Wonders never cease."

I turned to lay the full weight of my gaze on him. He'd said the right things with a tone that was all wrong.

"Angles, right? What's yours?" I asked.

"Can't a guy just be happy for his buddy?" He pushed off the wall and rolled his eyes, the tension gone with a snap. "God, you're so fucking paranoid. If nothing else, I'm glad you got laid. Your celibacy was disturbing, man. So congrats on the ass," he said as he passed.

I watched him walk to the drum cage. The bet was over. Now Ian knew I was with Val. Everything was fine. I had nothing to worry about.

Ian would never betray me.

I turned my gaze to Val as she set up her music. The light of her stand lamp highlighted the curve of her forearms, the curls framing her face.

And I hoped to God I was right.

VAL'S ARM SLIPPED INTO THE warm space between my coat and shirt when we hit the sidewalk outside of the theater. "I can't believe you survived dinner with my family."

I adjusted the strap of her trumpet bag so the case wouldn't bump her. "And I didn't even end up with my shoelaces tied together or poisoned or anything."

Val laughed. "I dunno. Pretty sure *Abuelita* wanted to drug you and keep you for herself."

"If she made me paella every day, I'd go willingly. Really, I'd be ripping her off."

"I told you my brothers were a nightmare."

"No, you said they were a furry hurricane. A furricane. And I'm not worried about them. They said as long as I don't make you cry, I'm safe. Little do they know that's already on my vision board."

"Oh my God," she said on a chuckle. "I just imagined you sitting in the middle of your bedroom floor, listening to Katy Perry while you cut pictures out of *Seventeen* and wallpaper them to your closet door."

"I prefer Taylor Swift and *Cosmopolitan*, but you're not far off." I tucked her into me a little tighter. "I had a thought."

"Mmm? What's that?"

"We shouldn't go dancing."

"No?"

I smiled at the trace of disappointment in her voice.

"No. We should go home instead and spend the night in bed."

She squeezed my middle. "Yes, please. Tomorrow, we'll dance."

"Tomorrow, your birthday."

A sheepish laugh. "It's not a big deal. Please don't make it a big deal. And tonight, your bed sounds like the only place I want to be."

"No promises. And good."

With a sigh, she settled into my side. We were quiet on the walk back, a content, introspective silence that never came between us. It was something we shared.

The night had held the potential for disaster, but I'd made it through unscathed. I had Dante's tenuous approval, had eaten the meal of a lifetime, and had played with her grandfather and bowed to a master.

It had been a good night.

I wondered if she'd ever brought a man home before. From what I knew about her, I'd be willing to bet the answer was no. But she'd allowed me to crash that dinner, and the allowance was a testament to her trust in me and her faith in us.

Worry licked at my heart like fog. She trusted me. And I was responsible for nurturing that, protecting it.

I didn't want to fail. Not at anything, but especially not at this. I couldn't fail *her*.

Ian crossed my mind again. I hadn't been able to shake our conversation, the sense that it wasn't over even though he'd said it was. At least, I thought he'd said it was.

It'd better be over, I thought, shifting to press a kiss into her hair.

Ian had no reason to bring it up again. There was nothing left to say.

Possession surged in my chest. Possession and protection.

She walked up the stairs of my building with me trailing behind her by a step. And when I looked up, all I could see was Val. The curve of her cheek. Her curly hair. Her shoulder, her arm.

All I could see was her.

I stopped, tugging her hand until she stopped, too.

When she looked back, amusement and curiosity flickered across her brow. When she saw I wasn't budging, she turned to face me.

She was far enough above me that I had to look up to see her. The hallway was dim, lit only by an old, out-of-style dome light, obscured by her head. The light lit her hair up like a halo, casting her face in shadow.

She cupped my jaw and smiled, lips together. "What is it, Sam?"

"It's you, everything about you. I want … I want so much. I want to earn your smiles, your laughter. Your heart. Your pleasure is my pleasure. I didn't know that your happiness would be my own, too. There's so much I didn't know."

Softly, she laughed. "And here I thought you were supposed to be teaching me."

I climbed one step, bringing me level with her lips. "Oh, no. It was you who were teaching me all along."

And before she could speak, I pressed my lips to her sweeter ones, breathed her in for a moment. Just a moment. Felt the curve of her waist, the warmth of her skin, the beat of her heart.

Up the stairs of my building we climbed. I opened the door, and she strode in, lazily stripping off her coat. She tossed it on the back of the couch and crossed her arms over her waist, grabbing handfuls of her shirt. With a glance over her shoulder and a seductive smile in my direction, her hands rose, her shirt rising with it, exposing first the curve of her waist, then her ribs, her shoulder blades. Her curly hair spilled out of the neck, brushing her shoulders. And then she tossed it away.

She never stopped walking.

I shed my jacket, my shoes, my shirt, following the trail of her clothes. She disappeared into the dark portal of my doorframe.

When I passed into the darkness, I reached for the light. And when the bulbs of my lamps flared, there she was.

She sat perched on the end of my bed, her eyes bottomless and lips wet. She was constructed solely of smooth, tan curves, shoulder and arms, breasts and hips, thigh to knee to calf to the tip of every round toe. Shadows sank into every valley, light brushed every peak.

And her eyes, those endless eyes, called me, whispered my name.

I strode across the room, caught her face in my hands, felt the silky strands of her hair against my knuckles, her skin against my fingertips. For a moment, I was a captive despite holding her in my palms.

And then I kissed her.

The girl who had hidden her body from me had gone, replaced by a woman who wanted to be seen. Those places she hated were forgotten in the safety of my arms—she knew I wouldn't betray her. She knew I wouldn't make her feel anything but perfect and desired.

Because that was the truth. And my honesty had affected her, changed her. Made her a believer.

She sighed into my mouth, her hands working my belt open,

then my pants down, reaching for me as I stepped out of them. Her fingers trailed the length of me, the tip of me. I leaned into her. She broke the kiss to sigh against my swollen lips.

"Lie down," she whispered, and I did, though not before kissing her again and not without taking her with me.

She lay a trail of wet, slow kisses down my chest, her fingers brushing my nipples. Down further, down the planes of my abs to the ridge of my hips. Her hands roamed, touching, teasing, never the place where I wanted her most. That place was aware of every fringe touch—a lock of her hair brushing my length, the curve of her cheek skimming the sensitive skin of my crown, the tip of her nose as she kissed the eager skin so low between my hips.

Just when I thought I couldn't take it, she wrapped her fingers around my shaft and stroked. Her face rose, her lips parting, her tongue darting out to slick them. I gathered her hair, cupped the back of her head, watched her, lashes down, nose small, mouth open as she descended. Hot and wet, soft and slick—the sensation overwhelmed me, amplified by the sight of my cock disappearing into her, inch by inch.

Her moan sent a vibration down my shaft and deep into my body.

No, this was not the same girl who had asked me to kiss her so she'd know the good from the bad. This wasn't the girl who hadn't dated and had never had an orgasm by a man. This was a new being altogether, one who touched me with all the confidence of a woman who knew what she wanted and what she needed.

And she knew exactly how to get it.

I lay there underneath her, holding her hair, trying to breathe, trying to hang on. She picked up her pace, bringing me up with her, my ass flexed and hips forward. She slowed, let me wait for only a breath before bringing me to the edge again.

I drew my hips away, held her head where it was, exiting her mouth with a quiet pop. I breathed her name, and she smiled, climbing up my body at my command.

She paused when she reached my lips to kiss me, still on all fours instead of spread across me. I grabbed her ass and squeezed, telling her where I wanted her, but instead of acquiescing, she broke the kiss and reached for my nightstand.

Her breasts were in my face, and I took the invitation, pressing them into each other, testing their weight, bringing the peaked tip of one to my lips, my mouth, my tongue. She sucked in a breath at the contact, lowering her hips enough that I could reach between her legs and stroke her.

But the connection was brief. She backed up, rose up on her knees, her hands tearing open a condom, her fingers on my cock, the condom rolling on. And I watched her, letting her do what she would. Because that was what she wanted.

And what she wanted, I wanted.

My hands shifted on her thighs, my eyes locked on the rippling flesh at the apex. She guided me, stood me upright, stroked herself with my tip. And she spread those legs, those glorious fucking thighs, and sank onto me, not stopping until she was flesh to flesh against me.

I pulsed inside her. She flexed in answer.

Her body was a wave, her palms resting on my chest, her breasts caught in the cage of her arms.

I watched, jaw clenched and hips high.

My eyes traced her curves, each one magnified, exaggerated by the stretch of her body. Her shoulders high and tight. Her heavy breasts bouncing with every revolution of her hips. The smooth trough from her ribs to the bend in her waist. The grand swell of her ass. I reached for that swell, held it in my palm, let my hand ride the rhythm of her body.

Faster she moved, tighter she held, her nails abrading my skin, her ass bouncing. Her face pinched, her eyes closed tight, her face turned to the side, covered by her hair. I traced her jaw, swept her hair away, and for the briefest moment, she opened her eyes. Fear was there, but when she met my gaze, when she saw me, it dissipated, softened her face, arched her back, gave her peace in her pleasure.

She lost herself wholly, committed completely. She took my hand and laid it on her breast, rolled her hips faster until her ass slapped my thighs. And she came, squeezing me so tight, I couldn't breathe. Gasping and writhing, she came to me, mewling and grinding. She came for me, wanted me to see her, wanted me to watch.

She granted me the gift of her fearlessness, of her brazen desire.

As she slowed, I sat, sweeping her up by the face and the neck to kiss her, to pull her into my body, to tell her I saw her. I understood. I wanted. I needed.

My arm hooked around her waist to flip her over, but she shifted in the opposite direction, stopping me. With her palm on my chest, she pushed me to lie down again, still astride me, riding me gently, knees buried in the bed, nestled into my ribs. Her hands trailed up her body, over her breasts, up her neck, into her hair, stretching the lines of her body out like art.

Once again, her hands braced my chest, and with a mournful shift of her hips, she released me.

Her smile said to trust her. And I did, though my hands sought every inch of skin they could touch.

I didn't realize what she was doing until it was nearly done. In a breath, she was straddling me again, though this time backward.

Her palms found my thighs, her feet tucked into my sides, her ass—God, that *ass*—in front of me. My hands were full of it, pulling her cheeks apart to feast my eyes upon the puckered hollow, the fluttering flesh beneath, her swollen lips. Her hips rose higher, and my hand slid to my cock, hooking the base, raising it to meet her.

Once again, she slipped the tip of me into her heat. Once again, she lowered her hips.

But this time, I could see everything.

She swallowed me whole, her skin pink and slick. Her ass spilling from my hands, the slap of our skin, the force I pulled her down on me. The vision of my body joining her body, of entering her, of her holding me, the hourglass of her body and the gentle moans in time to every thrust, every wave, every motion as we came together and fell apart.

Noisily, I breathed. Tightly, I held her. Deeply, I drove into the center of her until I reached the end. The end of her. The end of me. The end of my composure and the end of my will.

I came with a thundering pulse, hard and hot and blinding as she whispered her yeses in sighs and cries, and I moved her body at the speed mine needed.

And then I slowed her, settled deep in her. She shifted her hips side to side. I felt every movement from tip to root.

I sat, bringing my chest to her back, winding my arms around her waist, laying kisses across her shoulders, her spine, the base of her neck when she arched into me. But it wasn't enough.

Shifting, I rolled us, pulling out of her in the same motion. I held her against me as I lowered us onto the bed. Our legs tangled. Arms hooking and hands searching. And we kissed, skin to skin, heart to heart.

It was a long time before we slowed, a long time before we were sated.

For a moment, I just looked down into her face, and she looked up into mine.

This was what it felt like. Intimacy. I'd known so many women, known their bodies. But I'd never known body and soul. Mind and heart. They amplified every physical touch, threaded every breath with something deeper, something more.

I should have been afraid. I realized it distantly, like a light on the horizon, a curiosity.

But I wasn't afraid. Not of her. Not of my own heart or feelings. Because it was as I'd told her—I didn't do things even halfway. I went all in.

And now that I knew what I wanted, I committed completely.

There was no choice. Only fact. And the path before me was simple.

When she closed her eyes and pulled me in for another kiss, I knew I wouldn't miss a single step.

MAKE A WISH

SAM

The music bounced. We bounced. The whole world bounced with us.

I spun Val out and tugged to bring her back to me. Spinning and laughing and perfect and mine. The second I could reach her, I grabbed her ribs in one hand and her hand in the other, pulling her around with our hips and feet in perfect, harmonious time.

The club was hopping. Literally hopping, a sea of heads bobbing around us to the music. All except for one.

Ian stood near the edge of the crowd, eyes narrowed and locked on me.

On *us*.

I'd been ignoring his bitchy attitude all night, the snapping commands he'd thrown out during our set, the scathing looks that had been strikingly similar to the one he was directing at me right then. I found myself glaring back at him. But only for a second.

Then I remembered the girl in my arms and forgot all about Ian. Mostly.

The song ended, and we stopped to offer our applause.

Amelia appeared at Val's elbow. "Come on. You apparently have to take birthday shots."

She laughed. "Seriously?"

"House rule. That's what Benny said at least. Come on!" She tugged at Val's arm. "They're on the house. Ladies only though. Sorry, Sam."

I shrugged, laughing. "I'll try to move on."

"Well, if they're on the house, I guess I really can't say no," she said before lifting up on her tiptoes to press a kiss into my cheek. "Be right back."

"Be right here." I smiled like a fool, slipping my hands into my pockets.

She walked past Ian, not seeing him following her with his eyes like he wanted to douse her in gasoline and light a match.

My smile flattened, my jaw popping. I strode over to him, cool on the outside, molten fucking lava on the inside.

"Something on your mind, Jackson?"

He sipped his whiskey. "You're awfully fucking chipper."

"And you're awfully fucking bitter. What's your problem?"

"Just processing my disbelief over you and Susie Spitshine."

"I told you not to call her that, asshole."

He chuffed and took another drink.

"What do you want? What's your damage?"

"What do I want? God, you are so fucking naive. Guess. Guess what my fucking problem is."

My jaw clenched. "You're pissed you lost your wingman."

"Don't flatter yourself, Sam. Try again." He took a drink.

My brows drew together. "You're mad you lost the bet."

"Warmer."

And my frown fully set on my face. "You're mad because I won?"

"Hotter."

"You're mad ... because I'm with Val?"

"Ding, ding, ding. Somebody get this guy a drink."

"But why?" I asked, searching my brain like a man who'd lost something vital. "I don't get it. Why would you give a shit that I have a girlfriend?"

His eyes narrowed, his face pinched, his lungs expanded. And he snapped like a firecracker. "No, you *don't* fucking get it, do you? You are such a dumb motherfucker. Always the honest one, always the hero. Your fatal flaw? Taking everything at face value. You trust everyone. *Everyone.* Do you have any idea how easy it is to play you?" His jaw tightened, his spine stretching to give him a couple of inches over me. "One of three things was supposed to happen with the bet; you were going to feel like a piece of shit for leading her on, or you were going to hurt her. Or—my best-case scenario—both."

Fury rose in my chest, sending tingling heat down to my fingertips. "You didn't ever want her." I realized the depth of my mistake far too late. "You just wanted to fuck with me."

He shook his head at me like the fucking idiot I was. "*I'm* always the one who gets slapped or gets a drink thrown in my face. And you're always riding in to save the day. I'm fucking sick of it. I'm sick of living in the shadow of your high fucking horse. It's *your* turn to wear the black hat. It's *your* turn to be the bad guy."

"You're fucking sick, man."

"Sure, right," he said with a laugh. "Tell yourself that all you want. You act like you're so much better than me, but you're not." A smile as friendly as a knife slash split his lips. "Although I've got one card left to play."

Cold awareness shot up my spine. "Don't."

"I wonder what Val would think of our little wager. Think she'll be hurt when she hears the whole thing was a joke? That you wouldn't have asked out a fat girl if you hadn't been—"

My hands shot out, connecting with his shoulders, sending him reeling. His glass hit the ground with a crash and splash of whiskey and ice. A couple of people next to us squealed and jumped out of the way, watching us from a distance.

I took a step, arched over him, closed my fist in his shirt, and pulled. "If you ever call her fat again, I'll fucking rip your face off and spit down your throat. And I swear to God, Ian. Don't you say a fucking word to her about the bet. Not. One. Word. Or I will ruin you. Do you hear me? *Ruin.*"

Ian laughed. That motherfucker kicked his head back and laughed that cold, soulless laugh I hated so deeply. "Oh, Sammy boy. I'm not fucking scared of you. You always were kind of a pussy."

My hands tightened, one on his shirt, the other coiled to fly.

But in the second of my hesitation, his wicked eyes darted behind me. "Oh, hey, Val. Lookin' good tonight."

Her hand in the crook of my elbow was the only thing that stopped me. "Sam? Is everything okay?"

I let him go, smoothed his shirt, patted the spot on his chest too hard. "Everything's fine. Ian here was just leaving. Weren't you, Ian?"

"Who, me? Oh, no. I have the whole night ahead of me. Pussy to slay, secrets to tell." Evil. Pure evil in his eyes, behind his smile. "I'll see you later, Val."

I watched him walk toward the bar for a long moment.

Val twined her arm around mine. "What was that about?"

I looked down at her and smiled, feeling the thin veneer of the expression on my face. I was a fool. A guilty, sorrowful, unworthy fool. Everything I wanted was at risk, waiting under the hammer's shadow for impact.

I'd have to tell her—and soon. But not tonight. Not on her

birthday. Tonight, I'd keep her away from Ian. I wouldn't let her out of my sight. And tomorrow, I'd tell her the truth about everything.

Tomorrow, I'd find a way.

"Don't worry about it, babe," I said with my heart in a vise. "Gimme a kiss and let me take you for a turn, and we'll forget that asshole even exists."

She smiled and kissed me.

And for a moment, it worked.

VAL

Sam never stopped twirling me, and I never wanted him to. Death by spinning, aside from sounding like a punishment in Willy Wonka, wouldn't be a bad way to go. Especially not by Sam's hand.

I didn't miss his avoidance of Ian, nor did I miss Ian's constant appraisal of us. He stood on the fringes of the crowd, watching. Waiting for something. For what, I had no idea.

Honestly, I was too happy to care. My curiosity as to why Sam had been ready to pound Ian's face to a pulp had been watered down by the magic of the night.

All my friends were at the club—Amelia and Katherine, Rin and Court. Even Dante had come, and he'd been dancing with the same girl all night. I'd even say he looked happy, which was a feat of its own.

And all the while, Sam was by my side. When I went to the bar, he was ordering my drinks and carrying them back for my friends. Wherever I went, there he was. Always touching me somewhere— my hand, my shoulder, my back, my face, my hair—as if his hands were thirsty for me.

It wasn't until the night was over that he pulled me in for a searing kiss, dipping me to the whoops and whistles of the people around us.

When we straightened up, he smiled that smile that told me he was up to something and kissed my nose. "I'll be right back. Stay right here."

I laughed and leaned into him. "I won't move a muscle."

"Good." With one more kiss for the road, he turned and headed toward the stage.

When I looked to my friends, they were all tied up in conversation. So I turned to the dance floor and contented myself to watch.

"Heya, Val."

For a reason unknown, Ian's voice startled me. I tried to smile, unsure what my role was. I had no idea what had happened between him and Sam, but I didn't want to be rude either.

So, I gave him a halfass smile and said, "Hey."

"Kudos for reeling in the uncatchable fish."

I hesitated for a beat, not knowing what to say. I finally settled on, "Thanks."

"I mean, who knew our little bet would go so far?"

My heart stuttered, lungs frozen. "I'm sorry?" I whispered, turning to look at him.

He smiled amenably. "The bet. When Sam said he could date you for a month, I didn't believe he could do it. He sure showed me." His laugh was anything but happy.

A tingling crawled up my spine. I couldn't speak. There were no words, not in my head or mouth or the world.

His face softened in mock pity. "Oh my God. You didn't know. You really thought…" A laugh, a cold, cruel sound that matched the wind in my hollow chest. "You actually thought he liked you." His smile fell. "Sam is a player, Val. Always has been, always will be. There's a reason he's never had a girlfriend, and opportunity isn't it. He doesn't *want* one. You were nothing but a bet to him, a means to beat me in a game. I'm sorry he hurt you. But don't take it too hard, kid. It's just his way."

There was no air. I pressed my hand to my stomach and dragged in one shallow breath at a time as tears pricked my eyes.

"What was the prize?" I croaked.

"What's that?" he asked, leaning in.

"What was the prize?" I repeated louder, clearer.

He smiled his monstrous smile and answered, "Sleeping with you. What else?"

The music stopped, and the guitarist of the band onstage stepped to the mic as my world was reduced to the thumping of my pulse and the bomb that had gone off in my chest.

"Hey there, Sway—we've got a special birthday in the house. You guys might have seen Val around. She's played up here and shaken her bobby socks out there with you all, and tonight is her night. Happy birthday, Val! We're so happy you're ours. Come on, everybody, let's sing to her!"

The crowd in front of me parted, and in there was Sam, smiling and beautiful, a sheet cake in his hands and his face illuminated by candlelight. And three hundred people began to sing me "Happy Birthday" in what should have been one of the most epic moments of my life.

He stopped when he reached me and the song ended. And for a brief moment, there was nothing but silence.

"Make a wish, Val," he said, his voice velvety and deep and right.

I blinked back my tears and drew in a breath. Saw recognition cross his face and felt my heart break. And with my wish on my tongue, I blew out my candles, every one.

SAM

The candles went out, the crowd around us cheered, and my world came to a grinding halt.

The look on her face told me everything, named every sin.

"Val, let me explain—"

"I think I got the gist of it." The words were singed and smoking in trembling tendrils.

The crowd around us went on talking, the music starting up again, and we stood on an island in the midst of it all.

"It…it's not what you think—" I started.

"So you *didn't* have a bet with Ian about me?"

I opened my mouth to argue but closed it again.

She took a deep breath, her eyes gleaming with tears. "At least you didn't lie to me about it." Her eyes dropped when her feet moved, and before I could stop her, she was brushing past me. "Goodbye, Sam. Please don't ever fucking speak to me again."

I watched her helplessly for a moment with her birthday cake in my hands before shoving it at some faceless guy standing nearby.

"Wait," I called after her, reaching her easily. When I touched her arm, she jerked away from me. "Please, I didn't want to hurt you."

"Then you shouldn't have taken out a fucking *bet* on me," she shot, turning to me with hurt etched into every line of her face, shining in the tears collecting in her lashes. "I thought…I thought this was…" She shook her head, her chin flexing. "It was all a game to you. You never wanted me. I should have known."

Guilt. Horror. Complete abhorrence ripped through me like thunder. "That's not true. Val, you have to believe me—the way I feel about you is not a joke or a game."

"Believe you? How can I trust you when everything that's happened is a lie? I was a fool for ever thinking we could be more.

I was a fool for ever wishing for more." She backed away, her arms around her waist. "Well, you've won your bet. I hope it was worth it."

"Please," I begged, my throat closing up. I reached for her, and she let me pull her into my arms. "Please, Val. I only wanted to protect you. I didn't want to hurt you, and now…now, I—"

"It's too late," she said softly, her cheeks wet with tears. "Let me go, Sam."

Never, my heart called.

But my arms did as she'd asked.

I swallowed the stone in my throat.

"I'm sorry." The words were low, heavy with a thousand regrets.

She met my eyes with infinite sadness and said, "Me too."

And then I watched her walk away.

"Shame, isn't it?"

His voice flipped a switch in me, a murderous switch with a razor's edge. I turned. I took a breath that gained me an inch of height. And with a roar, I cocked my fist and let it fly.

The crunch of his nose and the searing crack of my knuckles did nothing to satisfy me.

Ian wheeled back, clutching at his ruined nose, the word, "*Fuck!*" muffled by his hands. Crimson streams ran down his lips and chin, and when his hand moved to his side to reveal a snarl, his teeth were ringed with blood.

"Fuck you, Jackson. How could you do this to me? To her?"

"Cry me a fucking river, you high and mighty son of a bitch. You thought you had it all figured out? Well, go ahead and fix this, asshole. Shouldn't have taken the bet if you weren't prepared to lose."

"I didn't have a choice!" I raged, reaching for his shirtfront again. "It was either take the bet or subject her to *you*, and I'd spare her that any fucking day, at any fucking cost. I can't believe I thought you'd let me win. That's not how you roll, is it, Ian?" I shook him. "*Is it?* I should have told her from the start. I should have blown this whole thing up in *your* face. I should have known you'd fucking double cross me the second you could."

"The second I could?" He laughed. "You don't even know how long I've waited. This is so much fucking better. I knew it would be, if I waited long enough. How's it feel, Sammy boy? How's it feel to be the villain? How's it feel to be the bastard everyone hates? How's it f—"

This time, my fist connected with his eye in a shock that shot up to my elbow in a blinding burst of pain.

When I let him go, he dropped to the ground in a heap. A laughing, manic heap.

"Poor fucking Prince Charming."

"Fuck you, Ian." My aching fingers clenched. My pulse charged. My vision dimmed. My heart was already broken. "I want you to remember when your life falls apart that you fucking asked for this. *You* asked for this."

"Hey, Haddad?"

I turned to Dante's voice without enough time to duck his fist. He caught me in the jaw with a hook that sent me spinning. My vision darkened, flashing with my pulse against the pain.

"Jesus fucking Christ," I choked, hand on my aching jaw. When I stood, my fists rose halfheartedly. "I don't want to fight you, Dante."

"I don't want to fight you either, you stupid son of a bitch, but I made you a promise, and I keep my word. I knew you weren't for real. I fucking knew it." He stepped into me, his face hard as steel. "Don't you ever fucking come near my sister again. I'd hate to permanently fuck up that pretty face of yours, but I will."

"You don't understand," I croaked.

He folded his arms. "Enlighten me."

"I can't lose her. This whole thing was Ian... I was trying to save her, but I didn't... I didn't know. I didn't know she was everything I wanted. I didn't know I'd fall in love with her." The words were past my lips before I could reel them back in, the admission hitting me deep in the empty cavern of my chest.

Shock passed over his face, but it was gone as quickly as it had appeared. "Well then, you're in deeper shit than I realized. I mean it, Haddad. Leave her the fuck alone. Don't come around. Don't call. Don't push her, or you will answer to me. Do you hear me?"

I ran a hand over my face with an ancient weight tethered to my heart. "I hear you," I rasped.

"Prove it."

I nodded once.

With every eye on me and the silence of the club pressing me into the dirt, I did the only thing I could.

I walked away, dragging my busted heart behind me.

PIZZA CAKE

VAL

A gentle knock rapped on my bedroom door. I didn't bother wiping the tears from my cheeks.

"Come in," I said, not really caring if the person on the other side heard or not.

The door cracked, then opened. "Hey." It was Amelia, bearing a tray of food and a smile.

Katherine followed her with another tray and Rin was behind her with a third.

I didn't move to sit. I didn't speak either.

I hadn't moved from this spot since the moment I fell into it last night. There had been no sleep. Only a drifting in and out of consciousness between long stretches of tears.

Everything hurt. My raw nose. My thumping skull. My aching body. My shredded heart.

"We ordered your favorite meals from your favorite restaurants to cheer you up."

"There's no cake, is there? Because I never want to see another slice of cake as long as I live."

"No cake," Katherine assured me. "Drunken noodles, veggie pizza, tacos, lasagna, and gelato, but no cake."

I peeled myself off my mattress and propped myself upright. They set the trays on various flat surfaces around my room.

"Where do you want to start?" Katherine asked.

I extended a hand. "Drunken noodles. I am not afraid to cry into noodles."

Rin handed me the paper carton, and I sighed, grasping the chopsticks stuck in the mass of noodles.

"Did you get any sleep?" Rin asked.

"Not really." I poked around in the carton, wondering if I was even hungry. My empty stomach lurched in answer. So I shoveled a rude bite into my mouth, hoping I could at least make my belly happy.

"I just can't believe this." Amelia's eyes were impossibly big and sad and crystalline blue.

Katherine wore a slight frown. "I never thought Sam would participate in something so asinine."

I tried to sigh, but my breath hiccuped as I drew it in. "I both don't believe it and am not at all surprised. I always knew it was too good to be true. I just had no idea how horrible the truth was. I was just a joke. He never had feelings for me. He never wanted to hang out with me. He never wanted to even talk to me, and if it hadn't been for the bet, he wouldn't have. Everything we had was triggered by that lie."

Rin nodded in thought. "But does that make his feelings any less real now? Does it matter how it got started?"

"It was started by a cruel wager—an unwanted girl and the man everyone desires. The man who never dates dating the girl he'd never choose. I hope his feelings aren't real. I hope it was all a lie, every word. At least that way it'd be easier to bear."

Katherine gave me a look. "You don't honestly believe that, do you?"

I fished around in my noodles like the answers were buried somewhere in the tangle. "I don't know what I believe anymore. I don't know how to feel or what to think. I don't know how I'm supposed to g-go to work tonight and see his face. Ian's face, too. G-God, I am s-so stupid." My tears fell freely. "I can't believe I fell for all of it. I can't believe I played along. Do you think that was always his plan? The tutoring and fake dates and e-everything—that it was all just a way to reel me in?"

"If it was, he's a sociopath," Katherine said. "Sam doesn't strike me as a liar. And seeing you two together? I don't think he could have faked that. I saw him look at you when he thought no one was watching. A man doesn't look at a woman like that if he's playing her."

Rin nodded again. "He said he was trying to protect you. From Ian, right? That sounds more like the Sam we know. Maybe…maybe there's some explanation."

"I'm sure there is," I agreed sadly. "I just don't know if I want to hear it."

"Why not?" Amelia asked.

"Because there's nothing he can say that will change what he did and how it made me feel to learn the truth."

Their faces softened, saddened.

"There's nothing that can erase my humility and shame, knowing he never wanted me in the first place. There's nothing that could undo the pain of giving my trust to a man who betrayed it in such a merciless way. Did he even think about how I would feel? Did he even consider me at all, or was he only thinking of himself?" I shook my head. "It doesn't matter. I don't even want to know." I stuck my chopsticks into the carton and set it on my nightstand.

The doorbell rang.

We all exchanged glances before bolting out of my room and to Rin's where we could see the stoop from her window. Amelia reached it first and clapped her hand over her mouth in a gasp. One by one, they reached the window, and I was last, having had to find my way out of my sheets first. And I knew before I reached it what I'd find.

Sam stood at my door, hands buried in the pockets of his coat and head hanging low. The stubble on his jaw was thick, and when he looked up at the window, his eyes were as hollow and haunted as mine.

The sight of him gutted me.

We bolted back as if it would undo the fact that he'd seen us.

Rin took my hand. "Do you want to talk to him?"

I shook my head and swallowed. Or tried to. The lump in my throat didn't budge.

Katherine put on her game face. "I've got this."

We followed her down the stairs in a pack. Rin and Amelia stood behind Katherine, arms folded like twin sentinels, and I pressed my back to the wall behind the door and out of sight.

I tried to breathe. That was probably the hardest part.

Katherine straightened up and opened the door. "Hello, Sam." Her voice was stern. It was her librarian voice, and she wielded it like a mace.

"Is she here?" he asked, the words thick and rough.

"Yes, but she doesn't want to see you. I'm sorry."

"I…I understand. But I just need to talk to her, just for a minute. Just once, and then I'll go. Please, I don't want the first time seeing her to be at work."

Katherine waited. I sensed her watching me in her periphery, so I shook my head.

"I'm sorry," she said again. "If you want, I can pass along a message."

"The things I need to say are for her and her alone. I have to…I need to…" His voice broke. A pause. "I know I hurt her, but you have to believe me when I say I never meant to. When I said I wanted to be with her, I meant every word. And when I said I only wanted to make her happy, it was the truth. It's still the truth."

I heard a shuffling, and then he spoke again.

"Give her this." His hand appeared, disembodied. In it was a box that he placed in Katherine's waiting palm. "Her birthday present. Tell her…tell her I'm sorry."

"I will," she said and began to close the door. "Goodbye, Sam."

He said nothing. And then the door was closed, separating him from me with deep finality.

The three of them turned to me. Katherine handed me the box.

I couldn't sort out what to do with it as I turned it over in my hands. It was small, a black box tied with a blood-red ribbon. The urge to pull the ribbon tip was equal to the urge to throw it into the fireplace and strike a match.

But I didn't do either. I just held it in my hands and stared at it.

"Are you going to open it?" Katherine asked.

"I don't know," I answered. My feet carried me to the kitchen, and when I reached the island, I sat on a barstool. My eyes didn't leave the gift, which I set on the granite.

"You don't have to if you don't want to," Katherine offered, resting a comforting hand on my back.

"I don't want to. Not yet," I realized, withdrawing my hands, placing them in my lap where they were safe. "Maybe not ever. But definitely not right now."

The four of us stared at the present in silence.

"Why did he have to come here?" I asked no one. "Why did he have to be so perfect? Why did I believe it was real?"

Rin's hand rested on my back. "It might have started on a lie, but that doesn't mean it wasn't real."

I shook my head. "When everything is built on a lie, there is no trust. What was real, and what wasn't? Every moment we shared has replayed in my mind, and I mistrust every one. Maybe someday I won't feel like I've been manipulated and betrayed. Maybe one day I won't feel like he stole my heart just to see if he could. Maybe, eventually, I won't miss him anymore. And until then, I have to endure his presence at work. There's no escaping him there."

"Do you think he'll try to talk to you?" Amelia asked.

"I know he will." A long, slow sigh slipped out of me. "If I wasn't terrified to lose my seat to a sub, I'd call in. But I've already lost my heart. I'm not about to lose my job, too." I slid off the stool. "Now, let's go back to my room where we will talk about anything other than this while we eat. Preferably until we're sick."

Rin hooked her arm in mine. "Anything you want, Val."

I wore a tired smile. "Thank you. Thank you for always being here. With lasagna."

And she smiled back. "Anything but cake."

Katherine bobbed her head. "I mean, lasagna is kind of like cake. Pizza cake."

Amelia shoved her. "Killjoy! Don't ruin it for her."

"Just don't put birthday candles on it, and we're good," I said with a halfhearted laugh, still holding out that someday, my wish would come true.

Because as badly as I hurt, as completely as my heart was broken, and as deeply as I missed him, I still never wanted to see his beautiful face again.

EAT YOUR HEART OUT

SAM

The pit was empty and quiet, the chairs still and solitary, the air humming with energy.

I knew she didn't want to talk to me. I knew what I'd promised Dante. I knew the right thing was to leave her alone.

And I would. As soon as I explained, I would leave her alone. As soon as I told her I loved her, I'd disappear.

I was already set up and waiting when musicians began entering in a trickle, then a stream. And then the pit was full, even a scowling, banged-up Ian.

Everyone but Val.

She almost missed the opening, sliding into her seat as the house lights went down. I watched her back as she readied her instrument. Her shoulders were stiff, her back ramrod straight.

I'd only caught a glimpse of her face, her eyes shining and swollen, her nose red from crying, her heart visible from across the room, shattered and glittering under the lights of my inspection.

Everything I'd been afraid of so long ago had come true. Only it wasn't Ian who'd broken her.

It was me.

I was overcome by the determination to make it right. To fix what I'd broken. To undo what had been done.

If she only gave me the chance, I'd do anything.

The show seemed to go on for an inordinate amount of time, and all the while, my eyes were on her. With bruised, aching hands, I played to her, played for her, wondered if she could hear me, wondered if she could feel me.

To see her and not speak drove me to madness.

When the show finally ended, I set down my bass and wound my way through the chairs and stands to her.

She was already standing, her case in hand and head down.

"Val," I started, still a row away.

She flinched but didn't look up and never stopped moving. I threaded my way through the pit behind her.

"Val, please," I said around apologies and excuse mes as I wove around chairs and music stands.

She disappeared around the corner.

I cursed under my breath and picked up my pace, finally catching up to her just as she pushed out of the door and onto the sidewalk.

"Wait, please," I said, reaching for her. "I…I just need to—"

She whirled around, her face bent. "Please, just leave me alone. You've done enough."

I retracted my hand, clenching it at my side, my fucked up knuckles flashing with penitent pain. "I know. I'm sorry. You've got to know how sorry I am."

"Sorry you got caught or sorry you took out the bet?"

"Both," I answered honestly, hating myself for the truth.

She took a measured breath, her jaw tight.

"Ian said if I didn't go after you, he would. He wouldn't have let it go. He wouldn't have stopped until he ruined you, hurt you."

"Neither did you."

The barb hit home, the ache in my chest focusing to the point of impact. "I wanted to save you from him, so I took the bet. And when you said you'd never dated, I found a way to save you *and* help you without misleading you. I thought I was doing the right thing, but then … then …" I swallowed. "Val, I think … I think I'm—"

"Please, stop talking." She shook her head, chin flexed and eyes brimming with tears. "Don't you think I'm smart enough to see through Ian? I wouldn't have ever gone out with him. I wouldn't have slept with him. I wouldn't have entertained even the idea of him. I didn't need saving, Sam." Another shake of her head, her eyes turning up to the stars in betrayal, as if they could have warned her against me. "But you … you knew you could have me. Am I that predictable? Did you think yourself that much above me? And never once did you consider my position. Not once did you think about how I would feel. Because if you had, you would have told me the truth right then and there."

"I thought … Val, telling you would have hurt you. I didn't want to hurt you."

"So you lied and hurt me worse. You once told me you'd never lie to me, not about anything But that was a lie too, wasn't it?"

I swallowed, my feet rooted to the concrete, my hands aching to touch her, to hold her. But I'd lost that right and all others I'd earned. "I only had your heart in mind. This … this is exactly what I was trying to prevent. And when I realized how I felt, what I wanted, nothing else mattered."

"To you. Nothing else mattered *to you*. But it mattered to me." She backed away. Her voice wavered like moth's wings. "Sam, you've got to leave me alone. You've got to respect this one request, please. After everything, this is all I ask. I can't tell you it's all right. I can't absolve you. Not right now."

There was nothing to say, nothing to do but nod my concession. I had to respect her request. I hadn't respected her enough.

I owed her this.

I owed her so much more.

And all I could do as she walked away was wonder if I'd ever have the chance to make it up to her.

It wasn't until I lost sight of her that I finally turned for the theater with my shoes full of lead and my heart lining the soles.

It all caught fire when I saw Ian leaning against the wall at the back entrance.

I didn't acknowledge him, not outwardly at least. Inside, every single molecule reached for his throat.

"You've exceeded all expectations, Sammy. Well done."

"Fuck you, Jackson." I passed him without looking.

"I mean, who would have thought you'd actually fall for her? Really, I'm impressed."

I stopped. Turned slowly. Met his hard eyes. "I'd say I can't believe you did this to me, but I'd be lying. I should have known all along. I should have walked away from you years ago. Maybe from the start. But I thought we were friends. I thought all these years meant something."

"Yeah, well—you always were a sucker," he said with disdain. "Do you have any idea how hard it is being the fuckup standing next to you? All I wanted was for you to be honest for one fucking second. Truth is, the whole fucking thing is tedious."

"That's what you don't get and what I should have realized—I can't turn you into me any easier than you can turn me into you. I thought I was helping you. Joke's on me."

"I don't need your fucking help, man."

"You and everybody." I turned to go.

"But that's what you do, isn't it? Save the day. Roll in on your white horse. Well, not this time."

I turned again to level him with a glare. "This is your fault."

"No, this is *your* fault." His smile was smug, superior. "She's hurt because of what you did, not me. All I did was tell her the truth."

"You told her your version of the truth, and you did it to hurt me. Honestly, I didn't realize you had such a fucking crush on me."

He chuckled. "The bigger they are, the harder they fall. And man, you had a long way to go. I'm not gonna lie, it feels even better than I thought it would."

My jaw popped, my hands flexing at my sides. "I can't figure out what the fuck you want besides another black eye. I'd break your nose again, but that just feels redundant."

Ian pushed off the wall, his face cast in shadow from the streetlights behind him. All I could see was the tip of his nose, the point of his chin, the gleam in his eyes.

"Just enjoying the fruit of my labor."

"Well, eat your fucking heart out." I reached for the handle, wrapping my fingers around the cold steel. "Don't bother showing up at Sway tomorrow night to play." As his smile fell, mine rose. "Or ever, for that matter."

"You wouldn't," he said flatly.

"I already did. When the guys heard what happened, they were mad at me, sure. But they were *furious* with you. And Benny…well, he's Val's number one fan. I couldn't get you back in if I tried. Which I won't."

"You've got to be fucking kidding me."

"You can't be surprised. Did you really think I'd let you stay in the band after this?"

"I'm not worried about finding another gig, asshole. But to get me kicked out of Sway? That's too far. Too fucking far."

"That was all you. Well, and Val. Benny caught her on the way out, and she gave him the gist. He would have kicked me out too, if I hadn't explained that I love her."

His face went slack. "You..." A disbelieving laugh. "Oh, Sammy. You'll never learn."

"Neither will you."

I stepped into the hallway, and the heavy door slammed behind me. I didn't see him again that night.

I wandered numbly into the pit and packed away my instrument, speaking to no one. The city was silent as I walked to the subway, the clacking of the train unheard, the murmur of voices noiseless. My footfalls on the pavement were marked only by the jolt up my legs, the sound of my key in my lock lost.

It wasn't until I was seated at my piano that sound returned, the notes of my loss ringing in the room, in my ears, in my heart. And every one was for her.

I loved her, and I couldn't tell her.

I loved her, and she didn't know.

I loved her, and I'd lost her forever.

PRÍNCIPE

VAL

I almost didn't go to dinner at my parents'.

It wasn't because the week and weekend had been unbearable—though it had been. I'd cried myself to sleep nightly and dragged myself to work an anxious wreck, only to find Sam gone. Some girl sat in his chair, doing her damnedest to upstage him, which was impossible in itself.

It wasn't because I hadn't been to the club since my birthday.

And it wasn't because the temperature in the city had dropped, riding a storm front that had been drizzling rain in thick, lazy sheets for days.

No, it was because I knew walking into that house, I would have questions to answer. It was the precise reason I hadn't wanted to bring Sam to dinner in the first place. Not that there had been any way to know that we'd burn out like a firework.

Distance hadn't helped me make any sense of my feelings or the things that had transpired between me and Sam. I tried to pinpoint the moment when things had shifted, if there was one. Tried to put my finger on the event that had taken me from a bet to more.

Because that was one thing I had realized. Sam cared for me, even if he hadn't at first. I just didn't know what was a lie and what was real.

That was the most maddening part of it all. Not knowing.

I climbed the stairs and entered the house, greeted by the familiar sounds and smells of home, though they did little to comfort me. With every step, anxiety tightened in my chest.

I found everyone in the kitchen, where they always were. They saw me the second I entered the room and rose to meet me. Each of them wore masks of normalcy, tightened at the edges of their eyes with worry.

They greeted me as they always did—with smiles and hugs, a few jokes, and a noogie from Franco.

No one asked about Sam. No one brought him up at all.

His presence in the room was heavy nonetheless.

I moved around the room, never staying in one place long. Once I made the rounds, Mama took pity on me and enlisted my help in the kitchen. I was cutting potatoes for *patatas bravas*, silently listening to my brothers one-upping each other, when *Abuela* sidled up next to me. In her weathered hands, she held the corners of her apron, and in the folds of fabric rested a handful of onions.

"*Ayúdame, cariño.*"

"*Sí, Abuela.*" I reached into the pocket of fabric to begin unloading them.

"I am sorry about your *príncipe*, Valentina."

I sighed. "Who told you?"

"Dante. He told the whole *familia*, you know how he is. *Fósforo* said he hit *pobre* Sam. Is he all right?"

I blinked. "He...he didn't tell me Dante hit him." I glanced over my shoulder at my brother and inexplicably wanted to punch him myself and curl into his chest and cry.

"*Sí*, he hit your *príncipe*. After Sam hit the other *desgraciado*. Twice."

I shook my head, turning back to my potatoes, so I'd have something to do with my hands. "What else did Dante say?"

"That Sam had a…" She paused, searching for the word. "*No entiendo, se dice apuesta*."

"A bet. Yes," I said softly.

She clucked her tongue, shaking her head. "*Lo siento, cariño*."

"*Gracias, Abuelita*. I should have known he didn't want me."

"¿Por que? Valentina, you are the prize, not the *príncipe*."

A humorless huff of a laugh escaped me. "He said the same thing."

She waved a gnarled hand. "Everyone knows this. No one storms the castle for the *príncipe*. They come for *la princesa*. But, *alma mía*, I am surprised. I know love when I see it on a man's face, and that man loves you."

Shock shot up my spine at the word. "No, *Abuelita*. Not love. It was too soon for love."

But she smiled slyly. "Is that what you think? I knew the moment I saw your *abuelo* that I loved him. It only takes a moment. You breathe his air, and you know he is yours. What comes after is just a matter of making sure he feels the same. And Sam feels the same. You are his air, *cariño*. He needs you to breathe."

A sheet of tears blurred my hands. I set down the knife, rested my palms on the cold countertop. "But he lied. He lied, and I don't know how to unthread what's the truth."

"*Sí*. He lied. He hurt you. But I don't think he meant to. Do you?"

I shook my head, swiping at my cheeks. "I don't. I'm just…I'm so humiliated. To know I was only a joke to him is just…I can't…" I pressed a hand to my aching chest, but there was no relief. "And I don't know how to trust him. He hurt me. He hurt me so bad."

She stepped into me, wrapped me in her arms, arms that had comforted me my whole life. Every skinned knee, every scrape, a few broken bones, and now, a broken heart.

For a minute, I just cried. That was all. I cried on her thin shoulder as she swayed back and forth, whispering to me in Spanish that it would be all right, to let it out, to let it go. But there was no letting Sam go. I think we both knew it.

When the tears ebbed and my breath steadied, I exhaled the last of it and stood. Her hands were still on my upper arms, her eyes dark and deep.

"It hurts. But if you love him like I think you do, you have to find a way to listen. You have to give him a chance to earn his way back from his mistakes."

"What if he hurts me again?"

"Then you know," she said with a shrug, wise and dismissive. "But, if you don't try, you will always wish you had."

Bawdy male laughter erupted from the table, nothing to do with us or me.

Abuelita let me go with a squeeze and shuffled over to the stove, leaving me to my potatoes. Her words circled my thoughts.

What I'd been so ardently avoiding was how badly I missed him. I'd asked him to leave me alone, and he had. He'd granted my wish, and I hated it. I needed it, but I hated it.

And I still wasn't past it. The shock. The pain. The betrayal and shame.

I didn't know *how* to get past it.

Because his intentions didn't change the truth of what he'd done or how that made me feel. Nothing could erase that. Nothing could undo it. And I didn't know if there was a way to put it behind me.

So I would choose myself over his intentions and hope that maybe, someday, I'd find a way to move on.

DINNER WAS UNEVENTFUL. THE CONVERSATION covered everything from relatives in Madrid to Franco's laundromat harem—there were apparently a dozen women frequenting his laundromat who were not only goddesses, by his description, but wanted to sleep with him. Several laundry sabotages had taken place, including a rogue red sock in a load of whites, a nefarious bleach spill, and a fair number of G-strings missing. I didn't catch whether or not that was the girls' infighting or Franco being a perv.

I was left alone, left to breathe and listen and interject when I had something to say. By the time we cleaned up, I was exhausted. It was that soul-deep fatigue that camped out in your marrow and twined around every vein, the kind that no amount of sleep could relieve.

I said my goodbyes, smiled and sank into one hug after another, each one containing a silent apology, an unvoiced wish, wordless understanding. When I reached the quiet hallway where my coat hung, I pulled it off the hook and shrugged into it, already dreading being alone again.

At least when I was around people, I could pretend I was fine.

"If you're not okay, just say so. I'd be happy to break Haddad's face again."

I tried to smile, turning to find Dante behind me. His expression was both sheepish and hard, hands in his pockets and a crooked smile on his face.

"I don't feel like I should reinforce your terrible behavior, but thanks. For sticking up for me, that is."

A shrug. "It's no big deal. He's not the first dumbfuck I've punched for hurting you, but I hope he's the last."

"Why? Did you hurt your hand?"

"Nah. I'm just sick and tired of guys thinking they can treat you like anything but the *princesa Abuela* says you are."

My mushed-up heart melted a little more. Pretty soon, it'd be leaking out of me. When tears pricked the corners of my eyes, I realized it already was.

"Well, thanks, Dante. For everything."

"It's nothing. I'm sorry for what he did. If he hadn't left Jackson's face covered in gore, I would have done it myself."

I picked up my bag, blinking back tears and sniffling against the itch in my nose. "Fuck that guy. Fuck him so hard."

Dante took a breath like he was about to speak but held it, watching me for a second. "For what it's worth, Sam really does care about you. I know what he did was fucked up—trust me, I could have broken his fucking arm in four places without feeling guilty about it. But…" He sighed, dragging his hand through his dark hair.

I folded my arms. "Are you… are you about to defend Sam? To your sister? Who he led on and had a fake relationship with because of a bet?"

He sighed again, this time with his face quirked like he was having some battle inside the muscles of his face. "Maybe. I mean, I'm just saying, Val. He's a total piece of shit, but maybe you should hear him out. You know? Because if you ever want to move on, whatever that means for you, you have to talk to him. Closure or some shit, right?"

I laughed. "Oh my God, Dante. Have you been reading self-help books again?"

"Listen, *Rising Strong* will change your life. Don't judge me for trying to be a better me."

I held up my hands in surrender, giggling. "Fair enough." But my smile fell as I spoke. "Dante, Sam was the one who moved us from friends to more. He was the one who asked me for that. I would have been okay. I could have moved on even though I've had a thing for him since the first time I laid eyes on him. I knew where the boundaries were, and I could have kept that last scraggly bit of the wall I'd built standing. But then he asked me for more, and it all came down. I lost myself, let myself fall. I knew I could get hurt, but this...this was so far beyond what I could have imagined."

"I know. But the guy I know wouldn't have asked you to be his girlfriend if he wasn't serious. He wouldn't have come here to meet us—to try to win *me* over—because of a bet with Jackson. He came here because he wanted to and because it was important to you. I'm not saying you have to forgive him. I'm just saying you should listen to him. Let him say what he needs to say, throw himself at your feet and grovel. Just...hear him out."

I nodded. "I'll think about it. Thank you, *toro*."

He smiled and reached for me, pulling me in for a crushing hug. "No prob, *conejita*. *Te amo*."

"*Yo también*."

With a final squeeze, he let me go.

He watched me walk away and out into the cold autumn evening.

I pulled my coat closed against the chill, buttoning it up as fast as I could before burying my hands in my pockets. But I could still feel the sting of cold.

It was only in part because of the weather.

I knew I'd have to talk to Sam eventually. Probably. I hadn't expected him to disappear from work like he did, and I think part of me believed at some point, we would speak again. I'd imagined a hundred scenarios. I didn't want to deal with any of them.

But Dante wasn't wrong. I'd have to talk to him if I wanted to move on.

Could I forgive him? Would I? If he stood before me and begged me for forgiveness, could I say no?

Should I?

They weren't questions I could answer. Fortunately, I hadn't had to.

I wondered again where he'd been, what he'd been doing. Why

he'd been missing work. It couldn't have been because of me. The image of him, unwashed and miserable, flashed through my mind, and I almost laughed at the absurdity. It had to be something else. His family maybe. A project. Something that had coincidentally aligned with our last argument and my request for solitude.

Maybe I could call him. My stomach flipped, and I amended that to, *Maybe I should text him.*

I didn't feel ready. But I didn't know if I'd ever feel ready.

By the time I got home, I had inched a little bit closer to the idea. The brownstone was quiet and dark, all the lights out, except one.

The light over the island shone down like a spotlight, and in the center, exactly where I'd left it, was my birthday gift from Sam.

No one had touched it in five days. We'd moved around it, eaten around it, no one daring to shift it even a millimeter. It was a silent beacon, one I'd forget about completely until moments like this. And then I couldn't think about anything else for a long while.

My eyes were on the box as I set down my bag and took off my coat, hanging it on the rack. I walked toward it like it had called to me, took a seat on the barstool where I'd sat when I placed it there. Picked up the box and turned it over in my hands.

I pulled the red ribbon.

The lid slid off in a whisper. Obscuring the contents was a note, written on thick, luxurious paper in a slanting, artful hand.

To the girl I gave my heart to.

Happy birthday, Val. I hope all your wishes come true, every one.

With shaking hands, I picked up the card, my eyes widening when I saw what lay inside.

Twin golden hair combs lay on a bed of black velvet, the heads adorned with gilded leaves and sprays of ruby petals. I picked one up. It looked very old, and as I tilted my hand to inspect it, the light caught the stones and filled them, making them twinkle and glow.

I closed my hand, closed my eyes.

This wasn't a lie. The gift in my hand had nothing to do with a bet. It was his heart in my palm, as honest and real as mine that I'd placed in his.

And that knowledge warred with the truth of the bet itself, with the fact that it'd existed at all.

He was an honest liar.

And I loved him despite it all.

My tears fell silently, the sharp angles of the comb cutting into the soft curves of my palm. And I whispered another wish into the quiet, dark room.

"*I wish he loved me, too.*"

TO FALL

SAM

One week. Seven days. A hundred and sixty-eight hours since I'd lost her.

My fingers moved across the ivory, the hammers striking the strings in the piano, the vibrations filling the room with the sound of my sadness.

There was nowhere to go. The club had become a place for her and me. The stage reminded me of her presence on it. The dance floor set my arms aching to hold her.

Work was impossible to consider. If her presence was felt at the club, the truth of seeing her would be too much to bear. I couldn't consent to leaving her alone if given the opportunity to talk to her. So I'd eliminated that opportunity by removing myself from the equation.

It was the only thing I could do to serve her. The only apology she would accept.

My absence.

Did she miss me like I missed her? Did she hate me the way I hated myself?

Would I ever find out?

I picked up my pencil and wrote. The movement was slow and deep, the cadenza haunting. Orpheus begging Hades to return his love to him. Psyche waiting for her lover in the dark. Echo whispering only the words her beloved spoke, words unheard and lost.

It was the best I'd ever written.

Pages and pages I'd composed. I hadn't eaten much, and I hadn't slept at all. I'd played and written and considered my regrets.

And I thought of her.

I sighed, turning on the bench, stretching my stiff back and neck when I stood. A glance at the clock told me I had to leave soon. Too soon.

I made my way into the bathroom, barely glancing at my reflection. Hollow eyes, unkempt beard, hair thick and shining. Shirt off, in a pile on the floor. Pants joined them. The shower was hot, pinging my back, my shoulders, my face when I turned, eyes closed.

I resolved to acquaint myself with the bottle of scotch I'd been avoiding. As soon as I came home from my parents' place, me and that bottle were going to get familiar. At least then maybe I could get some sleep. Sleep would help, just like the shower.

At least I don't smell like a dumpster anymore, I thought as I dried myself, discarding the towel on the floor with my clothes. I stepped into jeans, pulled on a fresh shirt. Stuffed my feet into boots and shrugged on my jacket. Snagged my keys and trudged to the subway.

My mind was sludge, viscous and thick, my thoughts amalgamated into nothing in particular and everything at once. And like a passenger, I accompanied my body to the Upper East.

When my mom opened the door, her smile fell. I saw her mind take in the sight of me, which, by most people's judgment, would have seemed fine. I stood straight, was clean and dressed, was there. I was there. I'd shown up even if I wasn't present.

I tried to smile and failed.

"*Qalbi*, what has happened?"

"I don't know if I want to talk about it, Mom."

She nodded once and reached for me. "Well, we don't have to talk. Come here."

I'd never understand how someone so small could make me feel so safe. I bent to hug her. Her arms wound around my neck, her hands on my shoulders, and she held me like that until I pulled away.

It was as she always did. Never once had she broken a hug, as if they were always for me to drink from until I was full.

"Come," she said gently, taking my hand. "There's food."

I followed her in, closing the door behind me. The house was quiet, lit by the slanting gray light of the overcast day. Dad was sitting on the couch with a medical journal in his hand, glasses perched on the tip of his nose. When he saw me enter, he assessed me over the top of his lenses.

"Are you all right, son?"

"No, but I suppose I will be eventually."

It was then that I regretted coming. I was in no state to chitchat.

"What are you reading?" I asked as I took a seat next to him.

He flipped it over in his hand and glanced at the cover. "An article about vascular grafts." He didn't elaborate, which was both welcomed and regrettable. "Everything okay at work?"

"I wouldn't know. I haven't been there since last week."

They exchanged a look.

"Did you quit?" he asked.

"No. I have someone subbing for me. I just...I've had some thinking to do. I've been composing."

Mom brightened at that. "Are you happy with what you've written?"

"It's some of my best. The best."

"I didn't know you were still composing," Dad said. "Not since Juilliard. How much have you written?"

"Scores," I admitted. "I write every day."

Confusion flitted across his brow. "Really? What have you done with it? Have you had anything picked up?"

"No one's heard any of it."

"Well, why ever not?" he asked a little shortly. "If it's good, why not do something with it?"

"Because it's mine."

He didn't seem to understand.

I assessed him for a beat. "Have you ever had something you loved so much, you couldn't bear for anyone to see it? Because if they did, it wouldn't be yours anymore. Then it would be *theirs*. That piece of you, that part of your heart."

"Yes, I have," he said simply. "You."

Everything in me stilled.

He went on, "I knew when you were very small that you would be great. It wasn't just a father's musings, dreams to aggrandize you as an extension of me. I *knew* by power of assessment. When you were three, you could pick out a tune on a piano. When you were six, you could tell me the key of a song on the radio. Your mother fed your heart and your mind, but I was afraid. What if you failed? What if you loved a thing that would never love you back? That would never provide for you? What if…what if you were hurt, damaged by the passion in your heart?"

Mom took my hand.

Dad shook his head and pulled off his glasses as if to see me better. "Samhir, I have been hard on you. I know this—your mother loves to remind me. But it is because of my own fear that I wish for more for you. It is my desire to see you succeed, to embrace what you love so it can embrace you back. But when your child loves a thing that leads them down a path of hardship, a path that so few find financial success in, it is difficult to accept without worry. So, I worry. And that worry, that fear, brings me to pushing you without need. It's never been easy for me to let go of that piece of my heart that I gave to create you."

I didn't know what to say, and he seemed to understand.

"I know you, son. I know that you are afraid, too. You're afraid to fail, afraid to fall. But what you've never understood is that without failure, there can be no success. It's all right to fall, Samhir. It's not all right to stay down. But I do not think this is about your work, is it?"

"No," I said, a single, thick syllable on my tongue. "It…it's Val."

"The girl you gave the comb? Your *friend* you called about last week?" Mom asked, searching my face.

I nodded. "I hurt her, pressed the deepest bruise she has. And I think…I think I've lost her."

"What did she say when you tried to talk to her?" Her eyes were dark, her voice soft and soothing.

"She was too upset to talk, to hear me."

"When was that?"

She was analyzing me, I knew. I didn't care.

"Last week."

"And you've avoided work—where she is."

I shook my head. "She asked me to leave her alone, and this is the only way I can guarantee that I will."

"We all need time when we've been wounded. No one heals, and no one can forgive without time," she said, reaching for my hand. "What would you say to her?"

"That I'm sorry. That I meant everything, every word. That I would never lie to her and that…that I love her."

They both stilled at the word.

"If you love her, if you've given her your heart, then you have to tell her. If not for her, then for you. This…this is the first time, isn't it?" Her eyes were soft, deep and dark.

"Yes," I said against the pain in my chest. "And I hope it's the last."

"Because you don't want to love again?" Dad asked.

I met his eyes. "No. Because I only want to love her."

A long pause. "Then you must tell her," he said definitively.

"But I've failed her," I argued. "I've hurt her. What if I do it again? What if my love isn't enough? What if I can't give her what she needs?"

"If you don't try, you'll never know the answer," he said. "Love isn't guaranteed. But you have to follow the song of your heart. Where will it lead you? Where will you find yourself if you shrug off the comfort of mediocrity and complacency and jump? Just jump, Samhir. You might fail, yes. But what do you gain if you succeed? What happiness will you know if you triumph? What joy if you thrive?"

I took a shaky breath and let it out.

"That is your choice, son. Will you risk your heart or deny it?"

When I searched for the answer, it was there waiting, a fact as simple and true as it always was.

That answer lit in my heart like a brazier, the flame licking the stars.

EVERY SONG, EVERY NOTE

SAM

"Come on in," Jason said, moving a stack of papers from his desk.

The office in the theater was shared by half a dozen people, crammed with desks and shelves and chaos. It was maybe big enough for three people to stand comfortably, four if they were friends, five and things would get real familiar.

That night, it was just the two of us. I closed the door, brushing my sweaty palm on the thigh of my jeans.

"It's good to see you, Sam. Glad you're ready to come back. Your sub is playing with unattractive desperation for your spot. Like I'd ever can you," he said on a laugh. "What can I do for you?"

I reached into my bag, my plan on my lips, riding every heartbeat. "Well, I have something I want to show you—"

The door burst open, and Ian filled the doorframe. His eyes were hot coals in their sockets, and when they landed on me, they flared.

"I should have fucking known I'd find you here. This is your doing, isn't it?"

Jason glared at him. "Are you accusing me of nepotism, Jackson?"

Ian swiveled his head to laser on Jason. "What if I am?"

"Well, I wouldn't think that'd be any way to go about getting your job back." Ian opened his mouth to speak, but Jason headed him off. "I fired you because I found someone better."

"You're fucking kidding me. Branson is a reject, a can't-hack-it wannabe from Des Moines. You're not seriously giving him my seat, are you?"

Jason's face hardened. "It's already done. Part of the problem here is your bad attitude. Case in point." He gestured to Ian. "But the bottom line is that Branson is better than you."

"Bullshit," he shot. "This is bullshit. This is all because of some stupid fucking bet, and now Sam's got his panties in a twist. I can't believe you got me fired, you son of a bitch."

"That's enough, Jackson. You've got two options—you can leave quietly, or I can call security. It'll be real tough to find a gig once everybody hears about your exit. But grace has never been your thing, has it?"

"Fuck you," he said, chest heaving with his rage. "Fuck both of you. I hope you're happy, Sam."

"Nothing about this makes me happy," I said, the truth of it hitting me deep.

But he was already turning for the door, passing the threshold, disappearing into the hallway.

Disappearing from my life.

The rubber band around my lungs let go, and I took my first full breath since he'd walked in. "I'm sorry, Jason."

"Don't be. I wouldn't have hired him in the first place if it wasn't for you—I've been wanting to fire him for a year." He took a seat.

"Now, tell me how else I can help."

And with an unbidden smile, I pulled the papers out of my bag and explained.

VAL

I'd told myself I was prepared to see Sam. He'd come back to work eventually, and there I'd be, head high, back firmly to him, and feelings locked neatly in my heart.

I'd had a whole week. An entire week, which was more than triple the time we had actually been together. I mean, together-together.

So seeing him will be a piece of cake, I'd told myself. *Easy-peasy. No prob, Bob. Nothing but a G thang, baby.*

Lies, lies, lies.

I felt him before I saw him, the air in the room tightening, electric. I turned to look—I had no choice, the reaction autonomous. And there he was, his eyes dark with regret and hope. But he didn't approach, didn't speak. He only nodded once, as if to say, *I'm sorry, I won't, I miss you.*

And all the bits of my broken heart that I'd collected, all the pieces I'd thought I'd put back together came apart like a house of cards in a breeze.

He moved to the back of the pit. I had to quit watching. I had to stop. I couldn't see him, couldn't think. So I turned to my music and flipped through it in a grand show of apathy that didn't fool anyone, least of all myself.

"Did you hear?" one French horn player to my left said to the other. "Jason fired Ian Jackson."

"You're kidding me," French horn two said.

"Nope. Jenny said she overheard the whole thing. Ian's *pissed*. He said something about Sam getting him fired and something about a bet. Have you heard anything?"

Tingling awareness slipped over me.

"No, but I'd pay good money to find out. Anyway, good riddance. If I had to put up with him hitting on me much longer, I would have complained to the union."

French horn one chuffed. "At least you didn't make the mistake of sleeping with him. That asshole is on my short list of regrets."

I couldn't imagine it was possible that Sam had the power to get Ian fired.

I couldn't believe he'd gotten Ian fired over *me.*

I chanced a look over my shoulder. Sam's eyes were down, his bass between his legs and hands moving as he played a tune that struck me with familiarity. But before I could place it, the conductor tapped her stand, bringing our attention to her.

And the show went on, as it always did.

It took all my energy to stay focused, especially during the music breaks and intermission. Intermission was torture. He didn't leave his seat and I didn't leave mine, but I could feel both of us wishing we could. I could feel his questions, feel the things he wanted to say. I could feel his apologies and his explanations.

The worst was that I wanted him. I wanted to hear every word, wanted to fall into his arms and tell him how I felt. I wanted to get up right then and beg him to tell me he wanted what I wanted, that he felt what I felt.

But I didn't. I stayed in my seat, wishing for things I couldn't have.

Somehow, I made it through the show and the curtain call. My plan after that was simple—grab all my stuff and run out of the theater like the devil was chasing me.

We held the last note until it was done. The conductor lowered her hands, we lowered our instruments. And I reached for my case to invoke my plan.

No one else moved other than to shuffle their music around, still sitting attentively in their chairs. I glanced around, confused, as the conductor's baton lifted and ticked off a beat.

Music rose around me as I sat, blinking stupidly in my chair, trying to figure out what was happening and why I wasn't in on it. The tune was familiar, the same Sam had been playing earlier.

The same he'd played that night, the night he'd played for me.

In my stupor, I didn't see Sam until he was in front of me. My body locked, my stomach swapping places with my heart as my eyes followed him. He moved my stand out of the way. Took my trumpet from my hands and set it next to my chair. Dropped to his knees at my feet.

And he took my hands in his, met my eyes and held them.

"I know I promised you I'd stay away, and I swore to your brother I'd leave you alone. And I will, Val. But before I can walk away, I need you to know that I love you."

Shock, a crack of lightning down my spine.

He loves you, he loves you, he said the words, he said them.

He didn't stop speaking. "I was wrong about so much. I should have told you about Ian from the start, but I thought I knew better. I thought I could save you, thought you needed me to. But I was wrong. It was me who needed you. It's me who *needs* you. I thought I knew what happiness was, but I was wrong about that, too. Because my life was empty until I met you, and it's been empty since I lost you."

"Sam," I breathed. My throat closed with emotion.

"I'm so sorry. I'm sorry I hurt you, and I'm sorry I didn't see this coming. I'm sorry I didn't tell you." He lowered his head, shook it gently. "I don't expect your forgiveness. I don't deserve your forgiveness. But you're the first girl I've ever loved, and I couldn't walk away without telling you. I love you, Val."

The music flowed around us, brilliant and sweet. It was the song of his heart. And the only truth that mattered in mine sat in the hollow of my mouth, on the tip of my tongue. It passed my lips without fear. "I've loved you for longer than I knew. I just didn't believe you'd ever love me. I didn't think you could."

He rose until we were eye to eye, his hands holding my face with adoration. "How could I not? It's like I said once before—you and I have become a fact. But I didn't know if I could give you what you needed, what you deserved. What I didn't realize was that I wouldn't have to try. Loving you is easy. Giving you everything I am is my joy, my privilege. Making you happy is all I want, Val. Love is music. You are music, and I want to learn every song, every note."

"Then kiss me and make me sing."

A twitch of a smile. A sigh he breathed that I breathed in. The tilt of my face.

His lips brushed mine with reverent disbelief, with the awe and grace of a man absolved. And with that kiss, I knew I would have always forgiven him. I would always forgive him. Because no matter what he had done, he'd done it for me. I knew this somehow, knew it in my marrow. In the threads of my veins, I knew.

With that kiss, that exchange of breath, the sharing of heartbeats, I gave him my heart.

It'd always been his.

DIAMOND & PEARLS

SAM

She loved me.

I held her in my arms, felt the weight of her, smelled the sweetness of her, tasted the honey of her lips as I kissed her with my heart and soul.

When our lips slowed and closed, when we opened our eyes, the things I wanted and the things I needed clicked into place before me, beginning and ending with her.

"It's your symphony," she said, smiling.

"No, it's yours."

Her brow quirked.

"*A Dance with Valentina*."

Her face went soft, her eyes velvety and filling with tears as she listened. "You...you named it after me?"

"I wrote it because of you. It was always you, every note, every phrase. It was you in my mind, your face in my thoughts when I heard every measure. I finished it and named it. And then I sent it to my agent."

Her eyes widened. "Did you?"

I nodded, smiling. "We'll see what happens. I didn't want to put this one in a drawer with the others. Because I've learned that if I'm afraid to jump, it's because what I want is worth the risk. It's worth falling for. It's worth failing for. Worth fighting for. Now my only fear is of *not* jumping."

"Just jump," she said. "Like you taught me."

I leaned in for another kiss, saying against her lips, "Like you taught me."

The brush of our lips was brief and sweet. The music around us came to a close, and the orchestra stood, clapping and whistling. And when the ruckus died down, the crew finally began to pack up. Val did the same, and when her instrument was in its case, I hooked it on my shoulder and pulled her into my side.

We strode out of the theater with her fitted under my arm, greeted by the crisp night.

"I've missed you," she said.

I kissed the top of her head. "You have no idea. I didn't leave my apartment but once since that night. I didn't shower for an unspeakable portion of that week either."

She chuckled. "What were you doing?"

"Writing. Contemplating my life choices. Missing you."

Val's free hand wrapped around my middle to join the one already curled behind my back. "I'm so sorry."

"Why are you sorry? You didn't do anything wrong—that was all me."

"I'm sorry that you were upset. I know it wasn't my fault."

"I lied to you."

"You did," she said. "By omission, but you lied. And you misled me. But you were being noble. A noble, lying asshole."

I chuckled against the ache in my chest. "He said he was going after you, and I knew he wouldn't stop. He wouldn't give up. But he did it because he knew I wanted you for myself. He did it because he wanted to hurt me. I don't think he even considered what it would do to you."

"Why were you friends with him, Sam? He's so…God, he's fucking awful."

"Loyalty, I guess. I've seen every side of him, and I thought I knew all his faces. He's thrown me under the bus before, but usually it's to save his own ass. This time, he just wanted to watch me fail. He got his wish."

"I'm so sorry."

"Stop apologizing, Val. Please. I can't take it."

She sighed. "At least you got to hit him. How'd it feel?"

"Who told you?"

"Dante."

"Ah," I said with a nod. "It hurt like a motherfucker and was simultaneously the most satisfying moment of my life, besides tonight."

Another sigh. This time, I could hear her smiling. "You wrote me a symphony."

"And you love me."

"And you love me, too. It's a night of firsts."

I didn't speak for a moment as we trotted down the stairs to the train. "Did you open your birthday present?"

She looked up at me, her face soft and open. "I did. I cried for half an hour afterward, but I opened it. Sam…they're beautiful."

We passed the turnstile. I was thankful for a second to process her crying for a half hour over me. It made me even sicker to consider that half hour had probably only been the tip of the iceberg.

"I used to watch my mom put on her makeup, and I'd dig through her big jewelry box that sat on her vanity. It was full of so many baubles, shiny gems, milky pearls. I used to imagine I was a pirate, and that was my treasure, piles of jewelry and gems I'd collected from the corners of the world. She has dozens of hair combs—beautiful, elaborate pieces. Some were my grandmother's, some older. But she would always tell me one day, I'd meet a girl and give her a hair comb, and she'd be mine. When she wore it, I'd think of how she belonged to me and how I would belong to her."

We stopped at the edge of the empty platform, the trough for the train dark and rough, metal and rock and oil. I turned to face her, pulled her flush to me, looked into the depths of her eyes.

"I thought of it like a fairy tale, as real as the possibility of my actually becoming a pirate. And then I met you."

Her cheek was warm against my palm, her skin soft beneath my fingertips.

"You're my fairy tale." I brought my lips to hers as the train flew into the station, the current of air twisting around us as we twisted around each other, lifting her hair, licking the edges of my coat, lifting us with force we couldn't see.

We felt it all the same.

The train stopped, the doors opened. And only then did I let her go, towing her behind me, then pulling her into me. We didn't speak. She held on to me, her face pressed against my chest, and I held on to her as the train took off, clacking down the track. Two stops, and we were moving again. Not a second had passed that we weren't touching other than our passage of the turnstiles. It was too much, the relief. The deliverance. I felt like I was breathing for the first time in a week.

Maybe ever.

In silence, we walked to my apartment, our pace picking up with every block. And then we climbed the stairs, crossed my threshold, closed the door, stood still in the quiet, dark room, face to face.

I traced the line of her jaw, held it in my hands. "I love you, Val.

I love every angle, every curve. Every freckle and every curl. Every smile, every laugh, every tear. I love you, all of you."

Forever, my heart whispered.

And I kissed her to seal the silent promise.

Our bodies wound together, my arms wrapped around her, her body melding into mine, the impression of every curve set into me where it belonged. Her hands slipped into my jacket, pushed it over my shoulders. I shrugged it off as she did the same, the kiss never breaking.

We were a blur of motion, of fluttering hands and hearts, of sighs and noisy breaths as we moved for the bedroom, shedding clothes all the way.

I broke away when we reached the foot of the bed, spent a long moment appreciating everything before me—her body, her heart, our future. Years later, I'd look back and realize this was the moment I knew without knowing that I'd love her forever. Until the day that I died, I would love Val.

And my greatest wish was that she'd love me in equal measure.

I kissed her sweetly until the kiss turned hot, deep and deliberate. Until it was desperate, delving and dark with desire. And then I laid her down. Kissed down her body. Held her breasts in my hands, kissed the tight tip with eyes closed, mouth warm. Felt her fingers in my hair, heard her sigh, smelled her heat as I kissed lower, lower. And when I reached the place where her thighs met, I cupped her sweetness, tasted her, kissed every ridge, licked every valley.

I didn't stop. I didn't want to stop, not ever, but she called my name, and I had to obey. Because I was hers.

Her pleasure was my pleasure. It always would be.

She pulled me up her body, kissed my lips, tasted the salt of her body on my tongue. I broke away only to reach into my nightstand, returning to her lips again as I tore the packet open, rolled the condom on. Settled between her legs, felt the give of her thighs, felt the slickness between, felt every inch of her from the inside as I slipped into her.

A pause, a breath, my eyes and hers, our hearts thundering and words of love on our lips. And I moved. My hips and hers, my hands buried in her curls and hers holding on, holding me close. Her legs parting wider, her knees drawing up, thighs bracketing my waist.

A thrust, and she gasped. Another, and she came. A third, and I was behind her, filling her up, letting myself go, giving to her and taking of her. Loving her and reveling in her love.

And it was over. But it wasn't.

Because when I looked at her, all I saw were beginnings.

THE RED ONE
VAL

"Tell me you don't have plans today."

I heard the words muffled through the rumbling of his chest where my ear lay and clear as day from the other.

I smiled. "Before last night, my plans included moping around like a sad panda and missing you."

"So, no?"

I laughed, shifting to rest my hand on the broad curve of one pectoral, propping my chin on the back. "No plans."

"Good," he said with a smirk.

God, he was beautiful. Dark and lovely and naked and wrapped around me like a spider monkey.

"What do you want to do?" I asked.

"I have a list."

"A list, huh?"

His smirk climbed, his eyes the color of honey. "Yup," was all he offered.

"Any hints? Clues? A treasure map maybe?"

"You'll see."

I wrinkled my nose. "Come on, give me a teeny-tiny hint. Just a little bitty baby hint."

His arms flexed around me, bringing me a little closer. "Nope. But let me know when you figure it out. Until then, you're on a need-to-know basis."

I chuckled. "When does it start?"

With a twist of his body, he rolled us over, hovering over me with his hair mussed and eyes warm. "Right now."

He kissed me, soft and deep, kissed me until we weren't just kissing, loved me with his lips, his hips, his hands and his body. He loved me right and thoroughly, and I loved him right back.

A FEW HOURS LATER, WE were walking through the Village, bundled up against the chill. My eyes scanned every storefront, anticipating where we were going.

"Is it brunch?" I asked when I spotted a new breakfast place. My empty stomach clenched at the prospect.

"Nope."

I scanned some more. We were heading toward my place, and I cataloged everything between here and there to try to figure out a pattern. "You're sure we're not going to my place?"

"I never said we weren't going to your place."

"Yes, you did."

"No, I kissed you instead of answering."

A laugh bubbled out of me. "You did, didn't you."

"I can't help it. I love kissing you."

"And you love not answering me."

"That too. Ah, here we go."

My face quirked in confusion as he pulled me into the grocery store. "Groceries?"

"Yup," he answered as he picked up a red plastic handbasket.

"Are you cooking?"

"Eventually."

"Eventually," I echoed. When he guided me away from the food and to the cosmetics, I frowned. "Are you gonna cook me tampons?"

Sam laughed, stopping in front of a display of dental care. "Do you like your toothbrushes soft or hard?"

"Hard. Always hard."

Another laugh. "Red. You're getting a red one." He grabbed it and dropped it in the basket, turning us around to the soaps. "What kind of shampoo do you use?"

"You can't get it at a drugstore."

"Do you have extra at your house?"

"I think I have a travel size under my sink. Why?"

"Good," he said, avoiding answering. "We'll pick it up when we go over to your place."

"Aha! So we *are* going to my place."

He shrugged. "I never said we weren't. I'll order some more so I can put it in my shower. Would it be weird if I used it every once in a while?"

I laughed. "I mean, it's just shampoo, so I'm gonna say no. You have to know I'm also going to ask you why."

"Because I have dreams about the way your hair smells, and I wouldn't hate for a second to smell like you for a whole day."

"That's fair. I have dreams about how you smell, but I have no idea what it is. Mostly I think it's just *you*, which is problematic. I can't exactly rub you all over myself to make me smell like you."

"I mean, it couldn't hurt to try."

I nestled into his side, laughing again.

"I don't know what it is. My soap maybe. There's this fancy lotion my mom uses that I stole from her because it makes my skin super soft."

"Okay, well, I'll definitely be using that."

"My deodorant? But that's not pH-balanced for a woman. How about we sniff test later and find out?"

"Are you asking me to smell your underarms? Because…okay."

He kissed the top of my head. "All right, do you want your own soap? Have a special toothpaste you like?"

"No, yours is fine. So, we're getting stuff for me to keep at your place."

"Your powers of deduction are astounding."

"I know, I'm a regular old Sherlock. But…I mean…you're not… you don't want to…"

"Move in together?"

I think I could hear him smirking still, which was reassuring because the thought of moving in made my stomach hit my shoes.

"I wouldn't buy you a new toothbrush, babe. I'd move the one from your place instead."

"Oh, thank God," I said on a sigh.

He leaned back to look down at me with that notched brow arched. "I know, wouldn't that be the worst?"

I rolled my eyes. "That's not what I meant, and you know it. I love you, but I'm not ready to share a toilet with you."

He laughed, this time lowering his lips to kiss mine.

We wandered through the grocery store.

"Okay," he said. "Mimosas or Bellinis?"

"Bloody Marys," I amended.

"My kinda girl. How about…poached eggs? Do you like eggs Benedict?"

"You know how to poach eggs?"

"I know all kinds of things. Like how to Manhattan Dip you on the dance floor and the fastest ways to make you sigh. So, hollandaise or no hollandaise?"

"Hollandaise, extra Canadian bacon. Okay, so toothbrush, breakfast—brunch? I don't get it."

"You will," he said on a chuckle as he loaded the basket with breakfast stuff.

Our next stop was a liquor store. He sent me in for Bloody Mary supplies, heading for somewhere else in the meantime. Where, I had no idea.

Until I stepped out. There he stood on the sidewalk with a grocery bag in one hand and a gorgeous bouquet in the other. Peonies, pink and salmon and cream, with soft green lamb's ears, purple thistle, and fern fronds.

But I barely noticed it. All I could see was Sam. The sweetness of his smile, the depth of love in his eyes. The black of his hair, the breadth of his shoulders. The soft pink against the dark of his jacket.

"Sam," I breathed, stepping into him, setting my bag next to us, so I could take the bouquet with both hands. I saw in the bouquet a few ranunculus, a bit of jasmine. It smelled divine.

He was divine.

I found my throat tight, my nose tickled with tears. I'd never thought I'd be a flower girl, but now, I got it. It wasn't about the flowers, the beauty or delicacy of them. It was about the man who'd chosen them simply because he wanted to make me smile, simply because he'd been thinking of me.

Simply because he loved me.

"They're b-beautiful." I buried my nose in the silky petals to hide the tears as they rolled away.

"I love you, Val. Don't cry."

"I love you, too, and I can't help it. How'd I get so lucky?"

He slipped a hand around my waist. "I'll be asking myself that every day, maybe forever." He smiled, searched my face. "So, have you figured it out yet?"

I considered, smelling the flowers again. Jasmine had always been my favorite. "Breakfast, toothbrushes, and flowers. Boyfriend material? Are you boyfriending me?"

He laughed. "Val, I'm gonna boyfriend you so good." And as he leaned in for my lips, he added, "And that's only the beginning."

EPILOGUE

VAL

I tipped the bell of my trumpet to the ceiling of the club, perched on Sam's shoulders. And I hit that high note with all the joy in my heart.

And that was saying something. My heart was so full that joy constantly spilled out of me.

I couldn't help it. I was a mess for Sam.

A year we'd been together, six months since I'd moved my permanent toothbrush in.

Well, truth be told, I had thrown my old one away. I much preferred the red one.

My favorite red dress pooled around his neck as he slapped the strings of his bass, and I played on through the end of our duet. And when I jumped off, I kicked my saddle shoes as high as I could, the force flicking the featherlight chiffon over my butt to flash my drawers.

The crowd went ballistic.

I fox-trotted around to face Sam, and for a minute, we played to each other, with each other, for each other in utter harmony and synchronization.

Tonight was different from the hundreds of others we'd spent at Sway only because tonight, we were celebrating Sam.

When the band joined in, I stepped back in line next to Chris, the other trumpet player, and we played out the rest of the song, our last of the night. I spotted all the faces we loved in the crowd. Hadiya and Ahmed jitterbugging, my mom and dad triple-stepping. My brothers, all with girls in their arms. Rin and Court bouncing, Katherine spinning in the arms of her boyfriend with her head kicked back in a laugh that held no abandon. Amelia and her husband slow-dancing their way through a fast song, lost in conversation with lovesick smiles on their faces.

How she'd gone from never being kissed to the first of us married was a hell of a story.

But that wasn't my story to tell.

With a long, climbing run, the song ended along with our set. The crowd stopped dancing just to cheer and clap as we bowed, and Sam took my hand as we trotted offstage. He paused, pulling me into his chest to lay a searing kiss on me, just like he always did after a show. As if he'd been watching me the whole set, just waiting for the second he could lay his lips on mine.

God, how I loved those lips.

Down the stairs we bounced, down to the dance floor and our friends and family. And then we were dancing.

Around and around we went, the adrenaline from performing zinging through us as we flew around the dance floor. He tricked me all over the place, using the flood of energy to fuel him as he flipped me over his shoulder, across his back, dropped me between his legs, dipped me. We didn't stop moving, not until I was breathless and giggling and a small circle had formed around us.

He pulled me out of a Charleston to bring me into his chest, spinning us around cheek to cheek, hip to hip. And the circle dissolved into dancing bodies.

Sam looked down at me, his lips tilted in that crooked smile I loved so much. "You're beautiful."

I laughed. "It's just this dress. My boyfriend says it's his favorite."

"Mmm," he hummed, pulling me closer. "He sounds like a smart guy."

"He really is. He just got a job composing a Broadway show."

His smile climbed. "You don't say?"

"It's true. I'm pretty sure he's on his way to being the next Andrew Lloyd Webber."

That earned me a laugh and a flash of his brilliant teeth.

"What can I say? I'm a lucky girl. He even got me these hair combs. See?" I turned my head to the side, smiling coyly. "He said when I wore them, he'd know I belonged to him, but really, they just remind me of how much he loves me and the moment he gave me his heart."

"I wonder what he'd think of this," he said just before he brought his lips to mine.

The kiss lingered, our lips parting in a slow, easy rhythm.

I sighed when he pulled away, gazing up into his face with a dreamy look on mine. "Oddly, I think he'd approve."

"Maybe we should ask your fiancé instead."

My brows quirked. "But I don't have a—"

I swallowed a gasp as he dropped to my feet, my hands in his. The music played on, but the people around us stopped. If I could see their faces, I would have noted I knew every one. But all I saw was Sam. Sam bathed in the golden light of the naked Edison bulbs, the same color as his eyes. Eyes that looked up at me with hope and love and nervous anticipation.

"Once upon a time, you asked me to teach you how to be brave. But it was you who taught me. You taught me how to love. You taught me how to jump. You gave me a reason to be brave, to be more than I was. I don't want to learn another lesson without you. Be with me always, Val. Marry me."

He held out the box, opened to display the ring inside—a band of gold set with small diamonds, and in the center was a square cut diamond the size of a meteor, faceted and twinkling in the amber light.

I didn't know if I responded or what I said, only that I was crying and reaching for him and kissing him and holding him. And he was holding me, his lips pressed to mine. And the ring was on my finger, and my heart was his.

And we were forever.

Everyone around us cheered and clapped. Distantly, I heard our names on the microphone, felt hands on our backs and arms and shoulders. But the only people in the world were me and Sam.

"Is that a yes?" he asked with that smile of his as he pressed his forehead to mine.

"That's a, *Yes.* That's an, *I love you.* That's a, *Please tell my boyfriend I'm sorry, but I've recently upgraded.*"

A laugh, the sweetest sound. "I love you, Val. I'll love you forever."

And the kiss he laid upon me left me without a single doubt that he would.

SNEAK PEEK:
BOOKED

AMELIA

Three more people.

The girl in front of me shifted the weight of her bag on her shoulder, the bulk of which rested under her arm like a pack mule, her body leaning in the opposite direction for balance. I eyed the bag, wondering how many books were inside like one of those *How many jellybeans are in the jar?* games I was terrible at.

There were eleven, if I had to guess.

I might not have had spatial awareness of jellybeans, but I probably could have sniffed that bag and determined how many books were inside.

Two more people.

Sweat bloomed in my palms as we all shuffled a few steps closer to the table where Thomas Bane sat.

All I could see between bodies was an unrecognizable sliver of face and bit of his elbow, clad in a black leather jacket. But there he was, and in two—*shit*—one person, it would be my turn.

Fortunately, the girl in front of me had plenty to keep him busy.

I took a breath—a deep, thick, anxious breath—and recited the words on the damp piece of paper in my back pocket.

It's nice to meet you.

I'm Amelia Hall with the USA Times.

Please sign that generic.

I'm fine, thank you.

Yes, I've read every word you've ever written.

No, I actually didn't enjoy them at all.

Okay, that last one wasn't on the list. And I'd never admit that to him—not aloud, anyway. I'd be lucky if I could do anything but squeak when faced with him directly.

I wouldn't have been standing in *Stacks*, a hip little book store in the East Village, if it hadn't been for my boss' insistence. *New* boss, that was, as I'd only recently gotten the gig book blogging for the *Times*. My personal book blog had, with a few viral reviews, essentially exploded, and the *Times* approached me to join their team.

This was my first big piece.

Cover the Thomas Bane signing, get a stack of hardbacks signed for giveaways, and try not to have a stroke when I had to actually have a conversation with him.

The girl in front of me unloaded her haul onto the table with shaking hands.

…Nine, ten, eleven. Ha!

A rumbling laugh from the other side of the table. He said something I couldn't make out, something in a snarky, smoky baritone that did something shocking to my insides.

I chalked it up to nerves.

I hadn't purchased groceries at the actual market in well over a year. I hadn't answered the phone for anyone but my best friends or parents in at least five. And I didn't go *anywhere* without a buffer who, in case of emergency, could speak for me.

It was almost always a case of emergency.

I wasn't sure exactly why it happened—my speechlessness. God knew I had enough words in my head, words in my heart, chittering, chattering words that never saw the light of day when the spotlight was on me.

It didn't even have to be a spotlight. A flashlight was plenty.

It was a physiological response to a psychological hurdle I'd never overcome. Such was my curse as the colorlessly pale, eccentrically shy daughter of the SlapChop fortune who had grown up with a speech impediment.

Not only was I an odd only child of inventors, and not only were we the wealthiest people in our provincial South Dakota town, but I couldn't pronounce Ls or Rs. It doesn't seem like that big of a deal, I realize.

When I was five, it was adorable.

When I was ten, I was a pariah.

Children are cruel, as everyone knows. And so, I cried in excess and escaped into books.

I had a million friends there.

Even when my impediment had been corrected with years of speech therapy, I didn't speak much. Not unless I was in the company of people I knew loved and accepted me.

Thomas Bane was not one of those people. And if he recognized my name, I was well and truly fucked.

I'd reviewed every book of his at three stars or less.

Three stars, you say, *but that's average!*

Not to authors, it's not. And there were few perks in being someone's top rated negative review on Amazon. At least for someone like me who hated disappointing people.

The thing was, my reviews weren't *bad,* per se. But they weren't exactly glowing either. They were honest, kind, constructive. I didn't shy away from what I didn't like, but always tried to present it in a way that was respectful and soft.

I cursed Janessa again in my mind for sending me here, wondering if she'd been intentionally cruel. Maybe she was hoping for me to return with some famous Thomas Bane quip or one liner. Or, if he was drunk, recount of a brawl.

Notorious bad boy Thomas Bane. Model dating, super rich, moderately famous, fist wielding, public drunken and indecent exposure Thomas Bane, fantasy author with a rap sheet the length of my arm.

"Did you want a picture?" I heard him ask. I thought I could hear him smiling.

"N-n-n-no, thanks," the girl stuttered.

My guts turned to ice.

She'd been talking her brains out with her friend not ten minutes ago with sword wielding bravado about how she was going to French kiss him there in front of God and everybody.

If *she* couldn't answer a simple question from him, I was never going to make it out of the building.

I took another breath and straightened my spine, stretching me to the extent that my five-foot-one frame would allow. When she moved out of the way, I almost went out like a candle.

His eyes switched from the parting girl to fix on me, and the air left my lungs in a vacuum that would have snuffed an entire *room* full of candles.

They were dark as midnight, the iris indistinguishable from his pupil, his lashes thick and long and absolutely ridiculous. Ridiculous, every inch of him. The cut of his jaw, covered in a dark shadow from his mildly kept beard. His nose, strong and long and masculine. Those cursed eyes, which had to be brown, but I couldn't make out anything but bottomless black. His hair, long enough to fall over his shoulders, waving and so thick, I bet his ponytail was at least seven times the diameter of mine.

But the most ridiculous part of his utterly ridiculous face were his lips, wide and full, the bottom in a constant pout, the top a little bit thicker, angled at a *ridiculous* angle that had me wondering what it'd be like to suck on it.

Which was ridiculous in and of itself. I'd never even been kissed. But whenever I was, God grant me lips like those.

Hands planted themselves on my shoulderblades and shoved.

Thomas Bane laughed, and I was unsurprised to find that his smile was ridiculous, too. What utterly unfair bullshit that a man should be that gorgeous.

I wondered if he went by Thomas and brushed the thought away. He was like Celine Dion, but with even better hair. No one called Celine Dion just plain old *Celine*. I imagined bet even her kids called her Celine Dion, yelling through their multi-zillion dollar home, '*Celine Dion, come wipe my butt!*' I also imagined that on Sundays, she wore a ballroom gown and tiara to lay around on the couch and watch Netflix.

I cleared my throat and unloaded the books the paper had sent with me for him to sign. I couldn't meet his eyes again.

"Hi…" He paused, probably looking for the name tag sticker on my tiny boob. "Amelia. It's good to see you," he said as if we'd met a hundred times.

Say hi. Say hello. Say hi, Amelia, goddammit.

I made the mistake of looking up, and my tongue tripled in size.

Don't look at him, you idiot!

My eyes darted back down to my hands. I swallowed.

"H-hi," I whispered.

God, I could feel him watching me. I could *feel* him smirking.

He took a book as I set it down, his hand entering my line of vision like a giant, manly, long-fingered version of my tiny pale one.

"Who should I personalize this to?" he asked.

"No personalization," I answered before I lost my nerve.

Another soft chuckle as I added to the stack. "No problem." The sound of a sharpie scratching the page filled the silence.

Say something! You are a mess, Amelia Hall. You have to tell him who you are. Janessa will shit a brick if you don't.

I swallowed the sticky lump in my throat, arranging the book pile without purpose. "I . . . I'm Amelia Hall. W-with the U-USA Times."

The book closed with a soft thump. "Amelia Hall? As in the blogger for *Halls of Books*?" The question was thick with meaning.

All of the blood in my body rushed from every extremity and up my neck in a blush so hard, I could feel the tingling crawl of it as my vision shimmered.

I looked up like a dummy anyway. An affirmative word was on my stupid, fat tongue, stuck there in my mouth like a gum ball in a water hose. So I nodded instead.

He was smirking, lips together, a tilted smile that set a glimmer of amusement in his eyes. "You're the blogger who hates me so much."

I frowned. "I don't hate you. I just hold issue with your idea of romance."

The words left me without thought or attempt or desire to reel them back in. I might not have been able to order a pizza over the phone, but I could stand up for a little old lady who someone cut in front of or the kid who was getting picked on. And my ideals. I could stand up for those too, especially when questioned.

The corner of his sardonic mouth climbed. "Well, lucky for me, I don't write romance."

A derisive sound left me. *Lucky for all of us.* "I don't hate your books at all, Mr. Bane."

He shrugged and took the next book off the pile to sign. "Wouldn't guess so from your reviews. My least favorite phrase on the planet is *unforgivable sin,* thanks to you."

The heat in my cheeks flared again, this time in defense. "Your world building is incredible. Your imagery is so brilliant, sometimes I have to set my book down and stare at a wall just to absorb it. But every hero you write is, frankly, a—" An asshole, that was what I was going to say, but landed on, "—an unkind man."

He nodded at the title page as he scrawled his name. "Viggo?"

"He left Djuna because she was pregnant with his half-breed baby. And she took him back, even though he wouldn't even commit to her for good."

"Blaze?"

I rolled my eyes. "He didn't come for Luna because he was more worried about himself. He could have saved her from the Liath!" My hand rose in the universal sign for *What the hell?* and lowered to slap my thigh with a snap.

"Even Zavon? He's everyone's favorite."

My face flattened. "He cheated on her out of spite. *That,* sir, is the ultimate unforgivable sin. And if that wasn't bad enough, she took him back for no reason. *He didn't even apologize.*" I said the words as if it had been *me* who he'd cheated on. Honestly it felt that way.

The curse of a reader.

He slid the book to me and picked up another. But he didn't sign it. Instead, he turned that godforsaken smirk on me which subsequently turned my knees into jelly.

"But he loved her. Isn't love enough to forgive?"

It was that tingle again, climbing up my face like fire. "Of course it is, but your heroes never make heroic decisions about the women who love them. In fact, they don't seem to love their women at all, not enough to sacrifice their own comfort. They're irredeemable. Why isn't love enough to make them act less like assholes?" I clapped a hand over my mouth, my eyes widening so far, they burned from exposure to air.

Something in his eyes changed, sharpened with an idea. He was otherwise unaffected, chuckling as he opened the book and turned his attention to his Sharpie again. "I mean, you're not wrong, Amelia."

The way he said my name, the depth and timbre and rolling reverberation slipped over me like a drug.

I blinked. "I'm not?"

His eyes shifted to meet mine for only a heartbeat before dropping to the page again. "You're not. Every time I publish a novel, I wait for your review to see if I finally won you over." He closed the book, pushing it across the table to me before reaching for the last. "I think you should help me with my next book."

Somewhere, a needle scratched. Tires squealed from a pumping of breaks. Crickets chirped in a chorus in an empty room.

Help him?

"Yes, help me," he answered. I hadn't realized I'd spoken the question. "I could use a critical voice on my team. I think they've been telling me yes for years when they should have been telling me no. I need a no. Are you interested?"

"Interested?" I echoed stupidly.

"Are you interested in being my no?"

I blinked at him. "What a weird question."

A chuckle through a closed, sideways smile. His eyes had to be black, black as sin. "I've got to admit, I'm usually asking for a yes, especially where women are concerned."

My face flattened, not only because he was a cocky bastard, but for the flash of rejection that I wasn't considered a woman worthy of a yes. "What would the job entail?"

He watched me with an intensity that made me want to crawl out of my skin, like it was too small for everything inside of me. "Be available for meetings to plot and character develop. Read for me when I send the manuscript and provide critical feedback. Talk me off any ledges. Or push me off them, if that's what you think I need. Help me make my stories better. What do you say?"

What *could* I say? Thomas Bane was a sensation, famous not only in the literary world but in the pop culture stream. His Instagram had seventy million followers. Page Six followed him around like he was their only job. He was, at that very moment, on a forty foot billboard for TAG Heuer in Times Square.

And he was asking *me* for help.

"Say yes, you idiot!" the girl behind me hissed, presumably the one who'd shoved me toward his table when my feet had failed me.

Thomas Bane's smile tilted higher. Otherwise, he didn't react.

Say something. You have to answer right now.

In the span of a handful of seconds, I weighed it out. He wanted my help, and I loved to help people. I'd beta read for authors a hundred times and had always found it fulfilling, to offer my advice in order to make a story the best it could be. In fact, I loved it and took every opportunity to say yes, should it arise.

So why wasn't I jumping at the chance to help Thomas oh-my-God-quit-smiling-at-me-like-that Bane?

On paper, there was no reason. Floating around in my head were a hundred, the topmost being that when he looked like that, I actually felt like my panties were on fire.

He watched me expectantly. But when that smile of his dropped incrementally, coupled with the almost infinitesimal draw of his brows, I caved.

He wanted my help, and I had to give it.

"No."

His eyes narrowed in thought. "Wait. No as in yes? Or no as in no?"

"I will happily tell you no at every opportunity. If that's what you want, I'm your girl."

There it was again, that smile that probably cost more than most people's cars. "I like the sound of that. I'll message you through your blog and we can set up a time to meet." He arranged the stack of books, straightening their corners before moving them a couple inches closer to me, the gesture strangely nervous and utterly disarming.

I found myself smiling. I picked up the books and deposited

them in my bag. "I'll look forward to it."

"Did you want a picture?" he asked.

I got the distinct impression he asked everyone that question simply because there was no way in hell anyone could have the constitution to make that request on their own. Not with his energy sapping everyone in a twenty foot radius of their wits.

"I...erm..."

He was out of his seat and stepping around the table before I could say no again, this time meaning the word in full. But there he was, approaching like a thunderstorm. My chin lifted as he approached. He was at least a foot taller than me, the air around him charged, everything about him dark. His hair. His beard. His bottomless eyes. His jacket that smelled like Italian leather and combat boots to match, the laces half untied and the top gaping open with irreverence.

My senses abandoned me completely. The effect of him was amplified by his proximity, and there was nothing to do but submit. And so, there I was, tucked into Thomas Bane's side with his arm wrapped around me like hot, heavy steel.

It took every ounce of willpower I possessed not to curl into him, fist the lapels of his jacket, and bury my face in his chest.

I couldn't have reached anything else if I'd tried. My nose came approximately to his nipples.

"Do you have your phone?" he asked, but the rumble of the words through his chest vibrated through me to the point of absolute distraction.

"Ah...um..."

"Here, we'll take one with mine." With a slight shift, he retrieved his phone, holding it out for a selfie. "Say *irredeemable asshole!*"

A laugh burst out of me. And then his hand lowered.

I stiffened. "Wait, did you take it?"

He nodded, smiling down at his phone. "I'll tag your blog on

Instagram."

"But...I mean...is it okay? I'm not..."

He looked down at me, and for a second, I lost myself in the vision of him this close, from this angle. I could see the fine lines in his lips, the thick clusters of his lashes, the depth of his eyes—the brown was finally visible, so deep there were almost hints of a deep, dark crimson.

"You look gorgeous. See?"

I tore my eyes away from his to glance at his phone and almost didn't recognize myself. My eyes were closed, my nose scrunched, my smile big and wide and happy as I'd unwittingly leaned into him.

A hot flutter brushed my ribs. "Oh...that's..."

He laughed, a short sound through his nose as he pulled away. "I'm glad you came today. Tell Janessa to email my brother if she wants any more books signed, and we'll send them to the office."

"O-okay."

The girl behind me cleared her throat, and I glanced back at her apologetically. She looked furious.

"Sorry," I said quietly.

"Ugh, life is just not fair." She brushed past me and plunked a stack of books on the table.

Thomas Bane's smiling eyes were on me as he took his seat, and I waved lamely before turning to walk away.

And I swear I could feel those eyes burning a hole in my back the whole way out the door.

BOOKED, coming January 24, 2018
Get a release email alert: http://bit.ly/1E3iJeO
Add to Goodreads: http://bit.ly/2P0Y7kX
Follow Staci Hart on Amazon: https://amzn.to/2DJIihi

THANK YOU

Once again, my husband Jeff gets the first thank you, as without him, I would not only be a soggy, lost, miserable mess, but would have no idea what true love was. You're the reason for everything, babe. Thank you for every bit of your love.

Kandi Steiner — Thank you for always listening, always making me smile, always granting me your love from thousands of miles away. I love you forever and always, more than tacos.

Kerrigan Byrne — You make everything better. Everything, always, all the things. Working with you, laughing with you, tearing my hair out with you, *everything* has changed me in the best way. Cheers to another book under our belts, and here's to many more.

Abbey Byers — Eights rule. Eights are basically the best thing to ever happen to the world (which we are sure to tell that to everyone who asks and all the people who don't), and you're one of the best things to happen to me. When we put our crazy eight brains together, magic happens. I am so thankful for you, for your time and energy, for your devotion and utter brilliance.

Jana Aston — Goddammit, woman. Working with you, plotting with you, laughing with you, has been one of the highlights of writing this book. I am so glad we glommed onto each other like barnacles and are working together daily. You make my days better and brighter and less lonely.

Kyla Linde — Blurb hound extraordinaire. Pinch hitting beta. My extra set of eyes and my daily dose of companionship. I am a richer woman for knowing you, and I am fortunate to call you one of my best friends. Thank you, thank you, thank you for everything.

Sasha Erramouspe — YOU, my darling, are an absolute gem. Once again, you read for me in a pinch, petted my hair, sent me all the feedback, listened to all my waffling, and laughed at my corny lines like a champ. I cannot tell you how much I appreciate your time and energy and brain and heart and soul.

Laura Leiva — Thank you so very much for taking the time to read this and correct all my Spanish, even those words that had no meaning and made no sense! Next time I'm in Spain, paella is on me.

Marjorie Whitehorn — To the President of the Staci Hart Hair Petting club, thank you for always reading my excerpts and telling me how pretty and smart I am. Some days, I really, really need that to go on, and you have always got my back for that.

Scott Kolman-Keen — Thank you for finding the time with your busy schedule to help me with the ins and outs of belonging to a pit orchestra. Your advice was instrumental to this process and story, and the life you breathed into this aspect of the novel is undeniable.

Carrie Ann Ryan — Thank you for the abundance of advice and support you've given me! You have helped shift how I see so many things in ways that have made a huge difference

Karla Sorensen — Thank you once again for reading for me, for your honesty and practicality. Your advice is so necessary in my life, and I'm so honored to be the neediest person in your life that didn't actually come from your body.

Kris Duplantier — Your notes are constantly my favorite. Your voice messages while under the influence of suspect cold medicine and a fever will be listened to for years to come. I love you, dude!!

Sarah Green — I love writing with you. I love sharing this

experience with you. And I love you so much for taking the time when you were so crazy in life to help me with this book. You are incredible, and I appreciate you!

Ace Grey — You are my GD hero, and I am so thankful to have you on my team. More than that, I'm grateful to call you my friend. Thank you for loving this book as much as you do.

Danielle Legasse — You are so appreciated!!! You never let me down, and your notes and advice helped make this book what it is. Thank you, thank you, thank you!

Kathryn Andrews — When your schedule was insane, you still agreed to help me, and I can't tell you how much that means to me. Thank you for reading, thank you for always being there, and thank you for loving this book. My asshole is **so relieved** that you did!

Tina Lynne — My right hand. My Teener. My love. Thank you for everything you do for me.

Jenn Watson — Thank you once again for your support and advice, for your positive outlook and your moxie. Thank you for everything you do, everything you've done for me. I can't wait to do it again!

Sarah Ferguson — Thank you for your hard work and dedication with every release of mine. Also, please tell me if you ever sleep or if you are, in fact, a vampire.

Lauren Perry — Once again, you have blown me away. Thank you for always being here for me, even when you're underwater yourself. You are incredibly talented, and I am so thankful for you!

Anthony Colletti — Thank you, steady hand. Your advice and support has made everything about this job of mine better and easier.

Jovana Shirley and Ellie McLove — Thank you once again for polishing up my words and making them shine!

Nadege Richards — You are a formatting wizard, and I ALL CAPS LOVE YOU.

ABOUT STACI

Staci has been a lot of things up to this point in her life: a graphic designer, an entrepreneur, a seamstress, a clothing and handbag designer, a waitress. Can't forget that. She's also been a mom to three little girls who are sure to grow up to break a number of hearts. She's been a wife, even though she's certainly not the cleanest, or the best cook. She's also super, duper fun at a party, especially if she's been drinking whiskey, and her favorite word starts with f, ends with k.

From roots in Houston, to a seven year stint in Southern California, Staci and her family ended up settling somewhere in between and equally north, in Denver. They are new enough that snow is still magical. When she's not writing, she's gaming, cleaning, or designing graphics.

FOLLOW STACI HART:

Website: Stacihartnovels.com
Facebook: Facebook.com/stacihartnovels
Twitter: Twitter.com/imaquirkybird
Pinterest: pinterest.com/imaquirkybird

Made in the USA
Middletown, DE
07 April 2021

37141881R00201